**SHE WAS SO TOTALLY
INNOCENT . . .
HE SO MUCH OLDER
THAN HIS YEARS!**

His lips came down on mine forcing my head
back. I was too shocked to move and felt sudden
panic as the violence of his kiss parted my lips.
His large hand moved to hold my face still against
his as his tongue entered my mouth, sending hot,
shuddering waves through my body. He went on
kissing me until an unfamiliar warmth began to
spread through my body and I melted against
him, hoping he would never stop.

KATHLEEN

FRANCINE RIVERS

A JOVE/HBJ BOOK

Printed in the United States of America

Library of Congress Catalog Card Number: 78-71574

First Jove/HBJ edition published June 1979

Jove/HBJ books are published by Jove Publications, Inc.
(Harcourt Brace Jovanovich)
757 Third Avenue, New York, NY 10017

I

A small candle flickered on the large oak desk, casting grotesque shadows on the wall of the darkened office. I stood straight-backed and tense with my hands clasped tightly over the back of the chair. Anna Bowen stood facing me, her eyes bright with excitement.

"I tell you it's true, Kathleen!" Her voice seemed agitated by my disbelief. "As God is my witness . . . let Him strike me dead this instant if I am lying to you!" She looked around furtively, lowering her voice to a whisper as she went on. "I'll be in real trouble if Miss Montgomery ever finds out I'm the one who's telling you! It must be the best-kept secret in this place!"

"I can't believe it!" My voice rose and cracked. Anna darted a glance over my shoulder toward the closed door, as though expecting the headmistress to burst in. "No," I choked, "I just cannot believe this!"

"Keep your voice down!" Anna hissed, her finger over her lips in an angry gesture. "Look! Read it for yourself!" Anna thrust a thick manila file folder into my hand, her green eyes sparkling unnaturally in the half-light. "It's all right there!" Her long-nailed finger poked at the folder in my hand.

At that moment, I hated her. I didn't want to know what was in the folder. It felt unreasonably heavy in my hand. What could this information bring me? More hurt? More pain? More rejection? Did I really want to know who I was? Did I really want to know how I came to be in this home for abandoned girls? And a strange home indeed, only twenty of us, when other orphanages harbored many scores more. Who was I? Who were any of us?

Turning the file over in my hand and looking at my name on the tab, I debated throwing it into the wastepaper basket and running from the room. Did I have the courage to open it and accept as fact what I would read?

Faces blurred in my memory, children come and gone, most finding families to welcome them. And then there was me, sitting in the upstairs schoolroom with Miss Montgomery, or more often by myself. When prospective parents came to meet us, I was always whisked off into the farthest section of the orphanage, completely out of sight.

Why? I asked myself.

What kind of dreadful blood ran in my veins that I was not worthy of adoption and happiness?

Confronted with the truth, I was terrified. I bit my lip, meeting Anna's flashing, cat-green eyes. Her posture told me she was impatient and angry with my hesitation.

"Kathleen! Hurry up, for crying out loud!" She stamped her foot. I could not expect her to understand. She knew about her parents. "Miss Montgomery will be back from town any time now. I've got to put that back where I found it so that she will never know you've seen it!"

"All right . . ." Sucking in my breath, my heart in

my throat, I looked at the file in my hands again with more determination.

Written in large red capital letters on the tab was my sur name: KATHLEEN WARDEN. I had always hated my name because it sounded just like all the other institutional names. A name chosen without care, stuck on a person like a label on a bottle. As I opened the file, I came around the chair and sat down. My knees and hands were trembling as I recognized the handwriting of Miss Josephine Montgomery, aging headmistress of New York's smallest, and jokingly referred to by its inmates as the most select, orphanage.

The first sheet of paper answered several of my questions. In a tight, neat hand, the writer stated, "Birth: January 23, 1870." That makes me just over eighteen, I thought before I continued reading. "Birthplace: New York," the form continued. "Mother: Brianna O'Reilly, actress. Died May 10, 1870. Father: William Stuart Benson, III." No further information followed my father's name. No information was needed. Everyone in New York had heard of William Stuart Benson, III, shipping industry tycoon.

"Kathleen, have you gotten to your father yet?" Anna's voice was strained with exhilaration. "William Benson! Do you realize he's alive, Kathleen, and he lives about ten miles from here! Can you believe it!"

I shrugged, hoping she could not see the tears that were in my eyes. I then read the short note penned at the bottom of the page.

Father agrees to pay agreed amount for the care and education of Kathleen Warden. Money will be sent each year for the duration of her stay in the Parkside Home.   —J.M.

A hard, painful lump stuck in my throat. This short paragraph explained a lot. "For the duration of her stay," I reread and thought how Miss Montgomery had encouraged me to stay on as a teacher when my schooling was complete.

"You are so good with the girls, Kathleen. We would be grateful to have you as an instructor." She had sounded so convincing about my capabilities. I had been happily flattered by the unexpected praise, and I had remained.

"Kathleen?" Anna's voice brought me back to the present, the darkened room and the heavy folder in my hand. "Isn't it what you wanted to know? Everything is right there." Her voice was thick with the excitement of discovery. Secrets were always romantic, never tragic. How little she knew! How little both of us understood what impact this information would have on my life.

"Yes . . . I suppose so," I replied in a hoarse whisper. "Did you read the little note at the bottom of the first page?"

"No, what does it say?" She sat on the hassock and peered into the file. For a moment her eyes flickered. "I wonder how much he sends," she breathed quietly.

"No wonder Miss Montgomery wouldn't allow my adoption . . . and encourged me to stay on at Parkside." I knew only too well how the home could use money, any amount. Perhaps I would be angry later, but now all I could feel was pain. Josephine Montgomery had always treated me with kindness, often with love. Love! No, I couldn't believe now that it had been love. Kindness and need. Need to keep the home going and the girls provided for in food, clothing, and the few little extras that were bright spots in our lives.

"William Benson! My goodness!" Anna's voice was awed and speculative. "My mother was a Catholic waitress and my father was from a Protestant storekeeping family." She stopped abruptly, pensive.

"You seem to forget that I am also illegitimate, the

daughter of an Irish actress . . . who was probably a . . . prostitute," I said, annoyed with her enthusiasm. The words nearly choked me.

"Maybe a little of her hot blood runs in those cold veins of yours," she retorted harshly. "Oh, Kathleen, be reasonable! Lots of people were born on the wrong side of the sheets. Why do you think most of these girls are here in the first place? Did you think they all lost their parents in some romantically tragic accident? Good grief, but you are stupid!"

"What are you saying?!"

"Most of them are illegitimate . . . Didn't you ever guess that, you silly goose!"

"But we're orphans . . . The parents are—"

"Oh, bosh! Don't hold on to your fairy tales, Kathleen. We're abandoned, or given over like you were. But unlike most, our backgrounds, our bloodlines are all written down in a file someplace. That's why so many of us are adopted. Didn't you ever wonder why so few of us remained for any length of time?"

"Bloodlines?" I repeated, dazed.

"Nobody wants a foundling . . . They'd always wonder if they had gotten the daughter of a murderer or prostitute," she continued. I winced.

My stomach turned over. "Nobody wants the daughter of a prostitute," I repeated. There it was. I was the daughter of a prostitute and a rich man with a family tree so deeply implanted in New York society that not even a hurricane could uproot it. A mismatched pair if ever there could be one, I thought. There must have been no love between them. Had there been even affection, would my father have put me in an orphanage? And the money. Why should he have even committed himself in that way? Was it to insure himself that I would never enter his life and defile his respectability?

"You don't know if she was a prostitute," Anna said with surprising perception and sympathy.

"Why else would Miss M. have carefully hidden me away in the schoolroom when prospective parents came to call?" I asked bitterly, and hated the self-pity that I heard in my voice.

Leafing through the papers, I discovered reports on my educational progress. At the top of each page was a concise evaluation, with a lengthier report below.

English: excels in writing clear and sensitive essays. Music: piano, good. Arithmetic: adequate, but beneath her capabilities. Reading: excellent; oral presentations show sensitivity and dramatic ability.

An inheritance from my Irish mother, perhaps, I thought drily.

What had she been like? Had she loved me? Had she wanted me? Or had the five-month-old baby in some way been responsible for her early death?

I went on reading, leaving the painful questions lurking in the back of my mind.

History: debates with instructors; interest high but prefers the romantic to the realistic.

This last comment brought a smile to my lips. Miss Montgomery and I had spent many an evening talking about events in history. And, as she had written, I preferred the more romantic interpretations of history to the real story behind the events.

Several loose pictures fell to the floor. Anna retrieved them.

"Look at these! There you are circled . . . in every picture. You are two here . . . five, eight, thirteen, sixteen—and here's one they took only a few weeks ago."

10

She handed me the posed group pictures of the Christmas dinner. On the back of each Miss M. had written my age. Anna withheld the last picture, studying it closely.

"I wonder if you look like your mother."

"Why do you wonder that?" I asked, startled and slightly perplexed by her interest.

"Well, I've seen pictures of William Benson in the *New York Herald*. I don't think you look like him. But I heard somewhere that people with blue eyes and black hair are called 'black Irish.'"

"My hair isn't black."

"Well . . . dark brown if you want to be that way!" Her brows came down angrily. "Anyway, I think you're 'black Irish.'"

I stood up and pushed the file toward her. "Put it back where you found it, Anna." She took the folder and raised her curious eyes to my angry ones.

"What's the matter?"

"Nothing," I answered, turning away from her. "I just feel a little sick!" Tears. I thought I had gotten over my sudden bursts of tears.

Maybe I did look like my mother? But was that where it ended? Did that necessarily mean I would become like her in other ways?

And my father. What about him. Was he shallow, irresponsible, and unfeeling in his personal life? How much was I like him?

"Kathleen? Are you going to stay on now?" Anna prodded, putting the file away. The lock caught and she put the key back in a small velvet box in the top desk drawer. I knew that she had been aware of this key for some time. It was in her face. Her sudden interest in a teaching position came to mind. If I were to leave, the opportunity would be open for her. And Anna was a determined, ambitious girl.

"No," I answered honestly, swallowing the addi-

11

tional hurt that choked me. Not wanting to look at her eager eyes, I went on staring at my clenched hands. People always looked out for themselves. I must learn to do the same. "I think I will look for a position someplace else . . . as far away from here as I can go . . . maybe even California."

Even for the pain she was causing me I couldn't feel angry with Anna. She had only shown me the truth, exposed the real reason for the kindnesses I had always received. No matter what the reason, she had given me the shears with which to cut the tie that bound me so closely to the home—and to Miss Montgomery. I was free to live my own life, no debts to pay, no past kindnesses to hold me.

"What will you tell Miss M.?"

"I won't say anything about you," I replied, realizing that Anna was worried about her part in my decision.

"I have a little money saved if you need it," she offered, and I knew she meant it. The sooner I was gone, the sooner she would be safe and established in her new job.

"I may need it," I admitted. Her deepset eyes almost disappeared with her grateful smile.

Her life, unlike mine, was secured.

When I returned to my small upstairs room, I sat in silence. I had spent over seventeen years in this very room. Years filled with loneliness, self-doubt, longing, with brief visits of happiness and joy brought by Miss Montgomery.

False happiness. False joy.

I looked around at the pastel walls, the yellow cotton curtains, the white knitted bedcover, the hand-braided rug. That rug had taken me two years to make, using the small scraps of material left over from the lessons in the sewing room.

12

My eyes caught the one beautiful thing in my room. On my apple-crate bedside table stood a small blue china vase with white painted flowers. Miss Montgomery had given it to me privately one Christmas after my best friend had been adopted. It was winter then, the loneliest winter of my life. There were no flowers to cut and fill the vase. But even empty, it had given me joy just to look at it. It was winter again. However, now there was no comfort in the porcelain piece.

In a furiously bitter moment, I grabbed it and without thinking threw it across the room. It crashed into tiny pieces against the wall.

And something fragile inside me broke, too. I stood up and moved across the room, kneeling down and picking up the pieces of the blue china vase. I looked at them lying in my hand, sharp little pieces beyond repair. Like me?

Crumpling over, I began to sob, wildly, heart-broken, wrenching every feeling from within me.

I did not go down for dinner that night. I sat alone in my room staring out the window. The night's stillness assaulted me with doubts and fears. I knew that I would leave Parkside. But what could I do? How would I make a living? There were so few positions for which women were acceptable. To take a position as a schoolmarm would be next to enlisting myself in voluntary servitude. I could not. Perhaps I could find a position as a governess someplace in the West. Still less than desirable, it was my only chance.

After completing my education, I remained at Parkside as an instructor because of my loyalty and indebtedness to Miss Montgomery. Now that loyalty was entirely gone and I wanted to be as far away from her as possible. I needed to feel free, to be away from sad memories, and to find some sort of genuine happiness for myself.

Didn't I have that right as much as anyone else?

Unintentionally, my thoughts turned to the little girls in my class. Would it hurt them if I were to leave right away? Would my father still be inclined to send some contribution to the orphanage if he were to learn of my disappearance?

Guiltily, I forced myself to be realistic with my emotions. Miss Montgomery was not a cruel woman, though she may have been so in her decision to deceive me. If I had never come to know the truth, I would have always gone on thinking of her as my sole friend, my benefactress, the only mother I had ever known.

With honesty, I admitted to myself, she tried to do everything she could to insure the well-being of her charges. Hadn't she proven that? Hadn't the money my father sent guaranteed that for the past seventeen years?

I pressed my hands over my face. I must not let myself feel bitter. It was not her fault. It was my father's . . . and my mother's for bringing me into the world. People do what they must to protect what is important to them. And Parkside was Miss Montgomery's life.

But not mine . . . not anymore. I didn't want to devote my life to the orphanage. I had to think about myself and what I wanted to do with my life.

But first I wanted to see my father.

The thought came unbidden and suddenly to me, as I lay on my bed creating scenes. I would borrow the carriage tomorrow to go downtown. Then I would drive up to his estate. Perhaps I would ring the doorbell and say, "Tell Mr. Benson his daughter is here to meet him." Or I would ask to speak privately with Mr. Benson. "Hello. Do you know who I am?" I would ask. "No, who are you, young woman?" he would demand in an irritated, I-haven't-got-time-for-unim-

14

portant-people tone. "Why, I am your daughter," I would answer nonchalantly.

I wanted to hurt him, to make him feel something of what I had felt. But something in me kept crying out, pulling at me. Don't do it, Kathleen! It'll only hurt you in the end! Leave him be! Forget him. You must make your own life!

When at last I fell asleep in the early hours of morning, I dreamt of a young man and woman. The man was a faceless blur and sat silently watching a young girl who looked like me. She sang an Irish ballad in a sad and haunting voice, while she kept her eyes on him.

Trusting me completely, Miss Montgomery did not question my request to make an unexpected trip downtown to shop. After all, I had a little money and had for some time intended to buy wool for a badly needed winter dress and cape. And it was Saturday, my one free day of the week. Sundays were filled with religious training and services in a neighborhood chapel.

"Would you like Joseph to drive you?" she asked from the top of the steps. I looked past her, still not quite able to look at her. The old brick building looked cold and impersonal, anything but home.

"No. Today is Joseph's day off. And I can take care of myself, Miss Montgomery," I answered.

"Is anything wrong, Kathleen? You don't sound yourself today," Miss Montgomery asked.

"I'm just fine, thank you," I replied, turning to climb up into the seat and take the reins. I could feel her gray eyes watching me curiously.

"It is really not at all proper for a young lady to be going unescorted, Kathleen," she said, and I sensed once again the familiar note of resignation that indicated she would not press her point.

"Don't worry. I shall be quite proper in my behavior."

"Well, do be careful, child. And for goodness' sake, do not talk to any strangers. They will be very interested in making the acquaintance of a beautiful young girl who is quite alone."

"Yes, Miss M.," I answered dutifully, feeling once again back in the schoolroom. I was eighteen and a woman now, but there were still times when she was capable of making me feel like a schoolgirl.

I had been downtown many times, but always with Miss Montgomery or one of the other instructors from Parkside. Now, alone, the rush and noise of people and carriages was a little frightening. At the same time, it filled me with excitement to be on my own. However, my purpose in making this trip brought renewed apprehension.

First, I will buy material for a dress and a cape—"my traveling outfit," I added aloud with satisfaction. Then I will pick up a couple of Western newspapers. I will read them later for positions.

Then, I will go to the Benson estate.

I found the brown wool I wanted shortly after entering the shop. I postponed departing by buying some small, brown pearl-shaped buttons, some hooks and eyes, thread, and several yards of cream lace. The transaction was completed all too quickly and I found myself standing on the sidewalk, a heavy parcel in my arms and no further excuses for delaying the real reason for my trip.

Putting the bundle in the box under the seat, I stepped up into the buggy and entered the thoroughfare. I drove slowly, taking more than an hour to reach the correct street and causing great annoyance to the other street travelers. My heart pounded heavily. I admonished myself for being so nervous and cowardly. I would not even be meeting my father, I had decided that last night. If it had been so terribly important to him to never set eyes on me, I would not hurt myself by

16

forcing him to meet me. But I did want to see where he lived, perhaps get a glimpse of him, to have some feeling of what he was like.

I brought the buggy into the wide, tree-lined avenue. Huge houses were well-spaced on each side of the street, richly landscaped and protected by gates. Slowly, I drew up next to a high wrought-iron fence. A huge, black *B* was soldered into the middle of the front gate. I looked through the fence at the house beyond. Large, square, brick, it looked coldly expensive. Trees and shrubs only slightly softened its appearance.

I stared again at the surrounding fence, which looked like a cage around the estate, as though it were keeping something inside as well as the world out.

Sitting as nonchalantly as I could, I stared through the fence at the wide lawns and cold façade of the house. I wondered if my father were like his house. It made me shudder slightly. Surely happiness could not abide in such a place.

Did my father ever think about me? Did he ever think of my mother?

Probably not. He was a very rich and powerful man. He probably had some office clerk send the money to Parkside each year. He would have long since forgotten both of us—my mother and myself. The affair was long over, and my future had been easily and swiftly settled. To his satisfaction, but not to mine!

How free was I really? I wondered angrily. Had things been different, what kind of life would I have chosen? Would I still have chosen teaching? I wondered with a jolt. Perhaps there would have been more strict limitations as William Stuart Benson's daughter. Society had stiff boundaries by which it ruled people's lives. Perhaps I was more free now than I would have been as a rich man's daughter. Independence as a female Benson would have been impossible. How would I have reacted to those limitations and restrictions?

The sound of an approaching carriage caused me to realize I had remained sitting near the gate far too long. I tightened my grip on the reins, preparing to drive down the avenue and start home, when an exquisite black buggy came up and stopped next to me.

"Well . . . well."

I turned to face a young man, smiling arrogantly down at me. Hardly noticing the older man whom he accompanied, I felt pierced by the younger's cold, blue stare. "Another curious tourist?" he asked. I did not answer, his manner being insulting. "Do you like the Benson estate?" he went on when I remained silent. His voice was no less arrogant.

"No, I cannot say that I do," I retorted boldly, disliking the tone the young man used in addressing me.

"Oh?" He raised his brows in astonishment at my reply, darting a quick look at the man beside him. I looked past the young man and for the first time saw the person he accompanied.

My heart began to pound violently and I felt a deep flush rise up in my face.

It was him! Even seated, he appeared tall. Leanly handsome, he looked well over fifty, though his age was reported to be in the mid-forties. His hair was almost white and something tragic emanated from his face, lines crinkling about his gray-blue eyes and full mouth. He looked at me curiously and I was unable to take my eyes from his.

Something flickered across his face. He tensed.

"You are an extraordinarily rude woman," the young man was saying, drawing my attention back to him. His cold eyes stared down at me with unveiled dislike. Then he smiled slightly, showing straight white teeth. His eyes swept down over me in openly devouring appraisal. I stiffened.

"And you, young sir, are an extraordinarily rude young man!" I sensed rather than saw the rage my statement caused.

My father leaned forward slightly, staring at me, a peculiar stark emotion in his face. Then his expression changed, the emotion gone as though a curtain had been lowered.

"In case you did not know, young woman, this is William Stuart Benson." The young man looked at his companion and then back at me with smirking satisfaction.

"I had guessed that it was," I answered casually, pretending to be unmoved by his introduction. His eyes widened with shock. "Did you expect me to fall on my knees, sir?" I asked, with surprising calm. His face blanched and then turned white with unsuppressed fury.

"You . . . are . . ." he stammered, his eyes like ice.

"Extraordinary?" I supplied. "Your vocabulary seemed limited to that word."

"I have a few other words I could—"

"David!"

My father's voice was deep and commanding. He lifted his black, silver-headed cane in an impatient silencing gesture. "Drive this carriage through the gate or I will take the reins myself!"

David looked at me as though he would like to say more. Then he shrugged. "If you will excuse us," he said, smiling almost pleasantly.

"You're excused," I answered with a smile. It was my turn to be arrogant!

The black carriage started forward with a jolt, almost racing down the road toward the square brick house. A Negro groundsman closed the iron gate, looking up at me with curious admiration.

Instead of feeling satisfied, I felt an unfulfilled longing and intense hurt as I watched the carriage speed away. What had I hoped to accomplish by coming here? Why had I lashed out so rudely at that arrogant young man? Who was he?

Perhaps I had hoped to make some kind of judgment on my father. Perhaps I had hoped to dislike him or just satisfy a curiosity about him. But now, having seen him, I felt only hurt and remorse—and a vague emptiness as I wondered what my life might have been had I known his love.

I flicked the reins and headed once more for the orphanage, needing the quiet solitude of my upstairs room.

That evening Anna brought a notice to my room. It had lain unnoticed on Miss Montgomery's desk for several days. Similar advertisements had found their way to the orphanage, but had been discarded. I thanked Anna for bringing the notice to my attention, and studied the brief and carefully written words that would change my life.

Wanted: Governess. Write to C. Matthews, Rancho Las Posas, Las Positas, California.

Over three thousand miles away. A continent. Mental pictures of wild animals, Indians, highwaymen, snakes, all the unknown elements flashed before my eyes, all those frightening wonders that lived in Anna's collection of five-cent novels.

Was the West really like that? I shuddered. Then, resolved, I started my letter to C. Matthews.

II

"We'll be in Las Positas in an hour, Miss O'Reilly!" the stagecoach driver shouted down from his jouncing perch while with one hand he held the reins expertly and with the other cracked a whip. For a moment, I sat wondering whom he was addressing, then smiled.

"O'Reilly." Kathleen O'Reilly! That's me! A new name, a new life.

"Thank you, Bert!" I called up to him, still not feeling accustomed to the casual friendship he had offered. He had become indignant when I had previously addressed him as Mr. Winters.

A cloud of dust floated in, giving substance to the rays of hot sun which beat down unmercifully on the coach. My muscles ached from constant bouncing, and I had long since given up trying to brace myself against it. My dark brown traveling suit was dusty gray and rubbed uncomfortably against my skin.

Though I was hot and exhausted, I was happy. Happier than I had been since Anna Bowen had shown me the manila folder, and more excited than at any time in my life.

I was free now! And so far from Parkside that nothing could make me return.

Taking my mother's name, I had started my trip West. No one would ever find me so far from New York. Anyway, why should they even try?

Reflecting on my last conversation with Miss Montgomery, I wondered.

As I had entered her office, I found her at her desk, round wire-framed spectacles slipping down her long, thin nose, her head leaning into her writing. She had looked up and given me her tight-lipped smile, indicating that my interruption of her work was not altogether welcome.

"Yes, Kathleen?"

When I hesitated, she put her quill down and pushed her glasses back into place. Her face relaxed slightly. "What is it? A problem with Ellen Collins again?" Ellen was one of my mischievous pupils, a little red-haired, freckled scamp who was forever in and out of trouble.

"No." I shook my head, still unsure of how to begin. "I see you are very busy," I said, losing my nerve. "I'm sorry I disturbed you. Perhaps later, I can . . ." It had been many weeks before I had received the reply to my letter to Rancho Las Posas. I could wait a few hours longer.

Miss Montgomery studied my face with open curiosity. "You've never made a habit of disturbing me without cause. Now sit down." She smiled, gesturing for me to sit in the chair opposite her. "Tell me what's on your mind."

Obeying, I met her kind eyes, and felt a smarting of guilt.

"I am leaving tomorrow, Miss Montgomery," I blurted out, and watched her eyes widen as full comprehension struck her. "It's the end of the term and

Anna Bowen is qualified to take my place," I added in a defensive rush.

Her mouth opened slightly, but before she could speak, I continued rapidly, "I have accepted a position as governess of two children."

"My God in Heaven, Kathleen!"

I had expected surprise, but the expression on her face shocked and frightened me. I thought for a moment she would have a fit of apoplexy.

"Why didn't you discuss this with me? You'll have to break the agreement, of course. Did you accept an advance to travel? Well, we can repay that." She spoke vehemently, not expecting any disagreement from me. I had seldom disobeyed her in the past.

"You don't understand. I am going. It is settled."

"But you must not!"

"Why not?!" I demanded, growing angry.

"Kathleen, there are reasons, believe me . . ." she cried out imploringly.

"What reasons?" I persisted. Did she really expect me to stay with no explanation of why it was so important that I do so?

"Reasons . . . real reasons I am afraid I cannot tell you at this time." Her voice shook with emotion, whether fear or anger I could not tell. Why should it matter so much whether I stayed or left? Was the home in financial difficulty, I wondered suddenly.

No, I would have heard something before this. I would not give up my life for Parkside.

"I know I have a father who is living," I stated flatly. "Is that the reason?" I had not meant to say it, but it had come anyway.

"How did you find out?" She yanked her glasses off and her eyes seemed to protrude from her face. There was no mistaking the fear in them.

"I also know that he sends money each year for maintenance of Parkside." So as, I thought with pain,

23

to insure I will remain out of his life forever. I bit my lip to stop the bitter tears and words threatening to surface.

"That's not the reason, Kathleen." Miss Montgomery clasped her hands and looked down at them, trying to decide what to say and what to do. Then she went on, her voice sorrowful. "You were never supposed to know about him."

"There are few secrets kept here. I always thought there must be a reason why I was hidden away every time prospective parents appeared. I always thought there must be something terribly wrong with me . . . so I worked very hard to be worthy of a real home. You came close to giving me that yourself," I said with sudden tenderness and regret, then went on: "It never entered my mind that I had a parent who was living, who did not want me . . . who would not let others want me either."

"Kathleen, you don't know his reasons. Believe me, he has reasons for his actions." She came around the desk and started to put her arm around me. I gave her a watery smile, but moved away.

"That my mother was a prostitute. That my birth would have defiled his reputation in high society?"

"No!" Her answer shot out forcefully and I turned to her.

"What then?"

"I cannot say." She put her hand up to her forehead as though her head ached.

"I'm sure he does have his reasons," I said without bitterness. "But, you see, I have my reasons too . . . for leaving Parkside." I moved farther away from her, speaking with more control. "I thank you for my education and your kindness." As the tears filled her eyes, I found it difficult to speak. This was *his* fault, I thought, hating my father.

"You mustn't worry, Miss M. . . ." I said, using the

24

affectionate nickname for the first time in several months. "I've found a place for myself where I can be happy." I hoped.

As I opened the door to leave, her voice, strangely tense and unfamiliar, stopped me.

"Kathleen! I beg of you! Do not leave Parkside!" I watched in astonishment as stark fear flooded her face. But I closed my mind and heart to her appeal.

"I must go, try to understand," I replied firmly. "I do not wish to hurt anyone. But I am eighteen and I have a right to my own life. I have a right to some happiness." I turned away from her.

"Kathleen . . . wait . . . just a few days . . . I'll tell you everything. But first I must go and speak with your . . ." her voice reached out to me as I raced down the hallway. "Kathleen! . . . Please! For God's sake, wait!"

Shortly after running from the office, I saw from my bedroom window that Miss Montgomery, still greatly distressed, had ordered the carriage brought around. Joseph stood waiting, holding the bridle as she stepped hurriedly up, grasping the reins.

I could hear her voice giving hasty, last-minute orders. The groundsman looked up toward my window just as I ducked back out of sight.

Did she propose to stop me?

I heard her crack the whip with authority, and again looked down furtively as the carriage sped down the driveway. Joseph stood staring after it with confusion, raking his fingers through his graying hair.

I knew then that if I did not leave Parkside immediately and without anyone's knowledge, I would not be leaving the home at all. Scurrying downstairs, I burst in on Anna in the office.

"Anna! I need your help."

"You scared me half to death bursting in here that way," she said hotly, her pen having scratched a black smear across the page. "And just look at this . . . I'll have to recopy—"

"Never mind! I've got to leave . . . now! I need the money you offered."

"Leaving . . . now? Why the rush all of a sudden?"

"I think Miss Montgomery is going to try to stop me," I explained quickly.

"Why would she, for pity's sake," she said disbelievingly.

"I don't know," I retorted impatiently. "But if you want my job, you'll help me get away right now . . . this afternoon."

She blushed and nodded at my frank understanding of her motives.

Everything packed in an old carpet bag, dressed in my gray day dress, with a little package of food and the few dollars Anna provided, I started down the back steps.

Anna, ever helpful when it concerned her future, distracted Joseph in the front lobby.

Now sitting in the stagecoach and so close to my final destination, I let the welcome feeling of relief and freedom fill me. Patting my handkerchief to my damp forehead, I turned to look out at the country through which I rode.

It was beautiful. Green hills were covered with the bright orange and blue flowers of early spring. The sky was a brilliant blue, fluffy clouds floating high above. And it was hot. The trees between Sacramento and Las Positas appeared few and far between at present. But off in the distance I could see darker hillsides.

No Indians! No highwaymen! I remembered Bert Winters laugh when I asked him if the last part of the trip would be dangerous.

The sound of the horses' hooves pounding on the

hard dry ground came to me. Faster, faster, faster, closer, closer they brought me to my destination. Less than an hour. On and on! Hurry! Hurry!

For yet another time since starting my journey, I pulled a frayed envelope out of my drawstring bag, opening it to look at the papers inside. A small clipping was first, the advertisement which had started this journey. Another paper, this one the short telegram that had followed my letter: TWO CHILDREN. MUST BE WILLING TO ADAPT TO RANCH LIFE. NO FRILLS. SALARY $15 A MONTH. SHALL AWAIT YOUR REPLY. C. MATTHEWS. The last piece of paper said simply: FARE ENCLOSED. SOONER YOU ARRIVE, THE BETTER. C. MATTHEWS.

For a moment, I felt guilty as I thought about my letter to Mrs. Matthews. I had not lied, I told myself defensively. I had stated my qualifications and capabilities, simply and honestly. But I had not volunteered information which I was sure would have prevented my immediate acceptance. I knew very little of what to expect from ranch life. I did not know anything about the West except what I had been told by Anna. And her knowledge came from novels.

Perhaps my duties as a ranch governess would be odious and ranch life would be intolerable. But I had to try. I could only hope that Mrs. Matthews, terse as she sounded in her two telegrams, would be willing to try me once I arrived.

Perhaps age and inexperience would not matter so much either. They had not been mentioned in the conditions of my employment.

I reread the acceptance note with mixed feelings of amusement and anxiety. "The sooner, the better," I read softly. What were these two children like to warrant such hurried acceptance? How little I knew about them. Not their ages, not their names, not even whether they were boys or girls.

I will not allow that to worry me, I reasoned. I have taught several classes in the past two years. And surely there could not be the problems with two that there were with twenty. And surely, if boys, they would not be much different from girls in their mischievous pranks.

"Well, there won't be a long time to worry about it now," I said with a laugh, for I could see the buildings of Las Positas not far in the distance.

The stagecoach slowed as Bert Winters pulled on the reins and shouted colorful profanities. He no longer shocked me with his language, but rather caused me to smile at his vehemence. The horses were never out of his control, but his agitated voice might cause doubt in one unfamiliar with him.

My first view of the main street in Las Positas brought immense relief. It was civilized! Neat buildings stood side by side along a wooden sidewalk. People buzzed in and out of the picturesque shops, dressed only slightly differently from New Yorkers. They stopped to talk to one another, however, in small friendly groups.

"Careful, little lady," Bert Winters warned gruffly as he prepared to hand me down from the coach. My muscles ached horribly and I was exhausted. Moving with stiffness, I braced myself before stepping down. His gnarled hand was strong and firm, steadying me. "Watch your step, Miss O'Reilly."

My free hand went to his hard shoulder and I could feel my shaky, travel-weary legs touch the ground for the first time in hours. I dusted myself off with a few hard downward pats on the folds of my dress. Brown wool peeked timidly through the dust.

Laughing happily, I looked up to meet Bert Winters' admiring look. "Thank you for the ride, Mr. Winters! I mean, Bert," I corrected quickly.

"We ain't so formal out here, ma'am," he explained again, and then asked me where I was planning to stay.

"I'm not sure yet. I'm a day earlier than expected. Do you know where I can get overnight lodging?" I took the bag he handed down to me and watched as he scratched his chest in concentration. I had the urge to giggle, but suppressed it.

"Well, there ain't but one damn hotel in this hole. Not fit for a lady like yourself."

"It'll do just fine. Where is it?" I smiled, amused and touched by his concern.

"You shouldn't be traveling alone, anyway. Ain't right. Ain't safe neither," he scolded gruffly, frowning down at me. "When you git your room, you lock yer doors and don't let nobody in. You hear me?"

"I'll do that," I agreed, feeling slightly nervous over his rough commands. Was this really such wild country as I expected to find? It didn't seem so from outward appearances. And Bert had said there was no problem with Indians or highwaymen now.

"Well . . . the hotel is right across the street . . . there . . . you can git your room there. You remember what I told you," he said, grasping the reins again.

"I will . . . and thank you."

"Pleasure, ma'am," he answered, showing a couple of broken teeth. He gave a quick nod of his head before lashing the horses on their way.

Looking down the street, I spied a town clock. Only eleven! The last couple of days had been the hardest, the trip from Sacramento to Las Positas dusty, hot, and uncomfortable. The train went no farther than Sacramento and so I was forced to learn that stage travel was anything but comfortable.

Now I was here . . . and famished.

I looked curiously around at the wooden buildings, which appeared sturdy but were frill-free. When compared to the brick and stone of the East they seemed almost temporary. But they had a warm, welcoming charm.

Several men on horseback rode down the main street. I noticed they glanced in my direction curiously, raising their hats slightly when I met their eyes as they passed. I must be a sight in my dusty travel suit, I thought with amusement.

I did not see many women and those I did had children in hand and were bustling here and there on apparently important errands.

"I'm here at last!" I whispered happily, hopeful that I would be staying for some time. I took a tighter grip on my carpet bag and looked across the street at a brightly painted sign which announced: HOTEL AND SALOON.

From my side of the street I could hear loud laughter and voices coming from within the building. My heart began to pound as I started across the street. I had never been in a hotel before and was therefore not sure what it would be like inside. I had seen many hotels in New York, but they had neither looked nor sounded anything like this one.

As I entered the open hotel doorway, I saw a large room off to the right. Round tables were placed here and there, at which men were sitting and playing cards. There was laughter, some music coming from an old piano, and much talking. Several brightly dressed women, in shockingly scanty outfits, served the tables with drinks. They exchanged jokes with the men, laughing easily. One man reached out and grabbed a woman around the waist, hauling her squealing gleefully into his lap. I felt my face turn crimson as she leaned over and planted a warm kiss on his waiting lips, then whispered something in his ear which made him grin.

Quickly averting my gaze, I saw a middle-aged man sleeping at the desk, his chair leaning back against the wall. I leaned across the counter and spoke in a light voice, hoping neither to be conspicuous to those in the adjoining room nor to surprise the clerk too suddenly from his nap.

His eyes opened slowly, and he snorted a little as he pushed himself forward, the chair making a loud thud on the floor.

"Huh?" he grunted. "What the hell do you want now?"

"Excuse me, sir, do you have a room available?" I asked softly, blushing at his indignant, sleeping expostulation, followed by his wide-eyed stare as he came fully awake.

"Pardon me, ma'am. I thought you was one of the whor—" he coughed and blushed. I was confused by his embarrassment. "We don't get many ladies through Las Positas," he stammered, explaining his surprise. He frowned slightly as he swung the register around. Much to my dismay, he banged loudly on a little bell, and silence fell over the adjoining room.

"How long will we have the pleasure of your company, ma'am?" he asked with a self-conscious formality that made him sound pompous. He straightened his shoulders, sucking in his well-rounded belly and pulling his vest down slightly. I almost smiled.

A low whistle issued from the cardroom and I looked around curiously, then returned my attention to the clerk.

"Only the night, sir. I'm expected tomorrow at Las Posas Ranch," I answered, keeping my voice low so that the words did not carry to the others who were listening. He swung the book around again, his eyes lighting with obvious interest.

"Rancho Las Posas!" he repeated, reading my name afterward. He came quickly out from behind the counter and moved to the doorway to the larger room. He snapped his fingers loudly and made a frantic gesture for someone to approach. I turned around again, standing in the hallway near the desk, and looked curiously into the room. The clerk's finger-snapping attracted more attention, and I saw several pairs of eyes studying me with interest.

"Holy Christ! An honest to goodness angel!" someone shouted, and laughter filled the room. I felt mortified with embarrassment. I looked away, studying with no interest the stairs, the walls, the pictures.

The pictures! My eyes widened with shock. I looked again at the stairs.

The clerk was speaking louder than I thought necessary, for the whole room could hear his every word.

"Joe, hurry up! Take Miss O'Reilly's bag up to room 4 so she don't have to listen to these apes." A boy picked up my bag and started for the stairs. I was relieved to follow and escape the bold stares. The clerk gave me a bow, which made me feel even more ridiculous, for never had anyone showed that kind of courtesy to me. My position hardly warranted it.

"Hold up there, Frank!" a strong voice called out, and from the corner of my eyes I saw a man of medium height approach. "Did I hear you say Miss O'Reilly?" The man's face was round and friendly, a small jagged scar on his cheek not matching his demeanor. He looked about forty, hard and trim, darkly tanned from the outdoors. He had a pleasant, easy smile as he met my glance with unconcealed curiosity.

"You heard right, Calhoun. Why?" the clerk answered rather curtly, and motioned Joe to hurry on.

"This is the lady I was sent to fetch," Calhoun explained and then looked at me, standing awkward with embarrassment near the stairway. "Ma'am, let me introduce myself." He inclined his head slightly. "My name is Jim Calhoun and I work for Clinton Matthews, your employer. He sent me in to fetch you to the ranch."

Suddenly he seemed greatly amused by something, for his face lighted with a wide grin. "I do hope, ma'am, that I am present when Clinton makes your acquaintance. You are not at all what he has been expecting!" He threw back his head and laughed. I blushed again, wishing I were somewhere far away from all the curious and amused glances.

"C. Matthews" was a man. I had thought all along that C. Matthews was the wife of a rancher.

"What was Mr. Matthews expecting, Mr. Calhoun?" I asked with tart defensiveness.

"Someone about twenty years older and not the least bit pretty, ma'am," he answered with a grin. "Oh, ma'am . . . I'm not laughing at you. Don't get your dander up, Miss O'Reilly. But . . . well, he'll be getting a big surprise," he chuckled.

"Oh, dear," I muttered under my breath, feeling more and more dismayed and nervous. It was shock enough to find my employer was a man, though I should have expected as much, for why would a woman want a governess? But now, as well as finding I would for the first time be working for a man—frightening enough since I had never been around men at all—I discovered that he expected me to be older and undoubtedly more experienced.

Jim Calhoun snatched the bag from Joe and took my arm. "Come on. We'll get the buggy and be on our way."

Unable to protest, I found myself escorted out into the bright sunlight again. I almost groaned audibly at the thought of riding another foot, but I apparently had no choice in the matter.

Moments later, Jim lifted me up into the large buggy. In an easy, fluid motion he jumped up next to me, taking the reins in his practiced, callused hands. And then we were off again.

"How far is it to the ranch?" I asked, hoping that

it would be a short trip. I was hungry and exhausted. My previous excitement was gone, nervous tension taking its place. Would they think me impertinent if I asked for something to eat shortly after arriving?

"We'll be on Las Posas in about five miles, but it'll be about three hours before we reach the ranch house," he answered casually, as if we were on a Sunday ride. I stifled a groan, trying not to think of my empty stomach and already bruised posterior.

"What is the Matthews family like?" I asked gingerly, hoping that he would not take my interest as nosy curiosity.

"Not much family left, ma'am."

Sand and dust filtered up from the hooves of the horses and I squinted my eyes against the glare. Mr. Calhoun snapped the reins and leaned over, resting his elbows on his knees while he explained.

"Clinton is the last Matthews left."

"But the children?"

"They're not his. They're his sister's. She and her husband died two years ago in a flu epidemic. The kids are Adamses."

"Oh," I said quietly. So I would be working for a widower, taking care of his sister's children. "When did Mr. Matthews lose his wife?"

"Wife? Clinton?" He laughed again. "No wife . . . he's a bachelor. Hasn't had much time for courting since his Pa died. He's been running Las Posas for seven years . . . through some mighty hard times too. His Pa died a couple years after his Ma. Seems like one thing after another has happened to him."

"What is he like?"

"That's a question I'll leave to you to answer yourself," he grinned.

"How old are the children?"

"Let's see." He tilted his head slightly and frowned. "Priscilla is eight and Steven just turned six last month

. . . but don't hold me to it." He paused a moment before going on, giving me a sidelong glance and smiling with amusement. "Clinton sent East for you because he wanted a good teacher for those two. He doesn't have much time to spend with them, being busy with the ranch and all . . . and he wants them to have the best education possible." He chuckled again and I couldn't see what was so funny about what he was telling me. "He tried to get Mabel to handle it, but she told him she had enough to handle with the ranch house and seeing to grub for the hands. She's the one that put him up to advertising for a governess in the first place. They had quite a time trying to find someone willing to come so far."

"Who is Mabel? A relative?" I wondered if she would be a friend.

"Mabel Banks. She runs the household. Been on the ranch since the beginning, I guess. She practically raised Clinton, but she's too old now for handling two young kids and she's smart enough to know it."

"Do you think she'll be disappointed?"

"In you? No. I think she'll be pleased." He grinned again at some private joke.

"What are you finding so amusing, Mr. Calhoun?" I asked with annoyance.

"Not you, ma'am. I guarantee. It's just the thought of what my boss was expecting me to bring to the ranch. A middle-aged, drab-looking schoolmarm. He's not been the least eager. That's what most governesses are reported to look like."

"Well, then, he might just tell me to climb back on this wagon and go back East," I said, half-convinced that would be my fate.

"No . . . ma'am," he answered with assurance. "Women like you are scarce in Las Positas. He'll not be sending you back, I daresay."

I didn't share his conviction.

After a long silence, he gave me an understanding smile. "What do you think of California, ma'am?"

"I like it, Mr. Calhoun." I prayed silently that I would have a chance to like it even more.

III

Jim Calhoun and I did not talk much more on the remainder of the ride. There did not seem to be as much dust farther on, or else I had grown too weary to notice. The sun was high and tormenting. I hardly noticed the beautiful, wild, hard country through which we rode.

Exhausted and famished, it was all I could do to keep my eyes open and myself balanced on the seat. I kept daydreaming about a nice cool bath, a cup of tea, and a slice of bread with butter and jelly. I was too tired even to think about Clinton Matthews and his possible disappointment and displeasure at sight of me. I didn't care anymore. So long as he let me have something to eat and a place to sleep for a couple of hours.

"There it is, Miss O'Reilly. We're almost there," Calhoun said sympathetically. I smiled at him and then studied the big house still a distance away.

It wasn't what I expected. Three stories high and beautiful, it was surrounded by shade trees and flowering shrubs. Everything was green and cool around it. It looked welcoming and homelike in spite of its size.

There were barns some distance from the house and mazelike fenced-in areas that Calhoun identified as the corrals.

A huge porch went around the front and sides of the house, hanging plants flowering between the posts. As we neared the house I could smell a mingling of flower fragrances.

"Is that Mabel Banks?" I asked, spying a heavyset woman who came out and stood on the front steps. She did not seem ominous or unkind as we approached, and she came down the steps to greet us.

"You're a day early, Jim!" she called out, her round face not seeming the least bit distressed or surprised by the inconvenience.

"Should I have waited?" Jim asked with a laugh.

Mabel Banks scrutinized me with raised eyebrows, her expression revealing neither pleasure nor disapproval. "You are Kathleen O'Reilly?" she asked finally, her tone indicating her surprise.

"Yes, ma'am," I answered quietly, smiling somewhat shyly. She smiled suddenly in return, a mischievous light flicking on in her eyes.

"You are most welcome here, my dear," she said sincerely. Jim Calhoun threw back his head and laughed. Jumping down, he lifted me from the buggy. I brushed myself off again but my traveling suit was beyond that, in need of a thorough cleaning. Every muscle in my body protested even another thought of movement, and I felt wilted from heat and hunger.

"Heavenly days, Jim. The girl is exhausted," Mabel Banks observed. "Jim, Mary will show you where to take her things." As he took my bag and started up the steps, she tossed another hotter comment over her ample shoulder. "You probably didn't even bother to ask her if she'd eaten anything before you dragged her onto that wagon." She looked back at me. "Did he?"

I smiled, giving a noncommittal laugh in reply.

"Follow me, dear, and I'll show you to your room. We'll get you some warm bathwater, some food, and then you can rest until Clinton gets back. How does that sound?" she asked with a warm smile.

"Wonderful, Mrs. Banks." I followed her gratefully up the front steps. I knew I would like her even more as my days at the ranch went by. If they were allowed to.

The room I found ready for me was large and furnished comfortably. I exclaimed my pleasure. Mrs. Banks smiled more widely with my praise, dimples showing in her sunburned, chubby cheeks. She opened the windows out onto a huge garden. A lattice of roses grew up and around, bringing a fresh fragrance into the room.

A tub was being filled with buckets of water as she pointed out the various native flowers of the area.

"It was a long dusty trip, wasn't it?" she said compassionately as a young dark-haired girl stood in the doorway watching me. She was attractive in an assured, almost bold way. I flushed slightly when she stepped into the room and Mabel informed me that she would help me bathe. "Your supper will be brought up when you finish. I'm sure you must be starving by this time." As she left, Mary Cramer immediately took command of the situation.

Quickly and expertly, she prepared the bath and then helped me disrobe. Although embarrassed by her presence when I started to undress, I found myself grateful for her assistance. I was too tired to move. She helped me with casual disinterest. Gathering up my clothes, she left the room once I was in the tub, returning a few minutes later to lay out carefully my meager, though practical wardrobe.

"Which dress would you like to wear this evening, Miss O'Reilly?" When I hesitated, not sure which would make the best first impression, she held up my

39

blue linen dress with the white lace at the collar and cuffs. "This one is very pretty. It matches your eyes very well."

"That one will be fine," I said, giving her a grateful, though shy smile.

"I'll press it for you." She disappeared, leaving me alone again. I leaned back in the tub, luxuriating in the rapidly cooling water.

Dry and wrapped in an enormous towel, I sat eating the supper of thick soup and fresh bread that Mary had brought in on a tray. The blue dress was pressed and hanging in the corner.

Soothed and clean from my bath, with my hunger appeased, exhaustion took control.

It was dusk when I awakened and sensed someone in my room, staring at me. For a moment I felt unreasonable terror. I sat up in bed suddenly.

Then I saw them.

The little girl was standing closest, and I saw her face more clearly than the boy's. Her hair was light brown and braided tightly down the side of her head, dropping down her thin little back. She was dressed in a simple yellow frock.

The little boy was harder to discern in the shadows of the room. His eyes were large and he looked younger than six. His hair was darker than his sister's and fell carelessly on his forehead, almost over his dark eyes.

"Hello," I said softly and smiled. They stared at me curiously. "You must be Priscilla, and you, Steven."

"Are you Miss O'Reilly?" The little girl spoke first, repeating the same surprised question that everyone had asked so far. She looked at her brother with a precocious smile. "She's pretty, isn't she?"

Steven did not answer or move. What a solemn little lad he is, I thought with pity. Not at all like a child should be.

Priscilla looked back at me unperturbed. "He's

shy," she explained offhandedly, as though reading my thoughts. "You don't look anything like a governess," she observed boldly.

"Oh? Have you had many governesses?" I asked with surprise.

"Oh, no. You're the first. But Uncle Clinton has told us all about governesses. He said they are old and grumpy."

"He did not!" Steven said forcefully, speaking for the first time.

"Well, then, what did he say, smarty?"

"He said a governess might be cross with us and that she might be about Mabel's age." I suppressed a giggle. I liked these children so eager for friendship.

"You're the first we've had," Priscilla repeated, ignoring her brother's heated correction. "Like I was saying. Will you be grumpy with us?"

"I hope not," I replied, laughing. The little boy still stood in the shadows, his eyes cast down. "Come here . . . please . . . so I can see you."

While Priscilla came forward readily, Steven approached more shyly. He seemed withdrawn, quiet, vulnerable. I reached out a hand to each of them. "I am very happy to be here. I think we will have lots of fun together. And we will be good friends." A flicker of a smile touched the little boy's face and then was gone.

"Naughty children," Mary Cramer said suddenly, entering the room and looking at them with mock anger. She wagged a finger at them. "Let Miss O'Reilly get up and get ready to meet your uncle. Off with you, now!" They went without question, Priscilla tossing a bright little smile over her shoulder as she pulled the door shut.

"I hope they didn't disturb you," Mary apologized as I still looked at the door through which my new charges had disappeared.

"Oh, no. They're charming." I rose from the bed, tossing the covers back. Then by force of habit I straightened the covers. Mary watched me for a moment and then said with some abruptness, "You don't have to do that, you know. I will make the bed." I stepped back, slightly embarrassed at my mistake. "Mr. Matthews just rode in," she said over her shoulder as she took over. "He will probably want to see you in an hour or so." Finished with the bed, she left the room.

Carefully plaiting my thick, waist-length hair, I tried to gain control of my tense nerves. I twisted the braid into a crown on my head, hoping the mature hairstyle would make me appear older. Would my being only eighteen really make such a difference? I wondered. I had finished schooling, something more than most women could claim, and had experience teaching children at the orphanage. Why would my youth be a detriment? After all, I thought, Mr. Matthews had never once asked my age in our minimal correspondence. Therefore, at this point, he could not, in all fairness, say it was a condition of my employment.

I looked in the mirror, distressed with my appearance. Little girlishly curling tendrils of hair escaped at my temples and no amount of combing kept them tightly in the braid. Finally resigned to the fact that my efforts to look more mature were fruitless, I let them curl.

As I heard a tap at the door, I stood up, straightening the blue linen dress more to ease my tension than to mend my appearance. Mrs. Banks entered, smiling.

"You look very pretty, Miss O'Reilly. Don't look so worried, child!" She smiled more widely. "One look at your blue eyes and there will be no thought about having older governesses."

My smile was stiff with fear as I looked back at her.

I wondered if he was already discussing an older governess before even seeing me.

As I followed her down the hall, I put icy palms to my cheeks to lessen the flush. My heart was fluttering nervously and I spread my fingers tautly over the blue skirt.

As we came through the parlor toward the double doors of the study, I could hear men's voices. I recognized the easy speech of Jim Calhoun. The other voice was deeper, holding more assurance and authority. It was almost harsh as it raised slightly and carried through to us as we approached.

"What the hell do you find so amusing, Jim?"

A sudden twinge of panic ran through me and I wanted to turn and run back up the stairs. I darted a look at Mrs. Banks. "More bark than bite," she answered my silent question. "You go right through those doors. Chin up, Miss O'Reilly. He's not half as bad as he sounds." She patted my shoulder, but I was not convinced of the truth of her statement.

The angry, demanding voice assaulted me again. "You have been smiling and laughing to yourself since returning from Las Positas. Let's have it! What's your impression of this Kathleen O'Reilly?"

I came slowly nearer the doorway, hesitating in my embarrassment, not knowing how to make my presence known most gracefully.

Both men had their backs toward me. For a brief moment, I had an opportunity to study Clinton Matthews. Taller than I had expected, he was neatly dressed in dark brown trousers and a heavy cotton shirt. His shoulders were broad and powerful, tapering into a narrow waist. He was lean-legged and when he moved impatiently, waiting for Jim's unhurried answer, there was an almost animal grace about him. There was an air of confidence in the straightness of his back. Light brown hair curled down over his collar.

"Miss O'Reilly is . . . a surprise . . . to say the very least, boss!" Jim answered, chuckling again as he finished the amber liquid in his glass and set it down. He had turned just enough to catch sight of me standing in the doorway. However, he did not bring my presence to Mr. Matthews' immediate attention.

"Well, damn it?" Matthews' voice rose in agitation, making my hand rise almost involuntarily to my throat.

"Judge for yourself, Clinton. She just came in." Jim laughed again, and I heard a muttered oath from my employer as he turned around to face what he expected to be a drab, old spinster governess.

"Excuse me, ma'am," he said respectfully before even fully turned. He stopped when he was facing me, his eyes showing unconcealed shock. My face flushed at my own surprise.

Clinton Matthews was ruggedly handsome, his jaw square, his brows flared slightly over eyes that were dark brown. His hair fell carelessly over his forehead much like Steven's did. But what surprised me most was his age. He did not appear to be over thirty, though there was a more mature air about him. His face showed strength, determination, a hardness and cynicism that I would not have expected in a man of his age.

Dark eyes swept over me in a slow, thorough appraisal that left me pale. I noted his jaw tighten and a muscle work in his cheek. Covering his surprise almost immediately, he could not hide his displeasure. Raising my chin slightly, I steeled myself against his cool scrutiny.

My effort challenged him. He raised one dark brow and then turned toward Jim Calhoun, who had missed nothing in the silent exchange. For the first time since I had met him, he was confused and not just a little embarrassed himself.

"I'll talk with you in the morning," Matthews said

44

with a growl of dismissal. All the amusement was gone from Jim's face. Frowning slightly, he looked between the two of us standing motionless in the quiet study.

"Good evening, Miss O'Reilly," Jim said, nodding his head and giving me an encouraging smile as he left the room. I felt as though my only ally had deserted me and I stood alone to face the enemy. Again, I met Matthews' cool appraisal. He moved past me and shut the heavy double doors with a snap. A heavy depression descended on me.

"Please sit down, Miss O'Reilly," he said sharply, indicating I was to come to a chair near the desk. Any other time, this room would have seemed almost cozy. Now it seemed a battleground.

"Yes, sir." My voice came out surprisingly calm and clear. I wanted to turn my eyes from his, which pierced me unmercifully. But I fought my inclination. If I showed my fear of him he would dismiss me then and there, thinking me nothing but a child unable to cope with life. As I sat opposite him, still holding his eyes with an effort, he spoke, his anger now all too apparent.

"You are not what I expected, Miss O'Reilly!"

My spine stiffened defiantly at his tone. "I can see that quite plainly, Mr. Matthews." My voice matched his in agitation. "What were you expecting?" I asked bluntly. Considering my question for a moment, he decided not to hedge.

"Someone older, more experienced. You are much too young," he informed me flatly.

"You did not make age a qualification for the position. I am over eighteen, sir, and have completed more schooling than most women you might think suitable."

"Oh, you're eighteen?" he exclaimed sarcastically. Then standing up suddenly, "Christ Almighty!" he exploded. "I send East for a governess and find myself saddled with a . . . mere babe."

Anger made me bold. "I cannot be much younger than you were yourself when you took full responsibility for the running of this rather sizable ranch!"

His immediate change of expression made me wonder if I had gone too far in my defense. Oh, why had I said that! Only force of will kept me from shaking before his glare.

"You know so much about me already?" His words were taunting. My fear was replaced by embarrassment. He did not even know me and he was already judging me in some insulting way from my hasty outburst. But he had been unfair, I thought frantically.

"Not so very much, sir," I answered, ashamed of my outburst. "I was told you were quite young when the necessity arose for you to take over. I know you have two children who need a governess. I am qualified as such and you accepted my word on that." I wanted to look away from those cold eyes, but met his glare with as much coolness as I could muster. "But you know nothing more of me either, Mr. Matthews. You did not ask much information. But I can assure you that I would not have accepted the money to travel across an entire continent if I did not believe I could fulfill my obligations to you." I tried to keep my voice low and calm, though my heart was pounding frantically. Not realizing I had done so, I stood up to meet his disapproval. His expression changed slightly, softening somewhat, a sparkle hinting at surprise and possibly even respect.

"Sit down, Miss O'Reilly . . . please," he added the last word almost as an afterthought. His tone was calmer, less fierce. "I am sorry for my abruptness, but I was expecting a much older woman." No longer agitated, I detected a certain note of apology in his deep voice. "You must admit . . . you do not look like the average governess."

I smiled slightly, not admitting that I had not met

another governess who could supply me with a comparison.

"You ride, of course."

"No, sir," I answered, depressed and expecting him to say this was a requirement he had neglected to mention, but which was part of "adapting to ranch life." Surprisingly, he did not.

"No?" He shrugged. "I thought not," he added dolefully.

"I can learn," I volunteered.

"You'll have to. Priss and Steven love to ride . . . and you will, of course, have to go along."

"I'm sorry if it will cause inconvenience . . . but I'm afraid there were no horses for riding where I was raised."

His dark eyes showed interest and suddenly I felt my throat tighten. I hoped he would not pursue my sudden admission with a pointed question about just what kind of background I had that excluded riding horses. An educated woman should be familiar with horses. If he pressed the point, I would have to evade his desire for specifics. But why should he now request information in which he had no interest previously. My application, vaguely stating my experience without volunteering references, had been accepted.

"Starting tomorrow evening, you will take your meals with Priscilla, Steven, and me in the dining room. I want you not only to teach them reading, writing, and arithmetic, but drawing-room manners as well. Polish them."

Smiling at him slightly, I thought he was sorely in need of some manners himself. He read my thoughts and frowned at my amusement. "I want an outline of what you will be teaching them, and weekly reports on their progress," he went on, his words curt and commanding.

"Of course," I answered, attempting not to show my hurt at his obvious distrust of my capabilities.

"Is everything clear to you, Miss O'Reilly?" he asked with cool indifference, though his eyes were sparkling strangely.

"Yes, sir. Thank you."

For a long moment we sat facing one another, sizing up the spirit behind the words just spoken. His expression was unreadable, his eyes still continuing their discomforting scrutiny. The silence was becoming oppressive, with the evening breeze in the trees outside providing the only sound in the room. He raised his brow in his curious way and I felt a sudden tremor go through me.

"Will that be all?" I asked, hoping my voice sounded natural. He did not answer for a moment, probably enjoying my discomfort.

"You may go."

Relieved, I rose from the chair and started for the door. He rose also, watching me curiously. I wondered if he expected me to say something more.

"Good night, Mr. Matthews. And thank you for allowing me the opportunity to prove myself." I gave him a shy smile, not knowing what else there was to say.

"Good night." I detected a hint of amusement in his tone, though I could not see his eyes.

As I left the study I saw two barefooted, nightgowned children scurry up the stairs and wait on the landing. A little loudly, Priscilla whispered, "Oh, I am so glad he likes you." I gave a little laugh and wondered if his manner was always so gruffly forbidding to those he had just met.

I hurried up the stairs, taking each child by the hand when I reached them on the landing. "Where are your slippers, you little scamps?" I asked teasingly, feeling lighthearted and gay now that my ordeal with Clinton Matthews was behind me.

A noise in the hallway below caught my attention. Matthews was leaning against the door jamb, hands in his pockets, looking up at us. I could not read the expression on his face, nor did I wish to delay long enough to try. I hurried Priscilla and Steven down the hall and out of his sight, the children's feet pattering gaily beside me.

Two full weeks would pass before I again had to speak with or face Clinton Matthews, the dark brooding man who was my employer. And for my reprieve, I was grateful.

IV

Nearly every waking hour was spent, happily, with the two children, either in studies or in play. Priscilla immediately took me in hand and gave me an animated grand tour of the ranch house. Spacious and warm, there were at least ten bedrooms, a sitting room, a den or study where Matthews usually locked himself to work when he was home, a small parlor, an upstairs schoolroom complete with large chalkboard, an enormous kitchen, a dining room, and a large entry hall.

As one entered the house, the stairs were straight ahead and sets of double doors opened to show the sitting room on one side and the study on the other; beyond the stairs additional doors led to the dining room and, farther along, the kitchen.

There were several small bedrooms on the first floor. Matthews' room was on the second floor as were guest rooms always ready for the unexpected visitor. On the third floor was my room, flanked by Priscilla and Steven's. The schoolroom was at the far end of the hallway facing the front of the house.

I particularly liked my room, for it had a lovely view of the gardens behind the house. The red roses climbing up the lattice made a lovely frame for the scene beyond. Fruit trees grew below, as well as a large oak and many flowering bushes and shrubs. Patches of annuals were planted so as to blend bright colors with the lush green foliage. Mabel said that Matthews' grandmother had first planted the garden, adding a tree and bush at a time. She had loved beauty, especially that created by nature. She had somehow added several lilacs which had since grown to tall trees, and there were hydrangeas and rhododendron which were now dormant but would bloom again in May.

Although most of the flowers were unfamiliar to me, I recognized some I had seen on my stage ride from Sacramento. Mabel identified them as yellow poppies, buttercups, blue wild irises, lupins, Indian paintbrush, and mustard. Several of these she termed weeds, but I thought them as beautiful as the planned garden into which they crept unbidden.

Each day Mary Cramer picked fresh blooms from the rose bushes to arrange in the dining room and sitting room. Priscilla and I both picked the wild flowers and arranged bouquets for our own and Steven's bedrooms.

As the days sped by, Steven became more and more special to me. Although I could not help but love Priscilla, she was happy and independent in spite of her tragic loss. Steven was solemn, sensitive. I could see the defenses go up just as I felt we were becoming close to each other. I wanted very much to pull him into my arms and tell him that I understood. That I too had felt that same longing for something which was gone. I wanted to tell him that it was easy to build a wall around oneself to prevent further hurt, but that this wall also prevented love from entering your heart.

It was still too early. He needed more time to accept me, to trust me and know my warmth and love toward him were sincere. I hoped he would reach out to me as

51

I was reaching out to him. But for now, my mission was to make him smile and laugh as a child should, to remove that mask of sorrow and solemnity behind which he hid.

For the first few days, Priscilla and I talked, Steven commenting now and then. Lessons would come soon, but first we must become acquainted. The children remapped the ranch for me as my guides, showing me the barns, corrals, and hills close by. I met most of the people who worked in and around the house, and a few of the ranch hands. Most, however, were "on the range rounding up the herd."

After the first week, everyone accepted me and no special attention was shown, for which I was grateful. I began to relax and lose the shyness I always felt with new people. And the children and I settled down to a daily routine of study and play.

The house and corrals were alive with activity by dawn. However, the children and I rose later, spending the first hour or two getting dressed and having breakfast in the dining room. The remainder of the morning was spent in the garden or schoolroom, depending on the weather. On nice days I found it was easier to get Priscilla and Steven to concentrate on their studies if they were allowed to do their schoolwork in the garden.

In the afternoon, after a light lunch the children rode their horses near the house where I could watch them. Sometimes we took long nature walks in the hills behind the house. Steven sometimes brought back things that he'd collected: a rock, an abandoned bird's nest, a cocoon, a walking stick.

Often I saw Mabel Banks watching the three of us while we were studying or at some child's game. It had taken me only a short time to discover that beneath her stern countenance, she was warm and understanding. She had fooled the children even less.

Only the ranch hands and house staff seemed in awe of her, trembling at her commanding voice.

Late one afternoon, while the three of us were out taking a walk through the garden, Mrs. Banks emerged from the back of the house.

"Miss O'Reilly," she called, an infrequent smile lighting her aging face. She looked at the children holding my hands. "Would you three be interested in some oatmeal cookies and milk in the kitchen?"

The children screeched their affirmative answer and turned without a second's delay to race for the kitchen door. I laughed at their scurrying figures darting through the garden.

"That was very nice of you, Mrs. Banks. Thank you," I said, as delighted as the children with the invitation.

"Please!" She raised her hands and frowned. "My name is Mabel."

"Then you must call me Kathleen."

"I planned to do just that," she answered. Taking my hand suddenly, she gave it a little squeeze. "You have made those two very happy again." The gesture and warm compliment were so unexpected that I felt a lump in my throat. She released my hand, and we started to walk slowly toward the back steps.

"They have made me very happy, too," I said at last. "This is the first time in my life I have felt I really belong somewhere."

"You have no family, then?" she asked, looking at me sympathetically but with a glimmer of speculation.

For an instant, I thought of my father, then answered softly, "No, I have no one."

"That explains why you understand our two so well. You know what they need . . . love and fun, as well as learning. Until you came here, nobody had any time for them. Clinton is just too busy running this ranch, and I'm too old for running after lively youngsters. They just wandered around, Priscilla into mischief, and Steven becoming more and more the little ghost every day."

"I wasn't sure Mr. Matthews would let me stay," I admitted. "Our first meeting was anything but pleasant."

Mabel laughed. "He's got his mind going in too many directions. The last couple of years have been hard. One year, little rain and poor grazing for his herd; the next, too much rain and the cattle drown in the gullies. One thing after another. Now you come, hardly what he expected in a governess. I suppose he sees trouble with your good looks," she explained, smiling with secret amusement.

"Why should I be trouble for him?"

"Oh, you won't be, dear. But men see trouble in a pretty face . . . one sort or another."

Mabel had me thoroughly confused, but I decided not to ask for further explanation. I didn't understand men. I had never been in contact with any with the exception of Joseph and little with him.

"How long have you been on the ranch, Mabel?"

"About sixty years. My folks died on the wagon train when I got here. The Matthewses took me on as a maid." As she explained how she had come to stay on at the ranch, the sadness in her voice was pronounced. "I've seen Matthewses grow up, grow old, and die. In the last seven years, I've seen all but Clinton taken. First Mrs. Matthews takes ill, a couple of years later she's followed by Old Jake. Clinton was just twenty, sowing his wild oats, when he took over. It put a quick stop to his youth, unfortunately. Then two years ago, Clarissa, his sister, and her husband, Jim, died of influenza, along with about fifty others in this area. With the ranch problems on top of all that, Clinton's had his hands and heart about as full as he can take without breaking."

"No wonder he seems so gruff and cold," I said, almost to myself.

"Gruff?" she laughed. "I suppose he is now. He used to laugh a lot. His pa wondered if he'd ever settle down and take life seriously." She hesitated and I thought of little Steven and how solemn he was. Perhaps the man was no different from the boy.

"Well, let's talk about you. Where were you before you came here? Clinton said your second letter came from Denver."

That was where Anna's and my money had almost run out. "New York is where I started."

"All that way! My goodness! There must have been lots of positions back there. What made you come such a distance?"

"Oh . . . I guess I just wanted to be a part of the West. Something like that," I answered tritely, evading the real reason. I could hardly admit to her that I wanted to get as far away from New York and my father as I could, nor that I would have been stopped if I had not fled immediately.

I knew that there would be no chance of being traced, now that I was so far from New York. And why would they want to search for me anyway? I had only accomplished what my father had wished all along. I was removed from his life, and even his proximity.

"Have you been a governess before?" Mabel asked curiously.

"No, this is the first time. But I taught for two years in an orphanage."

"The same one where you were raised?" I paled at her statement.

"Is it that obvious?"

"Don't look so upset, Kathleen. Where do you suppose most governesses come from nowadays? Rich families?" She was interrupted by Priscilla, standing with her hands on her hips at the top of the steps.

"What is taking you two so long? Can we start?"

"Go ahead, child," Mabel answered, making a shooing motion with her hand. "We'll be there in our own good time." Then returning to me, "That little one is going to be a handful for some man one of these days. She's like her grandmother." Then after a moment she went on, "If you hadn't decided on being a governess, what would you have done?"

"Continued teaching in the orphanage, I guess." I knew the inevitable question would soon follow.

"Why did you leave?" We entered the kitchen where the two children were installed on high stools. They were eating their oatmeal cookies with relish and drinking the cool, raw milk.

"Why does anyone decide to leave a position?" I answered noncommittally, hoping that my reply did not sound rude. She was curious about me, as I was about her. But I could not tell her more than I had.

Mabel shrugged at my question, but did not comment. She changed the subject almost immediately.

"Clinton will be in for dinner tonight," she announced, to the great joy of the children. My reaction was quite different.

Noticing the effect her announcement had on me, she smiled reassuringly, giving me a quick pat on the shoulder.

This was the first evening in two weeks that he would be present, the first time since our unpleasant first encounter that I would have to see him again. In spite of the things Mabel had told me about his life, I did not relish the idea of facing him again. I wondered if he would find my work satisfactory and the children's progress up to his expectations.

I was pleased with their enthusiasm for study and they both had quick minds. However, my expectations and those of Clinton Matthews might be entirely different.

My nerves went taut, my mind wheeling with defenses should he be displeased. What could I do if he decided to dismiss me? Where would I go? How would I repay him for the fare west from Denver? Only one thing I did know for sure.

I would never return East.

That afternoon, shortly after the children had gone up for their late-afternoon nap, I heard horses riding into the corral. Hurriedly, I went to my window and peered out, straining my eyes to see. Beyond the gardens, I could make out five or six dusty and tired men dismounting. It was not hard to distinguish Clinton Matthews. His tall, broad-shouldered figure caught my eye immediately. I could hear his voice distinctly, strong and authoritative. He left his huge sorrel with Ted Berns, the stable hand, and turned toward the house.

Moving back from the window, I could still see him taking his long, smooth strides toward the back of the house. He looked exhausted, unshaven, and dirty. And he looked angry.

"Will it be another battle tonight, Mr. Matthews?" I asked too softly for him to hear, my gaze lingering on him as he came through the garden. After he disappeared into the house, I remained at the window looking out into the garden through which he had walked, feeling a mixture of strange emotions that I did not comprehend.

I wondered why I should find Clinton Matthews so frightening. Perhaps it was because of my limited experience of men. I had no idea how they thought or reasoned. Clinton Matthews seemed cold and hard for all the things Mabel had said. Though she had perhaps helped me to understand him a little, she had not told me anything that stopped my heart from pounding with panic every time I saw him or even thought of him.

I prepared for dinner with special care. I dressed in my ivory dress with buttons down the back. This had been reserved for religious holidays at the orphanage. It was my best gown.

Mary Cramer had to help me fasten the buttons. I piled my hair high on my head, trying to cope with the curls that many Eastern women still wore. I found them impossible to manage. With my hair high, I looked taller.

Several minutes before six I went to check on the children. When I tapped on Priscilla's door, she opened it immediately, impatient to be downstairs. She looked pretty in a light pink frock with a ribbon tying her two neat braids together at her back. I smiled, pleased with her appearance and realizing that Mabel had also taken special care to make this evening right.

Steven emerged at my side, dressed in light brown knickerbockers and a white shirt. His bow tie was too tight, for he fingered it with a frown, and gave me an unexpected smile when I loosened it for him.

"You both look fit to meet a king!" I praised them. Priscilla smiled brightly, giving a deep though still somewhat awkward curtsey.

"We'll have to work on that a little more," I teased. Steven only blushed at my compliments, but I distinguished the excited sparkle in his dark, usually melancholy eyes.

"Shall we go?" I held out my hands, and the children each took one. As we walked down the hallway to the stairs, I could feel my heart racing nervously and my appetite wane. From the children's faces I knew Clinton Matthews could not be so terrifying. It was my imagination, my inexperience with men.

Priscilla chatted gaily all the way down the stairs,

but my mind was whirling in near panic as we neared the dining-room doorway.

I wish my heart would stop pounding so hard. I wish he liked me just a little. I wish I were older and less easily cowed by him. My mind went on. I could see candlelight brightening the table and I must have hesitated, for Priscilla pulled at my hand looking up at me in confusion.

"Is something wrong, Miss O'Reilly?"

"No. I think I have everything I need right here," I answered, giving their hands a little squeeze before walking into the room.

Clinton Matthews was not there.

A wave of relief washed over me and then I saw the disappointment in Steven's face. The sparkle died. His eyes were again blank and lost.

"Don't give up, sweetheart. He'll be here in a minute, I'm sure," I whispered softly, leaning over so Priscilla would not hear. How many times had I felt that same longing that I could see so plainly on his sad little face? How many times did I still feel that same pain at night when I was totally alone with myself?

"Good evening," Matthews said, entering behind us. My heart took a leap. "Sorry to be late."

Steven's eyes lit up with pleasure, and a smile followed.

As calmly and gracefully as I could, for my body felt stiff, I turned on cue with Priscilla and we sank into low formal curtseys. "Good evening," we three answered, rather ceremoniously. I was surprised to find my voice cool and controlled because my heart was thundering nervously as I met Matthews' dark eyes, now alight with amusement. A telltale tic started in his cheek and I found myself blushing slightly as I smiled back.

"So you've dressed up for me," he observed, pleased. "You're getting to look like a little lady, Priss!" Matthews smiled down affectionately at his young niece. She stared up at him with open adoration, twinkling with pleasure at his praise. He turned to Steven and grinned, but said nothing. He didn't have to.

"I want to be just like Miss O'Reilly, Uncle Clinton. Don't you think she's beautiful?" I was grateful that Priscilla's nature did not allow for an answer. She chattered on rapidly, not even permitting time for her uncle to answer the next question she posed. Steven looked at his sister with obvious annoyance.

As we walked to the table, Steven made a valiant effort to seat me. Matthews raised his brows as he watched, and I fearing he would laugh, gave him a pleading look. Following his nephew's example, Matthews seated Priscilla with a half-smile.

"I can see I will have to start minding my own manners," he said lightly, noting Priscilla's look of surprise and hearing her giggle. Then he went on to his position at the head of the table.

Dinner started smoothly and I stopped worrying about conversing. Priscilla hardly stopped talking, though Steven was quiet. Once he turned a shy smile on me and I felt my heart melt. Matthews asked him several questions, drawing him into the conversation, and he became more animated than I had ever seen him.

Once, I met Clinton Matthews' eyes as he caught me studying him. From that time on I kept my gaze cautiously averted.

The comments the children made about some of their lessons caused me some slight embarrassment, though I could not suppress a laugh. Matthews studied me in turn. Probably sizing up his adversary, I thought.

"How do you like living on a ranch, Miss O'Reilly?" he asked suddenly in his deep, cool voice. Thinking he only meant to draw me into polite conversation, I answered politely, without elaborating on my opinions. Surely he was not really interested in what I thought.

He waited a moment, as though expecting more, looking somehow disappointed. "We watched Jim break the mare yesterday," Steven offered, looking between the two of us.

"What did you think of that?" Matthews asked, addressing the question to me again. I watched his warning brow raise at my delayed answer.

"I felt sorry for the horse," I answered, the startled look on his handsome face making me feel incredibly stupid.

"Why? It wasn't whipped or beaten, was it?"

"Oh, no . . . it just seemed such a beautiful, spirited animal. I thought it deserved to be free. It fought so hard to shake that rider off."

"It was the black mare, Uncle Clinton," Steven explained and then turned to me with a worried expression. "He caught it himself," he said quietly, while I felt his uncle's eyes still holding on me.

"I didn't suspect that I had employed an animal lover," he said, smiling slightly. I knew he was ridiculing my Eastern softness, but I chose to make no further comment for his amusement. Dropping my eyes from his, I went on with dinner. My hand shook slightly when I lifted my wineglass for a small sip and I saw Matthews frowning at me from the end of the table.

"Shall we go into the study?" he asked after tossing his napkin down next to his empty plate. Relaxing again, I looked at Steven and winked.

Taking my cue, he challenged his uncle to a game of chess, a game for which we had been preparing for the past three days.

"You're on!" Matthews answered, and Steven smiled over at me. I silently thanked Miss Montgomery for her eccentricities, having learned the game from her. Few women played, finding it tedious and believing men did not like women to think. But I enjoyed the game.

While Steven set up the chessboard, I sent Priscilla up to the schoolroom for her embroidery sampler. When she returned and settled herself into a chair, one leg crossed under her and biting her lip in concentration, I thought it time to leave the family alone.

"If you'll excuse me," I started, but Matthews' quick glance made any thought of escape vanish.

"No. Stay here." It was a command, not a request.

Why? I was no pleasure to him, obviously. He did not like my company, but rather was annoyed by it. I walked to the bookshelves, deciding to stay in the shadows of the room. Running my hand over the beautiful leather-bound volumes, I came across a book of Shakespeare's plays. I took it down and started to read *The Merchant of Venice*.

Several minutes later an exclamation of surprise roused my attentions.

"Why you little scoundrel!" I shot a glance at Matthews but saw that he was speaking only in mock anger and that his face showed pleased surprise. "Who has been teaching you these underhanded tricks?"

Steven looked delightedly proud as he laughed and clapped his hands. "Miss O'Reilly! Miss O'Reilly!" He swung around with a triumphant smile. "It worked. I really beat him!"

"Wonderful!" I grinned at him, still hearing that first laugh and feeling triumphant myself. Replacing the book on the shelf and approaching, I surveyed the chessboard and the positioning of the pieces. "But now that you've shown him your mettle, he will be more careful. You'll have to keep practicing." Matthews leaned back in his chair, but all I could see was the radiance of Steven's face.

"We'll play again soon, Steven. But now, I think it's time you both hit the sack." Obeying his uncle,

Steven started to collect the chessmen, but was forestalled. "Leave them. I'm going to challenge your instructor. I want to find out what kind of game she's teaching you." Cocking his head, he locked his eyes with mine. "Come back down when they're settled in."

"As you wish, Mr. Matthews." Oh, no. I thought.

I would have preferred to stay upstairs and talk with the children. However, tonight they were almost eager to be settled. Priscilla watched me leave with a smile on her lips. Usually she protested going to bed, being a little night owl. I found her sudden acquiescence unusual and almost alarming.

As I stood in the hallway the house seemed very quiet. And it was only half past eight.

When I again entered the study, Matthews was standing by the bookshelves holding a volume. I hesitated at the doorway for a moment, studying his face. He seemed relaxed, deep in thought, the hard lines of his jaw softened by the candlelight. He had a handsome profile, his nose not too long, his mouth curving up slightly in a half-smile. Yes, indeed, he was very attractive. I wondered again what Mabel had meant by "sowing his wild oats." Women, undoubtedly. I could well imagine how many would find him handsome in appearance and desirable in wealth as well.

He turned suddenly as though catching some small movement I had made at the doorway. I blushed, feeling somehow caught in the act of studying him. The candlelight cast his shadow high against the bookshelf, and made him look like a menacing giant angry at being stared upon. As he approached me, I wanted to back away but stood stiffly.

"Come in."

Moving into the room, I still did not meet his eyes. "Do you like Shakespeare?" he asked, closing the double doors behind me. As they snapped shut I felt trapped. This was how our first meeting had started.

Would this one be the same? Would he yell at me again?

"Pardon me?"

"I asked if you liked Shakespeare?"

"Yes, I do, sir," I answered tremulously, looking up at him as he came around to stand in front of me. He seemed so much taller than I.

"Do you always speak so formally?" he asked rather sharply, staring down at me, too close for comfort.

"I am sorry. I'm afraid it is habit," I apologized, feeling more and more inadequate to the situation.

"Please sit down," he offered more gently, indicating a chair next to the chessboard. Those cool dark eyes! If only he would stop looking at me.

"You and the children seem to be getting along very well." Replacing the chess pieces one by one, I noticed his large, long-fingered hands, rather like those I would have expected an artist to have. They were, however, hard, strong hands, callused from ranch work. "You're good for them according to Mabel."

How much had Mabel told him?

"They're good for me, Mr. Matthews." I tried not to speak formally and antagonize him, but somehow the words came out stiffly. He glanced up, his eyes moving over my face and lingering slightly on my mouth. A tremor passed through me and I flushed, praying that the candlelight hid my confusion.

"Your play," he said finally.

The game progressed slowly, neither of us giving ground. I began to wonder if it was customary for the woman to play into the man's strategy, while he spoke.

"You're a worthy opponent, Miss O'Reilly." With his next few moves, I realized that he had never been out of control of his game while he tested me. I felt myself losing ground.

"I'd like to ask you some questions."

My hand shook slightly as I reached out to take my rook from jeopardy.

"In your letter you said that you had teaching experience." He hesitated, considering the chessboard, then moved his queen to take my castle. Leaning back, he went on. "I would like to know where."

My throat constricted. Why did he want specifics now? Was he not satisfied with my performance? Why had he never asked for this information before hiring me?

"Is something wrong?" he asked when I still remained silent, staring down at the chessboard.

"No," I answered, trying to keep my voice from shaking and pretending I was deep in concentration on the game. I made a move. "I taught in an orphanage."

"Where did you get your schooling?" he asked, almost casually, making a quick decision and changing the position of his knight.

"In an orphanage," I replied in a low voice, still staring at the board, trying to match my tone with his.

"The same orphanage?"

"Yes."

The blood drained from my face and my hands felt cold in spite of the warmth of the room. Reaching down, I made a hasty move as he watched me.

"That was very foolish, Miss O'Reilly." He made a swift move, placing his queen strategically, and pronounced, "Checkmate." Color flooded my cheeks as I saw the stupidity of my move.

Settling back into his chair again, he picked up his questioning again. "Now, where did you say the orphanage was?"

"I didn't say." I had not meant my reply to sound impertinent, but he took it so.

"Why not?" he shot back.

"You never asked before. Are you dissatisfied with

my progress with Priscilla and Steven?" I asked, trying to steer him away from my background.

"I already said I was pleased. I have no doubts now about your capabilities. The children's faces were enough to convince me you're right for them, even if you don't teach them a thing. I'm just interested in knowing more about you. Is that all right?"

He had every right to know all about me. But I wanted to forget all that, and how could I if I had to talk about it, remember it.

But I was remembering already. William Stuart Benson, Miss Montgomery, the cold granite eyes of the young man in the carriage, the fragmented china vase on my bedroom floor, Anna's bright green eyes. Again I was standing in my room at Parkside, watching as Miss Montgomery rode frantically down the drive after telling Joseph to watch me and prevent my leaving.

"Miss O'Reilly?" Matthews' voice cut into my memories. My wall had unknowingly crumbled before his eyes, leaving my emotions bare and raw for him to see. He looked startled.

"Why didn't you ask me before?"

"Your letter was enough to show me you were educated. But now I'm curious about you. Why shouldn't I be? And why should you hesitate to answer such simple questions?"

"It's personal . . ."

"You're evading me again. Have you done something wrong?"

"No!"

"Then . . ." he pressed.

"I simply quit my job and left. That's all. I'm eighteen. Do I need permission to leave?" My voice was sharply defensive, as though I faced Miss Montgomery and my father.

"Christ, you're touchy!"

"I'm sorry . . ." I apologized quickly, clenching my hand in my lap until the knuckles turned white.

"Why did you leave?" he persisted, curious.

"I wasn't fired if that's what you're thinking," I answered angrily. My emotions were in a flurry of confusion. Why was he persisting if he was just curious? He said he was satisfied with my progress with the children. Wasn't that enough for him to know about me?

"I didn't think you were. You just got through saying you quit," he retorted hotly. "Now I want to know why, without any more evasion." His tone was demandingly cold, and tears smarted my eyes.

"I wanted to live my own life," I answered quietly, controlling my voice with an effort. I wanted to leave behind the memories, false and empty. I wanted to leave behind a file that said I was the child of a prostitute and a man who didn't want me. I wanted to leave Miss Montgomery and her false affection, her false concern.

But hadn't that all come with me? Didn't I have nightmares frequently with all the faces of those people I wanted most to forget, and faces of people I didn't even recognize?

"Miss O'Reilly," Matthews spoke quietly, his eyes softening as I stared at him, yet beyond him to the others. "Do you think I am being unfair to ask these questions?"

"No," I answered.

"Did you hate it there so much?" he asked, his voice surprisingly gentle.

"No. They were always . . . kind . . . to me." Kind? Had it been kindness that had prompted Miss Montgomery's deception?

"Perhaps you misread their intentions and were a bit hasty, even ungrateful . . ."

"I did not do anything wrong nor anything that anyone else would not have done had they been in the same position. I owed them nothing . . . do you hear, Mr. Matthews! Nothing!" I shot out of my chair at his accusation, my hands digging into the folds of my skirt as I cried out at him. I swung around, my hand over my face, feeling choked with unhappiness and shame. He rose behind me and the noise of his movement startled me. I turned around, moving back instinctively as he stood looking down at me. When he stepped around the table my heart quickened with fear and I could see his angry eyes go to the pulsing vein at the base of my neck.

"Are you so afraid of me?" he asked with surprise, the anger gone. He reached out slightly, as though to touch me and I jerked away instinctively. "My God, you're terrified. Why?"

"I'm not," I denied, feeling suffocated by his closeness.

"I can see it in your eyes," he observed. "Do you think I want to hurt you?"

"I don't know," I admitted, shuddering.

"I won't," and then with surprising perception, "You've never worked with men before, have you?"

A heavy silence fell between us. I did not need to answer. "I want to know you a little better, Miss O'Reilly," he said finally. "Most women love to talk about themselves for hours. I can't get anything out of you at all."

"There is really nothing to tell. The only part of my life with any meaning and truth started here with Priscilla and Steven."

"I won't press you anymore now. You're good for the children. That's enough to know about you for the moment."

A weight of depression lifted from me and I reached out spontaneously, the unconscious gesture of human need for understanding and contact. Catching myself,

I dropped my hand to my side, my heart fluttering madly at his strange, curious look.

"May I go to my room now?"

"If you wish to go."

"Good night, then, Mr. Matthews. Thank you for the game of chess." I dropped a curtsey and turned to the double doors, opening one quietly.

"Miss O'Reilly?"

I faced him again. He was about to speak, but stopped. "Good night," he said simply, a half-smile touching his lips.

I smiled back, quietly shutting the door behind me.

V

Unlike my years at the orphanage, time on the ranch went swiftly, each day packed with children's adventures and fun. While teaching Priscilla and Steven their required lessons, I allowed them the freedoms that I had never had, and through them enjoyed the joy-filled childhood I might have had under other circumstances.

We laughed with each other, played games, read each other stories that we found in various collections. I tried to make their lessons fun, making games out of their grammar and math assignments, instilling in them the joy of learning as well as the material itself. Mornings were spent in the garden now that spring was past and summer begun. Priscilla and Steven were nose-deep in their books, eyes sparkling and minds active with a hundred questions about everything. I endeavored to find a reason for every fact they were to learn and spent time explaining the importance of building knowledge atop the proper foundation. "Later, your house of knowledge can take any shape you want, be it a simple log cabin, practical and unadorned, or a towering palace with a thousand extra rooms."

In the afternoon, I sometimes watched the children practice company etiquette. Often they turned the lesson into a nonsensical fair, one attempting to outdo the other. Priscilla had a natural grace, her curtseys executed with a precocious maturity. Only her expression gave away the hoydenish personality beneath the ladylike fluff and ruffled frock she donned for dinner.

Steven was another matter. Even at six, he had a certain ease and dignity. Unlike his older sister, he was more prone to seriousness in anything he did. Slowly, now, I watched him emerge from the shell in which I had found him during the first weeks on the ranch. Then I seldom saw him smile, nor heard him laugh. Now he shared in Priscilla's and my fun.

Each day made me feel more "settled in," as Mabel expressed it. And I felt at home with everyone, except Clinton Matthews.

He was often absent from dinner, busy with ranch business. Sometimes he was out on the range; other times, locked deep in work in his study, his account books open and the lamp on his desk burning. Mabel would take a tray in to him, hoping to entice him with the aromas of her fine cooking. Hours later, she would return the untouched tray to the kitchen, mumbling under her breath.

Since that night in the study, Matthews and I had not talked other than to exchange polite conversation at dinner. The less Clinton Matthews noticed me, the happier I was. Better to bear his indifference than his disapproval and curiosity.

When he did join us for dinner, he treated me with politeness. Sometimes I felt him watching me with an intentness that made me uneasy. He said little, showing even less.

When the children spoke about their daily activities, I sensed his interest in them was genuine, and for that I almost found myself drawn to him.

One morning, however, that all changed again.

Unexpectedly, Mary Cramer awakened me just before dawn. My head was aching from lack of sound sleep, having tossed and awakened several times during the night. The nightmare had recurred, a dream in which I saw my father, the young man in the carriage, Miss Montgomery, and Clinton Matthews. What roles they each played in my nighttime horror were nebulous memories, lurking in my unconscious mind. Awake, I could remember nothing but the terror.

Mary's tap made me awaken with a start and shoot upright in my bed, nerves wound tight. "Come in," I called uneasily, my shoulders still trembling slightly as I held myself up straight, watching the door. The room was still dark and shadow-filled.

I almost laughed with relief when Mary's head peeked in the door. Her face glowed from the candlelight on my bedside table and she glanced with surprise at the flame.

"I had a nightmare . . ." I explained, seeing her questioning expression.

"Mr. Matthews asked me to awaken you early this morning, Miss O'Reilly," she explained, coming quietly into the room. She was carrying something in her arms. "He wishes to talk with you downstairs as soon as you can get into these."

"Mr. Matthews wants to speak with me? What time is it?"

"Half past four, ma'am."

"Half past four?" I repeated dumbly.

"Yes, ma'am." She stood looking down at me nervously as I made no move to rise. "He's waiting now, Miss O'Reilly."

I climbed out of the bed, pulling the laces together at my throat. As I went to the basin to wash my face, Mary relaxed. She laid out a dark blue riding skirt, white shirtwaist, and matching blue jacket. On the floor she placed high riding boots, polished to a fine shimmering finish.

"To whom do these things belong?" I asked, rubbing the sleep from my eyes and then brushing my hair in long, hurried strokes.

"They belonged to Clarissa Matthews, before she was married. Mabel said she wore them when she was just sixteen. They've been in a cedar chest in the attic for about fifteen years." I stopped brushing my hair and looked at her perplexed.

"Does Mr. Matthews know Mabel unpacked these things for me to use?"

"He told her to get them for you."

"Oh, I see," I said, though I did not. Used to wearing hand-me-down clothes, I was not distressed by this offer. But I felt surprise that Mr. Matthews would allow me clothes that had belonged to his only sister, clothes that must have been cherished either by her or her family to be packed away and saved for so many years.

"They are beautiful," I commented, admiring the outfit and touching the soft fabric timidly. "Did you know Clarissa, Mary?"

"No, but Mabel often talks about her. She was very pretty from what she says about her . . . four years Mr. Matthews' senior, I think," she informed me. "She must have been something very special because Mabel thought so much of her. Mabel doesn't like many people, but she loved Clarissa. She feels the same way about you, too, I think."

For an instant, I thought I detected a touch of envy in her eyes as she looked away. I didn't know what to say, feeling that Mabel had taken me into her care with the maternal instinct so natural to her.

"Thank you, Mary. It's kind of you to tell me that."

She shrugged as though dismissing the information

73

as unimportant. "Will that be all, Miss O'Reilly?" I felt rebuked.

"Yes, thank you."

The riding habit smelled of cedar, a fresh, pungent fragrance. I admired the outfit, almost deciding to fold it up and put it aside. Somehow it seemed irreverent to borrow the clothes of someone so loved. But something inside me told me she would not have minded, for I was giving her children the love they needed so desperately.

When I finished putting on the clothes, I stood in front of my dresser mirror. The shirtwaist was snug over my breasts, but the skirt fitted nicely. The black boots were a near-perfect fit. And the final touches of the blue jacket and wide black leather belt made me feel very Western. I parried in front of my reflection, admiring the effect.

Never in my life had I worn such beautifully cut clothes. I was a good seamstress, and the clothes given to the orphanage had beeen adjusted to fit me, but I was far from professional. And our uniforms were straightly simple.

This outfit must have been made by someone in San Francisco or Sacramento.

I took one more turn around in front of the mirror and then left the room, excited and happy.

As I came down the stairs, Matthews stood in the hallway, slapping his leather gloves into his hand impatiently. I wished I had hurried a little more and not procrastinated in front of the mirror.

Before I was able to utter a word of thanks, or even be noticed descending the stairway, Jim Calhoun came striding into the hallway from out front.

"Clint, there's a little trouble out—" his voice dropped off slightly as he continued. A dark scowl filled Matthews' countenance and I heard him swear. "Good morning, Miss O'Reilly," Jim said, startled to see me coming down the stairs toward him and Matthews. He looked at my outfit and then darted a glance to his boss, a smile tugging at his mouth.

"Thank you for the loan of your sister's riding habit, Mr. Matthews," I said, smiling and feeling a fluttering under my breast at his look. He flushed slightly, cocking his head, and then turned toward Jim, catching his lingering half-grin.

I felt so happy. He, himself, was going to teach me to ride. Perhaps he did not dislike me so much as I had thought. The stairway rail slid unfelt under my fingers as I moved down the last few steps, my face flushed with excitement.

"Jim, give Miss O'Reilly her first riding lesson and take her around the ranch a bit so she can get familiar with the area." When he looked back at me in a quick appraisal, not smiling, my heart stopped. His cold stare at me and his hot glowering glance to Jim confused me. "It's about time she starts chaperoning Priscilla and Steven properly."

My spine stiffened. "I have always watched them carefully when they rode, sir," I sputtered, feeling myself fall back abruptly to stiff formality.

Matthews scowled, his eyes growing warningly narrow at my defensive retort.

"You agreed that you would learn to ride. You've been here for two months and still can't." His voice was low and accusing. My anger drained away and I stood silent, wishing I had never spoken at all. The happy glow was gone.

Jim shifted his feet uncomfortably. "Well, Miss O'Reilly?" he asked, gesturing toward the door and darting a puzzled look at his moody employer.

"I was going to teach you myself," Matthews offered and then added to spoil it, "but something important has come up."

By all means, take care of it, I thought, wishing I

were out of the house and miles away from him. He did not need to emphasize the indifference with which he had lately held me.

"Her horse is outside," he went on, his voice angry again.

Once outside and faced with the mount he had intended for me, I blanched. "Surely, he doesn't expect me to ride on this horse?" I asked hopefully, staring at the black mare, broken only a few weeks before. She stamped her hoof impatiently and snorted. I swallowed a hard lump in my throat.

"She's gentle as a kitten," Jim assured me.

"I'm sure," I retorted, unconvinced.

"Are you afraid, Miss O'Reilly?" he challenged me. "I thought the Irish were fire-eaters!"

"I'm only half-Irish."

"I heard you took a liking to that particular horse," Matthews chimed in from the top step. I turned to glare at him. So that was his game! Well, I'd take his challenge and make him eat it if it were the last thing I did!

"She *is* a beauty, isn't she?" I observed, turning back to Jim Calhoun. "I can't think of a horse I'd rather ride!" I went on truthfully, moving steadily toward the mare. My heart was in my throat and I prayed she would not bite me as I raised a hand to her silky neck. Her brown eyes turned toward me suspiciously, but she did not move.

"What do I do first, Jim?" I asked, smiling at him and pretending to be very relaxed. Jim grinned, giving me a quick, understanding wink. "That's the way, Irish! Just do like I do." I copied his actions and found it not difficult to mount the mare. Once on top of her, it seemed a long way down to the ground, however. Yet after a moment, I did not feel frightened anymore, but rather exhilarated and eager. I gave a little laugh, feeling truly relaxed and excited again.

"Okay, let's go."

We rode for some time, taking my lesson in slow, careful stages. Mount, dismount, mount again until it was a fluid easy task. Then we trotted. I bounced up and down, giggling, and Jim laughed at my expression. Once I urged the mare into a gallop just to see what it would be like. Jim let out a startled shout, darting after me on his gray.

"It's such fun!" I exclaimed, reining her in as Jim came up beside me.

"You scared me half to death, Miss O'Reilly," he scolded.

"But it's so easy."

"You're a natural rider . . . never seen anyone take to it so natural-like. Your other half Indian, maybe?"

I laughed. "Will you be giving me another lesson tomorrow morning, Jim?" I asked enthusiastically.

"Frankly, I didn't know I'd be taking you on this one. But you've got the basics, all you need is practice . . . and the kids will give you plenty of that . . . you willing." Then his eyes twinkled mischievously. "But I think I'll ask Clint if it's okay for a couple more lessons . . . I'd much rather ride with you than try to keep those rowdy ranch hands of his in line. They were at it again this morning," he went on.

We turned our horses back toward the ranch. Using the pressure of my legs on her side, I found the mare responded easily. Reaching down, I stroked her neck, feeling a companionship with her.

I was surprised to find Matthews back at the house. He stood with the children on the steps, watching our progress toward them. Priscilla jumped up and down, laughing and clapping her hands.

"Oh, you can ride now, Miss O'Reilly. Can we go riding this afternoon?" She skipped lightly down the steps and stood prancing next to the horse as I dismounted. "Please? Please?"

"How'd she do?" Matthews asked over Priscilla's plea. His voice was cool.

"Rides like an Indian," Jim answered, grinning. "You should have seen her. She thought I was going too slow and took off easy as you please . . . with control!"

Clinton Matthews raised his brows in surprise and looked at me for a second appraisal that morning.

So there! I thought smugly, though I only smiled at him pleasantly. His eyes twinkled with amusement as though he read my thoughts.

"If you and the children want to ride this afternoon, tell Ted to saddle Pepper and Lady for them . . . Consider this your mount whenever you want her."

"Thank you," I stammered, surprised at his generous offer of allowing me to ride the mare whenever I wanted. I was ashamed of my previous annoyance and arrogance.

"Can't you let me give her a couple more lessons, Clint?" Jim asked, his eyes sparkling with suppressed amusement.

"She'll do just fine without you if I can believe your report," Matthews answered, scowling slightly. "You've got more important things to do than give riding lessons." His last words spoiled my pleasure again and made my temper flare. What an annoying man! One minute he is kind, the next insulting!

The children's morning lessons went quickly, all three of us eager for our first ride together. As we set out from the stables, my legs were stiff, but they gradually loosened as we went.

We rode several miles from the house, enjoying the bright summer afternoon. The hillsides were still green, patches of wild flowers spattering color between the groves of oak, black walnut, and sycamore trees.

It was a peaceful, glorious countryside through which we rode. The hills rolled gently away from us on each side, climbing higher into another range beyond. Off in the distance a high mountain jutted above everything else around.

As I asked more questions about riding and caring for horses, Priscilla chimed in giggling at the momentary expression of discomfort on my face as my mount broke into a trot.

"That's the hardest thing to learn!"

"It sure is," I grimaced.

"Relax and let yourself go with your horse," Steven suggested from the back pony. Relaxing my muscles, I moved easier.

"Galloping is much more fun!"

Taking Priscilla's hint, Steven suddenly spurred his pony into a full gallop, darting away from us down the narrow valley and then turning up through some trees. "Bet you can't catch me!" he challenged over his shoulder.

Priscilla and I followed in hot pursuit. Some natural instinct told me to flatten myself down close to the horse's neck and loosen my grip on the reins. She picked up speed, her hooves flying over the grassy ground. Her mane whipped about me and I wanted her to go even faster.

"Go, girl!"

My hair ribbon tore loose and flew off, freeing my hair. It blew out wildly behind me like a dark cloud, and I felt that if I raised my arms in the air I would soar away like a bird.

Leaving Priscilla behind, I caught up with Steven easily, my mount much longer-legged and swifter than either of theirs. Reining her in was another matter, for she had taken the bit in her teeth, determined to run. She sprang past Steven's pony and headed farther up the hillside.

"Miss O'Reilly!" Steven cried out in alarm as I flew past him. "Wait! Pull her in!"

I tried. "Easy, girl, easy!" Don't panic, I told myself, trying to remain calm. I spoke gently to her, leaning into her neck, half of me frightened by her speed and fury and the other half wanting to let her run on and on.

Slowly I drew myself up, pulling the reins back steadily, my knees tightening on her sides. "Slow, girl. Easy."

She yanked hard, almost tearing the reins from my hands. I held on, the leather burning. She began to slow, tossing her head and snorting angrily, pulling hard for her lead again. For a moment, I feared she would rear and throw me off as she had tried to throw the man that broke her. Her front hooves bounced threateningly off the ground. Then she calmed. Blowing hard, snorting furiously, she stopped and I leaned down and patted her.

"Sorry, girl. I wish I could let you run." I turned her back down the hillside toward the children, who were frantically racing up toward me.

"We thought she'd run off with you!" Priscilla shouted as she came around a thick bush toward me.

"Are you all right?" The deep voice made my heart leap and I turned to see Matthews come through some trees to my side. I was struck by his attractiveness as he handled his huge sorrel with skill and ease.

"I'm fine," I replied, still breathy and excited. My heart had picked up speed again. The mare stamped her hooves on the ground. "I think she would be happy to run like that all day," I laughed.

"I'm sure glad you were around, Uncle Clinton!" Steven said, letting out a sigh of relief.

"I've got some strays down below," he explained to me. In the meeting of the hills below us a small herd of cattle grazed calmly. I must have ridden right past him, I thought.

"For a minute there, I thought I would be picking

up your pieces. But you handled yourself very well, Miss O'Reilly," he commented.

"Thank you," I smiled, uncommonly pleased by the compliment.

"We're going to ride up to the crest, Uncle Clinton," Steven announced, turning his pony up the hill again and taking off, Priscilla following. "We'll be back in a little while, Miss O'Reilly," she called as she darted away.

A breeze blew through my hair and I realized the appearance I must make. Windblown, face flushed and smiling, I must look like a hoyden. Watching the children disappear through the oak trees, I reached up and tried to straighten out my hair, pushing my fingers through the long tresses and flipping them back over my shoulders. I became acutely aware of Matthews watching me.

"I lost my ribbon," I explained unnecessarily, blushing at my unkempt appearance.

"So I see," he replied with a hint of laughter. "My mother had long hair. I used to watch her brush it. She'd bring it over her shoulder like that and comb it." My embarrassment disappeared as I heard the unguarded wistfulness in his voice.

I dropped my hands from my hair, feeling somehow closer to him for those few words. Maybe it was loneliness and responsibility that made him so harsh and unreachable.

"I was about seven or eight when I used to watch her do that. God, what a long time ago that was." There was unveiled sadness in his voice.

"When did you lose her?"

"Later, much later. I was sixteen when she died." My question brought him out of his memories, and once again he was the assured man. I wanted to know that other part of him. He glanced up the hillside toward the grove of trees through which the children had gone. "And you?" he asked suddenly.

"And me?" I repeated, confused.

"Did you miss not having your mother?"

"How can one miss what one has never had?" I answered with unexpected stiffness and a heaviness descended on me as I saw that familiar cooling look. "I'm sorry."

"I'm sorry I asked that," he said, frowning.

"No. Don't be. I am much too defensive about it," I admitted, wishing to bring back that sudden closeness I had felt for so brief a time. "Yes, I did miss not having my mother, but it must be worse to have a mother and then lose her."

He smiled, easily and with warmth. "I apologize for being so abrupt this morning," he said slowly. "There were some problems I had to handle myself."

"Important problems," I said, smiling. He chuckled. His horse pulled at the reins, bending to reach a high clump of grass.

"Have you been enjoying your ride?" he asked after what seemed to me an uncomfortable silence.

"Yes . . . very much. The children are so alive . . . so excited by everything around them. It's like being able to remold my own childhood the way I'd have liked it." I realized I was rambling. "I don't mean to say I didn't have a good childhood . . . it's just . . ." I stopped, realizing how close I was to admitting some of my more personal feelings. Why did I have this sudden urge to talk with him?

Matthews glanced down the hill toward the herd of cattle. I was boring him, like those other women he mentioned who always talked about themselves.

"I'm sorry to be keeping you. Please don't feel you have to keep me company," I said, feeling disappointed in his disinterest. What had I expected?

"I'm not in a hurry," he answered, quickly looking back at me. "Why don't we sit and talk for a while?"

Thinking he only meant to be polite, I answered, "I've interrupted you enough already with my wild ride."

"I can keep a watch on the herd from up here. And your strays will return in a while." Not allowing me a chance to speak again, he swung down from his horse and came toward me.

Again I became conscious of the easy manner in which he walked, his handsome features, his broad shoulders and narrow waist. He stood next to my horse. "Swing your leg over the saddle horn." I followed his instructions, my heart jumping as he reached up and took hold, lifting me effortlessly from the mare. My hands went to his broad shoulders as he lifted me down and I felt his hard muscles ripple. A strange sensation raced through my blood, and I flushed.

For a moment he held me suspended, his face very close to mine as he searched my eyes. My heart raced, my breath catching in my throat. When my feet touched the ground, I dropped my hands from his shoulders quickly, feeling a strange shakiness. His hands loosened slowly, and then he pulled them away suddenly, a disturbed frown appearing on his face.

He exhaled sharply, looking over my head. "I'll tie up your mount." Taking the reins, he led the mare to a tree and flipped the leather straps around a low branch. When he returned, he appeared relaxed and friendly.

"Let's sit over there," he suggested, indicating a shady spot between two large oak trees.

"Fine," I agreed, smiling and feeling more relaxed with him again.

Sitting down in the grass, I plucked a large red

flower. I smelled its heady fragrance and studied it curiously.

"It's a variety of tobacco," he said, answering my silent question. "The Indians use it for some of their ceremonies," he remarked, watching me hold the flower to my nose again.

"What do they do with it? Smoke it?"

"They smoke this part," he explained, pointing to a round section under the petals. "It brings on pleasant dreams even when awake."

"Really?" I looked at him smiling down at me. "Are you teasing me?"

"No, it's supposed to be true."

"Oh, then you don't really know."

"I tried it once," he admitted, picking a blade of grass and chewing at it. He leaned back, his elbow bracing him.

"What was it like?" I prodded when he didn't volunteer the outcome of his experiment.

"Nothing happened . . . except I coughed a lot. I was about ten at the time." He grinned, the blade of grass dangling jauntily out of the corner of his mouth, making him look a bit like the mischievous boy he was reported to have been. I laughed.

"It's so beautiful and peaceful out here in California," I commented after a moment, looking at the hills and twirling the flower between my fingers.

"You like it?"

"Uh huh," I replied, dreamily, leaning back in the grass and looking up through the branches of the oak tree. "It's not like anything I was told about California."

"What were you told?"

"To expect wild Indians, snakes, gunfights on every main street, stagecoach robbers, drought, and I don't remember what else," I informed him. Then I grinned. "It all came from a five-cent novel."

He laughed out loud. "I suppose most Easterners think that anyway," he commented after a moment.

"Well, your telegram didn't admit anything which helped to add to the image," I said, remembering the vague, "must adapt to ranch life." "It sounded ominous, somehow."

"Ominous? How so?"

I explained.

"That's probably why you came," he said, smiling. "You were curious."

"Well, it did sound interesting," I admitted, "and I wanted a change." My voice dropped. Yes, I had wanted a change.

Our eyes met and locked, something powerful and unexplainable passing between us. I sat up with a jerk, averting my eyes and looking down the grassy incline where the cattle grazed peacefully. The breeze blew playfully through my hair.

Why had his intent look made my blood rush through me like that, making me tingle all over?

The silence that fell between us became disturbing. "Would you tell me about the children's family?" I asked, wanting to end the tension.

"Their mother was my older sister, Clarissa. She married James Adams, a rancher who came from beyond that range of hills over there." He pointed toward the high mountain in the distance. "He was quite a bit older than she was . . . about twenty years . . . but he was a nice enough fellow."

"And they both died of influenza," I said, remembering what Mabel had told me.

"The children came through by the Grace of God."

"You've lost so many . . ." My voice was quiet; I felt a tender sadness as I watched his face.

"It's a hard life," he said briskly, "and the last few years have been harder than usual. Scarlet fever, measles, influenza . . . they've taken their toll from all the families in this valley. Not just mine."

"How long has your family been in the valley?"

"From the first. My great-grandfather was a Mexican patrone. My grandfather jumped ship in San Francisco and worked on some of the large ranchos out here. He was accepted as a guest on Las Posas, met and later married my grandmother." A note of pride entered his voice. "My mother came West on a wagon train."

"A wagon train . . ." I said dreamily, thinking how exciting that would have been. New land and a new life.

"Sometime, we'll go up to the crest and you can look out over the whole valley. It's beautiful."

I smiled at his polite offer, never expecting it to be fulfilled. Again something seemed to flash between us and all the ease I had felt vanished. I took my eyes from his with an effort, wrapping my arms around my knees. I was still all too conscious of his dark eyes studying me with that disturbing, yet exciting light in them.

"They've been gone for quite a while," I said, referring to the children.

"Don't worry about them. They'll be fine." After another long silence he asked a question about the children and I answered briefly, realizing it was only to break the silence.

"Do you like Jim?" he went on.

"Yes, he's very nice," I answered, surprised at his question.

After another long silence, I started to get up. He was on his feet and standing in front of me with his hand extended. I could hardly refuse and reached up to him. His fingers closed over mine with warm strength, pulling me up easily. My heart was playing tricks inside me again and I stared at him in a daze, waiting for something to happen to break the silence.

Some movement, some word to shatter the stillness and that strange vibration between us. I withdrew my hand from his slowly.

Just as he took a step toward me, the children's voices floated toward us, breaking the spell. I stepped back slightly and turned, looking up the hillside as they came racing through the trees toward us, laughing.

I wondered why I felt a pang of disappointment. What was the matter with me?

"Well, I'd better get back down with my strays now that yours are back," Matthews commented. A sharp whistle brought his sorrel. Mounting easily, he looked down at me.

"See you back at the house," he said casually. I watched as he turned and rode down the hill as though nothing had passed between us.

Perhaps, to him, nothing had.

I did not see Clinton Matthews again until dinner that night, though for the remainder of the afternoon, I could think of little else but our time on the hillside. Each time I relived the moment when he held me suspended and I trembled with a strange vibrating excitement. I wondered what it would have been like to let him kiss me, and then was shocked by my fantasy of such a thing.

When I came downstairs with the children, the muscles were like tight cords in my legs and back. Determined not to show any discomfort from my first day of riding, I moved slowly, drawing the children into conversation as we went down to join Matthews for dinner.

Once seated, I felt tense and flustered with Matthews, all the closeness of this afternoon working to make me slip back again behind my protective barrier. I wondered if he knew the effect he had had upon me and it distressed me to believe that he did. But now he again treated me with cool politeness, almost in-difference. Not reflecting on my own behavior, I was confused by his. I was hurt and slightly bewildered, but accepted the fact that I was a governess in the house of a young and much too attractive cattleman. His interest in me would be nominal and impersonal. I had been naïve to believe his friendly visit on the hillside was a hint of more interest than my position in his household warranted. I felt even more embar-rassed and ridiculous when I reviewed my afternoon of fantasizing.

Matthews relaxed in his chair, the deep creases around his eyes loosening. The children monopolized the conversation and I watched Priscilla laughing as she recalled stories and happenings not yet shared.

Steven's comments were limited to cattle and ranch interests, sometimes cutting in on his sister impatiently when she dragged her tale out too long. Matthews laughed and mediated between the two from time to time, while I sat in virtual silence, feeling somehow disappointed. This afternoon had meant nothing after all. Everything I had felt came from the depths of my own loneliness and imagination and not from anything he had done or said. But did it really matter if I knew that he no longer disliked me? Indifference was far better than disapproval.

"I'm glad you're taking such an interest in what's happening around the ranch, Steven," Matthews said. I felt him glance in my direction.

Steven perked up and responded: "Miss O'Reilly says the most important thing in the world is to feel you belong somewhere. But she said you have to give to belong. You know. Do chores, help people. She says if you don't help, you're being selfish." My face pinked as my pupil went on parroting my philosophy. His uncle sat quietly sipping his wine, one arm draped over the back of his chair.

"When we got back from our ride this afternoon, Ted came out to take Pepper and Lady. Miss O'Reilly told him that since we had enjoyed riding the horses, her black mare included, it was only fair that we should groom them and feed them . . . and would he show her what we were to do."

"Oh?" Those cool, dark eyes seemed to pierce me as he prompted Steven to go on. Priscilla answered before her brother could.

"Ted showed us how to curry the horses and then what feed to give them. And we had a lot of fun, Uncle Clinton. Miss O'Reilly taught us 'Camptown Races' and we sang to our horses," she said laughing gleefully.

The silence at the head of the table was oppressive. Well, why shouldn't the children take a little responsibility on the ranch, I thought defensively.

"What else is she asking you to do?"

"We are to keep our own rooms neat. She'll inspect them once a week. No more help from Mary or Mabel except for washing. We even make our own beds now. And when Mabel gives us cookies and milk, we clean up afterward so we don't make more work for her. Miss O'Reilly said it will teach us what other people are doing and give us an apprecia—aprec—"

"Appreciation?"

"Yes . . . appre-ciation of what is done for us." Steven beamed at having been able to inform his Uncle of something new before his sister had beaten him to it.

Matthews nodded, taking another slow sip of wine. "Not a bad idea," he said casually, giving me a smile of approval for the first time since this afternoon. Relief swept over me and I felt the tension suddenly ease. I smiled back.

"With all this training, Steven, I'll take you out on the range with me in a year or two. You can handle the cooking and camp work for me." Matthews leaned over and ruffled his nephew's hair playfully. The boy's face lit up with delight.

"Really? Can I?"

My heart swelled at the boy's eagerness and his uncle's affirmation. In the past few days I had noticed the change in Steven. He was becoming more animated and cheerful and, as on this evening, offering his own conversation rather than sitting quietly and listening while his uncle and sister talked.

"I had hoped to play another game of chess with you tonight, Miss O'Reilly," Matthews said, "but I won't be able to have that pleasure now. I've got some book work I've got to get done."

"Some other evening then, Mr. Matthews. And I hope I will have all my wits about me when we do play." As I answered his friendly statement, I realized my voice no longer held its usual cool formality, but was warm and friendly.

Matthews eyes lingered on me for a moment longer than usual before he left the room.

VI

The next day, after lessons and lunch, the children and I rode again. I had to go slowly, for my muscles were still crying their discomfort and stiffness from the previous day.

The countryside was even more beautiful than the day before, but I knew I was seeing it with the happiness of Matthews' warmth still fresh in my mind. The children took me to the springs after which the ranch was named. There was a small lake there, surrounded by willow trees and flowers. It was a garden paradise and we sat talking for a long time, plucking out pieces of grass and chewing them.

On the way back to the ranch house, we stopped and tied the horses up again, so that we could run through the tall yellow mustard flowers and collect handfuls for our rooms. Everything about this Western land smelled fresh and wild. How I loved it!

As we rode over the knoll which looked down on the house, we spied a large black carriage standing at the front steps.

"Oh, no!" Priscilla exclaimed angrily from beside me. I looked at her with surprise, for her normally cheerful face held a deep scowl almost comically like her uncle's.

"Who is it?" I asked, curiously, keeping a smile hidden. Steven's bright smile had disappeared too, and he looked solemn and withdrawn again.

"It's Miss James again," Priscilla explained and then made a face. "I don't like her! She's always fussing around Uncle Clinton. She's going to marry him someday!"

My heart seemed to rise and stick in my throat. I looked back down at the carriage again. So he had a woman he loved. So what! Why should that depress me, I wondered angrily, mentally shaking myself.

Priscilla glowered toward the house as if it were an offending portal. Then suddenly her face brightened slightly. "Well, maybe her brother came with her today. You'd like him! He's very handsome and nice, too. Almost as handsome as Uncle Clinton," she added with bias.

I couldn't shake the pain in my chest, but managed to smile and ask, "Oh, she has a brother?"

"I'm sure he will like you! He always likes pretty ladies," Steven reported, his voice sounding surly and anything but pleased.

"Don't like him too much, Miss O'Reilly. Promise?" Priscilla pleaded and I laughed at her sudden changes of mood.

"Why not, for goodness' sake?" I teased, but she took me seriously.

"Because we want you to fall in love with Uncle Clinton," she admitted ingenuously, and my laugh stopped with a croak.

"Oh, Priscilla . . . don't be silly. Your uncle is my employer. It would be unthinkable."

"Oh, he likes you a lot already. I can tell!"

I smiled at her, taking her childish fantasy lightly. "Well, don't talk about it or hope for it anymore, sweetheart. You'll only be disappointed." To myself I said he probably tolerates me at best, for the majority of the time I seem to irritate him. This time yesterday, I had hoped that we could at least be friends. But even that was unlikely.

Mary Cramer rushed out to the front steps to meet us. Her face was flushed with excitement and her eyes had a bright sparkle. "Mr. Matthews wants you to join him in the sitting room, Miss O'Reilly. Just as soon as you can change."

Then she added with impatient breathlessness, "You two run along upstairs and play. Hurry now! Miss O'Reilly has not much time."

The children scampered up the steps and disappeared into the house. I followed more slowly, until Mary looked back anxiously over her shoulder.

She helped me dress in my best gown again. The ivory-colored bodice was fitted down to my hips and pulled back slightly. The dress was simple, but my most flattering, for it accentuated my narrow waist and dark hair. My eyes looked darker blue than usual, shining brightly back at me as I twisted my hair quickly up into a chignon. Flushed and nervous, I pressed my icy hands over my cheeks.

Very tense, I descended the stairs and walked toward the sitting room wondering why Matthews had requested my presence. I heard voices, a sultry feminine voice and a man's deep, resonant baritone. I hesitated for a moment before appearing in the doorway, my heart fluttering. I wished there were an acceptable excuse to disappear upstairs and remain out of sight with the children. But I was more curious than nervous.

My heart sank.

Miss James was more beautiful than anyone I had ever seen before. Several years my senior, she was everything that I was not and could not be. In one quick appraising glance, I saw her as sophisticated, fashionable, blond, and highly curved in a voluptuous way. Never had I felt so dowdy, plain, and childishly inadequate before, and I felt a defensive anger at the man standing next to her for requesting me to come to the sitting room.

"Who are you?" I heard a deep voice ask and turned to meet the eyes of another tall stranger.

He was about the same age as Clinton Matthews, but very different. He had not the lines around his eyes, nor the hardness and strength that seemed so apparent in the other man. This stranger was handsome in the same way as his companion. His hair was sandy brown and thick. He wore a well-trimmed mustache that gave him a charmingly rakish appearance. Tall, as tall as Matthews, and broad-shouldered, he moved with casual grace and assurance, his gray eyes sparkling with interest.

I remained standing uneasily in the doorway, flushed as he scrutinized me from head to toe with a disturbing twinkle in his eyes. I wished he would not look at me like that, though I did not understand his intention. But something about his slow smile embarrassed and flustered me.

"This is Miss Kathleen O'Reilly, Priscilla and Steven's new governess," Matthews introduced in a flat voice.

The stranger took my hand and raised it to his lips, pressing a warm kiss to it and lingering longer than I thought necessary or appropriate. I pulled my hand away and stared at him with open distrust. Matthews went on in a somewhat harsher voice, "Miss O'Reilly, this is Cybil James and that . . . is her brother, Michael."

"I am pleased to meet you, ma'am," I said, giving a curtsey toward the beautiful young woman and ignoring the man standing next to me. Michael James laughed at my rebuke.

"I wish I were ten again, Clint . . . and that I had this beauty for my governess," he said with a teasing lilt. "Mine was middle-aged, very undesirable, and cross as an old crow!" I could feel his eyes resting on me in admiration and wished again that he would look somewhere else.

"Michael, don't you see how you are embarrassing the poor child," his sister admonished in a steely tone. I saw the irritation sparkle in her ice-blue eyes and I sensed her husky words were not directed at him. She swept her glance over me and then turned to Matthews, dismissing me from her notice. Her voice dropped and she leaned closer to him, murmuring. "Dear me, darling, isn't she rather young to be a governess. She hardly appears old enough to be out of the schoolroom herself."

Michael James took my arm gently and led me to the couch. He was speaking in a low, personal voice, leaning toward me slightly.

"I have never seen such Irish-blue eyes. They're like large sapphires," he said, expecting me to be flattered, I supposed. I was not.

"Thank you," I replied with stiff politeness.

Once seated, he turned and draped his arm over the back of the sofa, watching my face turn pink at his continued bold scrutiny.

"Do I have a fly on my nose, sir?" I asked pertly, feeling more annoyed with his continued perusal than flustered. He laughed, throwing his head back. Matthews looked across the room and met my eyes for an instant. He scowled, his eyes taking in Michael's position and becoming cold and hard.

"I don't wonder you kept this little lady a secret, Clint. Saving her for yourself?" Michael asked, laughing again. Cybil James's eyes flashed with cold fury.

"Clint, darling," she said, turning and putting a dainty hand on his arm. "I haven't seen your garden yet. Why don't we go for a walk and have . . . more privacy." Her voice began her speech with forced calm and ended it with a subtle promise that agonized me. As I watched them stroll slowly from the room a powerful emotion gripped and held me.

So he wants me here to distract this man sitting next to me while he is alone in the garden with his lady love, I thought. Their voices carried for a few moments as they passed the windows. I felt irritated with myself, wondering why it should upset me so much. What was that man to me? My employer! Nothing more! I was not sure that I even liked him anymore, I thought with childish rage.

"Where are you from, Miss O'Reilly?" Michael asked, cutting in on my thoughts.

"New York," I answered flatly. Why wouldn't he move away from me? Surely this was not proper to sit so close? And I couldn't move any farther away from him, for he had positioned me at the end of the couch. I stood up nervously, and moved toward the bookshelves.

"Do I make you nervous?" he asked.

"Yes, a little," I admitted frankly, wondering how much easier it was to talk to him than to Clinton Matthews.

"I do apologize for staring, Miss O'Reilly," Michael James said, standing up and coming to my side again. "But you are very beautiful, you know."

Flattery, empty of meaning, I thought and took it for its worth.

"Do you have anyone special waiting for you in New York?" he asked curiously. His eyes moved from mine, drifting over my face until they came to linger on my lips. My throat tightened and my hands grew suddenly clammy. I turned my head away and he took my silence for reprimand.

"I am sorry, that's none of my business, is it?" He

96

took one of my nervously clasped hands. "I don't suppose you would be a governess thousands of miles from your home if you were betrothed." He rubbed my hand between his. "You're cold . . . I don't mean to frighten you with my interest," he said sincerely, and I wondered how he could so easily understand what I was feeling. "Would you like a little glass of Madeira? I'm sure it was only an oversight of Clinton's not to offer it."

"No, thank you, Mr. James. I don't drink," I answered, wishing he had not taken his opportunity to mention Matthews' indifference to me.

"How do you like Priscilla and Steven?"

"They're wonderful," I answered easily, thankful that he had turned the conversation from me. I smiled up at him.

"Then that means you will be staying for some time."

"I do hope so."

His eyes sparkled at my answer. "Do you ride?" he asked after a brief hesitation.

"I'm learning," I laughed, drawing my hand away from him again. "My hand is warm now, thank you."

"You never let up your guard, do you?" He grinned. "Who's your riding instructor? Clint?"

"No, of course not. Jim Calhoun gave me my first lesson a couple of days ago and the children have taken over since then."

"How do you like it?"

"Very much . . . I love it."

"Then would you care to go riding with me this Sunday?" he asked, drawing the trap closed with a satisfied smile. "I assure you I can conduct myself as a complete gentleman if the occasion warrants it."

"I'm not sure I . . . can go," I evaded. What would it be like to be alone for any length of time with a man like this? Would I want to be several miles from the ranch house in his company? There was something different about him, pleasant and charming, but too assured, too confident and easy-natured. He made me nervous.

"Seven days a week and twenty-four hours a day, you're a faithful governess, I suppose," he teased. "I don't think Clinton would mind you taking a few hours off," he persisted. As though verifying his words, voices drifted in from the garden, one gay and laughing, the other low and deep. No, I thought with sudden anger, he would not care in the least. I still sat without answering and the voices came closer through the garden. Michael James flashed a look toward the windows and frowned slightly. "Now why are they hurrying back in here?" he muttered as Cybil's voice, slightly angry and petulant now, carried into the room.

"It has been over two years, Clinton. And you know Clarissa herself loved the Fiesta del Verano. I can handle all the arrangements."

As they appeared in the open doorway, I saw Clinton's arm looped around Cybil James's waist.

"All right. Go ahead and make the arrangements." He acquiesced without enthusiasm. Then he turned and looked directly into my eyes. His gaze moved to Michael, who was standing so close to me that our shoulders touched. I took a step away from Michael as he addressed Matthews.

"Clint. Old buddy! When do you give your lovely governess her day off?" I stared at him, totally mortified at his audacity, and was even more shocked as he continued: "I plan to take her riding at the first opportunity." He gave me another of his slow, disturbing smiles.

Matthews frowned darkly, answering in a curt voice: "Her Sundays are free should she choose to ride with such an infamous gentleman as yourself."

Michael laughed, undaunted. "He's only kidding, my love," he said in an aside to me.

Cybil James said something quietly which attracted Matthews' attention and Michael pressed his advantage. "Will you do me the honor of riding with me this Sunday afternoon, Miss O'Reilly," he said formally. The sparkle in his eyes made me suspect he was amused at my hesitation. It was a moment before I started to stammer a refusal, but he cut my words off and made me feel even more foolish. "I will not make any kind of advance," he teased.

It was Clinton's sudden laugh at something Cybil whispered to him that decided the issue. "All right, Mr. James, if you wish," I said, feeling a gnawing anger in the pit of my stomach.

"You're not afraid of me anymore, are you?" Michael asked.

"No, I am not afraid of you," I answered, slightly irritated. "I just don't know you."

"Well, we will take care of that Sunday," he said, smiling with definite pleasure and then reaching over to take my hand again while directing his next words to Cybil.

"Shall we depart now, dear sister. Our missions are accomplished. You've bullied poor Clint into holding the Fiesta del Verano again and I have convinced Miss O'Reilly that she will have nothing to fear in riding with me on Sunday." Cybil shot him an indignant look and turned back to Clinton.

"I'll see you soon then, darling. I've missed you lately." Her voice dropped into a sultry whisper and I averted my gaze as she went on to say something for his ears only.

Michael took this moment to kiss my hand again. "I'm really looking forward to Sunday," he said and I knew he was sincere. Matthews looked up and scowled in our direction again, noting that Michael James still held my fingers lightly in his.

As the carriage pulled away, Matthews turned to me, his annoyance obvious. He started to speak but seemed to force himself to silence. The voyaging muscle worked furiously in his cheek and he turned abruptly, walking off toward the stables, his shoulders stiff with rage.

A few minutes later, from my bedroom window, I saw him ride from the barn at a hard gallop.

What have I done wrong now? I wondered. I lay across my bed feeling depressed and unhappy.

Matthews returned late in the afternoon, his temper improved, though he was unusually quiet at dinner. The children also seemed subdued by the afternoon visitors, looking between the two of us furtively.

However, when Matthews asked me to play chess with him, they seemed to brighten, asking to be excused so they could go upstairs and play. Their uncle nodded his consent and they scurried out of the room, leaving us alone.

The tension was thick in the air once we were by ourselves. I followed Matthews into the study and watched as he set up the chess pieces without so much as looking at me. Any minute I expected him to shout at me, for his irritation had returned in to the level of our first meeting in this room.

"Start the game," he commanded, and I jumped at the intensity of his demand.

"Wouldn't you care to begin, sir?" I ventured, trying to smile and ease my own fears. He didn't answer, but moved the first pawn his hand came across. We played in silence for a time and I felt more and more nervous. He was playing ruthlessly, taking one man after another, though intentionally not putting me in checkmate. I tried to concentrate more on each play but still he picked the pieces off the board one by one.

As the game progressed, I began to feel equal anger at his unprecedented behavior.

"What is the matter with you?" I blurted out without thinking, looking up as he took my last pawn, leaving me with only four pieces left on the board. "What have I done to make you so furious?"

He stared across the chessboard at me with angry black eyes, but didn't give me an answer.

"You could have had me in checkmate ten moves ago! Here, take the knight too!" I grabbed the carved wood piece and made a deliberately careless move. He picked off the piece with his queen and leaned back in his seat with an unpleasant smirk on his face. "Checkmate."

"You are a child. Now, sir, you've had your fun. May I be excused . . ." I stood up but quickly changed my mind.

"No! I'll not excuse you!" he growled, almost rising out of his chair. I sank down, eyes wide with surprise and not just a little fright.

"Why did you accept Michael's invitation?" he demanded, fighting for control over his fiery temper.

"Why?" I repeated, astonished at his question. Why should it matter to him whether I went riding with Michael James or not?

"I don't want you to go riding with him. Is that clear?"

"I don't understand."

"It's not proper . . ." he answered a little lamely, looking for just an instant as though he were embarrassed. I remembered Cybil James whispering to him just before she left.

"Oh . . . I see," I replied stiffly, my temper flaring. Yes, I am a governess, after all. And Michael James was Matthews' fiancée's brother. I was hardly to be considered suitable for him. "Tell me, sir, if it were any other woman but your governess, would it be proper?"

"I don't give a damn about what other women do. I'll not have you riding with him."

"Why not?" I pressed with unsuppressed fury. "It was you, sir, who told Mr. James that my Sundays are free. What could I say to him then, pray? 'No, I am sorry, but I am not free on Sundays, Mr. James.'" My voice had risen in sarcasm, my hands clenched in my lap. "You left me no choice but to accept his persistent offer."

"What would you have had me say, Miss O'Reilly? That you are forced to work seven days a week as my slave?" He leaned forward, his eyes glowering, the muscle in his cheek twitching again. His fiancée must have asked him to forbid me to ride with her brother. Or was this his own decision that I was not good enough for the likes of Michael James? He stared at me until I felt pinned to the wall and then he went on in a quiet, more menacing and insulting voice: "I expected you to answer him as any other . . . lady would have. I did not expect you to accept the first proposition that came your way."

My anger dissolved in a flood of total embarrassment and shame. Was that what I had done, acted fast and cheap, the way my mother perhaps had done? No, I thought. I had accepted an invitation to go riding, nothing more. I had felt foolish for my hesitation in responding to Michael James's invitation and now I was told I had, in essence, acted as no lady should. But what could I have said to decline Mr. James's persistent proposal for a casual afternoon together.

"I did not mean to act unladylike . . ." I stammered. "I would never do anything to bring embarrassment . . ." I stood up in a daze, almost knocking the chessboard to the floor. I hardly saw Matthews before me, but rather a tall man, with gray hair and a silver-headed cane. He was staring at me with dislike and disapproval.

Matthews came around the table to stand in front of me. "I'm sorry . . . I didn't mean to say that," he said quietly, but I did not even hear his words.

I stiffened suddenly at my own self-accusation that I was like my mother. "I would never do . . . anything . . . to bring shame on myself or . . ."

"I'm not concerned about what you would do, for God's sake. I don't think you can handle yourself with a man of Michael's experience. He is . . ."

Matthews' loud words brought me back with a jolt. I turned and stared squarely into his eyes. "Handle myself?" I repeated, fury bubbling in my veins again. "What do you mean?"

"You know damn well what I mean, woman!"

"I do not!" I disagreed forcefully. "Tell me, if you will be so kind." My voice rang with sarcasm.

"All right!" His eyes sparkled, all the gentleness and apology gone. "He likes the way you look . . . the way you move." His eyes slid down over me as they had that first night we met. "He finds you damned attractive. That much was obvious even to you." He paused but went on before I could utter a word. "And when Michael is attracted to a woman . . . he does something about it. He has a reputation for . . . his conduct with the fair sex."

For a moment I thought I would burst. "Oh," I sputtered, "and you think that I would allow him to do anything he wished!" I glared at him venomously, my body shaking with anger. "He promised to conduct himself as a gentleman." Then, in my anger, I forgot myself and added vindictively, "Which is more than you have done since my arrival!"

His brows shot up in surprise. "Oh?"

"No!" I informed him. "At every opportunity you have shown me your disapproval and dislike for me. The only time you even showed genuine . . . politeness was the other day when you deigned to speak to me on the hillside for a few minutes. I should bow down and thank you for that . . . sir!"

"You think it's dislike that makes me ask you not to ride with Michael?" His voice rose in furious astonishment and disbelief.

"You do not ask it . . . you demand it!" I retorted hotly. "I am sick to death of having people tell me how to live my life," I went on, ignoring the warning in the back of my mind. He opened his mouth to say something, his face tightening, the cheek muscle locking. I saw him change his mind.

"Let it be enough that I forbid you to ride with him!" His looked dared me to answer.

"You have no right to forbid me to do anything," I said without even thinking. "As you said yourself, I am not your slave." I was astonished at my bold words, suddenly feeling the prickling fear that he might dismiss me. My hand almost fluttered instinctively to my throat, as if I felt my head on the executioner's block.

My God, what was I saying! My very life depended on this position and I was trying so hard to gain Matthews' approval. Now, in a vile rage, I was throwing everything away. And why? I did not care one twit about Michael James and his invitation to ride. Why was I so angry I was shaking?

"You little fool!" Matthews spit out, and reached out to grab my shoulders. "On what horse will you ride? Not one of mine!" He was in such a rage that his voice shook, his eyes flashing.

His words stung and before I could stop myself, my defensive retort burst out.

"Perhaps one belonging to Michael James . . . or, better, we could take a long walk instead of a ride."

Never had I seen anyone so angry, and I had a sudden fear that he would strike me. I tried to back away from him, a tremor of terror running through me, but he held me tight. He stared at me for what seemed an eternity, drilling into me with those dark eyes. Then his expression changed and he gave me an unpleasant smile.

"Well, Miss O'Reilly, let's see how calm and sure of yourself you really are." His voice had softened, but I sensed a worse threat in his quiet words. "Michael is most charming with the ladies," he went on in a vibrating voice. I tried to pull away from him again, still angry, but growing more and more alarmed and frightened at the intense emotion that stirred behind his eyes.

"Could you handle him if he took you in his arms . . . like this?" I felt Matthews' arm slide around my waist and pull me hard against him, flattening my hands on his hard-muscled chest so that I could hardly move. As I struggled to get away, I felt his heart pick up speed against my breast. With his other hand, he raised my chin, glaring down into my face. His glance swept over my eyes and then lingered meaningfully on my lips. My breath came in frightened little gasps.

"I'm sorry, Mr. Matthews. I shouldn't have spoken in anger . . . please," I broke off. "Please, let me go," I pleaded, terrified at the motion in his eyes and the strange feelings tingling through my own body as I twisted and fought against him.

"He wouldn't let you go," he answered lightly. "He would relish the feel of your body in his arms. He'd brush his lips against your neck, breathe soft, encouraging words in your ear telling you how very . . . beautiful and desirable you are." His voice was low and husky. "He's already told you that you are lovely." I felt Matthews' lips warm against the curve of my neck, raising as he spoke quietly in my ear and sent chills down my spine. "Then, when you yield just a little," he went on as I shivered against him, "he'll kiss you. Like this."

His lips came down on mine, forcing my head back. I was too shocked to move and felt sudden panic as the

105

violence of his kiss parted my lips. His large hand moved to hold my face still against his as his tongue entered my mouth, sending hot, shuddering waves through my body. He went on kissing me until an unfamiliar warmth began to spread through my body and I melted against him, hoping he would never stop. His kiss changed then, becoming more gentle, still exploring, still exciting beyond anything I had ever dreamed. His lips moved down to the violently pulsing vein in my throat, kissing, tasting.

"Kathleen," he breathed huskily. "Oh, my God, Kathleen," he said and then raised his head and kissed my parted and waiting lips again with fervor. My fingers spread against his chest, marveling at the power and fire I felt. When I started to reach up and put my arms around his neck, he suddenly stiffened. Disentangling himself, he held me away from him. His eyes were alight with an emotion I did not understand and he cleared his throat.

"You see what I mean," he said, smiling slightly, his voice strangely hoarse.

For a moment, all I could do was look at him, the strange warmth still running through me. Then I realized what he had said. I felt the warmth disappear. I wanted to die, to hide someplace and never come out into the world again. He had kissed me like that to prove his point, to make me feel ashamed for my feelings, my needs.

"Kathleen?" Matthews looked at me with sudden confusion, questioning. "Do you understand why I don't want you to go anywhere with Michael now?"

I slapped him, almost blinded by my tears. "You are hateful . . . and cruel," I managed to choke out. "How could you make me feel like that . . . just to . . ."

He rubbed his cheek, his eyes large and incredulous. He looked as though I had knocked the wind from

106

him instead of slapping his face. My lip quivered uncontrollably.

"Mr. Matthews," I said, straining to keep my voice in control. "It's my life . . . I will become friends with whomever I please . . . and not you . . . not my," I stopped and quickly amended what I had almost blurted out, "not anyone . . . has the right to dictate what I am to do."

Before he could speak, I turned and fled from the room, the tears pouring down my cheeks uncontrollably.

How little I really did control my life I would learn much later. Almost too late.

VII

Stiff-muscled, nerves wound tight, I awoke before dawn the next morning. I did not have to look in the mirror to know my eyes were red and swollen from crying myself to sleep. I put the back of my hand over my forehead, aching from too many hours of sleeplessness and intense emotion.

How he must be laughing at me!

Even now in my own room, hours later, my heart pounded at the memory of his searing kiss. And he knew what effect he had had on me. I could not even deny my infatuation with him. Not now. Had he wanted me for any purpose, I would have said yes last night. How could I be so weak and pliant? Was I really like my mother, yielding myself to passion? Was this what she had felt for my father?

The emotions I had felt were terrifyingly intense. But they seemed natural, beautiful, even sacred until he had shattered the magic with his casual, cruel observation, "You see what I mean." The words were burned into my mind.

Yes, I did see now. He knew my emotions better than I did myself. But how could he have been so cruel? How could he have used my feelings so insensitively?

And he had failed in his purpose. He had meant to prevent me from seeing Michael James. But I would see him! And I would be with him as much as I chose to be!

How could I have allowed myself to fall in love with Clinton Matthews? Cruel, moody, unfeeling, arrogant, he cared nothing for me, not even as a person with feelings which could be smashed by his actions. How is it possible to detest a man for what he does to you, and yet still be blindly attracted to him at the same time?

His kiss took a secure secret from me and left my emotion bare for him to see. And he had smiled, pleased that his lesson had worked. He had left me without pride, shamed and rejected. Rejection was nothing new in my life, I thought bitterly. I rolled over, burying my face in the pillow, despising my self-pity.

I got up as the sun cast feeling rays beyond the hills. Pouring cold water into my small basin, I held a cloth to my face. A light tap at the door startled me sometime later and I dropped the cloth, spattering cold water on my thin nightgown. Shivering, I went to the door as a second tap was sounded.

"Mary?" I asked, unlatching the door, surprised that she was so early.

"It's Mabel," came the answer. The housekeeper entered carrying a tray with two cups, a pot of coffee and several fresh, warm sweet rolls.

"I thought so," she observed severely, studying my face. "You've been crying," she announced unnecessarily.

"I have a little cold," I lied, unconvincingly.

"I found Clinton asleep in the study this morning,"

she went on, not believing my fib. At the surprised expression on my face, she smiled. "It didn't appear that he got much sleep last night either. He gave me this for you before he left this morning." Mabel set the tray down on a small table, pulling up two chairs. She held out an envelope.

"Left?" I said blankly, feeling even more desolate. Perhaps he was on his way even now to see Cybil James. Why should it matter?

My hand shook when I took the note from Mabel.

"He rode out to check the fences," she added, taking in my mood. "He'll probably stay in one of the line shacks tonight and tomorrow. He plans to return Thursday." She smiled again as I stood listening to her and praying she was right. "It must have been some fight you two had."

Trying to cover the flush of embarrassment, I looked quickly down at the missive I held. How much did Mabel really see? How much could she read in my face?

Nervously, I tore open the envelope and pulled out a single sheet of paper. His handwriting was barely legible.

Miss O'Reilly,

I hope you will forgive my behavior of last night.

I have some line work that must be done. It will give us both a couple of days to cool off.

The black mare is yours to ride when you want.

C.M.

I reread the note several times before putting it on my bedside table. Though Mabel asked nothing about the episode or the message, I knew by her expression that she had missed nothing. What she had not seen or heard, she sensed, with the intuition of a woman who knew the man well, and me also.

There was little comfort in that thought.

That morning and the next, I rode an hour by myself before the children got up. Ted, the stable hand, was surprised the first day I appeared shortly after daybreak. The second day, he had the black mare saddled and ready.

I tried not to think about anything when I rode. I wanted to enjoy the beautiful countryside, the wind whipping my hair, the sound of the land coming to life after the silent night. Alone and lonely all my life, my solo rides were strangely comforting. I sought to be alone, and felt alive, happy, and more free than I had ever felt before. The aching loneliness that had eaten away at my insides for as long as I could remember was diminishing and when it surged again, I found I could cope with it, push it aside.

Each day I rode a wider circle, farther and farther out, exploring the hills and valleys around the ranch house. I felt at peace, and for a while I could even forget that I was in love with my employer.

On the second morning after Clinton's departure, I rode with reckless abandon, wanting to escape my own tormenting thoughts. My feelings tumbled over and over in my mind, a confused mass of contradictions. He would be back now. I would have to face him again. Experienced, he knew only too well that I had enjoyed his kiss, wanted him to keep kissing me. And I had slapped him because of that, not because of the act itself.

When the mare pulled for it, I gave her her head, letting her run and run, not caring how far or how fast she carried me. She tossed her head, throwing her mane back over my hands, and galloped on. The ground flew by beneath us. A mile, another mile. I wanted her to go on and on, carrying me farther and farther away from the dark, mocking eyes that seemed to pierce me even now.

The horse took a sudden, sharp jump to clear a fallen tree and I felt the saddle lurch to the side. Instinctively, my hands flew out to break my fall, but my body whirled in midair and when I hit, I rolled and slammed into some rocks jutting out of the ground.

When I opened my eyes, I was not sure where I was or what had happened. I felt confused and dazed, staring around me. The black mare was gone and I was completely alone.

Slowly, I pushed myself into a sitting position, wincing from my aching limbs. I felt blood, sticky and wet, on the side of my head. The palms of my hands were raw and bleeding, and the blue riding jacket was torn and dirty.

When I tried to stand, I fell back with a wave of dizziness. Bracing myself and taking slow breaths of air, I tried to clear my senses of the sickening lightness.

How long had I been out here?

I looked up at the sun, squinting against the painful glare. It was high, perhaps midmorning by now. And it was getting stiflingly hot.

How many miles am I from the ranch house? Five? Ten? Less? More? Why had I ridden so far like a woman crazed?

I had to get back. Mabel and the children would be worried.

Again, I pushed myself up, leaning heavily against the fallen tree to steady myself. Slowly the dizziness waned but I still felt a light-headed weakness. My body ached all over as I walked around the base of the fallen oak and started in the direction I hoped was home.

The heat beating down on my shoulders was almost unbearable. I stumbled several times, tripping over rocks and roots that rose out of the grassy sod. When I looked around, I could find nothing familiar about the trees or hillside. Nothing I could remember helped me distinguish my position on the ranch. I was in a canyon, narrow and long, but that was all I knew.

"How could you be so stupid?" I muttered aloud, pressing the back of my hand to the beading perspiration on my forehead. My head throbbed from both fall and heat. My back and shoulders ached, my hands burned, I was lost, and now I was frightened. The last passed quickly.

A lassitude floated over me as I moved. Everything around me seemed abnormally bright in the afternoon sunlight. Things were clouded and vague, sounds muffled and distant. Even the unmerciful heat did not bother me anymore.

I sank down into the grass, too weak to move any farther. The dizziness returned in a wave of sudden nausea. When it passed again, I felt drained, emotionless, and outside myself.

"Get up and keep going."

"I'll just rest here for a few minutes," I answered the other voice.

"You'll get sunstroke. Get up and keep moving. You're miles from the ranch house. How do you expect them to find you? Get up!"

"I'm too tired. I want to rest." I leaned back in the grass and closed my eyes, ignoring the warning voice in my mind. A blackness swept over me without a pause.

"Kathleen?"

"Yes, Miss M."

"Did you write your essay yet?"

"Yes, Miss M." I held up a sheet of brown paper, covered with rounded, childish handwriting. "It's right here. I just finished copying it for you."

113

"What did you write about this time, dear?"

"My dream," I answered, and saw the usual frown creasing her forehead.

"The same one?"

"The one I always have. The one about the dark-haired lady who sings that song." I hummed a few bars of the tune, haunting and beautiful. "Did I know her, Miss Montgomery?"

Her eyes grew round and filled with tears.

"Well, well . . ." the young man said, stopping his carriage and looking at me. "Another curious tourist?"

"I don't like your house . . . it looks cold. What are you trying to keep hidden in there?"

"What an extraordinarily rude young woman you are!"

"David, drive this carriage through the gate or I will have to take the reins myself!"

"Father!" I started running toward the disappearing carriage. The gate slammed in my face. Grabbing the iron rods, I pulled frantically, trying to open it. "Father!"

"Go away!" he shouted back over his shoulder at me. "Don't you understand! I don't want you here! Go away! Go away! Hurry!"

"Father! Why didn't you want me?"

"He had his reasons, Kathleen," Miss Montgomery said, pushing her spectacles up on her long nose. The office was silent then, and dark.

"How much, Kathleen?" Anna asked. "How much does he send Parkside?" Her smile sparkled, her eyes turning emerald green and shining in the dark.

"I won't stay here another day!"

"When will you go?" Anna demanded impatiently.

"No, Kathleen, stay. Wait . . . I beg of you!" Miss Montgomery said, running after her down the long hallway.

"When will you go?"

"You can't go!" Long fingers reached out and tried to grab ahold of me.

"No!" I was running again. Oh God, my head hurts. I'm tired of running away.

"I'll just rest here for a few minutes."

"You can't!" Angry dark eyes stared down at me. "I forbid it!"

"You have no right. It's my life!"

Strong arms held me tight. Lips, hot and searing on mine, transporting me into a fiery world of longing. "Don't stop, Clinton . . . don't stop!"

"See what I mean!" he laughed.

"I hate you!" I cried, looking up at those mocking, dark eyes. "No, I don't . . . I don't!"

"You have such beautiful blue eyes, Miss O'Reilly. Like sapphires. We'll get to know each other. I can be a gentleman if the situation warrants it." Michael James stared at me, his eyes caressing my face and moving down to linger on my lips.

"Stop looking at me like that. Do I have a fly on my nose?"

"She hardly looks old enough to be out of the schoolroom, darling." Cybil James smiled up at Clinton Matthews. He was kissing her now, his fingers raking through her blond hair. Then he laughed, throwing back his head. His eyes were on my stricken face.

"See what I mean! See what I mean! See what I mean!" The words kept echoing in my mind.

"Don't laugh at me!" I cried out. "I can't help it if I love you. How can you be so cruel?"

"He has his reasons, Kathleen," Miss Montgomery said flatly.

"Go away! Leave me alone! It's my life."

"No, it's not!" a woman said, her hair streaming out around her, her eyes wild and black with hate.

"Who are you?"

"She's dead, I tell you! Dead!" my father was yell-

115

ing, his face agonized and gray. The woman was laughing wildly, tormenting him. Then she looked past him to me.

"You ruined everything. You killed our love."

"Father! Please, stop her! Father! I didn't mean to kill your love." I was searching the darkness for him, groping with hands outstretched for something to hold on to. "Father. Please. Don't hate me anymore. Help me . . . someone. Someone."

Someone's strong hands raised my head gently, putting a tin cup to my mouth. The water tasted good, moistening my parched throat.

"Easy, Kathleen." I tried to open my eyes but couldn't. I could hear the worry in that voice. I wanted to tell whoever was there I'd be all right in a few minutes. Just let me rest here for a few more minutes.

A wet cloth slid over my forehead and down the side of my face. I jerked as it stung.

"I'll try not to hurt you," the man said, and with a jump of my heart I recognized Matthews' voice above me. I opened my eyes with an effort to see him bending over me, his face taut and lined. He poured more water and wiped my face again.

"She going to be all right?" I heard Jim Calhoun ask, from somewhere behind him. My head was spinning again as I tried to sit up.

"I'll be fine in a minute," I said, unable to recognize the weak voice.

"Don't move yet, for Christ's sake!" Matthews commanded, his voice taking on a sharp, impatient, edge. I closed my eyes, struggling against the dizziness and depression at the sound of his angry voice.

His hands slid down over my arms, ribs, and legs. "You haven't broken anything," he announced more gently. His arm slid under my drooping shoulders, propping me up. I braced myself again, feeling a sickening sensation swim through me. He lifted me easily, holding me tight in his strong arms.

"I'm sorry . . ." I mumbled. "I'm sorry I lost the mare," I managed.

"You didn't. She came back to the barn."

"I've ruined your sister's jacket," I said, my voice sounding strange and distant. I started to cry softly as he cradled me securely against him. He lifted me up, setting me on the saddle of his horse, and then swung up behind me, pulling me against him again. I felt his hand stroke the hair from my tear-stained face. He pulled a blanket around me snugly, and I felt his hard-muscled legs tighten as he urged his sorrel forward.

I awakened again in my own room to see Steven looking down at me. There were glistening tears in his eyes and running down his face. When he saw my eyes open, he uttered a little cry, flinging himself down beside the bed.

"Don't leave me, too, Miss O'Reilly . . . please don't die!" His little shoulders shook as he sobbed, his fingers digging into the sheets and covers.

I stroked his head, feeling the softness of his hair. "I'll be fine, Steven," I assured him gently, understanding his fear. My head felt better and when I pushed myself up slightly, I no longer felt the wave of dizziness. "I won't ever leave you if I can help it, Steven." I lifted his trembling chin and gave him a reassuring smile.

"My mother said she wouldn't leave me either," he said accusingly, "but she did!" He searched my face, still unconvinced by my reassurance, the tears running unchecked down his cheeks. The fear still glimmered in his eyes and I felt my love tug hard inside me.

"Come here, sweetheart." I held out my arms to him and he crawled up next to me in the bed. He snuggled tightly against me, as though my warmth and the closeness were an assurance that I would not leave him. Kissing his forehead, I pushed the hair back off his face.

"I'm sure your mother wanted very much to stay with you. She must have loved you very, very much, Steven. But she and your father were very sick."

"If she really wanted to live, why didn't she?" he sobbed into my shoulder, his voice sounding tragically bitter.

"Did your mother ever tell you about God?" I asked quietly, remembering the comfort He had brought me during my years at Parkside.

"Yes," he answered tentatively, his sobs slowly diminishing as he listened.

"Steven, sometimes He gets lonely. Your mother and father are with Him in Heaven because He needs them there."

"Couldn't he have taken just one of them?"

I felt a hard lump growing in my chest and throat. I tried to search for an answer.

"When your father was away for a while on a cattle drive, was your mother very happy?" I asked, trying not to let my own longing and pain be heard.

"No," he answered quietly. "She used to tell me that when you love someone, you are lonely without them."

"Would you have wanted your mother or your father to be lonely in Heaven?"

"No . . ." he said and I kissed him on the top of his head, resting my cheek on his soft hair. He snuggled more tightly against my side, not wanting to talk about it anymore. I knew that no explanation I could give him would really help. No one can explain away the pain of loss and death. Finally I could hear his breathing gradually slow and deepen into an exhausted sleep.

My muscles ached. My head felt a little light, but it

only hurt when I pressed my fingers on a bump rising slightly on the side of my head.

I looked down at Steven sleeping beside me, his head resting against my breast, my arm cradling him. I touched the face with wonder at how soft and smooth he was. Still a baby, I thought, feeling tenderly maternal. And yet with a mature sense that came with loss, such as his uncle had.

"I'll take good care of him, Clarissa," I whispered softly into the night. "And Priscilla, too," I promised.

Somehow, I felt sure that she knew I would try.

How could a parent give up the joy of a child? How could my father have so easily discarded me?

I remembered his face as he looked at me and I wondered if he had known who I was. Did I look like my mother? Had I brought back unpleasant memories for him? Was that why he had given me to Miss Montgomery?

If ever I have a child . . . nothing will make me give it up. Nothing. And no one.

I looked down at Steven again. I felt as close to him as if he were my own flesh. But he wasn't mine.

Leaning back against the pillows, I thought of Clinton. Someday he will marry Cybil James. And I will leave then. I have to find my own life, my own happiness. As much as I loved Steven and Priscilla, I must remember, they were not my family. They were Clinton's and his wife's, when he married. There would be no home here for me and I must accept that. Cybil will be their mother and she will give them the love they need.

As sleep stole lightly over me again, the door opened with a creak. Thinking it was Mabel or Mary, I felt no alarm. Opening my eyes from drowsiness, I smiled up at the tall figure standing in the shadows at the foot of my bed. A shock went through me like fire as I met the dark, brooding eyes of Clinton Matthews.

"I thought you would be asleep," he whispered. "I just checked in to see how you were," he went on to explain in a low voice.

"I feel much better, thank you," I whispered back, my heart racing wildly.

He smiled down at the small form snuggled tightly against me, the small hand clutching at the ribbons of my nightgown. "I see you already have company." The tension was gone from his face suddenly, and a softness grew in his eyes. I nodded and smiled up at him again. I had been unfair in my thoughts of Clinton Matthews. There was gentleness, love, compassion in him. It was there in his eyes as he looked at his young nephew.

"How long have I been asleep?" I asked after a long silence. I did not want him to leave yet.

"Round the clock."

"I'm sorry I have been so much trouble to you," I said sincerely. "I didn't mean to ride so far. Is the mare all right?"

"Fine . . ." he answered quietly, a half-smile touching his lips. He came slowly around the side of the bed, taking a nearby chair. Our eyes met again and held, his seeming even darker in the candlelight.

"How do you really feel?" he asked.

"I ache," I answered, smiling. "But I don't feel dizzy anymore." I couldn't take my eyes from his and a flush crept up my face as I remembered the last time we had talked. He smiled at me, as though reading my thoughts. There was no mockery or judgment in his face.

"I'm sorry about . . . frightening you the other night."

"Steven was afraid I was going to die," I whispered, changing the subject quickly, afraid he would understand too much if we spoke of our argument. The same blank expression I had so often seen close down over

Steven's features, closed down over Matthews'. He stood up slowly, almost reluctantly, leaning down then to carefully gather his nephew into his arms. As he lifted him away from my side, our eyes held. His seemed to soften and lighten, and then a dim unhappiness reflected in the candlelight.

"Good night . . . Miss O'Reilly," he said. I wanted to say something to him to keep him with me just a few more minutes, but nothing came. I just stared up at him, feeling the warm empty space where Steven had lain beside me. I must remember who and what I am. I must remember that there can be no home for me here.

The door shut quietly behind him, leaving me alone and desolate in the faint candlelight. I stared for a long time at the closed door before snuggling down into the covers and going to sleep again.

Early the next morning, I climbed gingerly from my bed, testing my balance. Relieved, I stood up and went slowly to the mirror, wondering how bad I looked after my fall. Other than a slight swelling and bruise on my forehead and a blazing sunburn, I appeared normal.

I washed my face with the cold water from the pitcher, pressing the wet cloth to the bruise for a moment.

I was almost dressed when Mary Cramer came into the room unannounced, expecting me to be still asleep. She started violently when I said good morning, swinging around to face me standing by the basin. I finished buttoning my blouse and smoothed down my skirt.

"Mr. Matthews said you were not to get up today. You are to rest," she announced, and I wondered why she was avoiding my eyes.

"I feel fine. And as for staying in bed, that's utterly ridiculous."

"But Mabel . . ."

"I'm already two days behind in the children's lessons."

"She'll be furious with me if I allow you to get up!" Mary exclaimed, more alarmed than she should have been. What was wrong with her this morning?

"I'm already up. And I'll explain to Mabel that it was my decision."

She seemed on the verge of saying something more, but closed her mouth, remaining mute. "I'll tell Mabel you couldn't persuade me to stay in bed. It's really better if I get up, Mary. Please don't look so worried. I'll explain to Mabel and she won't be angry with you."

She looked at me then, her lip quivering slightly. "I'm sorry, Miss Kathleen . . . I'm sorry about the . . . accident."

Smiling at her, I turned to make a final check in the mirror after finishing the long braid and winding it into a loose bun at the back of my neck.

"You hardly had anything to do with that, Mary. It was my own stupidity." Her silence was strained.

The house was very quiet as I came down the stairs. I had expected Matthews and the hands to be gone for the day, but wondered at the stillness. Where were the children?

I wandered through the house looking for them and found them sitting, unusually subdued, in the kitchen with Mabel. They were not eating the fresh-baked rolls nor drinking the milk that sat before them.

"Miss O'Reilly!" Priscilla exclaimed, charging off her stool and flying toward me.

"For goodness' sakes, Priscilla, don't jump all over the poor woman!" Mabel ordered unpleasantly. "And what are you doing out of bed, miss?" she went on, glowering her disapproval at me.

"I was very lonely and bored up there," I answered, not fooled by her fierceness. "I feel fine, Mabel. Really! And I am very hungry," I hinted, grinning at her.

122

Relaxing, she laughed and got up to pull another plate out of the cabinet. Her heavy breasts bounced as she moved quickly to the stove. Placing two sugar rolls on the plate, she then turned and poured a cup of hot coffee.

"I guess you are all right if you're hungry," she said, putting some scrambled eggs next to the rolls and then adding a rasher of bacon. "Children! Hush!" she reprimanded as they both resumed their enthusiastic chatter. Priscilla and Steven stood effectively silenced, giving me secret grins as they slid obediently back up on their stools.

"Uncle Clinton was so worried about you, Miss O'Reilly," Priscilla informed me and gave a quick penetrating look at her younger brother. "Wasn't he?" she asked, demanding his collaboration.

Steven nodded in agreement, still not taking his eyes off me. The smile on his face was endearing.

"You had us all worried," Mabel frowned as she sat down on the remaining stool. "How in the world did you get so far from the ranch house? It was near dark when they finally found you."

"I wasn't thinking, I guess."

"When you didn't get back for breakfast, we were afraid something had happened. Uncle Clinton and Jim went out to look for you," Steven said.

"That'll teach me to be more careful. It must have been a real bother for them to do that."

"What happened?" Mable demanded.

"I fell off my horse," I said simply, giving her an embarrassed smile. "Typical greenhorn, you'll say. Nothing very exciting about that, now is there?" I said to Priscilla. "It'll teach me to check the cinches and the saddle before I ride again."

"You shouldn't have to be bothered checking the cinch," Mabel commented roughly. "Someone from the stables isn't doing his job."

123

From the corner of my eye, I saw Mary leave the room quickly, her face flushing suddenly. Mabel turned as the door swung shut, and then frowned.

"Now what has gotten into that girl this morning?" she said, voicing my own thoughts.

The children and I picked up our usual routine and early that afternoon we went to the stables to get our horses. Ted hesitated before saddling the black mare, saying that Matthews had not said anything about allowing me to ride again. I assured him that I was fine, and promised, with a smile, not to lose my mount again. He went into the stables, reappearing shortly with all three horses, saddled and ready.

We took our time, staying close to the ranch house and walking our horses. My muscles still ached, and the children had no desire to leave my side.

When we returned to the stables about an hour later, Steven asked Ted when his uncle would return.

"Don't expect him back for another hour or more. It's a long ride to the James ranch, you know. And I expect he'll not be in a rush to leave," he grinned.

His words hit me with a thud.

"Is anything wrong, Miss O'Reilly? Can I help you down?"

"No, thank you, Ted," I answered with false brightness. The three of us walked back to the house, leaving the currying and feeding to Ted this time. Both Steven and Priscilla were silent. I tried to sound gay and light as I spoke to them.

"I wish he wouldn't see Miss James," Priscilla blurted out. The last thing I wanted to talk about was Clinton Matthews' visit to Cybil James.

"Maybe Uncle Clinton like her," Steven commented with a shrug. "She is very pretty." So even little boys were affected by her beauty.

Priscilla froze, swinging on her brother furiously. "She is not! She is too fat . . . and she is ugly!"

"I didn't say I liked her!" Steven stormed back in equal fury, his face blackening at her accusing glare.

"Stop it! Stop it right this minute!" I said, shocking them to speechlessness by my harshness. I regretted my tone as soon as I had spoken. Softening slightly, I continued, still feeling, however, the unreasonable irritation.

"Miss James is neither fat nor ugly, Priscilla. It is terrible that you even say such things. And your uncle has the right to see anyone . . . and do anything he wishes. It is not for you to say such things about his friends."

"She just wants the ranch!" Priscilla insisted, her eyes brimming with tears of hurt. Doubting her exclamation, I looked at her waiting for my response.

"You don't really believe that, sweetheart," I said gently. "Miss James likes your uncle very much." I remembered all too well the sultry looks she cast in his direction while they were in the sitting room. "And your uncle likes her very much too." How could he help but love her? She was the most beautiful woman I had ever seen.

"He does not! He likes you more than her!" she burst out, stamping her foot on the ground.

"He likes me because I love you two," I explained, trying to show her the difference between Matthews' feelings for me and his interest in Cybil James. A pain tightened in my chest.

"That's not true, Miss O'Reilly," Priscilla answered back, starting to cry. "He worried about you when you didn't come back. Didn't he, Steven? He wouldn't worry about Miss James like that. I know he loves you. I know it!" She was crying in frustration now at my calm disbelief. "He just has to love you," she blubbered. "Don't you see. You marry him! Don't let him marry that . . . Miss James," she spit the name out like a foul word. "You marry him!" She looked up at me pleadingly. "Please . . ."

My astonishment and embarrassment were complete. Priscilla burst out with loud sobs, stamping her foot again. "Tell her, Steven!"

"Prissy." I put my arm around her and then Steven, drawing them to me. "You are very dear to want me to marry your uncle. But your uncle will marry whom he wants. You can't plan things like that for him . . . just to suit yourself. And I can't marry him . . . don't you see that?"

"Why can't you?" Steven demanded bluntly, frowning as he looked from his sister's tear-stained face to my embarrassed one.

"Because he loves Miss James." Priscilla cried harder. "And because I am your governess." They both looked at me with blank, confused stares.

"You're both too young to understand these things," I said lamely, falling back on the age-old excuse.

"Don't you even like him?" Steven asked with surprise and hurt as Priscilla wiped her eyes and continued to stare at me.

"Of course, I like him . . . I like him very much." I blushed hotly, wondering how much they really saw and sensed about my feelings for their uncle.

"If he asked you to marry him, wouldn't you?" Priscilla put in.

"There's no point in even asking me such a thing, Priscilla," I said stiffly. "Your uncle would never ask me such a thing." Her face crumpled again and I felt cruel to disillusion her. But she must know the truth. She must not build her hopes on fluffy clouds.

"Do you want your uncle to be happy?" I asked, a little hoarsely. She nodded, wiping her eyes. "Then you have to be unselfish and try to like Miss James. If he marries her, it will make him very unhappy if you don't even try to like her." Priscilla sniffled, frowning.

"When you get to know her better, you'll like her as much as you like me," I added, feeling a sudden sharp twinge of jealousy at the thought.

"No I won't!"

"Neither will I!" Steven added, determined.

"That won't be fair to her," I said. "You have to give her the same chance you gave me when I first came. Will you at least try?" They were stubbornly silent. "Will you try for your uncle . . . and for me too?" After a grudging nod, we went back to the house, their faces tragically unhappy.

We spent a quiet hour reading in the upstairs schoolroom. Nothing more was said about Cybil James, nor about their uncle. But as I watched them, I realized the conversation was still fresh in their young minds, as fresh and painful as it was in mine.

Steven jumped up suddenly, looking out the window. "Uncle Clinton's back," he announced, turning to us. "Come on, let's go down and meet him. He'll come through the garden after he takes his horse around to the stables."

Priscilla darted over to me and took my hand. "Come on, Miss O'Reilly." The hope in her eyes was depressing. I understood too well what she was wishing.

"I'll be down later. You two go and visit with him." I remained seated, not wanting to see Matthews yet. I knew it was unreasonable for me to feel hurt and betrayed by his visit to Cybil James. But the emotions were there, nonetheless.

When the children had gone, I went and sat in the window seat, leaning my head back, absorbing the afternoon sunlight and smelling the honeysuckle that climbed up the front of the house. The road from the house stretched out toward Las Positas and the stage stop. I wondered how long it would be before I would be leaving the ranch.

"What's this about you taking the children riding

today?" I jerked around at Matthews' angry accusation. He strode into the schoolroom, dusty and flushed from the heat of his ride home. "What are you doing up at all?" he demanded. "I left orders for you not to get up today!"

His tone made me defensively angry. "I am not sick, Mr. Matthews," I replied evenly. I noted quickly that he was neatly dressed in dark trousers and a soft leather shirt. He looked very handsome, I thought bitterly, my mind turning to his visit to the James ranch. Did he press hot, demanding kisses on Cybil James's lips? Did he kiss her the way he had kissed me in the study?

"I told Michael that you would be unable to ride with him tomorrow," Matthews announced, looking pleased at his statement. My annoyance increased.

"You did what?" I asked, standing up, my eyes sparking.

"I told him you had an accident and that you would not be able to ride tomorrow," he informed me calmly.

"That was for me to decide, Mr. Matthews," I said coldly. He raised his brows and then shrugged.

"It's done."

I glared at him as he dug his hand into his shirt pocket and pulled out a folded envelope. "Michael sent this," he said, holding it out. I snatched it from his hand still staring at him. For an instant he stood waiting, and then had the courtesy to look embarrassed. He moved away, allowing me to open the envelope in privacy.

"I haven't been up here for years," he commented, watching me from the window where I had been sitting. I looked up at him again and then turned my back to read the message he had carried.

Michael James, unlike Clinton Matthews, had neat, clear handwriting.

Miss O'Reilly,

Clint told me you would not be able to ride tomorrow because you were thrown from your horse. I agree with him that it would be unwise to ride again so soon, but I shall come over and keep you company in the garden.

Counting the minutes . . . ever yours,

Michael

I looked up quickly at Matthews, who was frowning at me. I smiled in apology. His stare dropped to the note in my hand.

"You don't appear to be angry with me any longer," he commented, an angry tic starting in his own cheek.

"I'm not."

"Oh," he responded, his gaze concentrated and suspicious.

"I'm sorry, Mr. Matthews. I was a bit hasty in judging your actions. Mr. James informs me here that you did say I could not ride . . . but that he will be over tomorrow and we will sit in the garden and visit." I paused wondering why he was scowling again. "I thought you had gone to tell him not to come at all," I explained further.

He flushed.

"As you pointed out so succinctly the other evening, Miss O'Reilly . . . I have no control over your life." He spun around and stormed from the room, leaving me feeling confused and unhappy.

VIII

Priscilla, Steven, and I were on our usual Sunday morning ride when Michael James appeared on the knoll. Hailing us with a wave, he rode down to meet us on a magnificent black stallion.

"I thought Clint was a little too casual when he told me you'd had a fall," he said, edging his spirited mount between me and the two children. Steven gave way grudgingly. Michael James's thoroughbred threw its head up and down, blew hard, and then contemptuously nipped at Steven's mount.

I found myself more aware of Michael James' attractiveness than on our first unexpected meeting. He sat his horse well, his legs long and well muscled. His shoulders were broad and held straight with the inbred assurance that wealth and security bring. The well-trimmed mustache he sported emphasized handsome features on a bronzed face.

Matthew's previous forbidding warning made Michael James even more intriguing and I looked at him with a new interest. I was not disappointed in what I saw.

"She did have an accident," Steven informed James,

with a glare at the black stallion. "She might have been killed. And it was my Uncle Clinton who found her." I was startled by Steven's unexpected rush of words, but more astonished by the angry scowl that darkened his face as he stared up at James. For a moment he looked very much like his uncle.

"Steven," I started, intending to silence his rudeness, but James gently intercepted.

"So you really had an accident," Michael said, calling my attention back to him. His eyes were sparkling with amusement.

"I just told you that!" Steven exclaimed, and I blushed at his arrogance.

"Steven, that is quite enough!"

"Why don't you two children ride on ahead while I visit with your governess?" Michael suggested with a cock of his head. His eyes flashed a warning at Steven, making the boy's face flush with even more anger.

"Come on, Steve. Let's ride up to the ridge," Priscilla said, spurring her pony into a gallop. Steven followed reluctantly, casting a venomous glare back over his thin shoulder at my companion.

"I am so sorry," I apologized, looking at the disappearing figure of my young charge. "I don't know what's gotten into him. He's never acted like that before . . . never."

"He's jealous!" Michael exclaimed with a laugh. Something in his expression told me that James knew how attractive he was and some of his charm diminished at my thought. Well, I thought reasonably, why shouldn't he know he is handsome? He is.

"There's nothing for him to be jealous about."

"Not yet."

"You're very sure of yourself, aren't you, Mr. James?" I said, more as an observation than a retort. For a moment he looked embarrassed, but finally smiled lightly again.

"I've a feeling that I'll not be so sure of myself from now on, Miss O'Reilly."

"How is your sister?" I asked.

"Fine." He shrugged, dismissing her from his concerns, and then asked with interest about my accident.

"There's not much to tell."

"That's not how Steven would have it," he persisted lightly. "How did it happen?"

"I was riding and my mare jumped a fallen tree. I fell. It was rather silly of me to be riding that fast in the first place."

"Who was chasing you? Anyone I know?" he teased.

"No one." A flash of my thoughts about Matthews that morning came to my mind.

"Then why are you blushing like that?" he laughed. "You have a charming blush, Miss O'Reilly. Has anyone ever told you that?"

Speechless with embarrassment, I spurred my horse away from him, tearing up the hillside through the trees at breakneck speed. I ducked down, pressing myself against the racing mare until we shot out into a meadow. I had ridden some distance before James was able to overtake me. He brought his powerful stallion through a grove of trees to cut me off, reaching over and grabbing the reins from my hands. He looked far from his usual calm when he pulled her in.

"You could have broken your neck riding through those trees like that!" he exclaimed.

"I don't like to be laughed at!" I retorted hotly, trying to pull the leather straps free of his hands. He held them tight. His stallion sidled close to the mare, nudging her.

"Stop that, Diablo!" Michael exploded, jerking the reins. His face flushed and I laughed at his expression.

"I thought never to see you discomfited, Mr. James," I laughed again.

"Then we're even," he grinned, and I felt foolish for my sudden flash of temper.

"What a temper you have!" he observed. "But at least I'm relieved that it goes as fast as it explodes."

"Not always," I admitted.

"I suppose Clinton has warned you about me," he said without preface, leaning forward and resting his forearm on his saddle horn. His expression betrayed the casualness.

"You might say that," I answered, frowning. I remembered Matthews' warning only too well—his warm lips on mine, my heart pounding wildly in response, and then his casual, brutal remark.

"He's right. I'd better warn you myself," James said seriously. "I haven't exactly lived a life of celibacy. But neither has my friend Clinton, I might add," he went on, more defensively. "He's not an angel either."

"That's hardly my concern," I stated with annoyance. "And why are you telling me all this?"

"Because I have the feeling that your employer has been saying a little more than he has a right to say," he replied bluntly. "And because, I want to make my intentions clear from the start."

"Oh. And just what are your intentions then Mr. James?" I asked, unexpectedly bold. "Are you warning me from the start how little to expect from any relationship with you?" Was that really me speaking to a man hardly more than a stranger?

"I was right then," he reported, raking his fingers through his hair in an angry motion.

"I'm sorry, that was rude and unfair," I amended. "I usually try to decide for myself what people are like."

"Oh, hell." He didn't seem to be speaking to me but to himself. He looked at me piercingly. "I want to put it to you straight, Kathleen."

My eyes widened at his sudden use of my name

133

and the intent way he searched my face. "I intend to marry you!"

"You what?" I gasped.

"I know it sounds crazy . . . but I'm serious . . . for the first time in my life." He looked surprised at his own words. Then he laughed as though he had said something that had been weighing heavily on his mind. "I've enjoyed being with a lot of women. But I've never fallen in love. I never expected to, and quite frankly, never wanted to either. I heard in town that Clint had a governess for the children . . . and that you were anything but the usual dowdy old maid. I was curious. It didn't take much to talk Cybil into riding over here with me so I'd have an excuse to show up suddenly. You were everything they said you were in town—more. The minute you walked into that room, wide-eyed and embarrassed, something happened to me."

"You must be mad! Or think I am a complete idiot!" I burst out. Was this what Matthews had warned me about?

"Quite the contrary," he said, undaunted.

"You don't know the first thing about me!"

"I know you're from New York, that you love children. You're well educated or Clinton would never have brought you out here to teach Priscilla and Steven. And you are beautiful. You stir me like no other woman ever has," he said finally, the last words seeming to him the most important. "Many people marry knowing and feeling far less than that."

"You don't know me at all," I repeated, for want of knowing what else to say under these strange and new circumstances. Was the man mad?

"I will!" he said, smiling. "I told you all this because I want it understood from the start what I want from you. I intend to tell Clint also . . . so that he won't be playing watchdog over you."

134

"Mr. James . . ."

"My name is Michael," he insisted. After a long pause, he frowned. "Please don't look so frightened. I don't plan to abduct you or force you to marry against your will. But I do intend to pay suit to you . . . for as long at it takes to convince you I am sincere and get an affirmative answer. I want you for my wife."

I couldn't think of anything to say. I just sat there on my horse staring at him in disbelief, astonished at his proposal.

"You actually look shocked," he said with a hint of amusement. "Lots of men must have fallen in love with you before me."

"Hardly!" I said at last.

"Maybe you just didn't know how they felt."

"I never knew any men."

"None?" He sounded surprised, but somehow pleased.

"None."

He reached over and took my hand, his fingers closing over mine with gentle strength. "No wonder you think I'm mad," he grinned.

The sound of galloping horses approaching drew my attention. Relieved, I saw Priscilla and Steven racing toward us and took the opportunity to withdraw my hand from Michael's warm grasp.

"Uncle Clinton just rode in," Steven announced as he reined in sharply. "We saw him from the ridge," he explained. "He's a friend of yours, isn't he? Why don't you go see him?"

"Steven!" Why did he dislike Michael so intensely?

Michael appeared unperturbed, smiling as he met the boy's glare.

"All right, Steven. I do have some things to say to your uncle . . ." His voice was friendly and confidential. Then he leaned forward slightly, lowering his voice: "But we both know I came to see Kathleen, don't we?"

Steven stiffened in his saddle. Priscilla noticed her brother's fury and moved her pony in, drawing his attention: "Steven." He looked at her, irritated by her interruption. "Remember what we talked about on the ridge?" she prodded him. He glared at Michael again and then nodded. "Well, then, come on." He turned his pony to follow Priscilla toward the ranch house. I wondered what they had decided on the ridge.

"Was that necessary?" I whispered to Michael as he rode next to me. The two children were several yards ahead and out of hearing.

"He might as well know now. I'll be coming to call on you quite frequently, and I don't want to have him interrupting us."

As we entered the gate to the ranch-house area and rode up to the front steps, I saw Clinton come out to meet us. Mingled feelings of excitement and dread raced through my veins. James glanced sideways at me and frowned, jumping down from his mount and coming to aid me.

"We take our own horses to the stables," I explained.

"Steven, you handle that," Matthews said and Steven took my reins.

"Did you have a nice ride," Matthews asked, and I was not sure whom he was addressing.

"Yes, Uncle Clinton," Priscilla responded hurriedly, taking Steven's hand and tugging him. "Come on." The boy glowered at Michael as he helped me down from my mount, his hands lingering on my waist as he set me on the ground.

"We have coffee waiting in the sitting room, Mike," Clinton announced somewhat curtly, ignoring me. Michael's eyes took on a cold glitter, but he grinned up at his host. He turned to me, lifting my hand to his lips and smiling over it with assurance.

"Thank you for listening, Kathleen. I'll be seeing

136

you soon . . . very soon." I wondered what he would say to Matthews.

I went up the steps past the silent Matthews and entered the main hall. I almost collided with Mary Cramer, who stood at the door, her eyes on Michael James in pained adoration. The color was high in her cheeks and her dark eyes were brilliant. With a start I realized she was in love with him. Mary Cramer was in love with Michael James.

She smiled as the men entered behind me and I stared in shock at her lingering gaze.

"Hello, Mary," Michael said casually from behind me.

"Hello, Mi—Mr. James."

"We'll have that coffee now, Mary," Matthews said, his voice sounding a little more natural. "Miss O'Reilly, aren't you joining us?"

"We decided I should talk to you alone," Michael answered for me. I looked at him with surprise and annoyance. The man was taking too much for granted.

"I have the children's lessons to correct," I put in and then turned to hurry up the stairs.

I felt guilty at the love in Mary's eyes. I couldn't see Michael James knowing how Mary felt. It would hurt her. He had hardly been serious about his proposal to me. Matthews had told me about Michael James and his unprecedented success with women. Perhaps this was his way of attempting to charm me.

I would eventually learn with a shock that I had underestimated Michael James's sincerity.

Some time later, I heard angry voices below my window in the garden. Michael's voice was slightly louder, though Matthews' was low and growling in rage.

"Don't you think she has the right to decide that, Clint? What is she to you anyway?" Michael was demanding. A long hesitation followed and then Matthews mumbled an answer too low to be heard. "Since when did my affairs with women concern you, anyway?" Michael sounded indignant, furious. "It's not as though I was informing you that I want to just bed the girl, for Christ's sake." Another pause and muttered response. "I'm going to marry her, Clint. And you'd better stay the hell out of it!"

"Marry her? You're out of your mind!" Matthews' voice rose in fury, blurting out his words. The assault hit more than its intended victim as I blanched and felt sick with pain.

"Perhaps we'll have a double wedding, Clint," Michael said, almost pleasantly. "That would make Kathleen your sister-in-law, wouldn't it?" he chuckled, but stopped suddenly at something Matthews said. "We'll see if you do!" James growled and I heard his angry footsteps go back into the house. The front door slammed so hard it was easily heard upstairs at the back of the house.

I sat for a long time just staring at the wall, utterly devoid of feeling. Then it slowly seeped back. First the hurt, then the anger.

Was I never good enough? Not good enough for adoption, now not good enough for the interest of a young rancher.

Mary entered without knocking. The cold stare she gave me sent a shiver down my spine.

"Mr. Matthews wants you to come down to the library," she informed me in a cool voice. I knew the reason for her sudden dislike and felt defensively annoyed. Jealousy was a raw wound on her face.

"You may tell Mr. Matthews that I am indisposed, Mary," I responded in like tone, meeting her eyes. "And that I would like to take my dinner in my room this evening . . . if he will permit it." My eyes were flashing by the time I finished. I would have refused James's attentions to prevent hurting Mary, but her present attitude toward me made me care little for her feelings. I had feelings of my own to satisfy.

"He will not like it, Miss O'Reilly," she challenged.

"I don't care if he does not like it, Mary. If he is unduly distressed . . . he may dismiss me for my insolence. I do not care one twit whether he does or not."

She looked shocked at my calmly spoken words of rebellion. She left the room with a smile.

Half-expecting Matthews to come storming into my room, demanding that I pack my bag and take my disobedient, arrogant self elsewhere, I sat waiting in the rocking chair.

Nothing happened.

I was almost disappointed there would be no confrontation.

The house remained silent.

Later that day, Mary returned to my room with dinner. In the silence of the room, I watched her set the tray down on the small table and leave without a backward glance.

I began to think more clearly, realizing that I had run away again, escaped to the solitude of a locked room, locking not only the wooden doors but the entrance to my feelings as well. The anger disappeared and the hurt returned, as well as shame for my childish pouting.

Admitting to myself it was not Michael's dismissal from the house that had upset me, I had to face what it was: Matthews' response to Michael's intentions. Surprise and disgust had hardened that voice in the garden. Surprise that anyone could really care for me, and disgust that a man like Michael James would reach below himself to pick a wife. That was the real source of my hurt.

I had obligations to Matthews no matter what his sentiments about me. He knew only too well that I was searching for love, perhaps searching too desperately. He meant to see that I remembered who and what I was and he would remind Michael James also.

"I'm a person with feelings," I said, quietly experiencing the frustration of a lifetime of bent feelings.

Feelings better kept under control, I corrected.

The children were my concern. Nothing more. Any desire to be more to Matthews was the source of nothing but future anguish. I had no right to care about him. He was not my concern. The children were my concern. Any love I felt for him was futile for me and unimportant to him.

Taking my shawl from the bed, I walked quietly from the room and down the back stairs to the garden. I sat for a long time listening to the night sounds. I took slow, deep breaths of the fresh night air, hoping to alleviate the pain that nagged at me.

Perhaps if I left the ranch and found another position, I might find some happiness for myself.

Tears stung as I thought of leaving Priscilla and Steven. And could I leave Clinton Matthews, even knowing that he cared nothing for me? Would being away from him change my feelings?

Perhaps I was being foolish in thinking Matthews knew what I felt. But how could he not know? Was I infatuated with him or really in love with him? Was I drawn to him only because he was the first attractive man with whom I had come in contact?

A shock of memory flashed. "Maybe a little of her hot blood runs in your cold veins," Anna Bowen had said. Was it true? Was I like my mother?

Only today I had noticed Michael James's attractiveness. And he wanted to court me. Would I find myself as easily drawn to him as I found myself drawn to Clinton Matthews? The thought brought sudden panic.

But my heart did not beat faster when Michael James looked at me, I thought frantically.

Maybe it will, I thought with Anna's words still ringing in my ears. Maybe I would come to feel the same intensity of longing for Michael James. A strange, mysterious need for something I did not have or understand. Would his kiss awaken the overwhelming feelings in me that Clinton Matthews' kiss had?

The doubts died. I knew that Michael James would never awaken those feelings in me, just as I knew that if Clinton Matthews ever wanted me, he had only to take me in his arms and hold me there. I would yield to him my very soul.

The realization was not comforting. I did not want to allow myself, as my mother had, to become involved with a man who cared nothing for me or my future. I wanted something in return, some warmth, some kindness, some genuine feeling.

"I should leave Las Posas," I whispered to myself. As I stood up the crickets stopped their serenade. "But I don't want to go. I want to feel alive inside. I want . . ."

"Kathleen?" A familiar voice from close by made me jump. "Are you alone?" Matthews asked gently, approaching through the garden. "I thought I heard you talking to someone," he explained, not waiting for my answer. It was the third time I remembered him using my first name and it sent a renewed thrill of pleasure through me.

I stood there staring at him in the pale moonlight, and forgot all the angry hurt of the past few minutes. All I felt was his presence and the warmth it sent through me.

"Sometimes I talk to myself," I managed to murmur.

"Were you very lonely as a child?" he asked with a note of tenderness I had never heard before. He sat down on the bench. "Sit down, Kathleen." I sat down beside him, trying to make out his face in the dark.

I wanted to answer, "Yes, I was lonely . . . I still am, oh, dear God, I am still so lonely," but I couldn't bring myself even to speak a polite word. My throat was filled with a hard lump.

"Why didn't you come down when I sent for you this afternoon?"

All the hurt flooded back, and I shook my head, unable to speak a word. He took my chin in his hand and turned me slowly to face him. "You overheard Michael and me in the garden this afternoon, didn't you?" he asked softly.

I didn't move, didn't speak. I was afraid of the rush of words that would come if I uttered even one. So easily, I could tell him every feeling I had ever experienced, every longing that he awakened in me, every hope that stirred me when I saw him.

"If it means so much to you, I won't stand in your way or his," he said, resigned and disappointed. It was so dark I could not see his face clearly, nor the emotion I had imagined in his voice. His hand dropped and the light from the house caught his profile as he looked across the garden. His jaw was tight, his eyes deepset under the frown.

"I don't have any feelings for Michael James," I admitted. "It doesn't matter, really."

His face swung around to me again, but I could not see his eyes. For a few minutes I could pretend I saw whatever I wanted to see. Even tenderness. Even love.

"Then why are you so upset?" he asked pointedly.

"I'm not," I prevaricated.

"You are. I can feel it just as easily as I can feel this." His hand slid down my cheek as he spoke with gentleness. I cherished the darkness and the hiding place it made for me.

"Tell me," he pressed. "Was it something you heard me say?"

"What does it matter," my voice sounded distant, unlike my own.

"I only wanted to keep you . . . from being hurt,"

142

he said with quiet anger. "The children love you so much, Kathleen."

The children, yes, the children are his concern also. "Steven is beginning to come back to normalcy. He laughs now . . . and today he was really angry. It's because he loves you . . . and knows he is loved by you." He hesitated for a moment, his voice becoming even more quiet. "It's so easy for them . . . to show how they feel about you."

"It's easy for anyone to care about people." I said quietly. You saw how I felt when you stopped kissing me, I went on silently.

"Not everyone," he replied. He didn't seem to be speaking to me anymore, but to himself. "Maybe I'm wrong about Michael."

Something in his tone made me want to reach out and touch him, and say, "I don't care about Michael. It's you I love." But I couldn't do that. I knew that it would only embarrass him to hear me admit my feelings, and it would only hurt me. But for the first time since I had met Clinton Matthews on that hillside, he did not seem remote, assured, untouchable. He was so very human, with human needs, with human loneliness.

Perhaps he was thinking of Cybil James. Was it hard for him to tell her that he loved her? Was he wondering what she would say about her brother wanting to marry her future husband's servant?

"When will you marry Miss James?" I asked quietly, hoping to draw him out of his depression. Perhaps I could be his friend if not more.

"Why do you ask that?" he queried harshly. The spell was shattered and I felt ashamed of having pried into his personal life.

"I'm sorry. I didn't mean to pry," I apologized. "It's none of my business, I know."

"Did Michael tell you that I was going to marry Cybil?" he asked, angry.

143

"No . . . the children," I managed to stammer.

"They've been hearing ranch gossip." I wasn't sure by his response whether he meant reports of his marrying Cybil were just gossip. "I guess people around here knew about my father's hope that we would marry. Her family was all for it too. Our two ranches joined would make a small empire. Did Michael tell you that he was supposed to marry my sister Clarissa at one time? Or our parents planned it that way? But Clarissa fell in love with Jim. And, of course, Michael didn't want to settle down anyway." He hesitated. "He seems to want to settle down now . . . with you."

"He's not serious."

"I think you might be wrong. He seems quite serious."

"I wouldn't accept if he were," I answered tiredly, now sure that this was the reason for Matthews' sudden openness. He wanted my assurance that there would be no marriage between Cybil's brother and me. He wanted no shadow on the family with my nebulous, mysterious heritage.

"I'm glad," Indeed, he sounded glad. Why shouldn't he?

"You're so quiet. Are you unhappy, Kathleen?"

"No . . . not really. All my life I have wanted to find a family. People to care about me, love me. Your nephew and niece have given me something I will always cherish."

"You sound as though you're planning to go away," he said, alarmed.

"Don't you think I should?"

"Go away? Why?"

"Because of Michael."

"You've got me confused. Why would I want you to leave because of Michael?"

"Because of what I am."

144

"And what are you?" He sounded slightly exasperated.

"A governess. Hardly suitable for a wealthy young rancher's interest."

"Good God. So that's what you've been thinking!" he burst out.

"I understand that Miss James would not approve of her brother's interest in me, Mr. Matthews," I said, looking at him, wondering if that had been his reason for being so irate at the idea of Michael's interest in me.

"She wouldn't have anything to say about it. Michael thinks for himself."

"But if Miss James were upset . . . you would be also."

"Upset, yes . . . but not because of Cybil," he said with a laugh that sounded bitter. "If that's what you really wanted."

'But you could tell both of them about . . ." I started, thinking of my response to his kiss in the study.

"Tell them what?"

"About . . . what happened in the study." My face flushed and I turned away, even knowing that the darkness covered my embarrassment and shame.

"That's between us. It has nothing to do with Mike or Cybil," he said softly.

"I'm not," the word choked me, "promiscuous." I thought of my mother.

"Promiscuous?" he laughed in surprise.

I was pricked by his mirth. "I'm not like that," I said quietly with a note of despair, wondering if he thought me so.

"You're serious. You really think I . . . Kathleen, for God's sake," he said with a tremor in his voice as he drew me into his arms. I struggled in near panic and he released me abruptly, looking down at me. I

145

was shaking violently, frightened at my own sudden emotions which were flashing to life again.

"I don't want you to think that I'm like that," I said desperately. "I'm sorry I let it happen. You must think that I welcome such actions all the—"

"You didn't let it happen," he interrupted. "I made it happen." His hand touched my cheek in a gentle caress. "I wanted it to happen." He moved his fingers down my neck and rested his hand over the throbbing vein. "Are you afraid of me?"

"I should go to my room," I answered quietly, my heart taking a sudden leap at his tone. But I couldn't move. I searched his face, unable to read the emotion there because of the darkness.

Everything was still, quiet, charged with expectation.

"Do you really want to leave?" he asked quietly, his voice deepening slightly. His fingers moved lightly over my temple, brushing the tendrils of hair back.

"No . . ." I breathed, and then, unable to stop myself, amended truthfully, "I don't know what I want . . . I'm afraid."

His mouth moved slowly down over mine. My lips trembled and parted as they met his. His kiss was at first warm and gentle. I felt his hand move to the back of my head, touching my hair. Then he moved his other hand around my waist and drew me against him, his kiss becoming somehow urgent, possessive, his arm trembling slightly as he held me.

I jerked away from him, shaking, my whole body alive with vibrating warmth.

"I don't want to be like my mother," I choked out, crying. Standing up, I moved away from him, trying to shatter the invisible bond between us.

"Kathleen . . ." His voice was thick and unsteady. "I won't ever hurt you." He moved slowly toward me to draw me into his arms again, but I stumbled away from him blinded by my tears.

146

"I just can't be like that . . . I don't want to be like that."

Before he could touch me or speak again, I turned and fled into the house.

IX

I was still trembling when I reached my room. Once inside, I leaned against the door, horrified with shame.

What must Clinton Matthews think of me now?

I had told him I did not want to leave the garden. Of course, that would lead him on to other assumptions, assumptions I did not want him to make. But was that really true? Hadn't I wanted him to kiss me again? Hadn't I wanted to feel his arms around me again, his lips on mine, making my blood run like fire?

Oh, dear Lord, what he must think of me now! What was I thinking of myself at this moment!

"But I broke away from him," I thought defensively.

"Yes, but you encouraged him to kiss you also," my conscience added critically. "You enjoyed it, longed for more, for something excitingly mysterious that will still that raging torrent in your body!"

"I didn't encourage him. I only said what I felt." I pressed my hands over my ears, but the thoughts were loud in my mind.

"You can't fool yourself, Kathleen Warden O'Reilly!

You could have prevented what happened . . . if you had really wanted to prevent it."

I dropped my hands to my sides.

"This time was different. His kiss was tender. It wasn't angry and violent like before." The other self softened but remained adamant.

"That only makes it worse. That made you hope for something you have no right nor possibility to fulfill."

"And it was dark . . ." I agreed dismally. Perhaps the mockery, the amused understanding was still there in his dark eyes. I couldn't see his face. I didn't know what was there in his expression.

But his voice. It had been so tender, so full of warmth and need.

"Your imagination, Kathleen," the silent voice answered. "Maybe a little momentary passion for you, but nothing lasting, nothing that really means anything to him."

Sinking down onto my bed, I spread myself across its softness. Looking to the side, I could see the moon, a sliver of light, through the windows. I rolled over and stared up at the ceiling. Shadow ghosts frolicked on the walls around me, dancing and twisting about as a warm night breeze blew gently through the rose-covered vines on the lattice.

The moving black figures reminded me of my nightmare and a sudden shudder ran down my spine.

Snatching my shawl from the bed, I rose and went to the open window trying to forget my sudden uneasiness. Leaning against the frame, I peered out into the darkness below. Nothing was distinct, one dark form flowing into another. I could smell the fragrance of the roses, strong and sweet, all around me. And I wondered if Clinton was still in the garden below.

What would he be thinking wherever he was? Did he ever have thoughts of me?

Excuses to go down to the garden again flew through

my mind. None was satisfactory. But I wanted to go back to him, to talk to him, to feel close to him as I had that day on the hillside.

"No!" I uttered in despair and was surprised to find I had spoken out loud.

Was I going through the same painful longing to which my mother had succumbed? Had she felt these same strange emotions when she met my father—he, a man stations above her? Had she loved him as I now love Clinton Matthews?

"It doesn't matter." I turned away from the window. My love would share the same promise hers had. Never a wife, only a mistress if ever anything at all. And though my heart strained toward him, my mind rejected the temptation of submission to him. I felt as though I were on the edge of a beautiful lake, flowers surrounding it, sky blue overhead, everything promising beauty and peace. But on the bottom of that lake I knew there was not sand, but mud and slime that would cost me forever in its vileness.

I went to bed, no questions answered, emotions raw. Sleep came with unmerciful slowness. And with sleep came my nightmare, terrifying, threatening, deadly.

When I awakened, the breeze was still, the room unnaturally quiet and ominous. Tangled in my blankets, shaking and wet with fear-inspired perspiration, my eyes searched the shadowy darkness. My breath still came in gasps and I felt as though I had been running for miles.

Gradually my heart slowed its hard pounding, my breathing grew quiet, and my instincts relaxed their vigil, again the imagination of night.

This time I could remember some of the dream.

Someone had been chasing me, someone from whom there was no escape, someone who was relentless, hating, wanting my destruction. I remembered I had been standing before the wrought-iron fence at the Benson estate, but I could not climb over. The footsteps had been hurrying toward me, but no amount of struggling or effort helped me to climb that fence, though it appeared so easy to scale.

I could not remember who had been chasing me. Nor could I remember whether I was trying to climb into or out of the Benson estate.

When sleep finally came again, it brought a merciful, dreamless, dead quiet.

The sun peeked in my window, its rays slowly traversing the braided rug to my bed. I stretched, yawned, and slowly climbed from bed, grateful that today was Monday and I would be busy with the children.

Relieved, I realized that I would not have to face Clinton for several hours more, for by now he and the hands would be out working for the day.

Quickly I washed my face, dressed, and arranged my hair. I tried not to think about what had happened in the garden the night before, but it kept wandering into my thoughts. The morning brought color, light, and warmth, and with it new hope and happiness.

Hurrying down the stairs, I planned to have a quick cup of coffee before awakening the children.

My heart stopped and the blood rushed to my cheeks as I came into the dining room and faced Clinton still sitting at the head of the table, a mug of steaming coffee in his hands. His eyes were stormy and in an instant I knew why.

Near the window, a cool smile still frozen on his face, stood Michael James.

"Oh!" I uttered, surprised and embarrassed for my intrusion. "I'm sorry, excuse me," I said, quickly starting to retreat, but Clinton's voice stayed me.

"Come on in and have your breakfast." His voice was cool, too cool.

"I don't want to interrupt."

"I came to see you," Michael informed me, pleasure and excitement lighting his face. My eyes widened and Clinton scowled. "I've been trying to talk your employer into allowing you another day off for a ride into Las Positas."

"It's Monday," I said, stupidly expecting that to suffice as an answer. Michael went on to say something, but I did not hear. Clinton had put his coffee cup down with a clatter and sat staring moodily at Michael.

"What do you think, Kathleen?" Michael's voice demanded my attention.

"What? I'm sorry. What did you say?" I asked blankly, meeting his inquiring gaze.

"I've got the buggy out front. It's a beautiful day for a ride. We could drive in to Las Positas and have a quiet lunch at the hotel. I'm sure your ride out here from New York was more tiring than enjoyable. Well, what do you think?"

Clinton was holding his mug between his hands again, turning and studying it as though something were written in the coffee grounds that sank to the bottom. Some subtle change came over him and though he seemed miles away in his thoughts I knew he had not missed anything that had been said.

"It's Monday," I repeated. "Priscilla and Steven have studies . . ."

"They would be more than pleased to have another holiday. Besides," Michael added with a quick glance to Clinton, "Clint says it's up to you. He doesn't mind one more day . . . if I don't make a habit of asking it."

I shot a look at my employer, who still sat silent staring into his mug. He ignored my scrutiny. Was he really hoping to solve the problem of my infatuation by throwing another man into the picture? But only yesterday he had discouraged this acquaintance. Why was he now giving his approval, even slight encouragement?

"It's a beautiful day, Kathleen," Michael said invitingly.

"Yes, but isn't it three hours from here to Las Positas, Mr. James?"

"Mr. James? We're back to that stage again?" Michael asked, pained. I caught Clinton smiling slightly at that. Noticing where my eyes were, Michael dropped his voice and touched my shoulder to draw my attention. "It won't take that long with me driving and it would give me a chance to talk with you again. We have a lot to learn about each other . . . and I don't want to waste time."

Clinton tossed his napkin carelessly onto the table and stood up abruptly. His eyes raked appraisingly over Michael. A mischievous grin tugged at the corner of his mouth. Then he addressed me.

"I think Michael's idea is an excellent one, Kathleen. It will give you the opportunity to become really acquainted with our countryside."

My heart sank. He doesn't care. If he did, he would not push me into Michael James's outstretched and waiting arms.

Michael was obviously pleased with Clinton's encouragement and was about to press his advantage, when Matthews continued.

"And, Michael. You, of course, won't mind a little extra company."

"What? Clint, what the devil are you trying to pull?"

"I have some business to take care of in town, so I will ride along with you," he explained politely, the mischief gone and a warning glint in his eyes.

"Business?" Michael growled sarcastically.

"I have a telegram I want sent right away," Clinton informed him, his eyes slipping over mine quickly. He smiled at Michael's cold expression of disbelief. "And, more important, we don't want the local tongues wagging about the Matthews governess being with the town ladies' man, now do we?"

After a sizzling moment, Michael spoke.

"You're right, Clint," he agreed, "I hadn't stopped to consider that." He gave an unpleasant laugh at Clinton's astonished countenance. "Don't look so surprised. We had this all out yesterday, remember? I meant every word I said." He bit out the words.

"We'll see," was the only answer he received.

"How long will it take you to get ready?" Michael asked me, the possibility of my refusal dismissed from his mind with Clinton's voiced approval.

I wanted to shout my demurral, but hurt pride and rejection stopped me. "I'm ready right now, Michael," I responded, more brightly than I felt. I smiled with forced enthusiasm at both men.

For the first several miles, there was tension and awkwardness as Michael and I sat side by side in the buggy, Clinton Matthews riding along next to us. Gradually, Michael talked animatedly, ignoring Clinton's very presence. And gradually, I relaxed also and began to enjoy his company.

Michael described his youth in riotous detail, from his father throwing him into the lake to teach him to swim, to his first stolen kiss behind the barn. I laughed often and easily as he related his wild, carefree youth. I suspected that he still had not outgrown it, despite his twenty-eight years.

"How many hearts have you won with that laugh, Kathleen?" he put in once, his eyes twinkling as he watched me.

"None," I responded with a happy smile that he would even think I had won any at all. "Don't you remember? I told you."

"Oh, come on. You must have been in love several times by now. How old are you?"

154

"Eighteen. And no, I've not been in love several times," I answered truthfully, thinking of Clinton.

"Well, anyway . . . now you can understand why I need a steadying influence in my life."

"Heavens, why?" I responded, laughing and chosing to ignore the appeal in his expression and pretending he had spoken only in jest. "You have had such fun. Why spoil it?"

"Kathleen." He started to put his arm around my shoulder, but stopped, remembering Clinton's quiet presence. He frowned at the horse-mounted rider.

"Michael, I would love to have led such a mischievous, free, fun-filled life. And you still seem so young yourself . . ."

"Ten years your senior, my love. And you weren't tucked away in a convent or something, were you?" he asked.

"Or something," I said, nodding. Some of the brightness dimmed. "I grew up in an orphanage on the lower Eastside New York."

He looked embarrassed. I smiled, well acquainted with the shock of people first realizing that I was an orphan.

"It really wasn't that bad. There were lots of girls. Only girls, as a matter of fact, and sometimes . . . sometimes it seemed almost like a big family." The fib came a little hard, but I knew it would be easier than telling him the truth. And why would he want to know it?

"How old were you when you were placed there?"

"I was a baby . . ." I hoped he would not ask me more out of curiosity, and tried quickly to turn the conversation. But he veered back again, wanting to know more.

"You're a foundling, then?" he asked quietly.

How many times had I thought of myself in that very way. Foundling! To be a foundling meant that one was unwanted, caused shame, a bastard to be discarded on the steps of an orphanage in the dead of night, to be forgotten as though one had never lived. It meant that one would never know about the blood —good or bad, honest or criminal, moral or immoral or amoral—that coursed through one's veins. There was always the blackness of that nagging doubt which would surround, forever, the child's life like a cloud of thick fog. It was unjust. It was cruel. It was fact.

"No . . ." I'm not a foundling," I murmured, a bitter smile touching my lips as I remembered that I did, indeed, have a father, and I knew who my mother had been. "I know who my parents are." My voice was unexpectedly brittle. I looked away, and with a shock met the eyes of Clinton Matthews. He was staring at me intently.

"Are?" Michael asked.

"Were," I corrected.

A thrust of shame stabbed me as I remembered my refusal to confide any information about my background to Clinton Matthews. And now I was telling Michael James, a man I hardly knew and to whom I owed no obligation. I felt the warning of tears prickling like nettles in my eyes and I blinked, averting my gaze to the horses in front of me.

"I'm sorry I pressed you about that," Michael apologized, taking my hand. "Don't get quiet on me, Kathleen," he said gently. "You know it's nothing to be ashamed of . . . You're well educated, better than most women; you're poised and . . . beautiful."

I smiled at him, my control returning. "You are a practiced flatterer, Mr. James," I said lightly, withdrawing my hand from his with a flush.

During the next mile or two the conversation turned to the valley and its families.

"My folks came after the ranches were all settled and well established. My father bought a couple of smaller holdings and built up his herd. We have about ten thousand head now and it's growing all the time. The only other ranch comparable in the area is Clint's Las Posas."

"And it's bigger," Clinton grinned, as he spoke for the first time.

"Shut up," Michael grinned back. I laughed.

"How long have you two been friends," I asked, interested and happy that Clinton had at last joined the conversation.

"About twenty years, I guess," Michael answered.

"Sometimes off . . . sometimes on," Clinton added lightly.

"We're rivals in reputation."

"Oh? What do you mean by that?" I asked, remembering the reputation with which Clinton had credited Michael.

"Until Clint took over the ranch after his pa died, he was as wild, maybe even more so, than I." There was a mischievous glint in Michael's eyes as he looked up at Clinton and smirked.

"You're hardly being loyal, friend Michael," Clinton said with a frown, but there was a hint of mockery in his voice.

"I'm very loyal . . . when it doesn't interfere with my own plans."

"And how was he wild?" I asked, very interested.

"The ladies love Clint."

"You exaggerate, Mike," Clinton said, a little piqued.

"Cybil seems to enjoy your company."

The silence that followed Michael's statement was charged.

The buggy came around a last curve in the road, and below, the houses of Las Positas lay nestled in the meeting of the hills.

"There it is," Michael announced, breaking the silence. "It's not exactly New York or San Francisco."

"I like it."

157

"I'll meet you in the hotel," Clinton said, spurring his sorrel into a gallop and moving quickly down the slope and away from us. A satisfied grin lurked on the edge of Michael's mouth.

"Don't hurry!" he called out, and then laughed.

I was confused by the sudden tension and hostility between the two men.

Michael drew the buggy up before the hotel and helped me down. When we entered the lobby he led me into a smaller room opposite the card- and barroom I had seen upon my arrival.

"I never noticed this room before," I admitted.

"You've been in here? Who brought you?" he asked with surprise, suspicion showing in his eyes.

"When I first came into town. I was a day early and the stagecoach driver said this was the only place to stay overnight. When I walked in all I saw was that big room over there."

"And all the staring cowhands, no doubt," he said, his voice returning to normal. "You must have made a sensational entrance."

"I just walked in, but I was very relieved when Jim appeared and took me to the ranch," I laughed, remembering all those staring faces.

We reached a small table in the corner of the room, near a window that looked out onto a small garden. There was a simple checkered tablecloth and matching napkins. Holding my chair for me, Michael leaned down and whispered close to my ear as I sat down.

"I'm glad we're alone, Kathleen."

His softly, intimately spoken words flustered me, and I was made suddenly nervous by his attention.

"It's not exactly Fifth Avenue, but the food is good," he went on more casually, taking the chair opposite. "We don't have much company either, luckily."

The room was sparsely, though comfortably, furnished with small tables. No one else was in the room, and it was quiet, except for the laughter and honky-tonk music that drifted in from the larger room, across the lobby.

The double doors to the back kitchen swung open and a buxom, attractive redhead bustled through them. When she saw Michael, she smiled broadly, showing straight white teeth. She walked with a pronounced swing to her hips, and a sparkle in her hazel eyes.

"Michael! You devil! It's been an age since you've been in here," she said in a voice that matched her appearance. She glanced quickly over me in appraisal, raising her penciled eyebrows accusingly at my host.

"Been neck-deep in work at the ranch, Rachel," he explained and then went on with a wink, "I've missed your . . . fine home cooking."

"I'll just bet you have, love," she retorted. "Well . . . you know where the kitchen is." She smiled, a peculiar twinkle in her eyes as she met his look. Taking our order, she turned and disappeared through the double doors again.

I could no longer suppress my smile and, noting my amusement, Michael grinned. "What do you find so funny, Miss O'Reilly?" he asked with mock severity.

"You," I laughed, feeling very relaxed with him again. "You're like a little boy in a candy store—and you just love candy, all kinds of candy."

"Not all . . ." he responded. "Not now." Then he frowned, his eyes still twinkling. "Didn't I make you the least bit jealous?"

"Terribly, Michael. I could feel my claws coming out when she invited you to the kitchen." His eyes darkened at my comment, and then changed slightly to speculation.

"I wish you would invite me to the kitchen," he said lightly.

"Aren't you rushing things a bit?" came a deep and familiar voice from behind us. My heart surged as I saw Clinton approach the table and sit down. Michael frowned at the interruption.

"It certainly didn't take you long to finish your important business," Michael said tersely, glaring at Clinton, who only smiled back unperturbed. The smile seemed misplaced in his face for his eyes grew dark.

"But I thought my presence would be sorely missed..." he said, "so, I hurried." He ignored Michael's threatening expression and turned to me. "How do you like Las Positas, Kathleen?"

Before I could answer, Rachel came through the double doors again, a tray held precariously above her right shoulder.

"Clinton! You, too! How lucky can I get in one day!" My stomach tightened at her intimate greeting.

"Rachel, how are you, sweet?" Clinton's face showed genuine pleasure and friendliness, and I felt an ache gnaw at me. He had never looked at me like that.

"Just fine, love. Working long hours, as always. Hoping for a little fun at night, now and then," she said, smiling at him in the same inviting way that she had at Michael. Only the effect on me was different.

"Kathleen, this is Rachel Hansen." Clinton darted a quick look at me. "Rachel, this is Kathleen O'Reilly, Priscilla and Steven's governess," he introduced quickly.

"I'm pleased to meet you, Miss Hansen," I lied politely, feeling the hypocrite.

"It's a pleasure," she said with like sentiments, looking right through me.

"What's the special today, honey?" He called her honey, I thought dismally, my previous bright spirits almost extinguished entirely.

"How about some wine, Kathleen?" Michael asked and I turned to smile at him, relieved for the chance to pull my attention away from Clinton and Rachel.

"That would be nice," I answered, not really caring.

160

"Rachel, sweetheart—bring us your best bottle of wine. Not the stuff Jack tells you to bring."

"Sure thing, Michael," she said sweetly, but her eyes darkened as she looked at me for an instant. She turned her attention back on Clinton. "Maybe I'll see you later, Clint. Hmmmm?" She smiled and winked.

"Maybe . . ." Clinton didn't return her smile, but did return her wink. She turned away, walking to the double doors with a voluptuous swing to her well-rounded hips. I noticed both men's eyes were riveted to her as she moved. For just an instant, I wondered if I could convincingly imitate her sway, but doubted it.

"Cybil would tear your heart out if she saw the way you were watching Rachel," Michael teased, meeting Clinton's eyes with a grin. "Good gal, Rachel," he went on, lightly, looking at the closed doors.

"Not my type."

"Is that so?"

"I've something else in mind."

"I've a suspicion what that is." All the pleasure and joviality went out of Michael's voice. There was a deeper conversation going beneath the casual words, but I failed to comprehend what it was. They spoke lightly, with smiles, but I felt a growing tension and hostility change the air every time Michael brought Cybil into the conversation.

Lunch was uncomfortably quiet. Except for the frequent and often unwarranted, attentions of Rachel, we hardly spoke at all. When we finished, I excused myself, less from necessity than from embarrassment at feeling unable to cope with the uneasiness among the three of us. For even the most casual conversation died. When Clinton tried, Michael did not. When Michael tried, Clinton did not. I finally remained silent, ill at ease, and wishing I had never come at all.

When I came back and stood hesitatingly in the doorway, Michael and Clinton were leaned over the

161

table talking in earnest. Their voices were low. When they saw me approaching, they stopped, both bolting up. Michael moved to my side, taking my elbow in a peculiarly possessive fashion. Clinton's eyes were still like black coals, though he smiled in greeting.

"I think we'll be starting back to the ranch," Michael informed me. "You needn't hurry, Clint."

But Clinton rode with us back to the ranch. The trip was quiet and tense, a cold wall of fury between the two men.

When Michael spoke to me, he kept his voice low and intimate, in an obvious effort to be inaudible to Clinton, though the latter appeared disinterested in us, riding several yards to the side of the buggy, silent, his shoulders stiff, his mouth a tight, hard line.

When at last we reached the ranch, Clinton rode off toward the stables without a word.

Michael turned to me, his eyes seething with rage. "Next time we are together, we will be alone. That son of a—" he cut off his sentence abruptly, "I'm sorry, Kathleen. It's not your fault."

"I'm not sure there will be a next time, Michael," I said, intending to uphold the decision I had made on the ride back to the ranch.

"What? Why?" And then more hotly, "Because of Clint?!"

"Because of both of you. I have no intention of being the cause, directly or indirectly, of the ruin of a longtime friendship." I moved to climb down from the carriage, but Michael put a hand under my elbow and held me in my seat.

"No! I'm not going to just ride off that easily. This isn't a casual flirtation, Kathleen." His hand slid down my arm and took my hand, holding it even more securely when I tried to draw it away. "Clint's got ideas about you himself, I'd say."

"That's ridiculous!"

"Is it?" He stared at me. "I suspect he's already made a move or two," he said accusingly, and my temper flared dangerously close to exploding for the truth he spoke.

"Mr. James," I said stiffly, grinding the words out with an effort to hold my tongue in check. "I am a servant in his household—a governess—with duties to perform for which Mr. Matthews pays me. That is his sole interest in me. If I were to be less than competent, or to attract scandal of any sort, which might indirectly affect the children, whether I were innocent or not, he would not hesitate to dismiss me. I respect and am thankful for Mr. Matthews' concern for my reputation."

"Reputation, ha!" he growled, glaring toward the stables where Clinton had since disappeared. "He undoubtedly has his own private plans to make you a little more than just a governess."

Tearing my hand away from him, I tried to get out of the buggy. He jumped down quickly and came around to lift me down.

"Put me down!" I commanded, furious, when he held me for an instant longer than necessary. He did, but held my shoulders tightly so that I could not go up the steps.

"Listen to me! I'm sorry! Kathleen, I'm sorry. That was a stupid thing to say! I didn't mean anything about you, Kathleen." I stopped struggling and glared up at him, seething. "But you're so beautiful, darling. A man could lose himself in your eyes. And Clinton is unpredictable, Kathleen." I tried to push his hands away from my shoulders, but he held me firmly facing him.

"I'm sorry I spoiled your day with this scene. But I'm coming back," he said decisively.

"Don't!"

"I will. And next time will be more enjoyable. We'll be alone."

"No!"

"Yes. And each time I come, it will get better."

"No."

"It will. And you'll come to realize that I love you and want only your happiness." He spoke with such quiet sincerity that my anger lessened and I looked up at him.

"I don't love you," I said with blunt truthfulness, though not wanting to hurt him. If I could accept reality, then so could he.

"Give me time to be alone with you. Give us a chance."

"Michael . . ." I said more softly, feeling sudden empathy with him.

"I'll see you soon," he interrupted, releasing my shoulders and raising my hand to his lips. "Soon!" he repeated, giving me a penetrating look and an assuring smile.

As he drove away, I turned and went up the stairs and into the house.

I would have no time alone to think, for the children were waiting in my room, all ears for anything I wanted to relate about my day in Las Positas.

X

I awakened suddenly that night, feeling someone's presence in the room.

Many times before I had awakened in the middle of the night to hear strange noises, but never before had my instincts reacted so violently, warning me against a deadly, imminent threat.

I did not move, but lay feigning sleep as I listened to the silence, hoping a sound would tell me where the intruder was. Nothing. I opened my eyes to stare into the darkness. I could see nothing. The room was filled with menacing black shadows, moving silently against the wall.

A small shuffling sound drew my attention. I still did not move, and perspiration beaded on my forehead.

A shadow dislodged itself from the others and moved toward the open window. Large and grotesquely distorted, it slid across the room with stealthy ease.

Whoever it was knew where each piece of furniture lay and avoided them.

Then it was gone, out the window and down the

lattice in a quick, fluid movement that was almost graceful.

"It's my dream again," I whispered hopefully.

I pulled myself up into a sitting position.

Then I felt it.

It slithered across my feet, freezing my blood.

"I must be dreaming. Dear God, please, let me be dreaming this."

A sound like dry leaves in a gentle summer wind started from the foot of my bed. The heavy thing stopped moving, coiling swiftly on my blanket-covered calves.

Had I screamed? My throat felt dry and tight. "Lord, please, let me be dreaming," I prayed, frantic terror rising inside me until I felt it looming over me like a deadly giant. One move, only one move and I'm dead. Control! Get control, Kathleen!

I must be dreaming. How could it be in my room? Why would anyone want to do this to me?

Pale light flooded the room as the door opened. Any doubt I had vanished as I looked down at the bed. My eyes flew to the doorway where Steven stood with a candle raised high in his hand.

"Did you scream, Miss O'Reilly?" he asked sleepily.

Stay calm! Don't alarm him!

"Don't come any closer, sweetheart," I said, surprised to find my voice calm and clear, though my heart felt still and cold with terror. From where he was standing, Steven could not see the creature which lay coiled on my bed. I prayed that he would not move closer and thus endanger himself. If I did not move, I was safe. If I did not move!

The rattlesnake lay encircled tightly across my legs. Its grotesquely primitive head was flat, dark eyes unblinking as its tongue darted in and out, sensing my presence and feeling my body heat. The light fell across it slightly as Steven took a step forward and it raised its tail, rattling warningly.

"What's that noise?" he asked rubbing his eyes and looking toward the bed.

It was all I could do to still the scream that filled my throat and choked me. I held myself with rigid fear, though wanting to throw the covers and jump from the bed. Instinct told me not to budge. In the time I would move my hand, the snake would strike. And this close it would hit me in the face, neck, or chest. Death would be imminent.

"As fast as you can, Steven, get help," I said, my voice shaking in spite of my concentration. "Have Clinton bring a gun, a sack, anything! Do you understand?" I never took my eyes from the loathsome reptile coiled on my legs. I felt rather than saw Steven's confused fright.

"Please hurry, Steven." My voice cracked and my fear penetrated him with a force no words could. He bolted out of the room and I heard him tear frantically down the hallway.

My breath was coming in rapid, shallow little gasps as I sat waiting in the dark. Seeing the snake was terrifying enough, but to be left alone in the dark with it still resting on my legs was almost too much to bear. My control was crumbling rapidly, nausea threatening.

One minute passed. Another. Then another.

No one is coming!

I strained my eyes to see the snake. It was only a black shape on my bed, a formless shadow like all those others that had frightened me in the night. But the shadow on my lap had substance; I wondered briefly if the others did.

My eyes flickered to the doorway, as light approached. My heart jumped with relief, as Clinton appeared, entering the room slowly, cautiously, and following my look to the middle of the bed.

"Christ Almighty!" he breathed with shock. I saw the handgun he held.

"Please kill it," I managed to speak, my voice trembling.

"I can't shoot it where it is without hitting you too," he said, quickly looking around the room for something else to aid him. "Goddamm it! How the hell did that thing get in here?"

"Someone put it there," I answered. "I saw him climb out the window," I went on in a choked voice.

"Don't move! Don't talk! Don't breathe if you can help it!" He looked frustrated, angry, even frightened. His fear made mine even worse. "Steven, get to the bunkhouse," he said to his nephew, who was standing in the doorway. "Tell Jim to bring a hook and a sack."

The boy was out of the room before all the words were out and his sudden movement was sensed by the snake. It tightened its coil, its tail raising again. I heard Clinton cock his gun, and my control snapped. My hand flew to my face as I saw the snake's tail quicken.

Mouth open, fangs glistening with deadly venom, seeming even larger than life, the snake lunged at me in the candlelight. At the explosion of Clinton's gun, its head splattered, the body dropping harmlessly onto my chest.

"You shot its head off," I said, and hysterical laughter bubbled up into my throat. Clinton grabbed my arm and roughly pulled me out of the bed, as my laughter turned to screaming. Yanking my hands away from my face, he slapped me twice, hard. The sharp sting jolted me out of hysteria and I sagged against him, sobbing.

"You're all right, Kathleen. You're all right now." His fingers raked through my hair, and with one arm he held me tightly against him.

"What's going on?" Mabel shouted, lumbering hurriedly into the room in her ancient flannel nightgown.

"What was all the screaming and the shot? Kathleen, are you . . . ?"

"Someone put a rattlesnake in here," Clinton cut in, still pressing me against him. I felt numb.

"My God!" Mabel exclaimed, horrified. "Who?"

"How should I know? Steven's gone for Jim. Stay with the boy tonight, will you, Mabel? He'll need you. I'm glad Priss can sleep through cannon fire . . ."

I didn't hear any more. The intruder, the snake, the terror drifted through me. Someone wants me dead. As I felt my knees buckling under me, Clinton's arms tightened and he lifted me easily from the floor.

In a twilight consciousness, I felt him carry me from the room. My body was trembling uncontrollably, and I felt ice cold.

He put me on a couch in the sitting room, and stared into my eyes for a minute.

"I'll make her some hot tea," Mabel said from beside him. "She'll be all right. She's just scared half out of her wits."

"Forget the tea. I think brandy will be better. I'll see to it. You take care of the kids." He pulled a blanket around my shoulders and then strode across the room to pour a liberal glass of brandy.

The numbness was going and my fear lessening slightly as I looked around at the warm sitting room. No shadows. No snakes. No threat.

And Clinton.

He looked raging mad when he came back, though I knew his fury was not directed at me.

"I'm sorry I'm making such a fool . . ." I tried to apologize, my voice unusually quiet.

"Shhh . . . drink this." He pushed the glass into my hands, placing the decanter on the table with a thud. "Drink it!" he commanded more forcefully when I hesitated. His eyes lost their violence as he looked at me. The episode had really shaken him too, I realized.

169

Obeying, I sipped the brandy. It burned in its course to my stomach, then warmed my body slightly. After the first couple of sips, I found the taste improved, though it was still not good.

"I think you need something yourself," I commented, trying to make my voice sound light and natural. He smiled.

"Maybe I do." He rose and went to the table to get himself a glass. Then settling back in the chair facing me, he lifted his glass and took a deep pull.

"Why would anyone want to do such a thing?" I croaked.

"I thought you might be able to enlighten me on that."

"I can't think of anyone—" I stopped.

"Did you see anything at all that might help figure who it was?"

"Shadows are deceiving. They all look large and frighteningly grotesque," I answered, my body shaking slightly. I leaned back into the couch as though bracing myself. Clinton frowned at his glass. He set it down on the table and then reached across to fill mine again.

"Thank you for coming to my rescue," I said, giving a hoarse little laugh. My eyes met his. Silence.

Jim dashed into the front hall. "In here!" Clinton announced loudly.

"What is it?" Jim asked, entering the room, his face taut. Steven followed him, puffing hard.

"Everything's all right now. Steven, you can go up to bed. Mabel will be in your room for tonight." The boy started to stammer a question but Clinton shook his head. "In the morning. Now go on up." When Steven left the room, Clinton turned to Jim, who was looking at me curiously.

"There's a rattlesnake in Miss O'Reilly's room. It's dead. Get the damned thing out of there and bury it somewhere."

170

"How the hell could a rattlesnake get upstairs?" Jim sputtered, astonished.

"We'll try to figure out who put it there in the morning," Clinton answered.

"This makes the second time then . . ."

"In the morning," Clinton commanded. Jim left the room without further comment.

"The second time?" I asked. "Has this happened before?"

"He was referring to something else, Kathleen. Forget it!" He dismissed Jim's comment. "Take the rest of that. It'll relax you."

After a while, my head began to feel strangely, pleasantly light. I wasn't cold anymore, but was almost too warm. Clinton took the empty glass from my hand and set it on the table.

"Are you feeling better now?" he asked, a twinkle of amusement lighting his eyes.

"Yes," I smiled. "I feel very good as a matter of fact." My voice sounded strange. I thought he chuckled as he turned to put the decanter aside.

"I wonder who did it. I don't think anyone particularly dislikes me," I started babbling while at the same time I wondered why I was saying so much. "Or has reason to dislike me, except you, of course." Why had I admitted that, for goodness' sakes?

"Me?" he repeated, looking at me with surprised confusion. "What makes you say that?" he asked angrily.

"Oh, I don't blame you for not liking me," I went on, wishing I could stop talking. His frown deepened as he watched me. "I was not exactly reasonable when I refused to answer the questions you asked me. And then I started to blab all to Michael James . . . and I don't even owe him the information." I put my hand to my forehead. "I don't know why I'm saying all this.

I feel very queer all of a sudden. Please forgive me . . . I always seem to irritate you."

"Let's say you disturb my peace of mind," he said, more lightly.

My head started to whirl a little. "Well . . . I didn't lie to you, Clinton. Really." His expression suddenly changed and I was not aware that I had used his first name.

"I never thought you did," he answered, the anger gone from his eyes, some other warmer emotion lighting them. "I don't think it's in your personality to lie. If I had, I would have dismissed you that first day we talked."

"I was so afraid you would make me go," I said. "The first time I saw you, you were so disappointed and angry with me."

"Not with you . . . with the situation you would put me in."

"What situation?"

"This isn't the time to talk about it."

"Oh." The chill had left me completely and a warm euphoria spread through me. I felt more intensely aware of Clinton looking at me. "It's warm in here, isn't it?" I shrugged the blanket down on my shoulders. He didn't respond, but sat studying me. "I'll answer them now, if you like," I offered.

"What?"

"The questions you asked me before," I explained, wondering why I had felt it necessary to hide my background from him in the first place. It all seemed foolish now and I, even wanted to talk about my life at Parkside.

"Tell me what you want me to know," he replied, not pressing, but I could see his interest sparkling.

"I can't even remember now what you asked me," I laughed, leaning back again.

"Why did you leave the orphanage?" he asked.

172

"I couldn't stay after I found out why Miss M. had kept it from me."

"What?" he asked, thoroughly confused. "Who's Miss M.?"

"Miss Montgomery, she's headmistress at Parkside. She encouraged me to stay on and teach after I finished my schooling. I felt grateful to her for the hours she had spent tutoring me. But . . ." I stopped for a minute, feeling the happy, warm euphoria diminish with my thoughts. "Well, you see, I couldn't stay after finding out."

"Finding out what?"

I pulled the blanket around me, feeling cold again.

"You're cold?" he asked, solicitous.

"A little."

Clinton poured a small amount of brandy into my glass and handed it to me. "I don't think I should have any more," I said.

"Drink it. It'll warm your blood up a little." I took it, drank it slowly, and looked at him sitting in silence waiting for me to go on. When I finished, he took the glass and set it on the table. "Now, go on with your story," he encouraged. I could hardly refuse now, especially when I had volunteered to answer his questions.

"A friend of mine found a file in a locked drawer of Miss M.'s desk. It was a file about me. All about me." I looked away for a minute. "It said . . . my father was alive." I tried to laugh, but it came out a croak. I bit my lip. "Miss Montgomery used to have me stay in my room when people came to adopt one of the girls. They would meet all the children and then come back several times until they found a child that suited them and that they suited." I stopped, looking down at my clenched hands holding the blanket snugly around me.

"Why were you kept in your room?" Matthews asked.

I realized that he did not speak with simple curiosity. Something in his face told me that he sensed the pain I had felt and he wanted me to share it, talk it out, release it.

"I thought it was because something was wrong with me . . . that I was a foundling, and my blood was bad. You never know what kind of parents you had when you're a foundling. Maybe your father was a murderer, or your mother was a—" The word wouldn't come. My thoughts flashed to my mother. "I always thought I was a foundling," I said, forcing myself to stay on the track I had started. "But at least Miss Montgomery cared for me. I thought she did. But she didn't . . . not really . . . no, not at all, I guess." My voice broke. I stood up and walked to the windows quickly so that Clinton would not see the tears filling my eyes. I clenched my fist, brought it down on the sill. Clinton didn't speak but I felt his eyes on me and I fought for control.

"Anyway, the file said my mother was dead . . . just a few months after I was born. She was an actress named Brianna O'Reilly. I changed my name to hers when I left New York. The file also said that my . . . father . . . was sending Miss Montgomery money each year and it would keep coming as long as I stayed." The tears filled my eyes and spilled down my cheeks. But I didn't utter a sound, and was not aware that Clinton could see my face in the reflection of the window.

"He even lives on a big estate. He's very successful and powerful. Anna said that made me a 'thoroughbred.'" I attempted a laugh, but it came out sounding like a choked-off sob. "Well, thoroughbreds are bought and sold, aren't they?" A long silence fell and slowly I gained control again.

"What's your father's name?" Clinton asked finally.

"What does it matter?" I shrugged, turning around

174

to face him. "If it was so important to him to go to all that trouble to have me out of his life . . ." I couldn't finish. Clinton stood up and came to me, brushing the hair off my forehead and cheeks in a tender, compassionate way.

"Are you tired?" he asked.

"No." I shuddered involuntarily at the thought of returning to my upstairs room and to the shadows and memories that waited for me. "I don't think I could sleep up there just yet." I looked up at him. "Do you mind if I just stay here for a while?"

"Not if you don't mind company," he said and smiled.

"You don't have to stay, Clinton . . ." His name dropped from my lips and I flushed. "I mean . . . Mr. Matthews."

"Why change now?" he grinned a little roguishly.

"Oh."

He smiled again at my discomfort. "How about a game of chess, Kathleen?" he asked, dismissing the subject.

"At three in the morning?" I laughed, feeling warmed by his casual, warm invitation.

"Are you afraid I might win?" he teased, raising his eyebrows in challenge. He looked younger, the facial lines smoothed out except those around his eyes.

"Well, I don't know why I would think that. You have only won every game we've played. But I accept the challenge," I answered, following him into the study. I watched as he carefully set up the chess pieces.

We started the game and I quickly found myself on the defensive, his moves aggressive and sure. I tried to concentrate, but felt too warm and conscious of him.

Was I really alone with him at this time of night? Did he really want to stay with me?

Gradually, I became more involved in the game and

it began to turn slowly in my favor. When I captured his last rook, I looked up with an exuberant, smug grin.

"Your play," I said happily.

He hadn't heard me. He was looking at me with a strange expression, his eyes warm and lighted.

"Your play," I repeated. He focused his thoughts.

"You have me at a definite disadvantage," he said, and moved his eyes down over me. I became acutely aware that I was clothed only in my white cotton gown, hardly appropriate and not altogether concealing.

"Oh . . ." I blushed hotly, pulling the blankets up and back over my shoulders and breasts. I felt strangely excited as he continued to look at me with an emotion that stirred my blood. A slow smile crept across his face.

"It's your play," I managed to murmur.

He directed his attention to the chessboard and made his next move. Still feeling embarrassed and yet warm, I made several foolish moves and quickly found the game over, myself in checkmate.

"You almost had me," he said with a grin.

"Thank you for the game, Mr. Matthews," I responded, getting up and realizing that I must return to my room if I wanted to keep my resolution. The thought of the snake and intruder threatened my calm, but I dared not stay here any longer. My own emotions were more distressing. If he kissed me again, I could not be sure I would even try to stop further advances.

"You don't want to go upstairs," Clinton said, standing up. He quickly removed the chess set, replacing it in the desk drawer. He faced me and smiled slightly. "There's a room on my floor which you can use tonight."

I knew where the guest room was and also that his

room was just across the hall. I felt shaky, meeting his eyes and wondering how I could possibly think of using that room. He would be only feet away from me.

He smiled at my hesitation. "There's a good lock on the door, I might add."

My face turned crimson and I looked away. "I didn't think . . ."

In a gesture that seemed quite natural, he took my hand. His fingers were warm and hard. He took me up the stairs to the second floor. My heart was pounding nervously when he opened the door.

He left me standing self-consciously in the doorway as he entered. I heard the scratch of a match, its small flame casting a welcome glow in the seldom-used room. It was a large room, made up for unexpected company.

My heart raced as he moved back across the room toward me. He smiled.

"I'm across the hall if you need me," he said, leaning down to plant a light fraternal kiss on my forehead. "Good night, Kathleen." He looked at me for a moment longer. "Lock your door," he said quickly, closing it quietly behind him as he left.

When I heard his bedroom door open, I quietly shot the bolt.

XI

When I awakened late the next morning after a fitful sleep, I met Mabel in the hallway on her way up to check on me. She informed me that Clinton had taken a sudden and unexpected trip into San Francisco and would not be back for several days. She didn't know why he had gone nor the exact day of his return.

"He'll have to make it a fast trip though, because he's got the cattle drive downstate to handle," she added.

"Cattle drive?" I asked, my dismay all too obvious. "How long will that take?" I asked, trying to conceal my interest.

"Couple of weeks at least . . . usually takes about a month or so to get the other ranchers' herds together and make the trip to the southern market," she replied, giving me an amused smile. "He's going at the perfect time!"

"What do you mean?"

"Cybil James will be turning this place upside down and inside out preparing for the Fiesta del Verano," she answered with a scowl.

The closest she came to referring to my experience

of the night before was to ask if I had slept all right in the guest room, and to inform me that my room was "refreshed" and the windows had a latch added.

"I'll fix you a good hearty breakfast. I baked some cinnamon rolls this morning," she said as she bustled through the double doors to the kitchen and left me in the dining room. Mary came out a few minutes later with a cup of steaming coffee. Giving me a furtive glance, she set the cup down near me and turned hurriedly to escape. I watched her curiously as she disappeared into the kitchen.

I suddenly thought it strange that we seldom spoke anymore. But then, was it so strange the look I had seen in her eyes when she watched Michael James? She was in love with him.

That would explain the strain in our relationship, the loss of even casual friendliness. But surely, I had made it clear that I was not seriously interested in Michael. Hadn't I?

I had made it clear to Michael. I had stated my feelings to Clinton Matthews. Perhaps I had overlooked the one person who needed that reassurance more than anyone else. Mary.

Could jealousy have been a strong enough motive to wish me dead? My intuition revolted against the thought. Mary was in love with Michael, but she was not capable of murder.

"Miss O'Reilly?" Mary stood unsurely before me, my breakfast platter held precariously in her shaking hands. I studied her eyes and found no animosity. No, I would never believe that she was capable of such an act.

"Thank you, Mary." She lowered the laden platter. "Mabel must think I'm starving," I exclaimed as I looked down at the omelette, two cinnamon rolls, sliced ham, bowl of peaches, and a fresh pot of coffee. Mary grinned. Then her pleasant expression dimmed.

"Jim told me about the snake," she commented. "Someone must have put it in your room, Miss Kathleen. Snakes don't get up on beds," she informed me, trembling slightly. "Did you see who it was?"

"No," I answered abruptly, not ready to think about the episode of the previous night, but relieved to see only concern lighting Mary's dark eyes. She would hardly have broached the subject had she been the one responsible. "I didn't mean to sound abrupt," I apologized, seeing her hurt at my curtness. "I just don't even want to think about it." I shuddered, stopping any further thought.

"Would you like more coffee?" she asked, ready to pour. But I had lost my appetite. Even my favorite treat of cinnamon rolls failed to reawaken it.

"Jim will be staying in the house until Mr. Matthews comes back," Mary said.

"Oh? Is that the usual practice?"

"No . . . but nobody will dare sneak in with him here," she smiled. "I think they're watching out for your safety."

"My safety?"

"Mr. Matthews ordered it," she stated, smiling slightly and looking at me speculatively. "They don't want anything to happen to you."

When I returned to my own room, I wondered if the previous night had only been a terrible dream. In the light of day, the room was shadow-free, bright and fresh. The bed was made with a new white coverlet, a vase of red roses stood on the bedside table, and the window was open, boasting a new heavy brass latch that had not been there before.

No snake. No blood. No shadows. No reason to be afraid. Yet, I still felt the uneasiness, the apprehension, the feeling that something more was going to happen.

Life went on much as usual with Clinton gone. He returned to Las Posas only briefly after his San Francisco trip, and then was gone with several of the ranch hands to take the cattle south, leaving Jim again in charge. I found I missed his commanding presence in the house, the excitement of knowing I would see him in a few hours looking at me from across the dining-room table, the stolen glimpses of him as he strode through the back garden, dust-covered, bristle-bearded, and tired from a night on the range.

Even Priscilla and Steven were most introverted during his absence, and dinnertime was a quiet hour with little to say.

Our days were routine, lessons in the morning, lunch and a nap afterward, then an afternoon ride. One day we had a picnic lunch at the springs for which the ranch had been named. It was a quiet place, and one to which I would ride often myself over the time I would remain at the ranch.

Michael dropped by several times a week and rode with us. Priscilla enjoyed having him with us because he was charming even with young girls, but Steven was quiet and moody in his presence. I was relieved to find Michael's promise could not be kept. We were never alone. Steven made sure of that.

The nights were long. I lay awake often, listening to the sounds of the house and watching the shadows dancing on my wall—remembering. The crickets in the garden rubbed songs to one another and their bliss soothed my fears until sleep came to me.

It was during the third week of Clinton's absence that Cybil James began coming to Las Posas each day. She was making all the arrangements for the Fiesta del Verano which would culminate in a cattlemen's dance and barbecue. Cybil attempted to gain command in and around the house with an arrogant display of will that eventually sent the children and me to hiding in the garden at her arrival.

Mabel was the only one who refused to follow her instructions. From the first day, it was evident that Mabel detested the beautiful young woman. For each time Miss James summoned her, she refused to budge from the fortress of her kitchen.

"That young miss doesn't own this house yet, and until she does, I'll not take orders from the likes of her!" Mabel's eyes were glass-hard and determined as she stated her decision to me and the children sitting on the three kitchen high-stools. Mary, having brought the unwelcome command for Mabel to appear in the sitting room, stood hovering in the doorway.

"But, Mr. Matthews said she was in charge of . . ." Mary pleaded, and I felt sympathy for her. I would not wish to take Mabel's message back to the waiting Cybil.

"The Fiesta del Verano, not the house!" Mabel cut in abruptly, darting a look at Mary that said she would allow no trespassing on her domain. Mary seemed about to say something more, but gave it up, her shoulders slouched like a chastised child as she turned to take the answer to Cybil.

Mabel Banks would answer to no one but herself. Even Clinton knew better than to interfere.

I could well understand why. I remembered the story she had told me about her life. Mabel Hanson and her parents joined a wagon train in Independence, Missouri. They survived the hardships of weather, Indians, hunger, and exhaustion on the long trek West. When they reached their destination, the Indians, angry at the plundering of a previous wagon train, had fallen upon the unwary travelers with a vengeance. Mabel's mother and father had been killed in the first attack.

The wagon loaded with the family's few possessions burned, leaving Mabel with nothing but the clothes she wore during the ensuing battle. Those were ragged and bloodstained from the attacks and then tending the wounded and dying in the aftermath. She was sixteen, tired, hungry, and determined to find her own way.

She did.

Mabel arrived at Rancho Las Posas several days after the Indian attack. She had mended her clothes and washed them until they were almost threadbare. Her mother had taught her the basics of good housekeeping and passed on several well-guarded family recipes. And these she offered to the Matthews family with a dignity they could not refuse.

She started as a housemaid to Clinton's mother and soon after took charge of the kitchen.

A wandering cowhand named Jed Banks came through the area. He met, courted, and married the eighteen-year-old Mabel. They both worked on Las Posas together.

The year after they married, Mabel gave birth to a daughter. The child died two years later of measles, and only outlived her father by a year. Jed Banks was killed instantly by a fall while breaking a horse.

Mabel had remained at the ranch, sinking her heart and life into the Matthews family. Clarissa was born, and received the love pent up within the cook-housekeeper. And then came Clinton, another to feel her devotion.

But even then, Mabel was to be familiar with grief. First, Clinton's mother died, soon followed by her grieving husband. And then Clarissa and her husband, leaving behind their two orphaned children.

There remained only Clinton, the last of the Matthewses. All her hopes lay with him.

And Cybil James was not included in her plans.

"I'll not answer to that chit!" Mabel's indignant voice called me back from my thoughts. I wondered if she had underestimated Cybil James and the authority Clinton had given her.

Cybil was not undetermined herself. Used to having

her own way, she tried to skirt around Mabel's authority and control the household staff through direct orders. Her efforts failed, and she acknowledged her temporary defeat. Her dislike of Mabel, however, became even more vindictive.

"She'll be the first to go when I marry Clint!" I overheard Cybil state to Michael on one afternoon. "I don't care if she's been here a hundred and fifty years!"

"Don't be too sure of your success in getting rid of her, sis."

When the two women unexpectedly came upon each other, Cybil became furious at Mabel's cool, quiet refusal even to acknowledge her presence in the house. Finally, to everyone's relief, the hot war chilled. Mabel retained her territory and Cybil moved her authority into the barn where the preparations were taking place for the cattlemen's dance. She also took command of setting up the display stands where the women from Las Positas and the surrounding area would proudly show their handicrafts.

The two women avoided each other, and the tension of the first week eased noticeably, while life went on almost as usual.

However, one afternoon, I went to the kitchen to visit with Mabel and found her fury again on the verge of dividing the household. Cybil had come into the kitchen and thrown a rage such as the ranch-house staff had never seen. Her screams at the housekepeer could be heard on the third floor.

Luckily, the children and I had been out of the house and riding at the time or we would have been in the middle of the ruckus.

Mabel related with pleased malevolence how Cybil had lost her temper so completely that she had stormed from the house and ridden off wildly toward her own home.

"And good riddance! I couldn't resist a wave at her

as she left!" I could picture Mabel standing at the front door waving with a smug smile.

"Mabel, Mr. Matthews will be terribly upset when he hears about the quarreling that's been going on between you and Miss James."

"Ha! Who'd tell him? She won't tell him a thing because she knows he would be angry that she tried to take over my authority in the house . . . and no one else on this ranch will have the courage to tell him either," she answered with assurance. She smiled slightly, her eyes twinkling with the old amusement again. "She was pretty mad when she left." She chuckled, pleased with herself.

"From the sounds of it, you didn't help things either," I mused.

Defensive, Mabel growled with disgust, "She's been chasing Clinton since she was old enough to notice the difference between boys and girls! And she'll probably find some way to trap him, too, if he's not careful. Her kind usually does, no matter how long they have to stoop."

"Does he love her?" I asked, feeling my heart twist inside me.

"Love her?" She frowned at me. "He's a surefire fool if he does!"

She was kneading the bread dough roughly. Punching it hard, she flipped it over and punched it again. For a moment, I wondered if she was pretending Cybil James was on her bread board.

She went on, "I'm sure he's had his times with her. Men will be men, especially when the woman is so willing . . . and God knows how willing that chit is. But Lord help him if he's idiot enough to marry her!"

"Had his times with her?" I repeated blankly, not understanding what she meant. She darted an amused look in my direction and laughed.

"You're a babe yet, Kathleen O'Reilly!" She shook

her head, still smiling over her private mirth at my naïveté. I was no clearer on her meaning than before. Perhaps he'd had his times with me also, in the study and in the garden.

"Cybil is her father's daughter. Ambitious, calculating, determined, ruthless! Monte James has wanted to get his fingers into Matthews land for years. He hoped to marry his philandering son off to our Clarissa. That didn't work. So now he's encouraging a match between Cybil and Clinton."

"Will her father be at the fiesta?" I was curious to see this man.

"I doubt it. He's not interested in socializing. And he lost a leg in the Civil War. It's made him something of a recluse." She shrugged, indicating that she could care less whether he came or stayed home. "Cybil has the same ideas about land as her father. But I suspect that she also chases Clinton for more pleasurable reasons, too. He is a fine specimen of a man!" She had a glint of pride in her eyes.

I paled slightly, wondering if he kissed Cybil as he had kissed me that night in the study. Mabel studied my face, stopping her kneading momentarily.

"Why, child, you're in love with him," she stated flatly, catching me unguarded. She seemed immensely pleased with her sudden discovery.

"I'm not!" I exclaimed, blushing hotly and thus betraying myself.

"Don't deny the obvious, child!"

I averted my eyes, feeling tears of embarrassment and exposure threaten.

"It's written plain as daylight on your face, dear." Mabel's voice was gentle and motherly. Walking over to me, she lifted my chin with her flour-covered fingers and smiled at me affectionately. "Now, you would be good for him," she said with a nod. She brushed the

186

flour off my chin with her apron and took on a look of deep concentration.

"I work for him . . . I'm just a governess," I mumbled, unable to deny my feelings for the man.

"And so what of that!?" she said hotly, cutting me off a little angrily. She became quiet and pensive, turning to look at me from side to side and up and down.

"What's the matter?" I asked, uneasy at her scrutiny. I felt like a heifer being taken to market. I looked down at my blue linen dress.

"You're prettier than Cybil James any day, like a breath of good, fresh air."

"She's beautiful," I dismissed the compliment. There was no comparison between me and that woman who held Clinton's amorous interest.

"Ha!" Mabel ejaculated, putting her hands on her ample hips. "You're no judge, miss. Michael James would hardly be drooling over you if you were plain or even just pretty. What you need is something to make Clinton notice you. A new dress, that's it! I am going to make you a very beautiful dress for the dance," she informed me with a decided set to her chin. "Not like this high-necked sack!" she added, flipping with disdain the lace around my collar. I stared at her from where I was seated, wondering what was wrong with my dress. It as my best day dress. Mary Cramer had said it was very flattering that first day I arrived at the ranch.

"But it's—"

"Hush!" she commanded. I closed my mouth in obedience. "How do you expect to compete with the likes of Cybil James who wears low-cut dresses, when you wear sacks that cover everything you've got." I thought of Cybil's low-necked gowns which revealed the voluptuous swelling of her more than ample breasts, and understood only too well what Mabel was saying.

"It's sweet of you to want to make a dress for me,

Mabel, but if you're planning any matchmaking, there's no point in even wasting your time."

"I have some yellow swiss," she said, ignoring me, "and lace I bought for Clarissa. With your dark hair and blue eyes you will look beautiful!" She clapped her hands together, making a little cloud of flour.

"Mabel, I don't think you should waste your time," I said, trying to sound calm and reasonable. Her excitement was infecting me with hope. And I did not want to hope and be hurt again.

Ignoring my plea, she continued determinedly: "You come to my room tonight after dinner and the children are tucked into bed, and we'll discuss the pattern. No . . . on second thought, I'll decide on the pattern. You just come and I'll get your measurements."

"Mabel . . ."

"Not another word of doom from you, miss!" she commanded, and then continued in her excited voice: "I can hardly wait to see that boy's face when he sets his eyes on you!"

"It won't make any difference if he does notice me. Don't you see?" I said, a little desperately. I was embarrassed enough about my feelings for Clinton Matthews, and I did not want to add humiliation to the problem.

"I thought you had more fight in you than this," she reproved, and I felt like a child rebuked. "You've got to fight for him if you want him, Kathleen! Not disappear into the woodwork and let Cybil have her field open!"

I could see that her decision was made and, as with Cybil, there was no chance of my changing it. I knew, as she commanded, that I would report to her room that evening and she would take my measurements. But I knew also that every effort she might employ to attract Clinton's attention to me would be of no avail.

Why would he look at a moth when a butterfly flutters near?

Each day I stayed with Priscilla and Steven, keeping out of the way of Cybil James. She amazed me with her vitality, almost turning the ranch upside down in her efforts to prepare for the Fiesta del Verano. I wondered if Clinton realized what he had done when he gave her permission to proceed with her plans.

She had the largest barn cleaned from top to bottom, moving the horses into the smaller barns, and the overflow into the corrals. She had the hands build display stands, and added several riding posts where visitors could leave their mounts.

There seemed no limit to her energy, nor to her ability to antagonize and alienate the workers with her arrogance. They did what she ordered, seething beneath the polite smiles they turned toward her for Clinton's sake. But later, in the bunkhouse, they made known their displeasure at doing a woman's bidding. Jim Calhoun gladly escaped to the house in the evening, having put up with Miss James during the day and not looking forward to listening to the angry grumbling in the bunkhouse at night.

"I wish Clint had let me go on the drive! He could have left Miss James to run the damned ranch!" he growled over dinner one evening. His comment was greeted with mute agreement and empathy.

Although I tried my best to avoid meeting Cybil, she seemed to make an effort to search me out. At least once a day, we faced each other. Coming in from the garden, halfway down the front stairs, in the hallway, on the veranda, she would meet my eyes with an indifferent glance which turned me cold. Sometimes she would make a comment carefully aimed to hurt. She seemed to gain pleasure in baiting me with her biting words. I answered with strained politeness when it was necessary to speak at all.

189

One day, she stopped me in the sitting room where she was taking an afternoon break and drinking some of Clinton's expensive Madeira.

The children disappeared out the double doors to the garden. Priscilla took a high-nosed look at Cybil before closing the door behind her. The object of her haughty behavior laughed. But I could see a hard jealousy in her eyes as she turned her brittle smile on me. I wanted to flee.

"Michael has been coming to see you quite often, hasn't he, Miss O'Reilly?" Her eyes twinkled coolly and I felt my back stiffen as I prepared for some sort of attack.

"Yes. We are good friends," I answered evenly, knowing she was planning her next words with careful concentration. She sat smiling at me, cocking her blond and beautiful head to one side.

"He usually doesn't show such constancy in his infatuations," she remarked, her cool brown eyes surveying me from head to toe. I blushed slightly, though I could not understand why her examination should be insulting. She watched my face pink and smiled a little more pleasantly. "Why do you blush so, Miss O'Reilly?" she asked, increasing my discomfort. "Surely you have kept your virtue well guarded?"

So that was her tactic for the day. "If you will excuse me . . ." I said, starting to move toward the doors to the garden.

"Oh, now don't be in such a hurry, miss," she said, her eyes flashing. "I am really quite interested to find out what my brother sees in you. You may, after all, become my sister one day soon."

I raised my head defiantly at her tone. "I'm sure that will not happen, Miss James. And as for why Michael remains interested in my friendship, I suggest you ask him."

"I have," she replied casually, pleased that her baiting was successful this time and my temper was flaring. "But I didn't find his answer satisfactory. You see, Mike has never carried on such an innocent relationship as he purports to be having with you."

"I can assure you, Miss James, that your brother and I are only friends."

She smiled mockingly. "Really? You can assure me of that? Well, I do wish I knew your secret for keeping a man in hot pursuit, Miss O'Reilly, when you only offer friendship. Of course, I've no fear that you will turn your charms on my Clinton," she smiled sweetly, her voice coolly certain. "He is quite satisfied with what I have to offer him." I met her eyes, not showing the effect her words were having on me. And she continued, "You know, of course, that Clinton and I will be married . . . soon."

"I hardly interest myself with your affairs . . . or his," I answered politely and wondered why her face suddenly darkened.

"Affairs?" she repeated.

"Now, if you will excuse me." I turned. "The children are waiting in the garden." I walked out of the room feeling her cold dark stare follow me.

"By all means, you are excused," she hissed.

When I entered the garden, I was still seething with anger at her rudeness and insinuations. What could she possibly think I was doing with Michael? What was he telling her about our relationship? But even more powerful than the anger I felt was the agony she had caused by her announced betrothal and impending marriage to the man I loved. And he had said he did not plan to marry Cybil James. Why had he bothered to lie to me?

After that encounter with Miss James, I tried even harder to stay away from her. I attributed her obvious dislike for me to Michael's interest. I wondered, however, why she singled me out now to be the carrier of her messages to Mabel. I supposed it was due to my friendship with the older woman. However, my messages were greeted with the same disapproval as Mary's. Miss James's reception of my relayed answers was insulting and demeaning. I was thankful at least that she did not vent her spleen on Mary as she chose to do with me.

Each evening after the children were settled in for the night, I went downstairs to Mabel's room. She measured and fitted each part of the dress as she cut it. She did not confide her plans in me, but stitched and stitched by the hour as she talked about Clinton's childhood. I never tired of listening to her.

"He was always a cheerful little boy." She frowned at my disbelieving smile. "He was. He's got reasons enough to be hardened."

"I wasn't laughing, Mabel. It's just that I find it hard to believe that Mr. Matthews was ever . . . cheerful. He seems so cool and controlled to me."

"Only recently has he become that way. He used to laugh a lot, take life gladly by the horns. I think Clarissa's death wiped the laughter from him. They were close. I hope he'll learn to enjoy life again." She spoke wistfully, her fingers pausing their incessant stitching. "He will!" she said with satisfaction, the needle penetrating the swiss expertly. "You'll see to that!"

On an impulse, I went to her and hugged her, feeling tears of apprehension stinging. "Mabel, you'll be disappointed. I couldn't bear that. Please don't . . ."

'Hush!" She commanded again and then reached up and patted my cheek. "You'll not disappoint me, child. Even if nothing happens with Clinton, you'll still be more beautiful than you ever thought you could be. The young men will come swarming around you like bees to honey . . . and someday you'll have a home of your own. A family that's really yours . . . a man you'll love." She touched my cheek tenderly, her own eyes brighter than usual. "I've loved every minute with this family, Kathleen. I want to see it happy again . . . what's left of it." She stopped abruptly and more like herself, patted my cheek again. "Enough of this sad talk . . . you just stop your disagreeing, miss."

Several days before the fiesta, the dress took its final form. And standing in front of the mirror Mabel had provided, I opened my mouth in stunned dismay.

"Oh, Mabel, it's beautiful but I just can't wear it!" I flushed as I looked at the swelling of my breasts above the scalloped neckline. I felt unclothed and exposed.

"I am not going to cover you up to your neck, young lady!" she answered tartly, vexed at my glance.

"But it's as low as Cybil James's dresses," I protested weakly, feeling the full power of Mabel's determination.

"There is a big difference."

I laughed suddenly, looking down again. "Yes, there is!"

"You don't have cow udders like her," Mabel added with a frown at my mirth. She attempted to look threatening, but I was not fooled. "Now you leave the sewing to me. If you are so embarrassed to show a little flesh, I will put some lace around the neckline under the scallops," she said. I smiled gratefully. "But just a little lace," she said forcefully.

The day before the cattleman's barbecue, nearly five weeks after Clinton's departure, Mabel finished the dress. Standing before the mirror, I modeled it. Mabel had added only a little lace, as she had warned. But I would have to be content.

"Oh, Kathleen! It's perfect . . . even if I do say so myself!" she exclaimed, delighted with the effect of her dressmaking.

"It's the most beautiful dress I have ever seen," I praised truthfully, realizing the love in each stitch made it even more beautiful. I still felt exposed and uncomfortable with the low neckline. The bodice fitted snugly, my breasts swelling above the almost too-low scoop. The dress accentuated my waistline and then flared out and down softly to the floor. The sleeves were soft and fluffed at the shoulders. It looked very fashionable to me and I liked it.

"Leave your hair down and put a ribbon in it," she suggested, handing over a narrow velvet tie. But I would not take her suggestion, for I wanted to look older, not younger.

"You are beautiful, Kathleen. Even you should be able to see that now." Mabel's face was alight with prideful pleasure.

"That's what Michael keeps saying!" I laughed, not quite believing either of them. It was the dress. Anyone could look beautiful in such a dress.

"Michael is known for his taste in women," she said in agreement, taking my words literally though she knew my feelings. Watching her face in the mirror, I saw the excitement and triumph lighting her gray eyes.

"Mabel, don't be disappointed if Mr. Matthews . . . doesn't pay any attention to me," I started to plead, afraid of her hopes.

"I'm not worried," she interjected, chuckling and meeting my eyes in the reflection. "I know my boy."

With all my heart, I hoped she was right. But I refused to let myself dwell on that remote possibility.

That night I lay awake for a long time thinking about the barbecue only hours away. Clinton had still not returned, and I almost hoped that he would be delayed longer and miss the activities. Then there would be no possibility of disappointing Mabel with my failure.

If he came, he would spend the evening with Cybil,

holding her in his arms for the dances, standing beside her, talking with her, looking at her.

"I'm torturing myself. I must not think about him, I must try to have a good time with the other people I will meet," I told myself quietly in the darkened room. There will be lots of women from Las Positas. I could spend time with them.

And, of course, Michael would be there.

But my thoughts kept returning stubbornly to Clinton Matthews. Would he notice me? Would he look at me as he had before, the strange dark heat coming into his brown eyes and sending shivers down my spine and warming my blood to fever pitch? Or would he have eyes only for Cybil James, dressed in her usual, sensually stirring fashion? Would he dance with me even once? Or was I hoping for the impossible?

With an effort, I forced my thoughts away from Clinton, for dreaming about such an impossible hope would only increase my pain in the inevitable disappointment. Perhaps someday I would meet a man of my own station and we would fall in love. If not, I could still involve myself with other people's children until they no longer needed my care. I still had Priscilla and Steven in my charge.

But for how long? Would I be allowed to remain if Cybil James became Mrs. Clinton Matthews?

Her words to Michael came back to me: "She'll be the first to go!" she'd said of Mabel.

Would I be the second? I did not doubt it. They would remove me from Michael's life, which was Cybil's purpose in continually tormenting me.

The mere thought of leaving Priscilla and Steven almost made me panic with unhappiness. They were a part of me now. It would be like cutting away my own flesh and bone. Or was that being totally honest? Could I stay, knowing and seeing Clinton's love for his wife? Could I bear to watch him touch her, look at her, laugh with her?

While I knew that I should leave for my own sake, I knew I would not go until told to do so. No matter how much I loved the children, I loved Clinton more. A part of me would die with his marriage, but I knew somehow I would survive the agony. I would remain as long as I could, just to be near him. I would live for the children, and the memories.

Memories of Clinton's arms around me after I fell from the horse, the closeness we had shared for those brief minutes on the hillside, the tender kiss in the garden, and . . . the fire I had felt grow in him as well as myself as he took my heart and soul in the study.

I would only forget the mockery in his eyes, the anger I had so often provoked without understanding how, the cool indifference, and the quiet acceptance of my presence in his household.

An exquisite sadness encompassed me as I realized the life I was describing to myself. Fantasy, living in the past, perhaps not living at all.

Somehow, when the time came, when Clinton took Cybil for his wife, I would have to search myself for the strength necessary to leave and find my own happiness elsewhere. Surely, somewhere something was waiting for me. Surely . . .

"Mother . . ." I cried softly. "Was this the pain you felt?" What had my father felt for her? Had it been my mother who loved him and sacrificed her honor and self-respect for his attentions? Or had he loved her too, even a little?

No. If he had loved her he would not have placed her in such a position. If he had cared for her, even some small bit, he would not so easily have discarded her only child by him—me. His child. The hurt of rejection began to build in me again. Not just my rejection now, but my mother's also. And then the anger came.

I remembered Clinton's words of assurance in the garden. He had denied his engagement to Cybil James. He had kissed me, wanted me to stay with him. Was he then offering what my father had offered my mother? Or was I reading too much into a stolen kiss in the moonlight?

Michael had said several times that he wanted to kiss me. His questioning glances and low-spoken words, however, had never left me breathless and curious about how his lips would feel against mine. But I had never been taken unaware by Michael, nor had he simply taken me into his arms and done what he said he so wanted to do. He had only taken my hand and pressed a passionate kiss into the palm. But it had not affected me, other than to make me mildly annoyed by his advance.

Would I feel the same excitement if I allowed Michael to kiss me as Clinton had? Would his kiss also stir my blood to liquid fire?

If my mother had been a prostitute, could I be like her? In love with one man, how could I think of kissing another?

Slowly my mind succumbed to sleep, the crickets chirping in soothing constancy outside my window lulling me away into a dream world. The moon cast a soft beam into the room through the rose vines, but no wind stirred the shadows into motion.

Then it was daytime again. I was standing in the garden and found Clinton miraculously standing in front of me, looking down into my eyes.

"I'm so glad you're home," I said, unafraid of expressing my love. My heart turned over as I looked up at him and saw his eyes warm and passionate as they held mine.

Slowly he drew me into his arms, his warm mouth coming down to cover mine possessively.

Suddenly, he thrust me away from him, wiping his mouth with the back of his hand as though he had tasted something vile and unthinkable. "What am I doing kissing you!" he gasped with repulsion. "You're a whore's child!"

As I looked up with amazed anguish, it was not the face of Clinton Matthews I saw, but another man's. Who was he? I was horrified, putting my hand across my face as though to wipe away the fog or to blot him out.

But he was there. He was real.

The man's face contorted grotesquely. "Your mother was nothing but a streetwalker. She was not an actress . . . that was a ruse to attract men to her. She was a whore! Do you hear that?" He grabbed my shoulders, digging his fingers in so hard that I screamed out in pain and terror. I tried to pull away from him but he held me tight to face his wild eyes.

I couldn't breathe as he shook me. I struggled in panic, reaching up and clawing his face with my fingernails. The blood dripped down onto his white satin shirt like red wax from a candle.

"Your birth brought nothing but shame and misfortune. You should have died along with your mother. He hates you! Do you hear me?" The voice changed to an inhuman screech. "He hates you! He hates you! He hates you!" It was like an echo in my mind.

My father was sitting calmly in his carriage, his face turned away slightly, so that I could only see his handsome unmoved aristocratic profile, like the marble of a statue. He did not look at me but said in a quiet, authoritative voice, "Drive on, we'll be late. Drive on."

I was running then, the breath searing my lungs. Fences. Fences everywhere. High, curling, iron fences.

I could hear running footsteps behind me. Looking

198

around frantically, I could see no one, nor could I find escape except to climb. I pulled myself up on the iron fence.

Higher, higher, higher, I climbed. There seemed to be no top. My arms were tired and I couldn't find a foothold.

Someone was behind me, hot breath touching my ankles. My hands were slipping.

"No!!!" I screamed in terror, the fence sliding through my tightening fingers as though it were melting. I started to fall, twisting in the air to catch myself.

Below me a woman waited. Her smiling face turned to one of rage and hate. Her eyes became wild, her hair streaming out away from her as though it had life of its own. She started to laugh, high-pitched and spine-tingling.

"You ruined everything! And now I've got you at last!" she screamed, pulling a knife from behind her. I was still falling, so slowly I seemed to float toward her. It was taking forever, the ground and the shining blade coming up toward me slowly as I floated down to it like a piece of paper dropped from a high building. The woman held the knife below me, waiting to impale me. I screamed again and again, clawing frantically at the air.

"Mother! Mother!"

Someone was holding me, calling me, shaking me. My eyes flew open and I jerked upright, feeling the first light touch of the blade.

Jim Calhoun's face focused above mine and I realized it had been another nightmare. I collapsed in relief against his chest, sobbing like a frightened child.

"You're fine, Miss O'Reilly," Jim said in a soothing voice. "It was just a nightmare."

"I'm sorry . . ." I was able to say finally. "Did I awaken the children?"

"They're all right, don't you worry about them," he answered and looked embarrassed as he took his hands away from my shoulders, his eyes glancing curiously down over me. "I heard you scream and thought someone was in here again," he explained. "Are you all right now, ma'am?" he asked, and I knew he was in a hurry to leave.

"Yes, thank you. I feel fine now," I replied, pulling the covers up over me and wishing that he would stay for just a few minutes, until I had lost the unreasoning fear of my dream.

"Good night, then, ma'am," he said and turned to leave. He went out into the hallway again, quietly closing the door behind him. I lay there for a long time, my heart still pounding fast and furiously. I did not want to fall asleep again for fear the dream would recur.

Why had I screamed for my mother? Who was the woman waiting for me? Was that my mother? Had she wanted me dead? Had I ruined her life? Had she been mad?

"A whore's child," the young man had screamed at me, or had it been Clinton saying it first? Was I really a whore's child?

I rolled over my bed, pressing my face into the pillow. I will not think of my mother that way. I can't let myself. I must think of her as a woman in love with a man too high to reach. I must not think of her as a whore.

I am part of my mother. She is a part of me!

XII

It was midmorning when Clinton returned from his cattle drive. Priscilla, Steven, and I were sitting in the garden having just finished breakfast when we heard a sudden burst of activity in the house.

Thinking it was Cybil James again, we were not in any hurry to investigate the commotion.

"So here you are!" a deep voice exclaimed, and I felt a sudden surge of my heart. I turned to see Clinton taking long strides toward us. He was met halfway by two flying children.

In one glance I noticed he was clean-shaven and neatly attired in brown pants and a crisp white shirt. I wondered why he had not returned dusty and bristled and then remembered Cybil's presence. Of course, he would want to look his best before arriving home . . . for her.

His laugh rang in the garden as he scooped up the children and hugged them, kissing Prissy's upturned cheek. Her eyes sparkled mischievously.

"I missed you," he announced, and looked over their heads to me. Putting the children down, he walked over to the bench where I was sitting. A tremor of excitement went through me as I watched the way he moved with easy grace. "It's good to be back," he said to me as the children chattered excitedly. He did not seem to notice them as his eyes locked mine.

"The children missed you very much . . . as you can see," I answered and smiled. A half-smile touched his lips.

"Only the children?" he asked, his eyes questioning. I detected a teasing sparkle and took his question in the light way it was meant, but before I could think of an equally casual reply, Cybil's voice sounded in the garden with a sweetness not heard in it for weeks.

"Clinton! Darling! You're back at last!" She approached swiftly, floating across the garden, her arms outstretched. Clinton had turned slightly so that I could not see the expression on his face. I was thankful. I could not bear to see the love that would light his eyes.

Giving him a hug, Cybil reached up, touching his face with a tenderness I had never known she possessed. She drew his head down to meet her waiting lips and as they kissed my heart stopped. I felt all the life in me squelched into silent stillness. Then an agonizing pain grabbed at me and I looked away.

"I missed you so, darling," Cybil said, a little breathlessly. "You are terrible!" she added, looking up at him with pouting lips. "I was beginning to wonder if you would miss our first Fiesta del Verano!"

Quietly, I stood up and took the children's limp hands, hoping to make my escape. They were equally distressed by Cybil's display. Clinton was holding Cybil's arms and mumbling a low answer. Her pout became a frown.

"You must go on a tour with me, darling," she said, smiling again, "and see the improvements I've been making." She raised one hand to touch his chest. He caught her hand.

"All right," he answered, without much enthusiasm, and turning slightly toward me. His eyes caught mine for only a second. "When is this shindig?" he asked.

"Oh, you're just asking that to make me angry, Clint!" Cybil exclaimed. "You know very well it's today. People will be arriving any time."

"Good God!" he said, dismayed.

"The rooms are all ready for them," she said as though by her doing and not Mabel's. "They've started cooking the sides of beef already. Everything is arranged. All you have to do is greet your guests."

As I reached the back door, Cybil's voice called me. "Oh, Miss O'Reilly, before you disappear completely, go into the kitchen and instruct Mabel to set out more plates. There weren't enough the last time I checked." Her voice was condescending and cool. I was sure that Mabel had set out enough and this was just her way of reminding Clinton that she was in charge of the fiesta and that Mabel and I were both servants in his household. He hardly needed reminding.

She turned back to Clinton, taking his arm and leading him through the garden. I was glad his face was averted, for my cheeks were flaming with indignation at her unfair dig at Mabel's preparation and my feelings.

People began to arrive in buggies and wagons almost immediately after the children and I left the garden. Men and women's voices were heard everywhere as they walked in small groups, talking animatedly about ranch problems, local gossip, valley politics and the handicrafts brought for display.

The women went first to the display stalls to set out their work. Patchwork quilts, jars of preserves, knitted garments, crocheted doilies and tablecloths, wood carvings, pottery, dolls, baby clothes, and many

203

other things lay for others to admire. Women exchanged ideas and hints on their various arts, while sipping apple cider.

The children had disappeared from my side as soon as other young ones had arrived and I found myself free to wander by the stalls and admire the displays. Fingering a beautifully crocheted shawl, I complimented the elderly woman who had made it. She was pleased, proceeding to tell me in great detail how it had taken her several months to complete it.

I saw Clinton only once that morning after he and Cybil had left the garden. He was standing with her, talking with several other young couples. Her hand rested possessively on the curve of his arm. The voices were gay and loud as they drifted across the cut grass toward me.

I wished I could escape the steady stream of conversation with the woman who had made the shawl, but did not wish to be rude. So I remained and listened.

A young man standing with Clinton's group asked loud enough for me to hear, "When are you two going to tie the knot, Clint?" I watched Cybil smile beguilingly and lower her eyes, but as Clinton answered she frowned, looking up at him and then giving a little laugh.

I looked away, feeling a stifling agony in my chest. So this is what the Fiesta del Verano had in store for me? I stood quietly offering light questions to my companion who wanted my encouragement to tell the history of her dress shop in Las Positas. As she spoke, my mind wandered again to the group close by.

Will I have to look at them all day? Will I have to listen to Cybil's cooing voice and husky laughter? My head ached with the thought.

I have to find a way to escape this event, I thought

with determination. I have to find an excuse not to go to that dance tonight.

The droning voice of the woman went on and on. I smiled and asked the usual polite questions, feeling guilty for my lack of attention and not wanting to hurt her feelings by turning on my heel and walking back to the house to shut myself in the solitude of my upstairs room. After all, my present state of mind was not her fault.

The same young man with the loud, carrying voice, was speaking again. "Who's that girl over there with Mrs. Tibbets?" The woman with whom I was standing stopped her conversation and gave me a slow wink.

"You've attracted a little male interest, Miss O'Reilly," she said, smiling pleasantly. Oh, no, I thought. That's all I need is some sarcastic attention on the dim-witted Matthews governess.

Cybil's soft voice answered and I heard a slight chuckle from the man. "Well, Mike will have a little competition. How about an introduction, Clint?"

"Will you excuse me, please, Mrs. Tibbets?" I said to my companion with pleading eyes.

"You're not going to run away, are you? The young man is asking to meet you, dear," she remarked with surprise. I nodded, giving her a self-conscious smile. However, before I could take more than half a dozen steps toward the house, Clinton called my name, making escape impossible. I could hardly pretend I did not hear my employer's commanding voice. I turned around toward him dutifully, wishing I were in my room, in the kitchen, riding in the hills, anywhere, in fact, but where I was.

Mrs. Tibbets had approached me again. "Mrs. Tibbets," Clinton asked with just enough charm to make my companion grin at him, "would you excuse Miss O'Reilly for a moment or two?"

"Why, of course, Clinton. We both heard Tom asking for an introduction," she laughed. "Go on, dear. No more thought of escape. The boy won't bite," she went on, as I looked at her feeling chicken-hearted and embarrassed.

As we crossed the short distance to the group, I sensed rather than saw Clinton's annoyance. He did not once meet my eyes directly as he escorted me across the grass. Everyone in the group turned curious eyes in my direction, and I tried desperately to control my nervousness.

"Miss Kathleen O'Reilly, this is Tom Whittaker," Clinton introduced me first to the young man who had requested my presence. Then he went on to the others in the group. I looked at each person directly, chin held straight and sure, smiled and nodded. The young women were cool, while the young men were curious, studying and smiling. It was the man named Whittaker who reached out and took my hand.

"It is indeed a pleasure, ma'am," he said, and I noted the smile that curved his thin lips. He was several inches shorter than Clinton but still stood several inches taller than I. He had the same carelessly attractive air that Michael James did, though he was not nearly as handsome. His hair was black, thick, and curly. He wore a beard and showed excessively white teeth.

"Thank you, Mr. Whittaker," I answered, disliking his open appraisal of me from head to foot. Cybil stared at me coolly when I met her eyes. Touching Clinton's arm, she whispered something to him as he leaned down. He shook his head and straightened, looking again at Tom Whittaker, who was still smiling with that annoying intimacy. When I met Cybil's glance again, there was no mistaking the animosity in her cold, blue eyes. And the silence in the group was becoming embarrassing.

"Please excuse me," I said, "but I believe Mrs.

Banks needs some help." I curtseyed, turned, and moved away, relieved to find escape so easy after all.

Tom Whittaker stopped me before I reached the drive, a hand under my elbow. "I'll excuse you only if you promise me at least one dance this evening," he said. Clinton was still standing by Cybil but I saw that he was watching us, an unreadable expression on his face.

"Thank you for asking me," I evaded, drawing my arm from his hold.

"That's no answer, Miss O'Reilly," he observed, smiling. "How about that dance?"

"If you wish, Mr. Whittaker," I answered with a smile. His voice was low and his manner not overly studious. I liked him better. "Excuse me now," I said and turned to continue to the house.

Mabel was standing over a steaming pot of beans, her forehead beaded with perspiration. She turned and smiled at me as I entered.

"Your dress is pressed and waiting for you, Kathleen," she informed me, her smile fading as she looked at my face. "What's the matter?"

"Nothing," I lied, my smile brighter than I felt. "I'm just a little nervous, I guess." How could I tell her I didn't want to go to the dance?

She looked at me curiously, and then I saw her eyes raise to someone behind me. She grinned suddenly and said in a mock-angry voice.

"What are you doing in my kitchen?"

"I've an idea you know the answer to the question, Mabel," Michael laughed, and I turned to meet his sparkling eyes. "Cybil said you were in the kitchen, Kathleen." He took my hand in an affectionate gesture. "Come on, I want to introduce you to some of my friends . . . Tom Whittaker excluded." I caught Mabel's twinkling eyes as I looked back at her. Michael did not share the same place in her heart as his sister.

As we left the kitchen, Michael's attitude changed subtly. "I was told Tom got you to promise him a dance," he said casually, his face taking on a look that I had never seen before. He was jealous, I thought with surprise.

"I didn't know what else to say to him, Michael," I explained truthfully. "Anyway, I'm not sure I will be going to the dance at all," I went on, remembering Clinton and Cybil standing together in the group, her hand on his arm as though she belonged to him . . . and him to her.

"Why not?" Michael asked with surprise. "Clinton hasn't got you watching over the kids, has he?"

"No," I answered quickly, hoping that he would not guess the real reason for my reluctance.

"Well, then, there's no question that you will stay until the very end of the dance. I'll allow Tom one dance and I'll probably have to fight the others away all night. But I intend to have you in my arms tonight. You can't object this time . . . since we will be dancing and others will be present." He was teasing me again, but I was surprised at the possessiveness of his hold on my hand, his eyes penetrating mine.

As the afternoon progressed, I realized that Michael intended to stay very close to me during the fiesta. I was slightly dismayed, for I began to feel stifled as he kept a possessive hand on my elbow at all times. He introduced me to several of his friends and from various comments I heard from them I gathered that he had already spoken to them about his feelings about me. The thought was distressing.

Smelling the barbecuing beef and watching as Mabel and her helpers set the long tables with food, I realized I was famished. Fresh oven-baked bread, cakes, hot steaming pots of beans, cornbread, corn on the cob, fruit, so many things to entice the appetite.

"Chow's on!" someone shouted, clanging a triangle,

and everyone began talking even more loudly at once as they moved toward the food and stacks of dishes.

"You sit here, Kathleen," Michael instructed, spreading a blanket for me to sit on just outside the circle of display stalls. "I'll get your food so you won't have to fight the mob." He moved away into the crowd.

I saw Clinton and Cybil among the people. For a moment, I thought I saw him looking in my direction. Then his head bent down to listen to something Cybil was saying.

"Well, finally, your guard has departed!" Whittaker said as he unexpectedly appeared above me. "I was waiting for an opportunity to talk with you," he said, sitting down on the blanket next to me. "Michael keeps a close eye on you, doesn't he?" He smiled at my silence. "Never mind. I was just teasing. Clinton says you're quite a governess.'"

"That can be taken many ways, Mr. Whittaker," I said, smiling. "I think I have disappointed him more than once."

"I doubt that, Miss O'Reilly," he said, matching my tone. He surveyed me carefully and I felt unnerved by his bold scrutiny. I looked at the crowd of people milling around near the food-laden tables, wishing Michael were back.

"Priscilla and Steven are nice kids," Whittaker commented. "They have sure taken a liking to you. I was just talking to them a few minutes ago."

"Oh? Where are they?" I asked, interested and glad he had changed the subject. "I lost them a while ago."

"They're over there getting some chow now. Don't worry about them. They're having a great time with the Anderson kids." He tilted his head a little to look at my face. I stared back at him curiously.

"Is something wrong?" I asked.

"Not at all . . . not at all," he answered. "You are very beautiful, Miss O'Reilly."

"I knew I could depend on you, Tom," Michael's voice cut in. I looked up with relief at his return. "The minute I'm out of sight you wolves make a move," he went on, his eyes meeting Tom's in a penetrating look which belied his good-humored tone.

"You got a claim on the lady, Mike?" Tom asked easily, and I saw a challenge pass between them.

"Maybe," Michael replied lightly, giving me a quick glance. Whittaker raised his brows and turned to me.

"You're going to marry this ladies' man, Miss O'Reilly?" he asked in obvious disbelief, a telltale twinkle of mischief in his eyes.

Michael flushed slightly as he looked at me.

"Michael and I are very close friends," I answered and then feeling something more was needed to prevent Michael's unfortunate statement from causing him further embarrassment, I added with a slow smile at Michael, "for the moment."

Michael's eyes lighted up and he grinned, pleased with my answer.

"Well, friendship isn't marriage," Tom commented, the twinkle slightly dimmed. "So I'll still hold you to that dance you promised me." He winked, got up and moved away, leaving Michael to glare at his back. Then he shrugged.

"What's one dance?" He turned and smiled at me. "I'm glad you added those last three words. It gives me reason to hope," he said, taking my hand and kissing it.

"Michael, I would rather you did not imply that we are going to be married," I said a little stiffly, still angry with him for his casual remark. His smile flattened. "We aren't, Michael. I've made my feelings very clear to you. We are friends . . . good friends . . . but nothing more." My voice softened.

"Give it a chance, sweetheart. In time, you'll change your mind," he said with forced lightness. "You've never even let me kiss you," he teased. "That might change your mind."

It was late in the afternoon. The women started drifting toward the house to change into their dancing dresses. Michael walked back to the front steps, his arm brushing against my shoulder as we walked, his hand lightly touching my waist.

"Would you like me to wait here for you? We could spend a little time in the garden," he said.

"I think I'll rest for a while, Michael. But thank you. I'll see you a little later at the dance," I said, smiling and wishing to be by myself for a while. To not feel his presence, like a guard, next to me every moment. I saw Clinton walking across the yard with Cybil. Our eyes met briefly over the distance, and I turned to hurrry up the steps into the house.

Only minutes after I arrived at my room to change dresses, Mabel knocked.

"I'll help you," she informed me with a smile, her gray eyes twinkling. "How's it going?"

"Tom Whittaker has insisted on one dance, and Michael has been by my side since he arrived," I reported, giving her a fading smile. "Michael is very nice," I added, feeling disloyal for my feelings of annoyance at his possessive presence.

"You're not after Michael," Mabel teased.

"Mabel . . ."

"I saw Clinton looking at you," she reported, and gave my cheek a little pat. "He was scowling. That's a good sign. I think he's jealous!"

"He's probably angry because I am with Cybil's brother," I corrected her. "And she has made her sentiments quite clear about Michael's interest in me. Besides, he scowls at me all the time. That's nothing new . . . nor is it a good sign," I commented, giving a little laugh to cover my unhappiness. Then as though torturing myself deliberately, I added more seriously, "He's noticing a good deal of Cybil James though."

"Hmmmmmph!" Mabel dismissed the comment, but did not argue the point.

I stood before the mirror in the yellow dress, Mabel smiling broadly as she carefully fluffed the delicate sleeves and the long full skirt. It was a beautiful dress, I thought again. I did feel almost beautiful in it. My skin looked more fair, my hair more dark, and my eyes more wider, and bluer. I flushed a little as I looked down at the neckline again, my breasts swelling almost seductively above the scallops.

"I wish we had made the neckline a little higher," I commented nervously, still looking down. Mabel laughed.

"It's perfect, Kathleen. Alluring. Promising of . . . well, we'll leave the dreaming to the men." She winked, her broad cheeks flushing with excitement and pride at her creation.

"I don't think I'll go down just yet. I don't want to be among the very first there," I explained quietly. I knew that I would be unable to avoid going, but at least I could delay my arrival.

"Well, be generous and let the plain girls and old ladies have a dance or two," she said. She looked at me long and kindly. "You are beautiful, Kathleen . . . and even more so because you don't know you are."

I sat for a long time in the rocker, looking out into the garden. The dance music had started and I could hear laughter in the distance, the lights from the barn casting a glow against the horizon.

The longer I waited, the less I wanted to go. My heart pounded nervously and my hands felt cold and damp. I could not let Mabel down, even if it meant watching Clinton and Cybil in each other's arms all night. She had worked so hard on this beautiful dress.

I owed her whatever small success I could make tonight.

A light tap sounded on my door and I turned to see Priscilla and Steven standing in the doorway.

"There you are!" she said, relieved. "Michael sent us up to look for you. Where have you been? The dancing has started and he's waiting at the barn." Priscilla rushed over and took my hand, while Steven stood shyly in the doorway, dressed in his best jeans and white shirt. They both looked adorable in their neat clothes, scrubbed and combed. I stood up and leaned over to give them both a hug.

"Gosh! You're so beautiful!" Priscilla exclaimed, and I saw Steven's eyes widen.

"You're much prettier than Cybil," he added, and I wondered if he could read my doubts or if Cybil infected everyone's thoughts. My heart swelled at the love I saw in their eyes and I didn't care about that woman anymore.

"That's because you like me much better, sweetheart," I said, running my hand gently over his soft, brown hair. He took my hand in a spontaneous gesture that touched me deeply. It was the first time he had taken my hand without me reaching out to him first.

When we entered the barn, I noticed several heads turn in our direction. I did not see Clinton and Cybil, but noticed Tom Whittaker and several of his companions turn toward me. A young man in his group looked over his shoulder and said something to which Whittaker nodded.

"Where have you been, honey?" Michael asked, and I felt his warm hand slide around my waist possessively, edging Steven away. As I turned toward him, his eyes dropped in surprise. I started to raise my hand instinctively, but he caught it. Raising his eyes, he grinned.

"I promise not to stare," he teased lightly, noticing my blush. "You are beautiful, Kathleen. Shall we dance?" he went on, already drawing me more closely into his arms and taking me into the rhythm of the dance. He held me a little closer as we moved, his breath against my hair. "I thought I would never get you in my arms," he said, his voice strangely tense. I smiled up at him. As we danced, I saw people looking at us and whispering to one another, smiles on their faces.

A young cowhand cut in on Michael and danced with me around the floor a couple of times. Tom Whittaker claimed his dance almost immediately, and again I wished fervently that Mabel had made the neckline of my dress higher. Relieved, I saw someone tap Whittaker's shoulder. I looked up and smiled almost gratefully and met Clinton's dark eyes.

He gave me a slow smile, raising his brows as his gaze dropped to my breasts. I turned crimson as he drew me into his arms and started to move with the music. Unlike Michael's touch, Clinton's hand on my back sent waves of warmth through me, and I parted my lips feeling slightly breathless as I looked up at him. I couldn't quite believe that he was really dancing with me, holding me in his arms.

"You made quite a sensation a while ago, Kathleen," he teased, his eyes looking into mine. He pressed me more tightly against him and grinned. "I like your dress."

"Mabel made it," I said with difficulty. The words sounded stiff.

His eyes dropped to my mouth. My heart was pounding and I wondered if he could feel it, for my whole body seemed to pulse with its accelerated beat.

"Where is Miss James?" I asked, almost in a panic for something to say.

He shrugged. "You're beautiful, Miss O'Reilly," he

said softly, bending slightly closer to my ear. His warm breath sent shivers through me, and I felt myself tremble slightly against him. He smiled warmly as I dropped my eyes and began nervously studying the buttons on his shirt. He moved his hand down a little to the small of my back and pressed ever so slightly.

Suddenly the music stopped. He hesitated for a second before releasing me, giving me a look that made me tingle. Then looking over my shoulder, he said drily, "Well, Michael is wasting no time."

"Oh." I could not disguise the disappointment in my voice. As I turned I saw Cybil walking with her brother, her eyes resting on Clinton. She was smiling demurely.

"How very sweet on you, darling, to dance with your governess," she said, giving me a brief dismissing look. I felt a heavy pain descend on me as she reached out and put her soft, long-nailed hand on Clinton's arm again.

"It was my pleasure," Clinton commented with a brief glance down at me. I smiled at his politeness, turning as Michael drew me into his arms for another dance.

As the evening progressed, and I danced with Michael, I noticed a subtle change in his behavior. He now seemed angry when anyone cut in and several times I noticed him standing with a small group of men near the punch bowls. Only once did I see him dancing with anyone else.

The woman was Mary Cramer. She was dressed in a pretty, flattering green dress, and she looked radiant as he held her in his arms.

Tom Whittaker cut in several times. I did not like the way he looked at me. I felt he was mentally taking off my clothes, piece by piece.

In spite of all the attention I was receiving, I was unhappy and somehow disappointed. The evening had been more than I expected, every dance taken. But still I saw Clinton and Cybil.

It was after twelve. I was tired and warm from dancing for several hours. And I wanted to escape.

Michael suggested a walk in the night air. I smiled my acceptance, relieved to have an excuse to leave the dance and not have to see Clinton dancing again with Cybil.

Michael took my arm in his as we walked. He talked in a low voice, but I was too deep in my own thoughts to listen to what he was saying. His hand slid down and took mine. "Have I told you how very beautiful you are this evening, darling?" His voice was deeper than usual, and not quite distinct. I looked at him in alarm, wondering what was the matter.

"It's sweet of you to say that, Michael," I answered finally.

"Sweet . . ." he repeated, "that's what you are, my love. Sweet. And innocent . . . and very desirable."

I began to feel an uncomfortable tension. We were farther from the barn and the lights than I thought and I began to feel more and more uneasy as he went on talking of his love for me in increasingly flowery terms. There was a strange tautness and urgency in his voice that frightened me.

Michael stopped walking and, almost frantically, I looked back at the lights some distance away.

"I think we should start back, Michael," I suggested quietly, feeling more and more apprehensive at his strange manner. His arms came around me, pulling me toward him abruptly.

"So all those men can put their hands on you?" he demanded harshly.

"Michael, let me go! What's the matter with you? Please don't!" I said, leaning back away from him and putting my hands up against his chest. His heart was pounding violently, sending a sudden chill of instinctive fear through me.

"I don't want to go back just yet," he said huskily. "I love you." I could smell brandy on his breath and as he moved his face closer, I realized that he was determined to kiss me. I turned my face from his, twisting against him, trying to get out of his grip. He went on speaking, his mouth close to my ear, pressing me against him. "I've wanted you since I first saw you. Do you know that? Do you know you're the only woman I've wanted and haven't bedded," he said without bragging. He laughed then. "Don't struggle so much, honey. I promise you I will be very gentle."

"Michael, please . . ." I begged, breathless with fear, trying to push him away. But he drew me even tighter against him, pinning my hands against his chest.

"Marry me, Kathleen," he breathed against my neck. "I dream about you . . . in my bed, soft, warm, yielding." His lips traveled down, tasting my skin. "I need you . . . God, I can't wait any longer to have you. I'll be gentle. Don't fight me." One of his hands slid up my back and his fingers fumbled at the ribbon in my hair. He scattered the pins on the hillside, raking his fingers through the mass of hair as it fell loose over my shoulders. When he pressed his body tightly against mine, attempting to mold me to him, I felt the change in him.

Struggling violently, I managed to pull one hand free, striking ineffectually at his back. I tried to cry out, but his mouth came down over mine in a passionate kiss that left me cold with terror. His fingers, more sure now, began to undo the buttons at the back of my dress, touching bare skin as he slid his hand beneath the fabric.

The longer he kissed me and the more I struggled, the more incensed with passion he seemed to become. Impatient, he pulled roughly at my dress, the material

217

ripping at the shoulder. He started to pull me down on the grassy hillside even as I fought frantically against his overwhelming power.

Michael's hand pressed hard over my mouth to keep me from screaming, his burning mouth sliding down the side of my neck as yellow spots of suffocation formed before my eyes. My struggles were weaker and I heard him laugh slightly as my head began to swim in a fog. His warm hand touched my breast and then traveled down to raise the hem of my dress.

"What the hell are you doing?" I heard someone say in a deep, raging voice. As though in a dream, Michael was suddenly torn away from me and I collapsed on the ground in a near faint, gasping for breath.

Someone was cursing violently and I turned to look up as Clinton swung Michael around and hit him full in the face. The blow hit with sickening precision and Michael dropped in an unconscious heap. But Clinton's fury seemed to grow, for he grabbed Michael by the front of his shirt, dragging him up again. He struck him several times more until, regaining my senses, I cried out:

"Don't hit him again, Clinton!" I scrambled to my feet. "My God, you're killing him!" I grabbed onto Clinton's arm to stay his next brutal swing. "Please! No!" I pleaded breathlessly, holding his arm tightly with all the strength I could muster. "He didn't know what he was doing! He's been drinking. He's never done anything like that before. Oh, Clinton, don't hit him again."

He let go of Michael and let him drop to the ground in a moaning heap. Then he swung on me, his eyes still glazed with his hot fury.

"Why the hell did you come out here with him?" he demanded. I had never seen such fierceness and it was frightening. His eyes dropped to survey my dishevelment and I crossed my arms in front of me, hug-ging the dress into place. I looked down at the ground, feeling tears coming.

"Turn around, dammit!" Clinton commanded and I obeyed. He buttoned the back of my dress with easy skill. As he touched a bruised spot I jerked slightly. Turning me around, his voice was quiet but still choked with anger. "He hurt you, Kathleen. He almost had his way with you and, by God, you stand here and tell me not to lay another hand on him!"

"I'm all right," I said, still too numb to fully understand the emotion riding him. His hand came up warm against my face. "I only wanted some air," I explained, looking up at him. "Thank you for helping me," I murmured, becoming all too conscious of his touch. "I only wanted to go back to the house," I added, my lip quivering at the look in his eyes.

"I'll walk you there," he said gently, and I knew he believed me.

"Won't Miss James be waiting for you?"

"Why are you always asking me about Cybil?" he demanded angrily. "Let her wait, dammit!"

Michael groaned and started to push himself up into a sitting position, rubbing his bruised jaw.

"Clinton, what on earth is going on out here?" Cybil's voice drifted to us through the semidarkness as she appproached the three of us. Looking down at her brother now struggling to rise, she gasped.

Clinton took my arm tightly. "See that Michael has a lot of coffee, Cybil," he directed coolly as he turned to walk me back to the house.

"Where are you going, darling?" she demanded in a high, petulant voice. I felt Clinton stiffen beside me as he turned to answer.

"What concern is that of yours, my dear?"

A silence fell between them for a long moment. I could almost see the thoughts flying across Cybil's face as she retreated and regained her forces.

"Will you come back as soon as you see your wayward governess to her door?" she asked, ignoring his angry demeanor. Then more rapidly, her anger getting the best of her intelligence, "Really, Clinton, the chit brought this on herself. She's been leading Michael around by the nose since the first day he met her. You've seen it yourself. Mike's a man . . . and he's not to be played with."

My face flushed with anger at the twisted words she spoke to slander me.

Clinton was motionlessly staring at her. I could feel his rage. Cybil seemed to wither before his cold glare, then she smiled slightly, her lips trembling to betray her calm.

"I am sorry for saying so, darling," she said, attempting to break the ominous silence. "Perhaps that was a bit of an exaggeration," she amended. "I was only . . . well, I am concerned about my brother's feelings, you know . . . and people would talk if you are gone too long. I'm sure that would not look good for anyone . . . especially Miss O'Reilly in view of her reputation," she added, her voice dropping a note as she saw success near. I could see the venomous glare in her eyes as she met my embarrassed glance. Had I heard a threat in her words? Was my reputation so easily destroyed?

Considering his next statement, Clinton raised his brows. "See that people do not talk then . . . if you really are concerned for everyone involved. Including yourself, my dear. After all, the James name is involved." He turned away from her abruptly and started to walk toward the house. I could hear Cybil saying something in a furious low tone to Michael as she helped him to his feet, but Clinton was walking me so swiftly toward the house that I had to almost run to keep up with his long, angry strides. And his hand dug into my arm painfully.

"I'm sorry to be the cause of any disagreement between you and Miss James," I said breathlessly. "You don't really have to walk me back to the house. I'll be quite all right now, really."

"Really?" he asked sarcastically, looking down at me.

I could hardly see his face in the darkness now, for the glow of lights was behind us. "Well, I'd better see you there just in case you end up in the arms of another one of your admirers," he said bitingly, almost dragging me along beside him.

We reached the house and he stopped at the steps. Grabbing my hand and looming above me like an angry giant, he growled out his next words: "Just what does Michael James mean to you? Are you going to marry that poor bastard or just keep him dangling?" he demanded. I was astonished to see the cold fury in his face.

"Pardon me?" I muttered numbly, shocked by the expression on his face and hardly hearing what he asked me. He pulled at my hand, drawing me up a step closer. He stared down into my face and then, turning, pulled me up the steps so quickly that I stumbled and almost fell. As he yanked me into the hallway, he slammed the door and turned on me again. I gasped, pulling back away from him.

"I asked you what Michael means to you, damn you! You heard me! I want no more of your games!"

The house was still and silent, everyone gone. I flinched slightly as his hand squeezed mine brutally. He saw my grimace and loosened his grip, yet didn't allow me to pull free. "I want an answer!"

"Michael is a friend," I choked. Why was he so furious with me. Had he really thought Cybil's accusation was justified?

"He doesn't seem to think so!" he growled. "You knew he told me he wanted to marry you. Didn't you?!"

His voice raised again. His eyes raked over me and I could see that he did believe Cybil. A cold hurt anger rose up in me to match his.

"He has told me also, Mr. Matthews," I answered in a quiet, tight voice. "But that does not mean that I share his feelings." I yanked my hand away from him.

"I warned you about Michael once," he snarled at me, his eyes flashing dangerously, but I was too angry myself now to take warning.

"You warned me that his intentions were not . . . honorable," I retorted, clenching my fists and standing rigidly facing him.

Clinton threw back his head and laughed. The sound was sarcastic, insulting, unpleasant.

"Oh, that is right, isn't it? And his intentions tonight were more than honorable, were they not, Miss O'Reilly? My God, if I had known that was what you termed honor, I would have made my own way to your bed long ago."

I paled at his assault. "I've already told you he had been drinking. He didn't know what he was doing," I stammered; "he's never treated me with anything but respect."

"Men aren't used to having a woman tease them to the extent which you seem to take pleasure in doing . . . churning up a man's insides until he's . . ."

I didn't hear any more. His words, spoken in rage, hit me harder than if he had struck me with the force he had Michael. My body sagged against the brutal attack; my eyes flooded with tears.

"I told Michael from the beginning that I did not love him and never would . . . I told him . . ." I couldn't finish. I strained desperately to gain enough control to speak again, to defend myself against the accusations being made.

Clinton saw my struggle and the blow he had so

unfairly struck. His hand flew out to my shoulder trying to prevent me from running away from him again.

"Kathleen, I'm sorry. I didn't mean to say that. I know it's not true."

I whipped myself away from him and backed toward the stairs. He took a step toward me, his voice low and gentle, apologetic. "Kathleen, listen to me." His eyes searched my face.

"No, I've listened to enough," I cried at him.

"I'm sorry I said all that," he said, his face pained.

"No, you're not! You meant every word of it! You believed everything your fiancée said. You even lied to me about her. You are going to marry her! She told me herself . . . in the garden." The tears spilled down my cheeks. "And I don't care," I went on more quietly. "You will do well together."

"Kathleen," he said, and reached out to stop me, but I swung around and moved up the stairs away from him, and then turned to face him again.

"Thank you very kindly, Mr. Matthews, for seeing me back to the house . . . safely," I said with pronounced sarcasm.

"Dammit, listen to me! You're driving me . . ."

I ran up the stairs before I could hear what he was going to fling at me. A few minutes later, the front door slammed with such force that it seemed to shake the entire house.

XIII

I awakened with the sun the next morning, my eyes swollen and red. My carpet bag was packed and lying hidden beneath the bed.

I felt depressed and exhausted, but I could not go back to sleep. For a long time, I lay in bed, listening to people moving around in the rooms below. Turning my head toward the window, I listened to the mockingbird singing his last song before departing as the activity increased in the garden.

Pushing myself up, I sat on the edge of the bed just watching the sun's rays enter my room. Taking my time, I dressed and fixed my hair, hoping to avoid meeting anyone that morning. From the house and garden the voices of guests saying their good-byes and thank-yous rose to my ears.

The beautiful yellow dress on which Mabel had worked so hard lay discarded across the foot of my bed. The torn seam at the shoulder would have to be repaired before it could be worn again.

I would never wear it again. It would remind me too vividly of the Fiesta del Verano and Clinton's words that still rang in my ears.

A key turned in the lock and the door opened. Mabel, who was carrying in a large tray, pushed it shut with her foot. "How did you know I wouldn't want to come down for breakfast this morning?" I asked, careful to keep my voice light and natural.

"There are no secrets around Las Posas," she answered, winking as she set the tray down on the bed beside me. My face crumpled and I felt humiliating tears rack me again.

"My Lordy, child! What is all this?" Mabel asked with surprise. Slipping a comforting arm around me, she rocked me gently against her.

"I ruined your dress," I mumbled evasively.

"It's your dress . . . and Michael had a little to do with that, I hear."

"I'm going to leave Las Posas, Mabel," I said more calmly, brushing the tears off my cheeks and straightening my shoulders. "I can't stay here after what Mr. Matthews said to me."

"What?" she ejaculated with astonishment. "He punched Michael James in the nose when he needed a good thrashing," she laughed. "That's no insult, little one."

"He thinks I have been leading Michael on . . . teasing him deliberately." I looked at her and shrugged. "And I don't care what he thinks."

"Oh, Kathleen . . ." she gave me a broad smile, dimpling slightly. "He must have been very angry to have suggested foolishness like that. And, of course, you care. Why else would you have cried yourself to sleep last night? Why else would you be wanting to run away?" She brushed the dampness off my cheeks with her apron. "Eat something and you'll feel better."

Mabel left me alone then, but I was not hungry. I remained motionless on the bed, listening to the commotion below, the mingled voices in the garden, the

225

buggies and wagons leaving, children laughing, a few dogs barking.

"Miss O'Reilly?" Mary called, tapping lightly at my door.

"Come in," I said blankly, not looking at her when she entered.

"Michael wants to speak with you before he leaves," she informed me, her voice quiet. "He's waiting in the study."

"I don't want to see him," I responded quietly.

"He said he wouldn't leave Las Posas until he talks to you . . . and Mr. Matthews is about ready to explode."

I knew he would wait, and I could hardly stay hidden in my room all day. Embarrassed, unhappy, and not a little angry, I turned and faced Mary. She had been crying, too, I could see. Men, I thought, hating them.

"All right, Mary. Tell him I'll be down in a few minutes."

After pressing several cold rags to my face, I started to the door. As I came down the stairs, I heard Mary's voice in the study, high, indistinct, and very upset. Michael answered her with a curtness that verged on cruelty.

"Mary, I'm sorry. I was roaring drunk last night. I'm sorry but it didn't mean we were going to start in again." His voice dropped as he continued. She mumbled something back and then I saw her rush from the room, her hands pressed over her face.

I empathized with her. Clinton could cut me to the quick too.

As I entered the study, Michael was pacing uneasily near the bookshelves. His head swung around as he heard me.

"Kathleen," he said softly, not moving for a moment. His eyes showed his shame as he devoured mine ques-

226

tioningly and then moved. He crossed the room when I avoided looking at him, remembering too well Clinton's accusation that I was teasing him. Was it teasing a man to show him friendship, to like him as a person but wish no further involvement?

When he tried to take my hand, I drew away from him. He let his drop to his sides and stood searching my face silently, anguished. He went to the doors and closed them behind me.

"Please forgive my deplorable behavior last night. I had too much to drink and didn't know what I was doing," he said, a desperate pleading in his voice and eyes. "No, that's not completely true," he said more softly, looking down. I stared up at him in surprise.

"I've wanted you all along . . . I've told you that . . . but I lost my head last night. When I touched you, I couldn't seem to stop. I felt you stop struggling and I thought for a moment you wanted me too."

"Michael," I said, looking at him directly and squelching my desire to defend myself, to tell him I had almost fainted. What did it matter? People believed what they wanted to believe. "I did a lot of thinking last night," I began. "It was my fault it happened at all."

"No! . . ." he tried to interrupt.

"Yes. It was. You've made your intentions clear from the very beginning. You said you wanted to marry me."

"I still do. Oh, darling, just say the word." His hand took mine and tightened. It would be so easy to just say yes. I could make him happy perhaps, but I could never really love him. I would never be happy.

"Michael, I'm not in love with you. I like you very much . . . but I don't love you." My hand shook as I drew it purposely from him, letting it drop into my lap. He did not seem surprised nor hurt by my quiet declaration.

"I know that," he said after a time. "But you could learn to love me in time, Kathleen. I know I've lost your trust because of last night . . . but . . ."

"Nothing will change," I said, looking at him imploringly. "Time won't help. Mr. Matthews thinks that continuing this friendship is leading you into hoping for—"

"I don't give a goddam what Clint thinks," he growled. "It's what you and I think that matters, isn't it?"

"Yes. But I think he's right. And what I think matters too. I don't think we should see each other anymore, Michael." I could tell by his face that I should never have mentioned Clinton. Now he would believe this decision was not my own. Was it? Wasn't it Clinton's accusation that had made me consider my relationship with Michael at an end? Or was it truthfully my own decision? It was the only thing that could be done under the circumstances if Michael truly loved me. I could never fall in love with him. And I could not marry without love.

And, in spite of what had happened, I still loved Clinton Matthews. An impossible love that would never know fruition, but I knew that I loved him nonetheless.

The only answer was for me to leave Las Posas.

Why couldn't I fall in love with Michael? Life would be so perfect then. I would be happy.

"Because of what Clint said, dammit?" Michael demanded suspiciously.

"No, because I think it's the only way to handle this situation." Michael, still angry, did not believe me.

"What's it to him anyway?" he demanded, taking my hand again and holding it so that I couldn't pull away from him. "Kathleen, I love you. I'm not expecting miracles . . . but give me time. I'm sorry about last night. Please try to forgive me for that. I'll never let it happen again."

I began to feel desperately trapped by his love. How could I make him see that there was no hope of my ever loving him in the way he hoped? How could I explain without telling him that I was in love with someone else?

"Michael, please. I'll only make you miserable. I can't love you," I said frantically. He looked at me strangely then, but gave me a gentle smile.

"Kathleen, you're the only woman I've ever found that I could love . . . I mean really love, not just want. Even if you never fully love me, I want to be near you . . . to feel that you could depend on me at least as a very close friend." He touched my cheek, his eyes loving and tender. "I can see that you're trying to be fair to me. But to never let me see you again would be torture." He ran his fingers over my lips when I would have spoken. "I won't press you about marriage again, I promise. If you change your mind, you have only to say the word," he finished. I could see pain and hope in his eyes.

In a few days, maybe even hours, it would make no difference. I would be gone and it wouldn't matter anymore. He would return to Mary Cramer, Rachel Hansen, or any number of others he had loved before me. He would forget me, I knew. Clinton would marry Cybil and they would arrange for another governess to care for Priscilla and Steven. Maybe my leaving would even hasten the marriage date.

I didn't care where I went anymore. I would even return to Parkside. What did it matter?

We left the study a few minutes later and walked down the front steps to Michael's buggy. Near panic hit me when I saw Clinton and Cybil standing next to the carriage. Michael's sister spoke in a low, pleading voice and Clinton seemed not to be listening to her. When she saw me approaching with Michael, she stared at me coldly, her eyes squinting like a cat's.

"Well, Miss O'Reilly. So you've forgiven my brother after all. I thought you would," she hissed, giving me a tight smile as her eyes grew filled with hate. "And how are you this morning, brother dear?"

Clinton turned to me at Cybil's first mention of my name, but I did not look up to meet his eyes.

"Shut up, Cybil," Michael answered tartly and then, still holding my hand, turned to me and said in a low intimate voice, "Don't let her upset you, darling. I'll be by later this week, Kathleen. We can discuss things again then." I could see Clinton's body stiffen at Michael's words.

"Are you ready, Cybil?" he said, turning to his sister.

"Yes," she sighed, giving Clinton a long look. Clinton met her eyes and gave her a slow smile.

"Good day, my dear," he said, his voice caustic. "And thank you for handling everything so thoroughly." I felt an undercurrent of hidden meaning in his words and looked up between them. Cybil darted a look at me and then looked back at Clinton with a cold glare. Michael jumped up next to her and took the reins.

As brother and sister wheeled out of the yard, Clinton swung around to me. His brows knitted in the center of his forehead, his face clouding over.

"Kathleen, what in God's name . . ."

Several people approached and I took the opportunity to turn and walk away from those searching, angry eyes.

Returning to my room, I pulled my suitcase out from under the bed. I would leave later when all the people were gone. I needed time to explain to the children that I could no longer stay. Perhaps I could tell them I was needed at my old home. Oh God, I just wanted to die.

By one that afternoon, everyone had left for home. The children were starting their lessons in the garden.

We were sitting on the far side of the oak tree and I was searching my mind for some way to tell them I was leaving Las Posas.

"Uncle Clinton! Over here! Are you looking for us?"

My heart raced with dread and I wondered frantically if there were a way to remove myself from his sight gracefully. I still felt the sting of his accusations and did not want to meet those mocking, brooding eyes. I just wanted to leave quietly as soon as I could and never see him again.

His footsteps approached. Steven was smiling up at him.

"Last night was fun, Uncle Clinton," Steven said, putting his book down and standing up to meet his uncle. "When will we have another fiesta?"

"Very soon, I hope, Steven," his uncle answered after a pause. I could feel those dark eyes on me, but I still did not look up at him.

"I'd like to talk with Miss O'Reilly for a while, you two. Why don't you run along and make this a holiday?"

My hands started to tremble. So he wasn't finished. I bit my lip, feeling suddenly miserable. Couldn't I just leave without him saying anything more to me?

"Come into the study, Kathleen," he ordered. Standing up, I followed him. His shoulders were rigidly erect as he walked and I could sense his building, brooding, anger.

San Francisco, I thought suddenly. That's where I'll go. Having paid my debt to Anna, I had enough money to get me there. The little that would remain after a stage ticket would keep me for a few days until I could find some kind of work. Perhaps when I found a place of my own, Priscilla and Steven could come to visit. Would he let them come?

As I entered the study, Matthews closed the doors.

He remained standing there for what seemed an eternity, silent, pensive, and tense as he watched me.

"Sit down, Kathleen." His voice had softened. I did as he instructed me and then waited again. He sat down opposite me, his eyes trying to catch mine.

Finally, I raised my head and looked at him. Frustration and anger were warring in his face and when he finally spoke, his frustration was the victor.

"Are you going to marry Michael now because of what I said last night?"

My face must not have shown the surprise his question gave me, for suddenly his expression showed something very near desperation.

"Kathleen, don't be a damn fool! You don't love him!"

"What made you think I was going to marry Michael?" I finally stammered.

"Then . . . am I to understand . . . you aren't?" he persisted.

"I'm not going to marry Michael. I'm not going to marry anyone."

"Well, thank God!" He leaned back heavily in his seat, suddenly relaxing as though that had been the cause of his tension. I could hardly believe that. The accusations, the insults, the mockery were still to come.

He saw me stiffen slightly in the chair as I prepared myself for the onslaught, and looked at me curiously. "You didn't listen to me last night."

"I listened," I mumbled, thinking that I could not stand to hear his cruel assumptions again.

"I'm sorry about what I said to you. I was raging mad," he said quietly, and I looked up with widening eyes. "That was what you didn't hear," he explained with a slow smile. "It was untrue and unfair . . . what I said."

My hands were still trembling from nervousness.

Then the tirade would not fall on me? He only wanted to apologize?

Of course, he did. He needed me to take care of Priscilla and Steven until Cybil came to the ranch permanently. He would even make this concession to soothe my hurt feelings.

Perhaps that was unfair, and untrue. Perhaps he was sorry for what he had said. But that could not, would not alter my decision to leave. I must leave Las Posas. I could not stay here any longer. Not when I was in love with him. Not when he even suspected for a moment that I might take anyone's feelings so lightly as he had first thought last night.

"I'm leaving Las Posas, Mr. Matthews. Today."

Clinton bolted forward. "Why? Because of what happened last night?" When I didn't answer, "Because of the things I said to you?" he pressed further.

"That and other reasons as well." My voice was so soft I was not sure he had heard me at all.

"What other reasons?" he asked. He was growing angry again. Why did he always have to be angry with me? I couldn't let it matter now. I couldn't let his dislike hurt me. "What other reasons?" he demanded again.

"I'd rather not . . ." I started, but stopped when Clinton's hand raised my chin and forced me to look at him.

"Look at me when you tell me," he commanded. "Now, what other reasons?"

I could feel the tears prickling my eyes, but stubbornly I held them back. "I'd rather not talk about it." He let me go, his hand dropping.

"I'm not going to accept that as an answer, Kathleen." He stood up and jammed his hands into his pockets. "You're going to have to explain to me."

"But I can't!" I cried out pleadingly, wishing he would just let me go and not torment me with questions I would never be able to answer without humiliating myself further.

"Does it have something to do with Michael?" he asked quietly, not looking at me. "Something to do with your earlier conversation with him?"

"No." I shook my head violently. Was he really so blind that he couldn't read my feelings for him? I was thankful at least for that. But he was ever speaking of my relationship with Michael. If nothing else, I wanted to salvage my pride by remembering that he would never know how I felt about him. I would never have to see the embarrassment in his face, the shock that I would feel such love for him.

"Then I don't understand," he said, and came back to sit down again. "It must have to do with what I said last night. It was a stupid thing to say, Kathleen, and I am sorry. But that's no reason for you to leave Las Posas."

He waited for my answer. It didn't come. What could I say to him?

"I thought you were happy here. Are you having difficulty with the children that you haven't mentioned before?"

"Oh, no!" I looked up at him and felt the tears prickling again. "I love the children!"

"Has someone on the ranch been bothering you?"

"No . . ."

"Then it is me, isn't it?" he pressed. "I've said and done something to hurt you . . . something other than last night."

He sounded unhappy and I looked up in surprise, my love for him shining unguarded for an instant. But luckily he was looking down at his hands.

"It's nothing you've done or said, Clinton," I answered. He looked up at me.

"Then tell me why you want to leave." His face lit up slightly and, looking away, I searched my mind

234

desperately for words that would satisfy him, yet protect me.

"I don't want to cause any more unhappiness," I answered truthfully. "Not to you, not to Michael, not to myself," I added silently.

"How are you causing unhappiness?" he asked, not satisfied.

"Michael isn't happy," I offered lamely.

"Oh, Michael . . ." A long-drawn-out silence fell between us.

"And you."

"Me?" He looked up again, confused.

"Miss James doesn't approve of my friendship with her brother. I'm sure that must upset you also. And I was the cause of a . . . disagreement last night between you and your fiancée," I went on quietly.

His face darkened in anger. "I told you once that Cybil and I are not betrothed. She is not my intended wife whatever she may say . . . and I have no, I repeat, no plans to marry her. Didn't you believe me?" he demanded hotly. "I don't happen to be in love with Cybil."

He waited before continuing and his voice dropped in uncertainty as he confided, "I'm in love with someone else."

My heart lurched. I could feel a sick pain in my chest. I didn't want to know whom he loved. What did it matter whether it was Cybil James, Rachel Hansen, or some other woman?

"I don't want to know!" I blurted out. He looked struck, and his eyes became bleak. "It doesn't matter . . . it's still the same," I went on, putting my hands over my face.

"What do you mean?"

"You're not trying to make this easy for me. I have to go away. Can't you just take my word for that? I can't stay here any longer. Can't you spare me some of my pride?" I pleaded for him to stop, able to take no more of his questions.

"I don't intend to make it easy. I want you to stay."

"You want me to stay?" I repeated, surprised and filled with a sudden surge of hope. I squelched it. "Oh . . . it won't take you long to find someone to instruct the children. And the next governess will find it as easy to love them as I have." I looked away so that he would not see the agony in my face. But I had not missed the suddenly intense expression that sprang into his eyes.

"What about me?" he asked gently, reaching across to take my hand.

"You?" My eyes flew to his, as I pulled my hand back.

"Yes, me," he repeated, giving a brief, deep-throated laugh.

"I don't understand . . ." I stammered, confused, not daring to believe what the words could mean if spoken to anyone else but me.

"You don't, do you?" He smiled then, and I felt my heart race as I recognized the look in his dark eyes. He pulled me to my feet as he stood up and his arms came around me in a tight embrace. His mouth came down over mine in a passionate, prolonged kiss.

My heart began to pound so violently that I thought I would faint. Finally, he raised his lips from mine, and leaned down to press his mouth to the hot, pulsing vein.

"You feel it too, Kathleen," he breathed, his voice strangely husky and deep. "Your heart is pounding almost as fast and hard as mine. You want me too, don't you?"

A wave of shamed exposure spread over me like a cold blanket. Pushing frantically against him, I felt the hurt and humiliation fill me as it had once before in this same room.

"Let me go!" He released me, looking down with surprise. The words welled up inside me, my anger at myself and at him for taking advantage of my feelings. "I thought you understood!" I cried out at him. "I thought you would at least respect my feelings."

The words almost choked me. "I am . . . illegitimate . . . Mr. Matthews. Do you know how that makes me feel . . . how it makes any child feel? I can't forget that . . . ever . . . ever, even if I wanted to . . . tried to with every ounce of my willpower. My mother died. My father didn't want me. He was ashamed of me and he cared so little for my mother that he . . ." My voice cracked, but I couldn't stop or control the flood of words that spilled from my heart. "He discarded me. She was *nothing* to him . . . *nothing* . . . but his mistress . . . a whore . . . with no feelings . . . no love . . . he didn't care a damn about her . . . or me, the aftermath of their affair."

"What do you think I'm—" Clinton tried to interrupt, reaching out to take me by the shoulders, but I dodged away from him as though he were Satan himself.

"What do you think I am?" I cried out, backing toward the door, feeling the hurt fury of rejection destroy my last thread of control.

"Kathleen, for God's sake, listen to me!"

"No! I will not listen to your mockery of my feelings anymore. Do you think I care so little for my self-respect that I could become . . . like my mother. That I would even consider a life like hers?" I dodged away from him again.

"Don't you touch me!" I screamed at him. "First you accuse me of leading Michael on. That is immoral, shameful . . . untrue! And now you offer me less than he ever did."

Turning, I started to run to the door, but he reached me. Grabbing me, he swung me around roughly and

237

pulled me into his arms again. I tried to push away from him, struggling in rage and frustration, but he held me tight. Slowly, my fury and bravado vanished and only the pain remained as I leaned against him too deeply hurt to even cry.

"Let me go," I pleaded. "Please . . ." I begged, as he lifted my face and held it between his hands. He kissed my lips gently, blotting out everything but my love for him. I couldn't bear to look at his face and see his triumph as I felt myself begin to respond against my will. Tears trickled unheeded down my cheeks.

"Clinton . . . please, let me go. Leave me something," I pleaded, tasting my tears as he kissed my wet cheeks and then my mouth.

His voice was rough with emotion when he finally spoke.

"You little fool," he said, making the words sound infinitely tender. I opened my eyes to look up at him. "I don't want you to be my mistress. I want you for my wife."

XIV

"Don't make fun of me!" I begged, staring up at him in disbelief. He smiled slightly and bent to kiss me again, but I pulled away from him. "Please . . . I can't bear you laughing at me." Clinton frowned.

"I love you," he answered simply, his eyes dark with emotion. "I have from the first." He didn't try to touch me again, but stood watching me as I moved slightly away from him. "You must have ignored your woman's intuition." He watched me retreat.

"I've frightened you again, haven't I?" He didn't move but his voice was touched with worry. "I did once before in this room when Michael told me he wanted to marry you." Clinton's face became withdrawn. "You're so incredibly naïve. I thought you would believe everything he would say to you. I was afraid he would hurt you. I almost went mad thinking of him putting his hands on you . . . making love to you like all his other conquests."

"But he never—"

"Not until last night . . . I know that now. He really is in love with you, Kathleen." His voice was harsh. "At first when he told me he wanted to marry you, I

239

thought he was just attracted to you . . . that he wanted you like all the others. So I tried to warn you about what he was like, and then . . . I acted the part of an animal myself." He looked at me, his eyes seeking understanding and sending a shiver of joy through me.

"I won't touch you again, Kathleen. But don't leave Las Posas."

I loved and wanted Clinton so much that I was afraid to believe that he could really love me in return. I stood motionless, staring at him with every trace of control scattering. And then finally I could speak:

"I couldn't bear to see you . . . and . . ."

"And?"

". . . and Cybil," I finished. "Every time I saw you last night, you were holding her. I couldn't bear to watch you love her . . . and know you thought of me with nothing but dislike and contempt."

His eyes suddenly blazed to life and he was next to me in two long strides. "It was mad, raging jealousy that made me say those idiotic things to you." He was so close to me I could hardly breathe for the longing I felt. He reached out to touch my cheek and then stopped himself, remembering the promise he had so recently made. "Say what you really mean, Kathleen. Tell me why you really wanted to leave." It was a plea for me to admit my love, to guard myself no longer from possible hurt, but willingly commit my feelings instead. Hadn't he? This wasn't my imagination. This was real and each moment I delayed tortured him further.

I looked up at him, touching his chest with the palm of my hand, feeling his heart pound faster. "I wanted to leave because . . . I love you, Clinton. Because I could not bear to watch you love someone else."

When he bent to kiss me, I reached up to him, clinging to him. Feeling my answer, he crushed me to him and kissed me until I thought we would never

240

have enough. I could feel him tremble, and knew that he felt the same passion for me that I did for him. After a long time, he held me away. He laughed suddenly, a pleasant, joy-filled laugh.

"We'll get married right away!" he announced, his eyes glowing and his voice strange. "Tomorrow morning!" He held my face again and pressed a kiss to my lips. "We'll go in and have Reverend Heath perform the ceremony. I'll send Jim in this afternoon to inform him of our plans." He kissed me again, and then pulled me against him before I could speak. His kiss was wildly passionate, drawing me out of myself until I felt a part of him.

When he stopped, I could hardly breathe. My face was flushed, my lips parted. My body ached with a strange longing I could not comprehend.

"Tomorrow?" My voice sounded strangely raspy, unsteady.

"I'd marry you now—this minute—if Heath were here," he said, and then added teasingly, his eyes taking on a sparkle, "I can't have you sleeping upstairs, all alone, so close at hand . . . knowing you love me. As it is, I'll be hard pressed not to come to you tonight." He grinned and I blushed, my heart racing again. Looking at me with that dark emotion flaring in his eyes, the emotion that drew me to him like a magnet, he said, "I love you, Kathleen."

When I didn't speak, he looked at me curiously. "What's the matter?"

"Nothing," I said quietly, dropping my eyes away from his. "It's just so sudden."

"Do you want to wait?" His bright mood dimmed.

"No . . . if you're sure you want me." I reached up and touched his face, hardly realizing that I did so. He turned his face against my palm and kissed it. His lightest touch made me sparkle inside. "I always thought you disliked me," I admitted.

"Never."

Then I asked the question every woman does when she finds she is loved. "When did you know you loved me?"

Clinton chuckled, drawing me tighter against him. "That hour on the hillside. And then again when I kissed you. I was mad . . . raging mad because you were pushing me too far already . . . and then Michael was the last straw. The minute I kissed you I knew I had to marry you. I wanted you to be mine. Up to that point I had dismissed any thoughts of you . . . and there were a lot of them. I thought about you when I was on the range after first meeting you. I kept seeing your eyes. But I told myself you were a child . . . too young, too untouched, the kind of girl a man doesn't make love to without marriage. I didn't want to get married just yet. But every time you turned your eyes on me . . ." My face was turned up to his and he bent to kiss me again, his lips warm and hungry. ". . . I wanted you."

He laughed again. "Once I considered seducing you," he informed me with a twinkle in his eyes.

"When was that" I asked, embarrassed yet pleased. I was not sure what the word meant but it sounded pleasant.

"The night you got drunk on my apricot brandy and let the blanket fall away from you," he teased. I gasped, my face flaming. He laughed heartily. "Oh, my love, if you only knew how you made me squirm."

"But I wasn't drunk . . ."

"You were, sweetheart," he disagreed.

"If I was a little . . . it was because you kept pressing it on me," I replied defensively.

"You'll have to get over that."

"What?"

"Your embarrassment. I'm hardly modest myself . . . and I have no intention of allowing my wife that

242

habit." He smiled at me, running his hand down over my back. "That pleased you, didn't it?"

"What . . . ?" I asked vaguely, my mind still on his last statement. What exactly did he mean?

"To know I wanted to seduce you."

"Why didn't you?" I asked with surprising boldness. I remembered only too well my own feelings of that night. If he had knocked at my door, I would have opened it to him and to all it would have meant.

"It was the way you talked about your parents. I didn't want you to think that was the way I wanted you. And you were too vulnerable after that experience."

I shuddered, thinking of the snake and shadowy intruder who had made a horror chamber of my room.

"I would have let you in," I admitted, pushing the other thoughts away.

"I knew that," he said seriously, running the back of his hand over my cheek. "You're so soft, Kathleen," he added with a note of wonder.

"How could you have known I would open my door to you and not have known that I loved you?"

"I can ask you that same question, Kathleen. You knew I wanted you, but every time I came close to you, you fled. And you would never hear me out."

"I love you so much, Clinton." I reached up to him again, and he leaned down to kiss me, urgently. I never wanted him to stop.

When he released me, he was trembling slightly. "God, what a long night is ahead of me," he muttered and moved away. Then he smiled. "If you look at me like that, I'll not wait for even one night." He looked away from me as though forcing his interest elsewhere, and after a moment he spoke again in a more natural voice.

"Let's go spread our news."

*   *   *

243

"I knew it would work!" Mabel said, smiling broadly as Clinton told her that we would be married within a day. He looked from her to me with confusion. I laughed with pure joy as Mabel explained her plan. "It was the yellow dress, of course."

"The yellow dress?" Clinton repeated, his face uncomprehending. "What are you talking about, Mabel?"

"I worked on that dress for days just so that you would look at this girl!"

He laughed. "Sorry to disappoint you . . . but I was already looking."

"I might have known," Mabel grinned. She looked at me, her eyes lighted with pleasure. "Kathleen can wear Clarissa's wedding gown, Clint. It's in the cedar box in the attic. I'll get it down and press it right away. It'll fit her perfectly." Her eyes twinkled brightly and then glinted with mischief as they rested on Clinton again. "You're not one to wait when you decide you want something, are you, lad?"

He grinned his response.

Slowly, the joy seeped through me as I began to accept what was happening. Clinton stood tall beside me, holding my hand tightly in his strong brown one. He really loves me, I thought with wonder. This is all really happening to me. All I have ever dreamt is taking place . . . now, in just the past hour.

Echoing Mabel, the children took full credit for bringing me to their uncle's attention. They related in humorous little sketches how they had contrived to do this. Clinton laughed with them as they told how they had often led me to the springs when one of them spied Michael riding over the knoll toward the ranch house. I, therefore, had missed several of his visits without even knowing it.

Steven in particular looked proud and satisfied.

"We were so afraid that you'd marry him before

Uncle Clinton would ask you," Priscilla said spontaneously. "I like Mr. James, but Steven doesn't. And I can't stand Miss James. And if he had not decided to marry you, Miss O'Reilly, who else would he have married but her. There is no one else around here that he likes. And if he had married her—ugh, that would have been awful!"

"Mr. James made me sick with all his lovey-dovey looks and the way he would lean over and talk to you," Steven added. Clinton listened, but didn't smile.

"Lovey-dovey?" he repeated, and then abruptly, "Well, friend Michael is now out of the picture." His voice was a little too curt and I looked at him with some surprise. Was he really still jealous of Michael?

"Are we going to have a big wedding, Uncle Clinton? With lots and lots of people, and a big cake and flowers and rice to throw and everything?" Priscilla asked excitedly. "Remember the cake and punch at Miss Tibbets' wedding last summer, Steven? And there was dancing, too, Uncle Clinton. Oh, will we have a wedding like that for Miss O'Reilly?"

Clinton frowned. "All that takes time, Priss. Too much time. I don't want to wait," he explained. I hoped that that was the whole reason he wished to marry me in a quiet, private wedding. Or could he be ashamed that he was to marry a servant in his household?

Stop it! I told myself. Don't always torture yourself with doubt. Isn't it just possible that he could really love you so much that he wanted to make you his wife right away? Isn't it possible that time is the only thing of which he is really thinking?

"You'll be our aunt!" Priscilla exclaimed suddenly, as though realizing it for the first time. The thought had not struck me, either. I smiled, pleased with the idea.

"What did you think she would be, dummy?" Steven

asked in a surprisingly mature tone and turned a radiant smile on me.

That afternoon Clinton left the house to work. He had sent Jim to inform Reverend Heath we would come in for the marriage ceremony the next morning, a Tuesday.

My head was buzzing from all that was going on around me. Mabel was working on Clarissa's gown. Mary Cramer was cutting and arranging flowers around the house. And the children were far too excited, as was I, to settle down to routine studies.

Mabel came up to my room after lunch, Clarissa's wedding gown in her arms.

"We'll try this on you and see if any alterations are needed," she explained, helping me to undress and slip into the white silk gown. After spending nearly half an hour buttoning the tiny loops over the pearl buttons, Mabel stood back to survey the fit.

"Well, we can take in a tuck or two at the waist, but I don't think we can do a thing about the snugness of the bustline. Just don't breathe too hard!" The long heavy silken train felt cumbersome. I did not want to look in the mirror and see the dress until tomorrow. Perhaps something would happen and this would all shatter like so many dreams I had had. Mabel's words broke into my thoughts.

"Well, let's get you out of it now and I'll make what alterations I can, have the dress repressed, and we're ready. I'll air it some more this afternoon. I can still smell cedar."

"Oh, Mabel . . ." I mumbled. "Everything is happening so fast . . . I'm afraid."

She didn't speak for a moment after my unexpected words. I wanted to ask her if she thought Clinton would be ashamed of me but I did not dare even voice the doubt. Speaking of my fears would somehow make them reality.

Walking across the room, she sat down next to me on the edge of the bed. "He loves you, Kathleen." When I made no reply, she went on: "He's not looked so happy in years."

"I'm . . . there's so much I don't know about him . . . and he'll find me so inadequate after Cybil," I said, trying to explain some of my doubts.

She patted my knee reassuringly. "You have nothing to fear, child." And then mistaking my apprehension, she went on bluntly, "Sex is very natural . . . and Clinton will be very gentle with you the first time."

I flushed with embarrassment. I had been referring to Cybil's social sophistication. She was from the same class as Clinton, while I was not. Cybil's sexual sophistication had not entered my mind and now Mabel's reassurance had raised other fears. Would I disappoint him as a woman? For I did not even know what would happen in the privacy of our bedroom. That part of my education had been totally ignored.

"You can believe me when I tell you that Clinton will much prefer to bed you than Cybil James," Mabel continued, seeing my mortification and fear. "He'll have the pleasure of teaching you the joys of the marriage bed. Now, forget those doubts of yours, Kathleen. Sometimes you're far too sensitive for your own good." And with that, my doubts, were dismissed, or so Mabel thought.

That night, I could not sleep. My mind was filled with bridal happiness and fear. And the opposing emotions warred with one another making sleep impossible.

Tomorrow I would become Mrs. Clinton Matthews! Kathleen Matthews! It sounded so wonderful.

"None of his friends will be there," the silent voice

247

in the back of my mind reminded me. "You'll be alone in the church with your joy—your marriage a secret among only those of Las Posas. Why?"

"What does it matter?" I argued. "Isn't it important that we love one another? Must others count so heavily in our lives."

"But will he lose his friends because of his marriage to you?"

"I will not disappoint him."

"He will think of Cybil, a full-blown woman, when the candle is extinguished and he pulls you into his arms. Will you know how to satisfy him as a man?"

I swung my face to the window, not wanting to continue the conflict between mind and heart.

A muffled sound in the hallway caught my attention. All my fears of the intruder of that night weeks before flooded back again. Quietly, I climbed from my bed, cringing at the creak of the springs as I lifted my weight clear. I tip-toed to the door, the wood floor cold and smooth. Pressing my ear against the door, I strained to hear what or who was on the other side. Something thumped heavily against the wall. I opened the door slowly so that there was only a crack through which I could peek out.

"Jim!" I exclaimed with relief, and his head spun around with a snap, reaching instantly for the rifle that lay across his lap. The chair on which he sat fell forward noisily, his surprise springing it away from the wall where he had leaned back.

"Christ! Ma'am! You aged me ten years!" His face relaxed and he grinned sheepishly.

"What are you doing in the hallway?"

"Tonight's my last night to look out for you. Clint said he'd have my job from tomorrow on," he explained, grinning even more broadly. I flushed slightly.

248

"I was pleased to hear the news, ma'am. You'll make him a fine wife."

"Thank you, Jim. But I still don't understand. No one has bothered me since . . . that incident."

"Nobody will either, ma'am, with me sitting here."

"But you haven't been here every night, have you?" I asked with surprise.

"Not me personal. But somebody has. And I've been staying in the house just to keep an eye on things." He was standing and leaning his shoulder against the wall as he spoke in his casual friendly voice, while I peeked only my head around the door. "Well, Clint got it all figured now anyway. His friend wired some information from New York. You've got nothing to be afraid of now."

"A friend in New York," I repeated, stunned. "Who?"

"Don't know the name . . . but he was contacted on the San Francisco trip."

"Oh."

What did it all mean? What had Clinton found out that gave him this assurance of my safety? And yet Jim was still guarding me? Why? I hadn't suspected that I was in any more danger and now the fear of that night was surrounding me like a malignant cloud. Who was Clinton's friend in New York? What had he found out? Was it someone there who wanted me dead?

My father?

Dear God in Heaven, was it my father?

Wasn't it enough that I was out of his life now? How had he found me? Anna Bowen?

"Good night, ma'am," Jim said as I slowly closed the door.

Suddenly, like a violent summer storm, all the fears of a lifetime poured down on me. My nightmare flashed through my mind, seeming more like a prophecy than imagination. How much of it was the horrifying fantasy of my tortured subconscious? How much of my nightmare was to be reality?

XV

My face peered back at me from the mirror, pale and drawn with exhaustion. The wedding gown was like a misty cloud of white encircling me, the lace veil about my face accentuating the wide, blue eyes that seemed larger and brighter from lack of sleep.

Mabel fluffed my skirts so that they draped gently around me.

"Clinton's mother made it herself," she informed me, admiring the gown. "You're beautiful, Kathleen!" Little tears beaded in her eyes as she looked at my face and quickly set to work arranging the veil over my face.

"Thank you, Mabel." My voice sounded hoarse and distant.

Mabel had flounced into the room early that morning, surprised to find me sitting in the rocking chair and staring into the garden. She had brought a silver tray loaded with covered dishes. One had a fluffy omelette, another held two slices of ham, and the last protected the fresh-oven-warm sweet roll. A red rose lay next to the small pot of steaming coffee with a brief note from Clinton.

"I love you! Hurry! C."

For a moment the numbing happiness of my wedding day obliterated the fears I had lived through the previous night. But still, I could hardly eat a morsel of the sumptuous breakfast Mabel presented.

Mabel and Mary carried in bucket after bucket of hot water for a lavender-scented bath. The young girl was flushed with excitement, her eyes sparkling brightly. I knew part of her pleasure was knowing Michael would now be free again. I hoped with all my heart that her dreams would be realized as mine had been.

"Come along, Kathleen. Clinton is chomping at the bit downstairs. He wants to get into Las Positas by ten-thirty this morning," Mabel said, pressing me as I still stood motionless, staring at the reflection in the mirror.

Was that really me? Did I really look like that? The exhaustion had disappeared from my face, a flush rising slightly in my cheeks as I thought of Clinton. My eyes were brilliant and a slight nervous smile touched my lips.

"Will anyone be going with us?" I asked.

"Well, Priscilla and Steven won't take no for an answer. But the rest of us will remain here. Mary is moving your things into the master bedroom. And I'll be working on your bridal dinner."

"I wish you were going with me." She patted my cheek affectionately in answer.

Clinton's eyes swept over me as I descended the stairs, my heart fluttering at the sight of him. Dressed in a dark suit, his rugged handsomeness and assured bearing made me feel even more shy. He continued to watch me and I tingled with his attentiveness. Not until I was standing in front of him did he speak.

"God! How beautiful you are, Kathleen," he said, his voice hushed and vibrant, his eyes sparkling like fire. He brushed the veil lightly with his fingertips. "I wish this were off your face." I felt a tremor of excitement run through me as I smiled up at him. "Let's go." He took my arm and steered me toward the door, taking a bouquet of red roses from behind his back and handing them to me without ceremony. "A bride can't be married without flowers in her hands."

Priscilla and Steven were waiting in the buggy at the front steps. As Clinton and I came down the stairs, they both stared, wordless. Finally, in what almost seemed a shy voice, Priscilla spoke:

"Ohhhhh . . . Miss O'Reilly."

"You might as well start calling her Aunt Kathleen, Priss."

"Aunt Kathleen," Priscilla corrected, smiling. Steven didn't say a word, but I could see his feelings as though they were written on his face.

We rode for several miles, silently. Then the children began to chatter. Though it was still early, the air was warming already, and I stared unseeing at the wild flowers on the hills around which we rode.

"Why are you so quiet, sweetheart?" Clinton asked, lowering his voice to a whisper and leaning against me.

"I'm happy," I whispered back. "I just can't believe this is really happening."

"It's happening," he said with a grin, his face crinkling slightly at the corners of his eyes. "You know, my father married my mother in much the same way I'm marrying you."

"Oh?" I turned curious eyes to his amused ones.

He laughed as he noticed the silence behind us, for the two children had stopped their talking and strained to hear the story also. He gave a quick snap of the reins, before beginning it.

"He was nearing thirty—like me—when a wagon train came through Las Positas headed south for Monterey. One of the scouts came by the ranch to buy a few head of cattle to replace those lost on the way or captured by Indians. He didn't need many because there were only a few wagons remaining in the train. My father agreed to supply a small herd for a good price and rode back to the train with the scout and a couple of ranch hands. That's when he saw my mother. He said she was beautiful. One look at her, he said, and he knew his bachelor days were numbered." Clinton smiled, looking out toward the hills and remembering his parents. "He claimed he carried her off that same day and married her."

"Oh, did he really do that?" Priscilla exclaimed, delighted with the romantic story.

"Evidently so, because my mother never disagreed with him. She'd smile at him across the room while he told the story. Sometimes I'd catch her looking at him and she'd wink."

"They must have been very happy," I said quietly, watching his expression sadden slightly.

"They were," he answered and then didn't speak for a moment. Finally he went on in a quieter voice: "When I was about sixteen, Mother got scarlet fever and died. I think that's when my father lost his will to live. Like my grandfather had after he lost my grandmother. While he was still alive, he used to talk to her by the hour as though she was still with him. When Grandmother died, everything that meant anything to him died with her." He paused for a moment and looked at me. "Matthews men love only once . . . and for a lifetime."

The tears nearly choked me as I felt such joy that I wanted to encircle the whole world. If only everyone could feel this.

Clinton's high spirits returned after his quiet words and he grinned roguishly at me.

"They all had something special between them. It'll be the same with us, Kathleen. All I needed was one look at you to get the fire going, but you wouldn't allow me to carry you off to the altar that easily."

I laughed at his teasing words. "You never hinted that was what you had in mind. You might have found me very willing."

"Would I?" he asked, raising his brow slightly, his grin cocking up high on one side. "It seemed to take some convincing."

Reverend Heath met us at the door of the church, his hand extended to Clinton in greeting. "Well, Clinton, I never thought I would be tying the knot for you." With anyone else but Cybil James, I added silently before I could keep the thought from coming. Reverend Heath glanced down at me as though he heard the words and he smiled. His thick cheeks dimpled slightly. "I wondered why the rush . . . but now seeing your beautiful bride, I understand."

Once inside the church, I hardly heard any word spoken. I repeated my vows almost mechanically. As Clinton's hands slipped the heavy gold band on my finger, they seemed the only thing real. I stood staring up at him when the ceremony was over, feeling strangely blank, wondrously numb.

"You may kiss your bride, Clinton," Reverend Heath reminded him with a hint of amusement.

Clinton lifted the veil and looked at me with those dark eyes, and my body flooded with life again.

"My wife," he uttered so softly only I could hear. And there was wonder in his voice. "My wife . . ." He bent slowly and kissed my lips with such gentle, awed tenderness that I could scarcely contain my joy.

We hardly spoke a word on the ride back to Las Posas.

I kept touching the thick gold band to reassure myself that this was not a dream. I was really Mrs. Clinton Matthews. Clinton would look down as I touched the ring and smile, his face aglow with happiness.

"I bought it in San Francisco," he informed me. "I wanted it especially thick and heavy to remind you who you belonged to." He took my hand, turning it over and kissing the palm.

Mabel met us on the front steps. I had never seen her so happy.

"Priscilla . . . Steven . . . you two can stay in the kitchen with us this evening," she informed them as they scampered up the steps full of excited chatter about the wedding. "You can tell Mary and me all about it later. For right now . . . scoot!" They hurried up and disappeared into the house.

Clinton lifted me down from the buggy, setting me on the ground close in front of him. Mabel's voice cut in on the magic of the moment: "As for you two, your wedding dinner will be ready as soon as you are."

"Yes . . . ma'am!" Clinton said, bowing and grinning up at the elderly woman commanding the moment.

"Kathleen, Mary is upstairs waiting for you. She'll help you get changed." Following her instructions, I went into the house and upstairs. Mary was waiting. The yellow dress was repaired and pressed, hanging ready for me. It brought back memories, some pleasant, some not. I wished that Mabel did not expect me to wear it. I would have preferred my ivory dress.

"Everything has been moved into Mr. Matthews' bedroom, Mrs. Matthews," Mary said, her voice dropping slightly. I smiled at my new title. She draped Clarissa's wedding dress over her arm while I stepped into the yellow dress.

Someone tapped very lightly on the door and I called for them to come in, expecting Mabel, or Priscilla.

From the mirror, I saw Clinton move into the room. Mary gave a little squeak and my eyes widened as she left the room, closing the door quietly behind her. I held the dress up, wondering how to button it, when Clinton walked over, surveying me from head to toe. My heart was racing nervously and yet with a trembling excitement.

"Turn around, darling. I'll do your dress for you." His fingers were almost as expert as Mary's as he looped the buttons. Then his arms came around me slowly, and I turned. When he bent to kiss me, I reached up and held onto him, feeling myself tremble in his arms. At my response, his kiss became more penetrating, more demanding, his hand moving down my back and over my hip as he pressed me hard against him.

Slowly he held me away from him, his eyes nearly black with passion.

"We'd better go down and have our wedding dinner, or Mabel will be up here demanding that we have the courtesy to wait at least an hour or two." He spoke slowly, thickly. He started to lean down to me again, but stopped. "We'd better go now," he said, smiling a little.

I hardly noticed what I was eating. I felt suddenly very shy with Clinton. The trembling expectation of the upstairs room was gone and I was suddenly afraid of what was expected of me later. His skillful fingers while buttoning my dress made me think now of his relationship with Cybil. Had he done that same service for her? How many times? And now he was married to me, and I knew nothing of what he would want of me.

Clinton filled my glass with champagne from the wine cellar, and my head felt light. I was aware of every movement he made, every look, every touch of his warm hand.

"Shall we go into the study for a little while?" he asked, understanding somehow my shyness. I nodded, grateful for his experience. He knew so much of women. And I knew nothing of men.

"You'll disappoint him," the silent voice started on me again. "He's used to headier brew than you will provide."

We sat on the couch together, his arm draped over the back, his fingers lightly touching my shoulder blade. "Would you like a glass of brandy?" he offered. "It relaxed you once before," he said with a twinkle of anticipation. I smiled with forced calm.

"Yes, I believe I would like some brandy," I answered, attempting to imitate his tone. I watched him walk across the room. He moved so easily, his shoulders moving in a graceful sway with each step. I became intensely conscious of every physical aspect of him. His broad back, narrow waist, long legs, and strong, long-fingered hands as they held the delicate glass and decanter, his hair that curled slightly over the back of his collar, and as he turned back to me, his dark eyes, and his mouth—his strong, yet sensuously smooth mouth. It was now curved in a half-smile as he looked over at me.

Frightened of my ignorance, shy of a man who would teach me the intimacies of our marriage bed, I watched him move across the room to me. My heart pounded in panic.

"You'll disappoint him," the silent voice repeated more loudly.

I dropped my eyes from his and sipped the brandy slowly, the warmth of the liquor having no effect on me. When Clinton took my hand and set my glass on the table, I shook.

"You're cold," he said, rubbing my hands and pulling me closer to him. My body grew taut in his embrace and he looked down at me with surprise. Suddenly, he gathered me in his arms and lifted me.

"We've waited too long," he said, looking into my

face. When we reached his bedroom, he pushed the door open with his shoulder and then closed it again behind us. My heart was speeding with fright and the blood drained from my face.

My fear burst from me. "I don't know what to do." My lips quivered with a mingling of emotions I couldn't even identify.

"You're not supposed to know, darling," he said with a quietness that soothed me slightly. "I'm going to show you." His mouth came down over mine in a tender kiss that sent flashes through my body. He kissed me until I began to relax against him, feeling the warmth loosen my taut muscles. He slid me down against his body until my feet touched the floor. My arms around him, clinging, and his kiss became demanding.

When he released me, I was breathless, my heart racing madly. My lips were still parted from his deep kiss and I looked up at him questioningly, wondering if this was what I had waited for. My body ached with heat and expectancy, but he did nothing.

Slowly, he took the pins from my hair until I felt it fall down my back. He lifted a curl, bending down to kiss me again. His fingers raked through the tresses, one hand holding the back of my head in the palm of his hand. With his other hand he undid the button loops until my dress hung loose. Then sliding his hands over my shoulders, he pushed the sleeves down my arms until the gown fell to the floor. With expert hands he removed my undergarments and pressed me against him again, stroking my back and hips, the feel of his clothes rough against my skin.

When he released me again, I watched him unbuckle his belt and pull it free. A bright flush rose to my cheeks and I swung around, closing my eyes, as he stripped his shirt off.

"You're beautiful," he breathed in a hoarse voice

as he turned me around again and looked slowly down over me I dared not open my eyes and look at him.

"Open your eyes, Kathleen. There's nothing to fear or be ashamed of about our bodies. God made us to enjoy one another . . . every curve a design of His own." He ran his hand down over my body. I opened my eyes, slowly looking up at him. He drew me against him again, his body warm and hard. My heart was pounding frantically as I felt his warm hands slide down over my shoulders and pull me even closer. He was so warm, I marveled, so comfortably, excitingly warm.

Gasping in surprise, I felt an unfamiliar rising eagerness of him. When I started to move away, he lifted me easily and moved across the room to the bed. He laid me down, sliding onto the bed beside me. He looked down at my body, catching my hand as it rose instinctively to shield myself from his eyes lest he be disappointed. He leaned down and kissed my shoulder, moving his lips down to the hard points of my breasts. I could not suppress a shudder of pleasure as his lips seemed to sear my flesh. He caressed me gently, slowly, exploring every inch of my body as if he had all the time in the world. I felt a growing hot tension building inside me as his practiced hands and mouth slowly moved over my body. His hand moved down and, feeling an aching I did not understand, I moaned, rolling on my side toward him. He drew me slowly against him, saying something unintelligible.

Then he slowly rolled me over onto my back, his knee parting my legs. I opened my eyes to see him above me, his face strained with what seemed pain, his eyes coal-black.

"Clinton . . . ?" My voice sounded strange to me, husky and breathless. I began to tremble in expectation, my lips parting as his mouth came down to cover mine, his tongue touching. He moved slightly

260

away, his hands tilting my hips up toward him. And then a quick sharp pain burned between my loins. I arched up hard, crying out more in surprise than pain. He stopped, his body trembling, his muscles taut. His eyes were closed tight and his breathing seemed labored.

"I love you," I breathed. "It doesn't hurt now." I reached up and touched him, no longer shy, running my hands over his chest and down to his stomach, every contact with him like a pulsing heartbeat. His body seemed to glisten in the candlelight, hot gold. His breath caught as I touched him and he leaned down to kiss me deeply, desperately. Slowly at first, and then more urgently, he began to move, his weight pressing me down into the bed. My body grew hot and tense and I clung to him until I felt a rising wave of shuddering feeling spread through me as I arched up against him, my body creating a rhythm of movement by its own power.

"Oh, Christ . . . Kathleen," Clinton groaned, burying his face in my hair. I felt him rise and press himself even deeper inside me.

Later, I still felt the wonderful, hot pressure of his body against mine.

"I love you . . . I love you," he murmured hoarsely, nuzzling my neck and turning sideways while still holding me tigthly against him. "You're not going to get much sleep tonight, Mrs. Matthews," he said huskily, kissing me again.

Holding him, I felt his reawakening desire make my body begin to tremble in response once more.

XVI

Two days after Clinton and I were married, Michael came to the ranch to call on me. Cybil accompanied him with the hope of making peace with Clinton.

The children and I were sitting in the garden. Priscilla sat frowning with concentration over her cursive writing, while Steven asked me questions about his addition problems. Suddenly, Mary burst through the doors and hurried into the garden. I knew by her face who had arrived, for her eyes sparkled with excitement and her voice was a little breathless as she spoke:

"Mrs. Matthews . . . Michael . . . and Miss James have just ridden into the drive."

Sudden panic and confusion rendered me immobile. I had up to now forgotten Michael's promised visit. Now I must face him, and Cybil as well, with the announcement that Clinton and I were man and wife.

How was I to tell them of our sudden and unexpected marriage? I expected Michael to be shocked and hurt . . . but Cybil? What would her reaction be? Violent, I was sure. And I would be her only target.

"Children, stay here and go on with your lessons.

When you are finished, you may play," I said gently, surprised to find my voice calm though my heart and mind were throbbing furiously. My head began to ache for tension and fear of what I was about to face within the house. I had the desire to run away again, but knew that would only postpone the inevitable confrontation.

I rose from the bench and followed Mary, words of explanation rolling over and over in my mind, only to be discarded as I tried to think of those more appropriate, less shocking, less hurting.

As I came through the double doors of the sitting room and approached the hallway, I heard, with sudden foreboding, Mabel's voice: "Good morning, Miss James . . . Michael." She sounded a little too polite.

"Well, Mrs. Banks," Cybil cooed. "I didn't know you had condescended to acknowledging my existence."

Please, Mabel, I thought desperately, praying my words would somehow transmit themselves to her. Don't tell them yet!

"I'll tell Mrs. Matthews she has guests!" Mabel's voice said, almost casually, and my heart pounded with suffocating terror.

Mary disappeared from my side as I stood in the doorway looking into the entrance hall where Mabel, Cybil, and Michael stood staring at one another. Mabel had a triumphant gleam in her eyes as she looked directly at Cybil. Cybil glared at her in disbelief, an unpleasant, almost violent sneer on her face.

"You old witch! What are you talking about?"

Michael had seen me from the corner of his eye and was looking across the foyer at me. His face, still badly bruised, was blank and whitened with shock.

"Mrs. Matthews, you have guests," Mabel said, giving me a proud smile. "Shall I serve refreshments in the sitting room?"

At least she was not going to desert me as Mary had so quickly done at first sign of a scene.

"Yes, Mabel, that would be fine," I answered her quietly. She turned and disappeared down the hallway to the kitchen.

The blood drained from my face as I met Cybil's eyes smoldering with hatred and smashed hopes.

"Shall we talk in the sitting room?" I asked, and gestured toward the double doors.

"I know where it is, Miss O'Reilly." Cybil pushed past me and into the room. I followed, feeling Michael's eyes reaching out to me with a pain I could not bear to see. Then suddenly, he spoke, his voice choked with emotion.

"Kathleen? What's this all about?" He took two long strides across the room, where I stood silently facing him. "For Christ's sake, is it really true?" He grabbed my left hand and raised it to stare at the heavy gold band encircling my finger. Dropping my hand, he shut his eyes.

"We were married two days ago," I answered softly, searching his face for some sign of how I could best make the announcement easier for him. When he opened his eyes they stared back at me with anguish. I could feel Cybil watching us, her eyes glittering. As we entered the sitting room, she closed the doors behind us. I felt the guest in Clinton's home and Cybil the mistress.

For a long silent moment, I stood in the room feeling both pairs of eyes on me—one hating, the other agonized. I could not speak.

"Did you know, Miss O'Reilly, that Clinton and I have been lovers for a number of years. No, I can see by your face you did not." She watched my face, hers changing subtly as she smiled slightly. "I pity you, you little fool. You must know that he will never really love you. He loves me and has for years. The only reason we haven't married is because I have repeatedly postponed the date. We argued about it just the other night, as a matter of fact. He was raging jealous because I danced with Tom Whittaker. He is always possessive about me. Did he tell you we had fought?" Her voice was calm, but filled with scorn. Then her attitude changed. She shook her head, tears glistening in her cold, blue eyes. She raised her lashes and watched me.

Clinton loved me, I told myself. I must remember that and believe it. Clinton would surely not lie. But as I looked at Cybil's beautiful face and body, I wondered. When my own father discarded me, was it possible a young man would love me?

I looked at Michael, experiencing a sick feeling in the pit of my stomach. Where was my joy of a few short hours ago? I wished desperately for Clinton's presence, the reassurance his look of love would give me. But Clinton was not there and I was alone.

"I don't understand," Michael was saying. "I just don't understand why you did it." He gripped my shoulders, searching my face. "How could you marry him when you knew I loved you so much?"

The door opened suddenly and I jumped, looking up in hope that Clinton would be there. Mabel entered with a tray of refreshments. She lookeed at me for a moment and then glanced between Cybil and Michael.

"Thank you, Mabel," I murmured, smiling at her. There was nothing she could do to help me. This was a situation I must handle myself.

"You may leave now, Mrs. Banks," Cybil ordered curtly, glaring at the woman malevolently. Mabel stood her ground. She looked at me and I nodded. She left the room, closing the door softly behind her. When Cybil looked at me, I was shocked by the fury in her eyes. I felt a shiver of fear run through me.

"Why didn't you tell me there was something between you and Clinton?" Michael asked in a low voice, his eyes penetrating.

"Michael, it all happened so suddenly," I started lamely.

"You're not going to tell me that he wasn't making love to you all the time," he said, his face losing its blank expression and darkening. He shook his head in disbelief.

"He never made love to me. He never said anything to make me guess that he loved me . . . until the day after the fiesta. Please try to understand, Michael. I couldn't love you because I was already in love with Clinton."

"Why didn't you just tell me that. Why did you let me think there might be a chance for me?" he demanded unfairly and took my shoulders again. I could feel his fingers biting into my flesh in desperation. Cybil's voice broke in with impatience.

"Michael, you're making a fool of yourself," she told him quietly. "She played for you and Clinton and she took the richer prize."

"No!" I cried back at her. "That isn't true!"

"Look at her face, Michael. Just look at her face." Something cold and speculative flickered in her eyes.

"Why don't you shut your mouth, sister?" Michael growled at her, his eyes blazing warningly as he moved toward her. Her eyes widened slightly in surprise at the intense expression twisting her brother's handsome face. "I'll kill you if I ever hear you say anything against Kathleen. Do you understand me?"

Cybil's courage returned. "I'll make allowances for your behavior, Michael. But I have more right than you to be upset. Clinton and I would have been married this fall. I pity us all," she went on, and her cold eyes filled with surprising tears. Michael looked at her with a curious expression.

"Miss O'Reilly may have married Clinton," Cybil sniffed, "but she will never have his love." She shook her head regretfully as though struggling for control.

She held out her hands in a heartrending gesture. "Perhaps he does desire her." Her eyes flickered again, growing chill beneath the veiling of tears, "but he can't love her. He is a man who loves only once and he loves me. Everyone in the valley knows that."

My self-assurance began to crumble under her calm onslaught. I remembered Clinton saying he would love only once. He had said he loved me, I told myself, trying to take strength in the short time we had shared. But if he loved me, why had he wanted so quiet a wedding? Why had he not invited any of his friends? Was his reason for wanting to protect me true? Protect me from what? Or was his real reason that he was ashamed to be marrying a foundling, a child even her father would not want or claim?

"Kathleen, are you in love with Clinton?" Michael asked quietly. I met his eyes. Was Michael even beginning to suspect my reasons for marrying Clinton?

"Yes. I thought it was hopeless. He never showed me how he felt."

"Because he really felt nothing but desire," Cybil said quietly, but her words were firm and direct. I swallowed convulsively, clinging to my belief in my husband.

"I tried to explain as much as I could when I asked you to stop seeing me," I went on, trying to shut out the image of Cybil. So beautiful she was. And Clinton had made love to her. He had been linked with her for several years, carried a love for her since they were children. My confidence was crumbling. Perhaps if I had been loved as a child I would have believed more in myself. But betrayals began to flicker in my memory. Miss Montgomery and her caring, and then the shock of finding out her caring had a price. My father. No. I would not think of my father.

"I was going to leave the ranch," I went on.

"I don't believe that, Miss O'Reilly," Cybil put in. "I believe that you brought about this whole sorry mess

267

with your cry of rape the night of the fiesta. You led my brother out on that hillside knowing he loved you and then cried rape so that Clinton would feel the great knight rescuing the poor, helpless maiden. A man can't resist that ploy, can he? Not even a man as intelligent as Clinton. He would be flattered and taken in by your defenselessness. For a while. Then it will bore him. He wants a woman, Miss O'Reilly. He needs a woman . . . not a little girl with tremors of fear for everything that surrounds her."

Cybil's eyes were sparkling as she watched my face gradually lose its color. I could hear horses riding into the ranch yard and heading for the corral. Cybil and Michael heard also.

"This marriage has been a tragic mistake for all of us," Cybil said, moving toward the door. "I'm going to talk with Clinton. Something must be done before nothing can be salvaged."

I started after her, but Michael caught my arm. "Kathleen . . . oh, God, Kathleen, why?" His voice was a whisper. "I could have given you so much love." Cybil was gone, and a sudden nauseating fear attacked me. I must stop her.

"Let me go, Michael. Please." My voice was shaking. I pulled away and started for the door. The afternoon sunlight nearly blinded me as I hurried across the front yard toward the stables. I saw the ranch hands, but Clinton was not among them. Cybil was not in sight. I was afraid of what she might say to him, what doubts she might plant in his mind about my love. Our love was so new, so untried.

As I came around the corner and started into the stables, I stopped, frozen. Cybil was standing in front of Clinton, her hand stroking his arm. He was listening to her intently. He said something low and Cybil moved closer, her arms encircling his neck. His hands went to her arms gripping her and she drew his head down, kissing him with desperate ardor.

I must have uttered a cry, for they were suddenly apart, staring at me. Clinton moved first, but Sybil's hand reached out and clung to his arm tenaciously.

"It's better that she knows now," she said, and there was a gleam of triumph in her brilliant blue eyes.

I turned blindly and ran. My hand pressed over my mouth to stifle the anguished sobs I felt tearing me inside. I heard someone laugh in the stables.

Someone was coming after me, a man's heavy footsteps hurrying across the yard. I was beneath the trees beyond the corral. I prayed it was Clinton. My heart pounded and I controlled my tears, the pain in my throat tight and agonizing. If it was my husband, I would know he cared. I would cling to any explanation he could give me for the scene I had just witnessed.

It was Michael who put his hand on my arm and pulled me around and against him, filling me with almost uncontrollable despair. Clinton had remained with Cybil. What I felt did not matter to him. What mattered now was a way out of a dreadful mistake he had made. What mattered more was Cybil and soothing her hurt. Was he kissing her now? Holding her? Cursing his rash marriage?

My body heaved with anguish. Michael's arms tightened and I felt his hand stroking my hair like he would a hurt, rejected child.

"Hush, darling. We'll find a way out of this tangle," he whispered, kissing my head. "I love you, Kathleen. I love you so much."

I put my hands against Michael's broad chest, pushing him away. I could not allow him to touch me. I still loved Clinton. It did not matter that Clinton loved Cybil.

Michael held my face, brushing the tears away gently. "I'll take you away . . . you won't have to see him

269

again." He was looking at me, his face charged with hope. "I'll take care of you. Oh, Kathleen, come away with me, now, this minute. I'll love you until you forget Clinton Matthews was ever born."

I felt suffocated with grief. I wanted to tell Michael that nothing was changed. Because Clinton loved Cybil did not mean that I could so easily turn my love to Michael.

"Michael . . ." My voice was choked, my eyes blurred with tears. He grasped my hands, pressing each with a fervent kiss.

"Get your goddam hands off my wife!" Clinton shouted. Michael swung around, dropping my hands like red-hot coals. His back stiffened for a fight as he saw Clinton take long, angry strides across the grass toward us. My husband glared at me with such fury that I started, stepping away from him as he reached us. All the emotion suddenly died inside me and left a numb shock. Hate? Was that what I saw now in his face?

Clinton turned toward Michael again. "Your sister is waiting for you in the carriage. Now get out!"

"Not until you explain a few things to me!" Michael tossed back in challenge.

"I don't have to explain a damned thing to anyone . . . not you . . . not Cybil! Now get out before I break your neck!" Caution gone, fury making him oblivious to the threat, Michael did not flinch.

"You selfish bastard!" he spat out. "I could understand your loving Kathleen, Clint. God knows how much I love her. But why the hell couldn't you have waited a few weeks! Couldn't you have given her a decent wedding so there wouldn't be scandal?"

"Scandal! What kind of scandal are you talking about?"

"You know damned well what will be said. And you let it happen! You know how the valley gossips will

270

tear Kathleen to pieces." Michael's voice kept rising and Clinton stood motionless under his assault. "You were the one to remind me of protecting Kathleen's reputation, remember? You goddam selfish bastard!" His voice was deep, and biting with unsuppressed jealous rage.

"If she had said yes to you, would you have waited, Michael?" came the cool reply, a sneer twisting Clinton's handsome face. But something in his eyes showed an instant of doubt.

"Yes, by God, if Kathleen had wanted a beautiful wedding, I would have waited."

"I thought you of all people would understand what it means to desire Kathleen," Clinton said softly.

Desire. The word was like a slap across my face. Michael's face went red and he opened his mouth to speak. I put my hand on his arm. Clinton's eyes were black.

"I think enough has been said." I looked between the two men, schooling my voice to calmness. "You mustn't blame Clinton, Michael. I should have waited. I know that now." My voice was a monotone, drained of feeling as I looked at them both staring at me. I caught something like the pain in Clinton's eyes. I tried to smile at him, understanding his regret.

"I'm sorry." I turned away from both and left them in the shadow of the grove.

It seemed like hours that I lay crying in my old room. I tried to think what was best to do. What a dreadful mess I had made of Clinton's life and my own. If I left the ranch he could find his happiness again with Cybil. Michael would be better off also. But where could I go?

A sudden crash startled me and I swung around to see Clinton standing in the doorway, his face black with rage. He stepped into the room and slammed the door so violently I thought it would crack and splinter.

"What are you doing up here? I've been looking all over the ranch for you!"

"I'm sorry," I apologized. "I needed to be alone for a while."

"What for?"

"To think things over," I answered vaguely. Clinton's eyes narrowed, an angry tic in his cheek.

"What did you need to think over?" I could not trust my voice to answer so I spread my hands inexpressively. His control seemed to snap. "Damn you! What did you need to think over?" He reached the bed and grabbed me by the wrists, dragging me up in front of him so roughly I was frightened of him.

"Are you making plans to run away with Michael?" Some strange violence seemed to be driving him.

"Clinton . . ."

"You do and I'll kill you both. I swear it!" His fingers dug into my wrists and I winced from the pain.

"I would never go away with Michael," I finally gasped. I looked away from Clinton's face toward the windows to the garden. I remembered how he had kissed me. He had wanted me, but he loved Cybil. Just as my father had desired my mother, but loved his wife. I shut my eyes. Clinton's hands loosened and I felt his fingers kneading the bruised flesh of my wrists.

"I didn't mean to hurt you," he said quietly. I looked up at him and wanted to cry, but knew I must not let myself.

"I know." I took a deep, shuddering breath before I went on. "I think it would be best if I left the ranch as soon as possible."

Clinton's face went white, his mouth set in a hard line.

"You're not going anywhere! You're my wife."

"Cybil should be your wife."

A silence followed my words, an ominous, chilling silence.

"Why do you say that? Because of what you believe you saw in the stables?"

"That and the things that were told to me . . . things I suspected before but didn't want to believe."

Clinton's hands pushed the hair back from my shoulders. "I didn't expect you to lose your faith in me so easily, Kathleen. I gave you my word in the church. Have you forgotten so easily?"

"And Cybil? Did you give her your word also?"

"I never loved her. I took her body, yes. She offered it to me when I was sixteen— But love her . . . never. And she knew it. Our affair ended long before you appeared . . . though she wouldn't accept that fact."

"Then why were you kissing her?"

"I wasn't kissing her. She was kissing me. She knew you were there in the doorway. She did it to hurt you, to make you doubt me, to make you turn to Michael." His voice grew harsh as he accused, "You did that soon enough."

"You didn't seem to object to her kissing you." I could not keep the words from coming.

Clinton stared at me, the angry tic appearing in his cheek again. "Did you see me pulling her into my arms like this?" he demanded, yanking me forward against him. "Did I bend to her like this?" His mouth came down cruelly on mine, forcing my lips open under his assaulting kiss. When he stopped his eyes were misted, still angry, but filled with pain. The blood was pounding in my temples, my hair messed.

"Who do you love, Kathleen? Me? Or Michael James?" The question seemed to tear from him.

"I love you, Clinton."

"And who will you run to when you hurt inside? Me? Or Michael? Who will you believe when you're told 'I love you'? Me? Or Michael?" His fingers were

273

in my hair again, pulling my face closer to his, though his eyes were still hot with slowly expiring anger. My lips quivered slightly as I tried to answer.

"Clinton . . ."

"I tell you now . . . I love you . . . I vow you my life . . . I'll give you my children." His voice was bitter. His eyes searched mine, frustrated, glistening. "Will you throw that all back at me because of what a woman like Cybil insinuates?"

I shook my head. "No."

"Do you think I could kiss any other woman the way I kiss you . . . feel what I feel for you? My God, Kathleen, how can you?"

I reached up to his face, touching his lips, imploring his forgiveness for my lack of faith. "Love me, Clinton." He lifted me, kissing me fiercely, punishing. Moving to the bed, he leaned down over me, and when he kissed me again, it was different: still passionate, demanding, but with tenderness, too. When he looked at me, I felt a sudden onrush of happiness.

"I loved you the minute I saw you," he murmured. "I love you now. Shall I prove it to you?" He gave a little laugh at my rise in color. "Or shall I merely tell you?" He leaned down, taunting me with a kiss. "Well, what do you say, my woman of little faith?"

"Prove it to me," I breathed, drawing him down.

Later, when we dressed and readied ourselves to leave the room, I straightened the bed.

"What are you doing, Kathleen?" Clinton asked, an amused gleam in his eyes as he buttoned his shirt.

"I don't want Mabel or Mary finding the bed that way. What would they think?" I answered, flushing as I pulled the coverlet straight and fluffed the pillows. Clinton threw back his head and laughed.

"Shhhh." I pleaded. Then smiling at his expression, I ran to him and hugged him with overflowing love. He pressed me against him.

"Oh, sorry. They might hear," he chuckled. His eyes twinkled as he scooped me up into his arms and kissed me again. "Next time I'll roll you in the hay so there won't be any beds to make." He put me down, still laughing, and patted me possessively on the bottom as I moved toward the door.

I thought my doubts had been resolved, but I had not reckoned with my own inner fears, my own lack of self-assurance. While I believed Clinton, I feared Cybil. She was so beautiful, intelligent, determined. I admonished myself for my childish insecurities, yet I walked in constant fear of the woman who had been Clinton's mistress.

Time would be the only healer. And until enough had passed, I vowed to control my apprehensions so that no one but I would know they even existed.

XVII

During the next few weeks my doubts concerning Clinton's love for me diminished. The jealousy and suspicions about his feelings for Cybil receded, but my fear of Cybil and her hold on him still haunted me when he was gone. Try as I might, she still remained in my mind, not foremost but still lurking like a waiting presence that, with time, might again have her opportunity to destroy our trust in one another.

Each time Clinton looked at me, I convinced myself that he loved me. That he felt nothing for Cybil James. But still, I remembered, with pain, that he had held her in his arms, kissed her, made love to her. She was so exquisitively beautiful, so voluptuous and seductive. How could he forget and not yearn for such a woman again? Did he still desire her? Did he ever regret our marriage, wishing he could once more be with Cybil, hold her against him and feel her hot, familiar response?

Then I would look again at my husband, sitting across from me during dinner, meeting me in the garden, waking me in the morning, and all I could see was that he did love me now. He seemed happier when we were together, his reticence gone. He responded more easily to the children's shows of affection, sometimes lifting Prissy for a spontaneous hug and kiss, which both surprised and delighted her. He spent more time talking with Steven during dinner and playing chess in the study afterward.

And he laughed often. The hard lines in his face seemed to soften and his eyes crinkled often with amusement, many times at my expense.

Even the children had changed. Steven's serious questions and comments often brought a smile to both of us. However, Clinton always listened with interest and then spoke to his nephew with an adult consideration. Sometimes the young boy would make observations that astonished and pleased his uncle. But Steven had also learned to enjoy his childhood. He laughed and played games, joining in the rollicking fun that Priscilla offered. And Priscilla became more compassionate toward her younger brother, still teasing but always careful not to call attention to his shyness. She often offered to help Mabel and me in our household duties, and took an interest in the responsibilities that were given her.

Clinton changed even more when it came to me. I seldom saw the scowl that had seemed almost habitual before our marriage. And now when he raised his brow at me, it usually warned of a burst of amused laughter. It seemed every time we saw each other, as he came in from work, a chance meeting while riding, checking on the children in the afternoon, he would draw me into his arms and kiss me.

How I loved him, I would say to myself every time I saw his tall, proud figure coming toward me.

At night when we were alone in our bedroom, the worries and responsibilities of the day peeled away, all my doubts disappeared. Often in these moments I found myself looking at Clinton and wondering that I

277

had ever thought him cold, hard, unfeeling. I wondered if the angry façade he had so often presented had been only protection for the sensitive man beneath. He had lost so much in so short a time. His mother, father, sister, and brother-in-law, all within a ten-year period. And the responsibilities of the ranch and rearing of two young children had fallen on his shoulders.

Now, he seemed to welcome that demanding responsibility. It was building him each day into a stronger, more assured person. And now he was warm, giving, open. He would spend hours lying beside me in the faint candlelight, drawing out all my feelings, telling me his plans and his dreams about our life together.

Sometimes I would awaken in the early hours of morning, the sun not yet up. I would lie there waiting for first light, listening to his steady, relaxed breathing. As the sun would peek over the hills and a faint, fairy light entered the room, I would study his face against the pillow. I was always surprised at his vulnerable, unprotected expression, his dark hair mussed and falling over his forehead like a small boy's, his face smooth, young, and carefree, his assurance and control gone.

I could never resist kissing him. He would awaken slowly, his eyes opening but not quite seeing through the fog of sleep. Then he would smile, the lines around his eyes crinkling. All the vulnerability and boyishness would disappear as he came awake, and he was again the man of strength, assurance, control, passion. Reaching up, he would wind his fingers in my long, free hair and pull me down to him, until our lips met. And we were frequently late getting out of bed.

Clinton's slightest touch or look made me happy almost beyond belief. His kiss could wipe away my doubts, my fears of him, though not always could I forget my self-doubts. He loved me . . . now. Would he always love me? Would I always be enough for him?

I could not imagine my life without him. He seemed always to have been a part of me. Sometimes the fear of losing him terrified me.

Slowly, day by day, week by week, the fears of Cybil diminished until they were almost gone. I had only my own inadequacies and weaknesses to conquer.

Then Michael came again.

Mabel announced him late one afternoon when Clinton had come back early from riding fence with Jim Calhoun. We were sitting in the study, Clinton in the big leather chair, me on his lap. I had tried to jump off at Mabel's footsteps in the hallway, but Clinton had just chuckled and held me tight.

"Clinton, Michael James is here to see . . . you and Kathleen." I could tell by her hesitation and the guarded look toward me that Michael had asked to see me alone. Clinton's cool reserve, which had so often bewildered me upon first meeting him, suddenly reappeared.

Why had Michael come? Why should he want to come after what had been said during his last visit? Surely he did not want to spoil my newfound happiness, my only happiness. A sudden uneasiness and suspicion flooded me.

"Tell him to go on into the sitting room, Mabel," Clinton said with unconcealed irritation. "We'll meet him there."

When Michael approached us as we entered the room, Clinton and he shook hands with an indifferent politeness that bordered on sarcasm. Michael smiled and then turned to me, even as my husband's face darkened with his guest's obvious attentions.

"Tell me, Michael. What brings you to Las Posas?" Clinton demanded, putting one arm around my shoulders and drawing me closer to him, as though to leave no doubt as to whom I belonged.

"I came to make sure that Kathleen is happy,"

Michael answered with frankness, his voice more cool that Clinton's. Then he smiled, his old friendly smile.

"Does she appear to be unhappy to you?" Clinton asked, tilting his head slightly. His voice had changed to a more casual tone.

"No."

"You don't sound particularly pleased with your observation."

Michael gave a laugh. "I would be a hypocrite to say I was." He looked at me with a warm, admiring smile as he continued. "I warn you, Clinton, should she ever become unhappy due to you, I will consider the door open to resume my interrupted courtship. I would not hesitate to steal her from under your nose if I could." Though he spoke in a teasing manner, I thought his tone held an edge of seriousness too. I recognized a certain sparkle in his eyes as they rested on me for a moment. I fully expected Clinton to throw him bodily from our home. However, to my surprise, Clinton's brooding manner was gone and only a warm camaraderie twinkled in his brown eyes as he surveyed Michael before answering:

"I'm sure you would not hesitate, Mike. But I don't plan to do anything to make my wife's affections wane for even an instant." My muscles relaxed and I smiled up at him and then at Michael. We sat and enjoyed a cup of coffee and some snacks prepared by Mabel. Clinton and Michael talked of ranching, exchanging news of the Las Positas area.

"Cybil is seeing quite a lot of Tom Whittaker now," Michael reported, and my heart slowed with dread. Why did he have to mention Cybil? Didn't he know how the fear of her tortured me sometimes?

"Really?" Clinton said without much interest. "Do you think it's serious?" I heard a hint of laughter in his voice.

"I think she's only trying to make you jealous and

sorry you jilted her. She expects you to return her affections before too long. She underestimates the charms of your wife." Michael smiled and turned to look at me. Clinton watched him and for a moment I thought he would say something. He remained silent, brooding.

The conversation then returned abruptly to business. I worked on my embroidery, listening with interest to the observations they shared on the marketing difficulties with which both were faced.

"Monte's even considered getting out and going East," Michael said of his father. "Cybil is considering the idea herself. She says she's tired of Las Positas, but I think she has Europe more in mind than the East Coast."

"Really? With Tom Whittaker dangling at her heels?"

"You'll have to talk with her about it, Clint," Michael said, and I saw an unpleasant smirk light his face. The room became still and I could feel the challenging emotions surge between the two men. "She might even be brought around to selling her share of the ranch to you . . . as a wedding present."

"And your father?"

"You'll have to make a trip over to the ranch and find out." Michael shrugged. He was becoming very uncommunicative all of a sudden and I wondered if he had come for his sister, in hope of digging a chasm of doubt between Clinton and me. Michael knew very well my fears and he was evidently going to use them if he could.

"I'd better get back," Michael said after a moment. "Would you trust your charming wife to walk me to the door?" he asked lightly, standing. I saw Clinton's eyes cool. his mouth tighten slightly. Did he suspect the same thing I did? Or more?

Michael turned to me. I looked at Clinton, feeling in the middle of the challenge now. Clinton could not refuse without saying he did not trust me, and Michael

281

knew it. Before I could say anything, Michael took my arm and walked me to the front door. Clinton leaned against the doorjamb of the sitting room, watching us. Michael grinned back at him and then turned to me. To antagonize Clinton, he bent and kissed my hand a little longer than necessary. Then, speaking in a low whisper which Clinton could not possibly have overheard, he said, "Should you ever be in need of a friend, remember I'll be there . . . always. I love you. Remember that."

"I have Clinton, Michael."

"You never can tell, darling. Just remember, I am always near you . . . and waiting." He closed the door quietly as he left.

I turned to Clinton. He looked at me for a long time, as though reading my expression. Doubt lurked in his face, a silent question passing between us. He turned abruptly and re-entered the study. I followed, feeling confused and rebuked. He sat in a leather chair, perplexed.

"What is it, Clinton?" I asked, dropping onto my knees before him and putting my hands over his. I looked up into his face as he considered me.

"What was he saying to you?" He frowned. "I do trust you, Kathleen. But I don't trust Michael in the least."

"He said he was still my friend and that he would always be near if I needed him." Clinton cupped my chin in his hands and raised it to meet his kiss.

"He'd like to see us unhappy," he commented, his eyes studying mine intensely. "He's still in love with you. He'd like you to doubt me, to make you think that I want Cybil."

I smiled a little tremulously and his fingers tightened. "Did he do what he planned, Kathleen? Do you doubt me now?"

"No, darling," I said. "Only you yourself could make me do that."

"Or you . . . Sometimes I can see doubts in your face. Your face shows everything, Kathleen. You still wonder sometimes whether I ever think of Cybil."

"Do you?" I couldn't help asking.

"Of course. But not as you think I do." He lifted me into his lap and kissed me, the kiss he usually reserved for the privacy of our bedroom. Then he held me cradled against him, running his fingers through my hair.

"Darling," he said and then paused, searching for words. "I have to go to the James ranch." His words shattered the magic of the moment, and he felt me stiffen against him.

"Not just to see Cybil," he went on. "But to see Monte. If Michael isn't exaggerating, I may be able to buy the ranch." I relaxed as I listened to the sincere excitement and hope in Clinton's voice. "I'd like to have that ranch, Kathleen."

"Would Michael agree?"

"That's what bothers me. I think he just wants to get me over there so that Cybil can try some trick." Her name was enough to make me dread his trip. "But I have to find out. If he really plans to go East permanently, I can't let that ranch go to someone else."

I suspected that Michael had accomplished his purpose. He had succeeded in getting Clinton to plan a visit to the James ranch. And what would be waiting there? Cybil, beautiful and sensuous, forgiving and loving, reaching out to my husband. I closed my eyes, but in my imagination I could almost see Clinton slipping away from me and into her arms. I wanted to beg him not to go, but I couldn't admit the doubts that assailed me. I had to remember that he loved me. He promised me fidelity and love for life.

Priscilla and Steven raced into the room, their homework assignments done. For the next few minutes, the four of us chatted animatedly about things other than the James ranch.

Clinton left for the afternoon to check the north pasture. He returned later in a pensive mood. Dinner and our evening passed quickly. We sat in the study, Priscilla and Steven trying a game of chess together, while Clinton studied his account books. Once he slammed his pencil down with disgust. I watched him with trepidation, wondering if he had found a way to buy the James ranch. He turned no pages but sat staring down at the book on his desk. Was he thinking of how much he could offer Monte James? Or was he thinking of Cybil and Tom Whittaker? Had Michael's intended jab hit its mark? It had most assuredly skewered me.

When he went to bed, Clinton gave me a light goodnight kiss. And for the first time since we had married, he did not pull me into his arms. I lay in silence, staring into the darkness. I knew he was not asleep, for his breathing was light.

I lay there for what seemed hours, feeling the pain of my own tormenting imagination. The cruel, ever-present, silent voice kept speaking to me.

"He's thinking about Cybil, Kathleen. Can't you tell?"

"No, he's thinking about money and how he can buy the James ranch."

The silent voice laughed at me.

Late into the night, he moaned and tossed in bed as I lay sleepless beside him. Was he dreaming of Cybil in another man's arms?

Rolling over, I pressed my hands over my ears, straining to prevent my imagination from winning over my rational mind. I, too, tossed and moaned in my sleep that night. For Cybil haunted my dreams, her smiling face taunting me as she beckoned Clinton into her outstretched arms. As he buried his face in her shoulder, his arms pulling her against him, she laughed at me as I stood watching.

"You see, Miss O'Reilly! He still loves me! Me! Me!"

And I ran and ran. But everywhere I went I could see them kissing, their passion flaring higher and higher to full flame. They were lying together on the grassy hillside where Clinton and I had sat together. Their lips were sealed together as their bodies were entwined in passion.

There was a gun in my hand, but it was not raised to them. I held it to my heart instead.

I would welcome death now.

Someone pried my fingers loose and dropped the gun. Clinton and Cybil were gone. Warm, loving arms pulled me tight against a hard-muscled body. Everything seemed to fade into oblivion and I floated without pain—without feeling.

XVIII

When I awakened, tense and thankful the night was over, Clinton was already gone. Starting up, I looked about the room. Where had he gone so early? The sun was hardly up. Why did my husband not awaken me as he usually did, kissing me lightly on the eyes and lips?

As my exhausted mind cleared, I remembered his plan to see Monte James . . . and Cybil. I leaned back on the pillows, miserable.

He could not wait until morning light to begin his ride to see Cybil James and her father.

Was I becoming mad with suspicion and unhappiness now? I wondered angrily, shoving the covers from me. Only a day ago, a short day ago, I was happy, secure in Clinton's love. It was in his eyes when he looked at me, in his hands and body when he held me.

Did it take only one visit from Michael to shatter all we had built in the last weeks?

I will not think of it! I will not! Clinton is my husband and he loves me, not Cybil James.

The silent voice laughed and my heart twisted in answer.

286

"The materials Clinton ordered from San Francisco have arrived, Kathleen," Mabel announced, coming through the swinging doors from the kitchen. "Jim will drive us into town this morning for your first fittings at Mrs. Tibbets." She smiled, setting my breakfast down before me.

"You look a little flushed, dear," she observed. "How are you feeling?"

"Fine," I answered, though I had noticed a mild nausea the past few days. "What materials did Clinton order?"

"For your wardrobe," she answered.

"He's never said . . ."

"He wouldn't. He's got his mind on other things. He said he was riding to Monte James's to make an offer for the ranch. I hope he gets the spread."

"So do I," I agreed. If he succeeded, perhaps Cybil would leave and I'd never have to see or hear of her again.

The long ride into Las Positas was quiet and beautiful. Mabel seemed to understand my need for silence and did not attempt to draw me into conversation. I thought about how much I loved Clinton, how very happy he had made me in the last six weeks as his wife. I pushed the thought of Cybil from my mind, reliving each day of our marriage.

Surely, if he wanted Cybil, he would tell me. If he admitted his mistake in marrying me, I would let him go. The thought came unbidden. I did not want to be the cause of any unhappiness for him. A deep depression started to steal over me and I tried desperately to shake myself free of it. I was sure of his love for me. I would not let Michael plant doubts for me to nurture.

"But he might love Cybil more. And fate has a way with making life what it was intended," that despicable voice challenged my peace.

Then I will try to make him love me more. I will

entice, enrapture, beckon, I thought with sudden re-solve. I smiled, amused at the thought. Couldn't I?

Jim helped me down from the carriage, holding me by the waist and lifting me down effortlessly. Mabel, he took by the hands and guided, her heftiness tottering precariously as she hopped down.

"I'll pick you two up in a couple of hours," Jim promised, climbing back up into the carriage driver's seat.

"Don't lose all your pay at the hotel!" Mabel remonstrated. Jim laughed and urged the horses forward to the middle of the street.

Mrs. Tibbets had seen our arrival and come out onto the wood-slab sidewalk to greet us, her thin white face friendly and open.

"Mrs. Matthews! Everyone in town has been waiting on seeing you!" she bubbled with a wide, welcoming grin. I remembered her spontaneous charm from the fiesta and was pleased to see her again.

Mabel grunted a reply to Mrs. Tibbets' announcement and the lady looked at her and laughed. "Mabel Banks. I'll bet you've been thinking Cybil James spread some rumors. She tried, mind you, but Las Positas women make up their own minds about people. And most of them had a good look at this young lady at the fiesta. They liked her a sight more than that fast little James hussy, I can tell you that for a fact!"

"That's a relief to hear," Mabel huffed. I flushed. So, as Michael predicted, I had been the topic of town gossip since my marriage to Clinton. Well, I had been warned to expect as much. But now, it seemed the gossip had not been vicious, but rather friendly acceptance and approval.

Rebecca, Mrs. Tibbets' only unmarried daughter of four, stood shyly behind the counter as we came through the shop door. She looked very much like her mother, not attractive, but with a natural vitality and friendliness that drew warmth even from a stranger like myself. She smiled at me as her mother showed me into the fitting room at the back. And I smiled back, liking her immediately and wishing for a chance to talk with her.

The afternoon passed quickly and pleasantly. Mrs. Tibbets' conversation was fast and entertaining as she showed me dress patterns after taking my measurements. She repeated much of the story she had started at the fiesta, for which I was grateful. I was now in the mood to enjoy her discourse.

"I ordered these patterns from New York. They aren't the latest, but they're newer than most, I expect. What do you think of this one?"

Bolts of materials were scattered around the back room, labeled "Matthews." Pearl gray, rust, green, and dark brown wools and heavy linens were selected for winter; red and lavender for evening dresses, lighter fabrics of blue, green, yellow, cream, and pink for spring and summer dresses, white silk, lace, and lawn were stacked for shirtwaists, undergarments, and nightgowns. Clinton had even ordered shoes, riding boots, and house slippers.

"Oh, Mabel, there are so many things here!" I whispered. Smiling, Mrs. Tibbets went out of the room for a moment to answer some question for a new customer.

"These were all ordered by Clinton," Mabel replied proudly. "He wants you to have everything you could possibly want."

"I never even dreamt of having such a wardrobe."

Mabel seemed to concur with my simple taste in patterns, only disagreeing adamantly on my selection of an evening dress. She insisted that it be similar to the one which she had made and which had been greeted with such success. The only pattern Mabel favored was even more exposing, but I finally gave in to her arguments, remembering my decision on the ride into Las Positas. How could I hope to be enticing if I continued to dress with complete modesty?

As we walked out of the dress shop to meet Jim outside, Mrs. Tibbets stopped me.

"I have something I would like you to have . . . as my wedding gift to you." She lifted a shawl I had admired from a nearby shelf and handed it to me.

"Mrs. Tibbets, I couldn't. You spent so many hours on this." I held the beautiful shawl reverently in my hands, its soft cashmere yarn like duck down.

"I want you to have it, Mrs. Matthews," Mrs. Tibbets insisted. She pressed it back into my arms. "I remember how you admired it at the fiesta. And I can't think of anyone I would rather see wearing it."

"Thank you," I said, smiling at her kind words. I held the shawl against my cheek to feel its softness. "It's beautiful and I'll cherish it always . . . as from a friend."

Jim lifted me to my seat and I smiled down at the elderly seamstress as Mabel stepped up alongside me, jostling the carriage.

"I should have a few dresses ready in a week. Would you like me to deliver them to the ranch, Mrs. Matthews?" Mrs. Tibbets asked. "I can leave Rebecca in charge of the shop."

"That would be very convenient for me if you could deliver them. Would you please plan to stay for lunch with us? We could talk," I offered, hoping she would accept my invitation and not send the parcels with a hired boy.

"I'd like that. Yes, I'll plan to come myself and stay for a visit with you." Her eyes sparkled with pleasure.

"Good-bye," she called as we started away.

Just as we reached the edge of town, a man came running across the street toward us. "Hold up, Jim!"

Jim reined in the horses and waited as the man puffed up next to the carriage. "Oh, I beg your pardon, ma'am," he said, staring up at me curiously.

"What's the problem, Mr. Wadsworth?" Jim asked.

"I'm glad I caught you before you left. Saved me a long ride. Would you be so kind as to give this to Clinton . . . it's mighty important, I think!" He handed the telegram up to me, darting a significant glance at Jim.

"I'll give it to him as soon as I get back," I promised, smiling at him and wondering why he was looking at Jim with such an intense expression.

On the ride back to the ranch, I forgot all my earlier depression. I leaned back and enjoyed the countryside in its late-summer stage. The hills had turned golden, still spattered with flowers. I felt relaxed and happy and Mabel and I enjoyed a long, close conversation about everything from mixing beeswax and turpentine for furniture polish to having babies.

Had I suspected the contents of the telegram that was hidden in my jacket, I would have feared for far more than my happiness. I would have feared for my life.

XIX

When we reached the ranch, Mary informed me that Clinton was in the study attending to some ranch business. I had forgotten for the moment, Michael's disruptive visit of the day before and went scampering happily into the room to thank Clinton for his generous gifts.

As I stood in the doorway, I saw him bent over his books, his hand bracing his forehead. I quietly tiptoed over to him, leaning down to kiss his neck. He started, so deep in concentration that he had not heard me at all.

Smiling at me, his eyes softened. He pushed his chair back and pulled me unceremoniously into his lap. Swinging the chair around so that anyone coming into the study would not see us, he pressed a kiss to my waiting lips.

When I was finally able to speak, my voice was shaky. "Thank you for ordering so many beautiful materials, Clinton. I have never seen so many gorgeous colors before." My breath was high in my throat, my heart beating excitedly. I leaned against him, kissing the sensitive spot on his neck.

Squeezing my waist, he grinned down at me. "I missed you today," he whispered, giving me a smile that suggested many things and then lightly kissing the end of my nose.

"I missed you too!" I giggled.

"I would have awakened you this morning, but I was still smarting from Michael's attentions to you yesterday," he added, a seriousness deepening his voice.

"Did you see Cybil?" I asked, not able to prevent the question from flying from my lips.

"Uh huh . . . and her father," he answered without sounding particularly cheered by the admission.

"And was Michael telling you the truth?" I persisted, wishing I could stop the constriction in my chest.

"No," he sighed.

"Oh."

"Monte hadn't even mentioned the idea of selling. But Cybil is considering a trip East."

"Oh."

"But I made an offer for the ranch and Monte didn't dismiss the idea of selling." He pounded his fist on the account books. "I've just been figuring out where we stand financially. I can swing buying the James ranch if he doesn't expect a king's ransom for it . . . though at the moment, I think he figures I'd be willing to pay it just to get his family out of the valley."

"Even Cybil?" The words burst out against my better judgment. He looked down at me and chuckled.

"Cybil, yes . . . but especially Michael." I smiled as wickedly as did he.

"Why didn't you kiss me goodnight the way you usually do?" I asked and then flushed at my question. Usually the kiss led to other things.

"You didn't exactly invite my advance," he retorted seriously. "You hardly said a word to me at dinner, or later. I guessed it was Michael's offer."

"And I thought you were dreaming about Cybil," I said, kissing him on the cheek and sighing with relief.

"Dammit, woman, when will you learn I love only you!" he growled, pulling my face up to meet his. His lips were warm.

"When you learn I love you," I answered, a slight lilt in my voice.

"Where are Prissy and Steven?" I asked when I was able.

"Out riding with some of the hands," he replied without much interest, nibbling at my earlobe and then kissing my neck again and sending shivers of delight up and down my spine. "Why didn't you shut and lock the damned door when you came in?" he asked huskily, a hint of teasing in his voice. His hand moved down to my hip.

"You wouldn't, Clinton," I started, sitting up slightly, but he held me firmly on his lap, giving me a suggestive look which made me gasp. "Not here . . . now . . . in the chair!"

"Why not? It's our home," he smiled, not discouraged. Unbuttoning my jacket, he slid his hand over my breast. I felt the familiar warm weakness that always came when he touched me. Darting a look across the room to the open windows, I saw the curtains pulled back so that anyone coming around the side of the house could see us plainly. "Clinton . . ."

"What's this?" he asked, pulling the telegram out of my inside jacket pocket and looking at it perplexed. "Who's sending you telegrams?"

"Oh, my goodness, I forgot all about it. Mr. Wadsworth gave it to me just as we were leaving town. He said it was very important that you get it as soon as possible. I'm sorry, darling, it slipped out of my mind," I added, surprised when he released me abruptly. I saw his old scowl as he took the envelope and turned it over.

I went to the bookshelves while he ripped it open and began to read the message. He shot out of his seat, frowning as he stared down at the telegram, lines of worry etching his forehead as he reread the message to be sure of its content.

"Is something wrong?" I asked, alarmed and concerned by his expression. He looked up, staring at me with frightening concentration.

"What?" he asked.

"What's wrong, Clinton?" I repeated, starting toward him. For a moment I thought he was going to let me read the telegram for myself, then he decided against it. He crumpled it furiously, walking over to the fireplace and tossing it on the grate. He turned to me then as I came to him. He took me by the shoulders.

"It's something I've got to see Jim about," he answered. He leaned down and gave me a quick kiss, releasing me and hurrying toward the door. He paused, looking back. "Kathleen . . ." he started, and then stopped. I could see the wheels of his mind spinning, emotions fogging his dark eyes unfathomably.

"Yes?" I waited, not pressing, but watching him curiously and wondering what had been in the telegram to cause the sudden violent emotions that flooded his face now.

"Never mind, sweetheart . . . just . . . take care," he said, giving me a smile that belied his more intense concern. He disappeared from the room and I heard the door slam as his hurried foosteps went down the stairs.

The telegram was charred and burning now on the coals.

There were still several hours of sunlight left and I decided to ride to the springs. I could think there, sort out my jumbled feelings and sensations from this confusing, eventful day.

Ted brought the black mare around from the barns.

It was not more than an hour's ride to the springs and back, I thought, and I wanted to be alone. Thanking Ted, I mounted, turned, and rode out of the gates toward the hills.

About two miles from the ranch house I began to feel uneasy. Someone was following me, I was sure. I stopped several times and looked back. No one was there. Shrugging off the uncanny feeling, I rode on to the springs, forcing control over my imaginings.

Dismounting and tying up the mare, I stood looking out at the springs burbling at the edge of the small lake. It was a favorite place of mine, a place where I could enjoy a warm solitude and yet not feel alone. Lady Nature seemed to be here, behind the willow trees or just beyond the wild roses.

The grass was warm and dry as I sat down. Closer to the edge it was green and patched with flowers. Leaning back, I looked up at the afternoon sky and listened to the birds singing and flitting about, darting playfully from one tree to another. I was not thinking about anything in particular now, just enjoying the warmth of the sun and the smells of Las Posas, my home.

A stillness fell around me and a chill of instinct made me immediately alert to every sound. I sat up abruptly and looked around, wondering where the birds had gone and what danger lay close by. A danger I could not see—but one I could feel.

No one appeared, nothing seemed out of the ordinary except the silence, an expectant silence. I had the urge to call out and see what threatened me. But I did not. I stood up slowly, moving with false calm toward the horse tied some distance away.

The sudden report of a rifle cracked from the trees on the opposite side of the springs. I felt a sting across the side of my head. I wavered slightly and then fell hard to the ground as a blackness closed upon me.

When I opened my eyes again, I was lying sprawled on my back in the tall grass. My head was buzzing, a numb feeling of disorientation still fogging my memory of what had happened. I thought I heard someone calling my name.

"Kathleen!" I heard it again, closer this time. It was Clinton. I tried to sit up, but fell back dizzy again. I lay there motionless with my eyes closed, letting it pass before I would attempt rising again.

"Oh, no . . ." I heard Clinton's low moan. "Oh, God, Kathleen, no . . ." His voice was vibrant with fear. I realized the picture I must make and forced my eyes open, pushing myself up as I heard him jump down from his horse and run toward me.

"Kathleen," he cried as he reached me, his eyes misting with relief, yet still showing a trace of the agony I had heard in his voice.

"I'm all right," I said when he would not let me get up. I touched the side of my head and winced. "It hurts. What happened?" When I looked at my fingers there was blood on them. Clinton yanked a scarf from his neck and poured some water over it from his canteen. When he looked at me again, his face was taut and unreadable. He wiped the blood away a little roughly, and then examined the slight wound. I was relieved when he was finished with his ministrations, for my head had cleared and the only pain I felt was when he prodded the slight wound.

"It's only a graze," he said, relieved.

"Someone shot at me . . . but why?"

"Did you hear or see anyone?" he demanded, not answering my question.

"No," I replied, trying to remember what had happened. "I noticed that the birds stopped singing all of a sudden. But no one was there."

I looked up at his face, seeing the concern and frightened alarm as the event registered with him. "I'm really all right, darling. It doesn't even hurt now. It can't be that serious . . . someone must have been hunting and shot at me by mistake."

"I thought I'd lost you," he breathed.

"I'm sure it was a mistake," I repeated, trying equally hard to convince myself. I shrugged, pushing the uneasiness away. Clinton lost his temper suddenly and I was surprised to realize it was aimed at me.

"Dammit! I've told you that you are never to ride alone! Maybe this time you'll be convinced and do as I say!"

"Stop yelling at me!" I said, struggling to my feet, glaring at him. "Why shouldn't I ride by myself? You do! Even the children do! Just because I was stupid enough to fall off my horse once does not mean that I will do so again. I am not a child, Clinton, and I can ride as well as some of your ranch hands!" I would not have the pleasure of riding alone taken from me because of some fool's mistake.

Clinton seized my shoulders in an iron grip. He shook me as though that would make me agree to his command. "This makes three times, dammit! Three times!" His fingers dug into my arm. "You didn't fall off your horse. The cinch was cut almost through. Someone wants you dead, you little idiot. And you provide them with their opportunity every time you ride out alone!"

"Clinton . . ." I cried, alarmed by his words as well as his violence.

"First the saddle cinch, then that damn snake, and now you're nearly shot through the head!" he went on. I stared at him, silent and frightened. "From now on, Kathleen, you are going to listen to me. You will not ride by yourself . . . you will stay near the house and you will obey me . . . I have to have time to clear this up."

"Clinton, you're hurting me," I whimpered.

298

"Do you understand?" he demanded, not hearing me.

"Clinton!" I twisted to be free of his cruel grasp.

"Do . . . you . . . understand?" he demanded, shaking me like a disobedient child who had pushed a parent beyond all patience and reason.

"Yes!" I cried. "Yes! Let me go!" He released my shoulders, which I could feel would be black and blue in a few hours. I rubbed them, shaking with fright and realization. Clinton stared at me and I could see he regretted his rash words, wishing he could retract them and leave me oblivious to what had been happening around me for all these months. Pulling me into his arms, he held me securely against him.

"I'm sorry . . . I didn't mean to hurt you like that. But, God, I thought I'd lost you, Kathleen! Why won't you listen? I couldn't find you . . . and then I saw you there so pale and lifeless. My God, Kathleen!" He held my face and kissed me, gently at first and then with rising passion that was born of his fears. I clung to him, meeting his kisses with a fervor and abandon of my own. I found myself caught up hastily in his arms and taken beneath the canopy of a nearby willow tree. Laying me down gently on the grass, he leaned over me, his kiss hotly demanding.

"Clinton," I gasped, reaching up to him as I felt his fingers impatiently undo the buttons on my shirtwaist while his mouth came down hot on my breasts. The growing fire inside me began to consume the fears of the past moments.

"Don't talk!" he commanded and stripped off my clothes, tossing them hurriedly to one side. His hands slowed to explore me. Caught up in his passion, I wanted him to hurry, but he would not. Pressing me down into the cool sweet grass, he continued his conquest of my senses until I lay breathless, floating in ecstasy. At last, he removed his own clothes and entered me, bringing me to fever pitch again as he thrust deep within me, all his control gone.

When he lay spent I couldn't speak, my throat feeling thick and hoarse. Taking part of his weight from me, he looked down, smiling boyishly through passion-fogged eyes.

"No beds to make this time," he mused.

Studying my face as though etching the features into his mind forever, he said, "I used to wonder what it would be like to roll you in the grass."

"When did you wonder that?" I asked, playing with the hair that fell onto his forehead.

"The first week you were at the ranch and I was on the range. I thought about you quite often."

I laughed, not believing him. "You were very upset about me as I remember. Something about 'being saddled with a mere babe.'"

"Well, maybe I was for a minute or two," he admitted.

"You didn't even like me," I went on. "I've never seen anyone so displeased as you were when you met me." I laughed again.

"You laugh, do you?" he growled. "Didn't you even guess what you did to me with those innocent blue eyes of yours?" He kissed me gently and moved against me with a roguish smile. "When I looked at you, I saw the end of my freedom." He made his voice woeful and full of mock regret.

"Don't sound so unhappy," I said seriously, and he laughed at me.

"Hardly that," he grinned. "You're all I want . . . and all I can handle." He laughed. "I'm exhausted."

I reached up feeling light-hearted and ran my fingers through his tousled hair. "You're a mess, Mr. Matthews," I teased.

"And what do you think you are, sweetheart?" he retorted with a chuckle. "Mabel will have a good laugh

300

when she sees the grass stains on your . . ." He started raising his brows with amused satisfaction at my flush.

"Oh, Clinton," I cried out, pushing against him as I pictured Mabel's all-too-comprehending grin when she saw my clothes. But Clinton only grabbed my hands and pinned them to the ground above my head.

"Too late to worry about appearances now," he teased, kissing a breast and nibbling at my collarbone. He rolled over, pinning me against him again. "Hmmmm . . . you smell like hay."

I laughed. "You're impossible."

"Have I ever told you I'm glad you're my wife?"

"No . . . tell me."

"I'm glad you're my wife," he chuckled. "Even if you're a wanton hussy."

"Oh, you!" I pushed away and pummeled him with soft blows as he laughed at me.

"I knew you would be, of course," he added, catching my fists easily and looking serious for a moment.

I flushed. "Why did you think such a thing?" I stammered.

"Hmmmm . . ." he grinned roguishly. "I knew it the first time I kissed you," he said and observed my deepening blush with satisfaction. "Your face was flushed bright pink . . . and here . . ." he touched the base of my neck with the tips of his fingers, "there was a pulse I could hardly miss seeing." He pulled me down to kiss him again, then whispered, "I damned near took you then and there!"

"You were just trying to prove to me how inexperienced and stupid I was when it came to men!" I retorted hotly, remembering that night clearly.

"You're serious," he exclaimed. "So that's what you thought! I always wondered why you slapped me."

"Well, weren't you?" I asked with surprise. "You said, 'See what I mean,' " I mimicked him, "and then you smiled so satisfied that you had made your point. I thought you would burst out laughing after I had made such a fool of myself."

"You are a little fool. I was trying to say I was in love with you myself. And I couldn't stand to see you with Michael!"

"But I thought—"

"Well . . . I can see how you would have thought something else," he admitted slowly. "You are a defensive little witch, you know . . . but I was jealous . . . purely jealous. You damn near drove me mad when you insisted on seeing Michael."

"Did I?" I grinned with unconcealed pleasure. "That's wonderful!"

"Why you little devil!" He pushed me over into the grass and stood up, grabbing his pants. I watched him dress, feeling warm and happy.

He saw me watching him with an amused smile on my face. Grinning, he leaned over and picked up my clothes, tossing them to me.

"I'm very glad, my dear, that you have gotten over your modesty. But get something on, or we will be spending the night here."

On the way back to the ranch house, Clinton again became very pensive. I watched his face and saw a variety of feelings fly across it. He seemed to be fighting something out in his mind, and I did not want to press him about it.

When we reached the stables, Jim came out of the corral and asked Clinton if he had fired Ted.

"No. Why?" Clinton's face suddenly hardened with suspicion. "Did he ride back in and ask for his pay?"

"He was here when I left," I commented before Jim answered. "He saddled my mare for me."

Clinton looked at me and then swung around to Jim. "Did he ride in?" he repeated harshly.

"He rode in."

Clinton jumped down from his horse. "When? And

where is he?" His voice was rough with anger as he darted a look toward the bunkhouse, his eyes taking on a dangerous glint.

"Gone . . . rode out about an hour ago. Said you gave him orders to pack his gear, collect his pay, and clear out."

"Damn!"

"What happened out there? Didn't you fire him?"

"Hell, no!" Clinton swung to me, and giving my horse a hard smack, he commanded me to go to the house and stay with the children. Obeying, I looked curiously back over my shoulder, wondering what he planned to do. He was talking rapidly to Jim and I overheard him mention the telegram I had delivered.

What had been in the message I had given him? Did it warn Clinton that someone was really trying to kill me? But why would anyone want me dead? No one had any reason. Or was that true? Hadn't my own father wanted me permanently out of his life?

As I hurried up the front steps of the house, I felt a dreadful chill run down my spine.

Clinton came in late that evening. He was dusty and grimy from hard riding, but I did not dare question him about where he had been. His expression was frightening in its intensity.

Later, in our bedroom, I sat at the dresser and unbound my hair. Clinton had bathed and eaten, but his mood was still strangely pensive. He lay back against the rough-hewn headboard and watched me silently, a slight frown on his face. I met his dark eyes in the mirror and smiled tremulously, wondering if I had displeased him again or if he were brooding over my folly of the afternoon.

The bed protested as he got up and moved across the room. I felt his hands in my hair. They moved down over my shoulders to the buttons on the front of my nightgown.

"I wonder sometimes if you know how much I love you," he said in a quietly restrained voice. I closed my eyes and leaned back against him, relishing the feeling that rose in me as his hands played over my skin.

"You couldn't love me more than I love you," I murmured. He gave a low laugh and pulled me up and into his arms. His embrace was painful. "You're a child . . . just a little older than Priscilla and Steven."

I did not find his description accurate and protested.

"You are!" He shook me and then stopped, cupping my face in his hands. "You take chances with your safety." He kissed me softly and studied my face, his own taut with anxiety.

"Kathleen. Your childhood friend . . ." He stopped, his expression showing doubt.

"Anna?" I knew something was very wrong and Clinton was debating with himself whether to tell me. "Clinton! What is it?"

"The telegram you gave me . . ." Still he hesitated, studying my face with worry.

"Clinton . . . she was my friend. I have to know." He made his decision. Closing his eyes, he drew me tightly against him.

"Anna Bowen is dead, Kathleen. She was murdered."

I pulled away and stared at him for what seemed an eternity. Then I shook my head. "No. You can't be right! No one would kill Anna! Why would anyone want to kill her?" My heart was racing as I tried to convince myself I had not heard Clinton correctly.

"Kathleen. Listen! There is no mistake. Anna Bowen was murdered. We don't know why yet." His hand was tense as he stroked my hair. I could feel the tears rising in my throat and almost choking me. And something else rose in me. Fear.

"You said you don't know why. Do you know who?"

Clinton shook his head, and then drew me back comfortingly into his arms. I could hear myself saying "Why?" over and over and Clinton's soothing voice trying to ease the pain.

Why had Anna been murdered? I was sure it had something to do with me. But what? And were others I loved in danger as well? Was Clinton now in danger? And what did my father have to do with everything? I was now out of his life as he had wished. Wasn't that enough? Or did he wish me dead as well?

I don't know how long I stayed in the comforting safety of Clinton's arms. His gentleness eased me and I clung to him feeling he was my only source of sanity and protection.

"Clinton?"

"Yes, love."

"Who sent the telegram?"

He hesitated and I could feel his body grow taut. "A friend," he finally answered, kissing me lightly. "Someone who cares very much about what happens to you."

My immediate thought focused on Miss Montgomery. She had been the only one who had really cared about me.

"Someone I know?"

"No."

I was about to pursue my questioning further, wondering who would care about me and yet not know me personally. But Clinton stayed my questions.

"Would you think me mad if I said I wanted to make love to you?" His hands pressed me against him, compelling.

"Now?"

"Now," he smiled down at me, kissing the tip of my nose.

"Oh, Clinton! You are truly mad, and I love you so much."

It was only later as I lay sleepless, Clinton's arms still tightly around me, that I wondered if his ardent lovemaking had been intended to silence my questions and dispel my doubts and fears. And for that attempt, I could only love him more.

XX

Prissy and Steven sat huddled together reading near the fireplace in the upstairs schoolroom. Outside the sky was an angry black, the first big storm of the year having hit in the early afternoon.

Rain spattered rhythmically against the windows, supplying the crackling fire with harmony. Pulling my legs up and holding my knees against my chest, I sat looking out into the garden from my cozy perch in the window alcove, my book forgotten. The roses had been pruned back, the trees were now just beginning to lose their leaves and the flowers of spring and summer were gone.

Beauty was resting in the cold autumn, drinking in the pounding rain to bring forth new life in the spring.

New life! My hand moved down over my abdomen and I smiled, secretly joyous. So soon Clinton's seed had taken hold in me. With some special sense I knew for certain it was so. It had happened the night Clinton had told me of Anna's death. From grief and fear, joy had come. It would be the miracle of creation I would remember now.

Tomorrow, I promised myself. Tomorrow I will tell Clinton that his child is growing within me.

"There you are!" puffed Mabel, startling me from my thoughts as she ambled into the room. "I looked in the sitting room, the bedrooms, then went to the stables to see if you were admiring the new foal. This is the last place in the world I expected to find you three on a Saturday!" she huffed, irritated by her needless and lengthy exertion.

Prissy looked up dreamily from her copy of *Jane Erye*. Steven sat deep in concentration, his hand bracing his forehead in a younger version of his uncle's pose. He did not even know that Mabel was in the room.

"We apologize, Mabel, but it was such a perfect day for a quiet, peaceful reading session . . . and a nice warm fire."

"So it is," she agreed, looking with renewed affection at her two temporarily serene elves. "Well. Anyway. Clinton came in from town a while ago. He's in the study and he would like to see you, Kathleen."

"I thought he was planning to stay over in Las Positas until the council had met on the water rights."

"He changed his mind, I guess. Left a proxy vote with Michael."

Slipping down from the high seat, I fluffed my skirts, making myself more presentable. It was one of my new dresses, a rust and dark brown. I wondered vaguely what I would do about clothes in a few months. My new wardrobe had just been completed and now I would fast be outgrowing it. I smiled at the thought, far from displeased at the prospect of gaining weight.

My heart picked up speed as I started out of the room. I always felt exhilarated at seeing Clinton, even after only a brief separation. And now, I had such news to tell him!

However, when I entered the study I immediately

knew something was wrong. Clinton stood waiting for me, leaning against the front of his desk, his hands jammed deep into his pockets. He seemed to sense rather than actually hear my arrival. As he turned and looked at me his face lighted, the frown of worry disappearing momentarily. He came to me, drawing me tightly into his arms, but something in his manner alarmed me. My resolve to not question him when I was afraid almost broke. I forced a smile and said as casually as possible, "How was your ride?" I noticed that his thick hair was still wet.

"You haven't even changed into dry clothes," I admonished with concern as I reached up to kiss him. Releasing me, he closed the doors as I surveyed him curiously. "What is the matter, Clinton? Did the council decide against—"

"Sit down, Kathleen."

"Only if you'll join me by the fire," I answered lightly, trying to dispel the growing tension I was feeling. He was trying to find a way to tell me something, something terrible. But what? Another death? Please, God! Not another death because of me!

"All right," he answered. He smiled and I could tell the acquiescense was only giving him more time to find words he needed now.

Quickly, with the expertise of years, he started a fire and then settled down cross-legged on the thick braided rug and stared into the flames. I put my hand on his knee, waiting.

"I got a telegram this morning," he announced, still not looking at me. My heart stopped.

"A telegram?" I repeated numbly, my thoughts darting to Anna's death. An image of Miss Montgomery flashed into my mind and I closed my eyes.

Clinton's hand closed tightly over mine. "From your father, Kathleen. He's coming to stay with us. He telegraphed from San Francisco." He gripped my hand harder as I jerked with the shock of his news. "He'll be here in a few days."

"My father!" I ejaculated, staring at Clinton, hardly believing his astonishing news. "How do you know my father?" I remembered Jim telling me about Clinton's trip to San Francisco and a friend he had contacted. Did the friend know my father?

"I never told you his name . . ." I murmured.

"Please don't look at me like that!" Clinton exclaimed with something of desperation in his voice. He tried to pull me into his arms but I strained away from him.

"I want you to tell me everything about your trip to San Francisco," I said coldly. I felt somehow betrayed. Why had he never told me he was in contact with my father? Why had he contacted him when I had explained my feelings?

"All right . . . but don't push me away, Kathleen," he said roughly and captured my hand. He pulled me down on the rug. "You'll stay sitting there until you hear it all," he commanded, his voice harsh.

I stared into the fire, refusing to look at him. I knew I was being childish, but his secrecy hurt me.

"Do you remember the day Michael took you to town . . . and I rode along on a business errand?" he asked. I nodded, still silent, still angry and hurt.

"I wired a friend in New York to find out which orphanage you came from," he explained and then put his hand quickly over my lips when I would have spoken. "No! Don't say anything! Just listen!" He paused for what seemed an eternity. I wanted to scream to him to go on, but I held my silence. "My friend finally contacted your Miss Josephine Montgomery at Parkside. He said she was almost frantic to know where you were. He only told her he was asking for a friend in California . . . nothing more. But he said she was frightened about something."

"Clinton . . ."

"Let me finish, dammit! I can see what you're thinking. But I was already in love with you. I wanted to find out everything about you . . . to understand why you became so defensive and nervous every time I asked about your background."

"But I explained all that to you! That night in the study!" I cried out angrily. "I told you how I felt—"

"Could you explain why someone wanted you dead?" he cut me off. He took my chin, forcing me to look at his angry face. "You told me just what you knew and that made my trip to San Francisco necessary."

"I told you everything I knew," I said, my voice now quivering, "except my father's name." I tried to stand up, but he pulled me down beside him again.

"You are going to listen, dammit! You found out you were William Benson's daughter. You took your mother's name and ran. And every time something hurts you, you run again . . . retreating further and further inside yourself. You damn near let Cybil plant suspicions in your mind about us . . . you almost let her come between us . . . and Michael, too. You're not going to let this destroy us. I didn't tell you because I didn't want you to lose trust in me. But now you've got to listen to me!"

"Why didn't you tell me? Why didn't you tell me you knew him?"

"Because your father made me swear I would not do that . . . because he wanted to come to you himself when it was possible to do so."

Smarting from the deception, I remained silent, my face averted. Clinton loosened his grip on my arm and went on. "He explained why he put you in that home . . . why there were attempts being made on your life . . . though he had no idea who could have found out where you were."

"Anna?"

311

"Anna. That's why she was murdered. She evidently sold the information to someone and then was killed so she couldn't tell anyone who was after you."

"Who was?"

"I can't say who. Your father will explain," he said tiredly, his eyes watching my face closely.

"Well, everything I know points to my own flesh-and-blood father," I shot out.

"There's a lot you don't know, Kathleen."

"But you know! And you've known for some time. Perhaps I should not have trusted you after all."

I felt immediately ashamed for the pain that flashed across Clinton's face. My hand shook as I put it to my forehead. "I'm sorry, Clinton. But don't you see," I pleaded. "That's why I left New York. Miss Montgomery said I was intended to stay there . . . for the rest of my life, I suppose. And why? Because a rich man had an affair with an actress and it produced an unwanted child. It wasn't fair! I had a right to live my own life, not one planned for me for the convenience of a father I never knew." Clinton sat listening and I went on rapidly. "I left when Miss M. drove off . . . I suppose she was going to warn my father or someone."

I reached out to take his hand. "Please don't let him come here! I don't ever want to see him again!"

"Again? What do you mean 'again'?" Clinton asked quickly.

"I saw him once," I answered, swallowing hard as I remembered all too well the feelings of that day. "When Anna showed me the file, I was curious about my father. I wanted to see where he lived . . . get a glimpse of him. I'm not sure what I expected. Maybe I hoped by some miracle he would recognize me. I don't know. I just sat looking in at his estate wondering about him. And then he and a young man drove up

312

and stopped alongside me. They wanted to know what I was doing there, I suppose."

"Did you tell him where you were from?" Clinton pressed when I remained silent, remembering the disappointment and rejection I had felt.

"No."

"Who was the young man?"

"I don't know."

"Did you speak with anyone else?"

"No."

We sat in silence before the fire, each deep in our own thoughts.

"Anyway . . ." I whispered finally, "all he said was, 'Drive on . . . drive on.'" I gave a brittle laugh. "I'll never forget that as long as I live."

"Did anyone know where you were going?"

"Anna found the notice advertising this position . . . she loaned me the money to reach Denver. She was afraid Miss M. would find out she showed me the file. She wouldn't have told anyone . . ." I defended her weakly, my voice now devoid of feeling.

"She did, Kathleen," Clinton insisted. "Your father knows who was behind all this, but not—"

"*Was* behind it—is it over then?"

"Yes. He'll explain everything when he gets here." Clinton leaned back on his elbows, staring pensively into space.

"Is that why he's coming now?"

"He's coming now because he can, darling," he answered, gently rolling onto his side and propping his head up with his hand. His face denied his casual posture. We looked at each other for a long moment.

"What's he like?"

"Brady said he's old beyond his years . . . unhappy . . . haunted by his memories . . . missing what he wanted most in life—you," he said, his words bringing me acute pain.

"How can I believe that after so many years . . ."

"More for him, Kathleen." Clinton watched me, his face not showing his feelings. I sensed his despair, and knew he was waiting for some sign from me that I did not view his secrecy as betrayal.

Reaching over, I touched his hair lightly. He sat up, catching my hand and drawing me to him. His kiss was completely tender, utterly sweet in the relief it brought.

"The rain has stopped," I said, listening to the stillness. His face glowed in the firelight as he looked at me. "I love you, Clinton."

"I love you."

I remembered that I had a secret also. "Clinton?" He waited, his face warm and questioning. I looked at him, loving him so much and feeling strangely free from the past. I did not want to think of anything but the present moment of closeness, and the future.

"What, sweetheart?"

"I'm going to have a baby," I told him quietly. His eyes misted for a moment and then he looked down at my abdomen.

"It doesn't really show yet," I said, smiling, feeling tears fill my eyes.

"How can you be sure so soon?" His hand slipped down and lay lightly over my womb.

"I just know."

He didn't speak then, but I could see the sparkle of happiness that lit his eyes.

That night my dream recurred with all its terror.

I was walking down a faintly familiar lane with high, dark shade trees. The branches seemed to be reaching down toward me, grabbing and holding me. I started to run, looking around me and dodging the grasping limbs. Ahead of me there was an iron gate standing high against the sky, a grotesque lion's head roaring silently above. The head seemed alive, warning possible

intruders against danger within. Below it was a large
iron *B*. I was more afraid of the trees that seemed to
be moving toward me, pressing me closer and closer
to the ominous wrought-iron gate.

Backing against it, away from the leafy tentacles,
I felt the gate swing back, and I stumbled and fell in.
Feverishly, I moved quickly behind the unlatched entrance and pushed it shut, the branches reaching
through the iron bars, just as I jumped away.

Somewhere in the distance, someone was laughing.

"Where do I go? Where am I?" I turned around
looking for some way to escape the strangely menacing
trees on the outside of the fence. " I must be mad!"

I saw an enormous white-columned brick house almost hidden among high-grown shrubs and trees in
the distance. The windows were like eyes watching
me.

I don't want to go there! No!

I turned and tried to run along the fence to find
a way out and away from the trees and house. But
every time I turned around I saw the face of the house
staring at me. No matter how fast I ran, or how far,
the house was still close, and I always came back to
the iron gate and the frightening trees.

Then I saw someone standing on the front steps,
waving. It was a woman, dark-haired, and even at a
distance I knew she was smiling. Feeling a surge of
relief and hope, I started to run toward her as fast as
I could.

"Mother! Mother!" I called, sure it was she. The
closer I came the more she was the reflection of an
older me. Except her expression . . . complete happiness, an acceptance of life and what it could offer
her, a look of serenity.

Someone was walking up behind her, his hand raised
high in the air and holding something sharp. I screamed
then, trying to run faster, but my legs became almost

315

frozen. Why couldn't she hear me? "Look out! Mother, behind you! Mother!!!" I screamed again and again, but no words came from my throat. My feet were stuck in a mire as I struggled to run even faster. The air was searing my lungs.

I saw the arm come down and strike her. It raised and fell again and again. My mother fell forward down the front steps. In her back was a long knife stuck in to the hilt, and blood bubbled out of the wounds, running down the steps as, too late, I reached her.

When I looked up, I saw a faceless evil walking down the steps toward me, my body cold with fearful perspiration. My throat tightened with nausea as I tried to back away from the approaching being. Who was it? What was it?

I strained to see the face more clearly but could not even tell if it was woman, man, or even human. As it reached the bottom of the steps, it reached down and pulled the knife from the lifeless body of my mother with a hard, sucking jerk.

A high, shrill laugh came from the foggy face. A woman's laugh! Her features started to clear as she turned to look directly at me, again turning the blade high in the air above her head.

My feet seemed rooted to the ground, some powerful force holding me motionless as the woman advanced toward me. She had long hair, blond hair, and her eyes became more and more like Cybil's ice-blue orbs. Her mouth was twisted in a demonic grin. She laughed again and the sound was more terrifying than anything I had ever heard. Her hand pinched down hard on my shoulder, swinging her other arm even farther back for her final downward thrust.

And it wasn't Cybil. It was someone else. Someone I'd never seen before.

Sound came. And I screamed and screamed and screamed.

"Kathleen! Kathleen!!" I jerked upright, my arms flaying against her, still screaming, and then I felt Clinton shaking me. My eyes flew open and cleared, and I sat, panting, shaking violently, the cold sweat slick on my body. The room seemed chilled and my lungs and throat ached.

"A dream! A dream!" I kept repeating, indescribable relief washing over me. "A dream!" But still the shaking terror lurked about me.

"It's not over, Clinton. It's not," I said with certainty.

"It was a nightmare."

"It was horrible . . ." I choked, the sobs now consuming me, my body racked by fear, as I clung to my husband.

"It's over. Everything is over. You're safe. There is nothing more to fear, darling." Clinton's voice was tense and worried. He held me tightly against him and down flat in the bed, pulling the warm covers high over us. "You're icy cold, Kathleen." He rubbed my back comfortingly and I cherished his warmth. He brushed the hair from my forehead and kissed me, his hand stroking me. For a long time we lay close, his warmth soothing me, making the terror of the nightmare slowly diminish and disappear until I was only aware of the strength of his protecting arms.

"Do you want to talk about it?" His hand rubbed hypnotically up and down my back.

"I don't remember anything about it now," I answered with surprise. "Nothing," I laughed without humor. "But I don't want to try to remember, either." I closed my eyes and pressed even closer, the hair on Clinton's chest feeling crisp and curly against my cheek. I could hear his heart racing. His hand pressed at the small of my back and as I moved against him, his lips touched mine, his tongue lightly teasing. He loosened his arms, his hand sliding down over my abdomen and lingering there. Then it moved again, stroking, caressing, exploring gently. The chill left me and inside warmth coiled expectantly.

"It's finished. You're safe," he assured me over and over.

He kissed my breasts, his hand wandering down my hip and then slowly upward.

"Clinton . . . please . . ." I pleaded. He rolled me over and pressed me down with his weight. I forgot everything but how much I loved and needed him.

XXI

Days and hours are torture when you wait—wait for something longed for since infancy and then is suddenly within reach, coming to you. Nerves slowly unravel and then rewind in another direction, twisting, agonizing, stomach-churning nerves.

So many years . . . so many years of raw wanting, wondering why it was beyond reach, hoping for something lost and without hope of being found again, and then only a few days, a few hours, a few minutes more, and it is there. He is there reaching out to you, his daughter.

Wanting and yet not wanting to meet him, I sat searching my heart for my true feelings about my father. Could I even know until I saw him again, talked with him, knew him?

But even while I wondered about my father, I wondered even more about my mother, and what he could tell me of her. What had she felt for him? Had she loved him? Why hadn't he married her? Why had he cast me into an orphanage? Why? Why? Why?

So many questions screamed at me from the corners of my mind, demanding to be answered. And only one person had the answers.

My father.

Each time a carriage drove into the yard, I felt suspended in an emotional limbo, half-dreading, half-praying I would peer out at the visitor below and see my father. But once it was Mrs. Tibbets. Another time it was Mr. Wadsworth. Another time it was Michael.

And I waited again.

A horse's hooves on the gravel in the drive, a knock at the door, Mabel's call, all set my heart to pounding with anticipation and apprehension. Trying to tell myself that I could not prevent this eventual meeting, nor did I really want to prevent it, I must learn somehow to control my emotions.

I no longer wondered how I would feel about my father, but I wondered how he would feel about me.

What would he think of me? Would I be all that he expected of his daughter, or would I be much less? Did I look like my mother? Could he tell me who the woman in my nightmare was?

As day by day time went on and he did not arrive, I began to believe that he had changed his mind. He no longer felt curious about me. Perhaps he felt it more sensible to forget he had a daughter at all and to continue his life as it was.

At the end of the first week of November, a carriage drove into the yard. By this time, I had steeled my nerves for disappointment and I believed that it would be anyone but my father. My father, I was sure, had decided against ever seeing me.

Priscilla jumped up and raced to the window, happy for an excuse to delay her dreaded arithmetic lesson.

"It's two men . . . a young man and an old one,"

she announced, still staring out the window. My heart constricted and I felt suffocated.

It can't be my father, I thought, relaxing again with an effort. He would be alone.

"Is it anyone you know, Prissy?"

"No . . . I've never seen them before . . . Oh, Aunt Kathleen," she turned toward me, her eyes sparkling with excitement, "it must be your father. He is very handsome. The young one, I mean. Who is he?"

The young man. Could it be the same young man who had been with my father in the carriage that day when I first saw him.

Hardly noticing what she was saying, I moved to the window, intent on seeing if it were really true.

Oh, my dear Lord, I thought with sudden nervousness, recognizing the men. What will I say? How do I greet them? How does one greet a father one has never known, or loved?

I had the wild urge to laugh. After all these weeks, days, hours, I had never stopped to consider how first to speak to him.

A hurried tap at the door announced Mabel. "They're here, Kathleen. Shall I answer the door when they come up or would you like to go out and meet them?" I had never heard Mabel nervous before and her usually steady disposition had helped to calm me so many times in the past.

"Where's Clinton?" I asked, needing his presence and support.

"Gone. What do you want me to do?"

"I'll answer the door—oh, I guess I'll go out and meet them." My voice quivered slightly as I made my decision. Wishing for all the world my husband was with me, I started down the stairs, Prissy, Mabel, and Steven excitedly tracing my steps.

"Oh, Clinton, where are you?" the silent voice called. "Help me!"

Straightening my shoulders and pushing my chin up a little, I opened the door and moved down the steps toward the approaching carriage. Feeling neither calm nor cool, I was at least relieved to find I could move smoothly and surely toward them.

My father was stepping down from the carriage, easily but hurriedly. Very gray and thin, he moved with surprising awkwardness for a man who was in his forties. He looked at me, long and awed, his eyes sparkling. He smiled with an anxiousness that showed his own nerves were far from calm. He was afraid of how I would welcome him, I realized suddenly—or if I would welcome him at all.

Clinton's friend had reported my father to be "old beyond his years, unhappy, haunted by his memories, missing what he wanted most in life"—me, his daughter.

And I could see some of that for myself now. In his face, in the way he stood expectantly, hoping, longing.

We stood staring at one another for only a moment, but it seemed much, much longer. Long enough for me to see there was a decided difference between the man I faced today and the man I had faced many months ago. The coolness was gone, as well as the reserve. And despite what I had seen before, he now looked young.

I couldn't speak, though I opened my mouth to welcome him. I stood frozen in my place, staring mutely at this tall, lean man who did not even seem the stranger I had expected.

"Kathleen . . . my beautiful little Kathleen," he breathed in wonder, and then took several long steps to me. Suddenly, I found myself embraced in his strong arms, his lips pressed to the top of my head.

Hardly realizing what was happening, I found my arms were around him and I was returning his embrace, tears streaming down my cheeks.

All the nervousness, fear, bitterness, anxiety were gone, wiped away by that one look, those few tender words, and the sight of him reaching out to me.

He held me away, his fingers turning my face from side to side. He smiled with joy, radiant with discovery.

"How many years I have waited for just this moment," he said, his eyes glistening. He went on with difficulty, "You look so much like your mother, Kathleen . . . so very much like my lovely Brianna."

Never had I seen such sadness in a person's face. He seemed not to be looking at me anymore, but past me to someone else. I did not even need to ask him if he had loved my mother. I felt my heart twist as I saw the mute tragedy of his expression.

"Father, aren't you going to introduce me to my sister," came an impatient voice. I became aware of smiling lips and cool blue eyes which could not disguise a chilling jealousy. I met those same cold eyes that had looked at me so contemptuously in front of my father's estate.

Father? Then was this a brother, a half-brother?

Slowly, emerging from a dream, my father realized he was being addressed. "I'm sorry, David. This is Kathleen O'Reilly Matthews. Kathleen, this is your half-brother, David Hale Benson.

"Haven't we met before, Kathleen," he smiled. "Yes, I remember seeing you once outside our estate in New York. Am I correct?"

"Yes." Why hadn't I guessed that he was my father's son? There was a pronounced similarity of jaw and eyes, though his coloring was much different— blond hair, light blue eyes, a more stocky muscular build that bragged of power.

"Had I known who you were at the time, I would have given you a more appropriate welcome," he said, smiling pleasantly, showing straight white teeth and a creasing in his cheeks. He jumped down from the carriage and came forward to kiss my cheek. His lips were cold, and I felt a strange tingling sensation at the back of my neck at his touch. I had the almost uncontrollable desire to pull away from him and run into the house.

"Mr. Benson! Wecome!" Clinton's voice rang out as he rode up on his tall sorrel and swung down. I caught his quick curious glance at David Benson, who met his eyes with a pleasant enough smile.

"Clinton Matthews, I take it? I am very pleased to make your acquaintance," my father said, extending his hand. Clinton caught it and shook it with a firm sincerity. "This is my son, David. David, Clinton Matthews, your sister's husband."

"Pleased to meet you, Clinton," David nodded. My husband surveyed my brother with cool concentration, then smiled with less enthusiasm than he showed in greeting my father. His appraising look was returned as the two men shook hands.

I felt foolish for my previous misgivings about my brother. He was friendly and open in his conversation as we entered the house. I accounted my qualms to my state of nervous anticipation, and his unexpected accompaniment of my father. Our first meeting had been far from pleasant and I had allowed that to shadow my impression of David Hale Benson.

Bags unpacked in their rooms, we met again in the sitting room. Clinton offered wine to our guests and both accepted readily. My stomach was a knot of excited nerves.

I watched William Stuart Benson with fascination. So many years in which I hadn't known that he even existed, and then he was suddenly discovered. During the last months, I had created my own image of what he would be like. He did not fit my creation's mold.

Soft-spoken and interested in Clinton's ranch problems, I found him more human than I had supposed. He was an enigma.

If he had cared so much for me, why had he put me in the orphanage? If he was an unfeeling man, why did my intuition tell me he was not?

Though the three men talked casually of masculine interests, I felt that I was the center of attention to each. My father's questions indicated that he was not unfamiliar with Clinton's holdings. David interjected questions showing his interest. Yet, I knew they were all delaying the real underlying reason for my father's visit. They were giving me time to collect my nerves and feelings. They were each in their own way studying my reactions to this momentous event in my life.

Clinton watched me with concern, offering me encouraging and reassuring smiles when my father and brother discoursed. My father's glances were a muddle of emotions, sadness intertwined with joy, hopeful expectancy, even pain. My brother surveyed me with cool impartiality and a lack of curiosity that I found mystifying. He looked at me in much the same way he would any acquaintance of some time. His smile offered neither friendship nor misgiving.

"Kathleen?" my father tested, searching my face openly before the other two companions. "Would you walk with me in your garden?" There was a plea which I could not deny, a look of appeal so exquisite that I knew my refusal would shatter him. I could not yet call him father and to call him Mr. Benson would be cruel. The first natural warmth of our meeting had dimmed to shyness and curiosity. I felt him again a stranger, a man of whom I knew nothing except that he was the man who had planted my seed.

325

I smiled, stood, and reached out to him. "Of course," I said, leaving off any polite or familiar salutation. I wanted to touch him, though I still felt terribly shy. He took my hand immediately, giving me no time to retreat within myself again. The strained sad tightness around his eyes and mouth slacked and his face lit up with gratitude. We walked together silently into the garden.

"You have a beautiful home, Kathleen," he commented, still unable to say what was on his mind, and mine. The garden was quiet, the cool breezes of imminent winter momentarily stilled. He looked at me with an exquisite sadness that almost overwhelmed us both. His eyes were misted and the lines in his face deepened.

"There is so much I must tell you, my little love. So much," his voice quavered as he spoke, vibrant with feeling. "Things about me . . . your mother . . . our life together."

Another silent voice inside me was calling out to him and to me. A voice I had only heard in my dreams, a gentle, haunting voice. And it told me to be kind to him, for any hurt he had caused me had been a hundred-fold worse on him.

I raised his thin hand to my cheek, and held it there. It was a warm hand, strong, and uncallused. He turned it and cupped my face, the tears now glistening in his clear blue eyes.

"You are like your mother, Kathleen. I knew you would be. When I saw you that day in front of the Riverview house, I knew you would be like her."

"You knew me?" I said with surprise.

"Oh, yes, my sweet . . . I knew you," he murmured with a smile.

"I look like my mother?"

"Her reflection . . . just as she was twenty years

326

ago." For a while he didn't speak but just stared at me with that sad smile touching his lips. His long fingers laced with mine and his breath made a cloud in the cold November air. I shivered slightly and he reached down to draw my shawl more closely around my shoulders.

"It's too cold out here. I should have been more considerate," he apologized, touching my cheek tenderly. "Is there someplace warm where we can talk? Or would you like to postpone this discussion until after dinner this evening?"

"No . . . I think I've been waiting too long already. Clinton's study is this way," I said, leading him through the back of the house, down the corridor and into the front study. I could hear Clinton talking with David in the sitting room across the hall as we entered the room. A fire was lighted already in the corner fireplace, offering a cozy welcome. I closed the doors, and then turned to face my father, who stood now unsurely before me, not knowing what my sentiments were.

I sat down opposite him in the same chairs that Clinton and I so often inhabited for our evening hours together after Priscilla and Steven were safely and snugly in bed.

"Tell me why you came after all these years," I asked without hesitation and without rancor. I wanted to know, now. My father smiled.

"To tell you that I have always loved you and wanted you to be with me," he answered simply.

"Then why wasn't I with you?" I responded with quiet disbelief.

"Because there was no choice."

Immediately the painful feeling of rejection assailed me again and I remembered that I was the product of an illicit affair. Why had he come to remind me of something of which I was well aware?

"No, Kathleen," he shook his head, reaching across to take my hand. "Not because I was not married to your mother," he said, reading my thoughts with surprising perception. "But because my wife would have killed you . . . as she killed your mother." His quiet-spoken words jolted me with shock and horror. His eyes never left mine, and before I could speak the questions that flooded into my mind he went on hurriedly.

"It was my fault it happened," he said with painful guilt, anguish twisting his face cruelly. "I loved Brianna . . . loved her and wanted to marry her. My marriage to Elizabeth was a horror I wanted to escape. We were married because of a family agreement to join our—oh, God, it doesn't matter why, it doesn't make any difference . . . except that you must understand that it was a loveless union.

"Shortly after I told Elizabeth that I intended to free her and myself from our marriage, Brianna was found murdered just outside the theater where she worked. The police said she had been robbed." His voice was grief-stricken and distant. "They never have suspected that my wife—a rather fragile-looking woman—could have committed such a hideous crime. But she admitted to it several months later . . . told me how she planned it for weeks before I told her of my intentions to divorce her . . . She said she knew I had a mistress . . ."

He ran his fingers through his gray-white hair and dropped his head. I thought I heard him sob but when he looked up at me again, there was no trace of tears, only an expression of haggard guilt and grief too deep for tears.

"I wanted to kill Elizabeth for what she had done. I wanted to expose her to the police. She laughed at me because she knew I wouldn't. It would have hurt my son, David." For a long time, he couldn't speak, and his face was gray and lined.

"She was mad. She almost drove me mad when I realized she was telling the truth . . . and then she started asking about the child—about you. She said that if you were dead also there would be nothing to stop me from loving her." His voice cracked with a bitter laugh, and for a moment he seemed incredibly old, all the animated excitement which had brought youth and life to his face when he had descended the carriage this afternoon wiped away.

"I told her that you had died soon after birth . . . but she never believed it. She became obsessed with finding you—destroying you. I finally arranged for you to be placed in Josie's care—she was an old and trusted friend of your mother's and was once betrothed to Brianna's older brother . . . but he was killed at Appomattox. She kept records of your progress, your accomplishments, your loneliness, your needs. And I sent her a yearly income to insure your care and the continuance of her orphanage."

'Was that why she kept me there?"

"No." He shook his head vigorously. "She was afraid you would believe that after Anna Bowen showed you the record file."

"How did you know about Anna Bowen?"

"She admitted what she had done when they found her. She had been shot."

"By whom?"

"She never had time to say more than 'I told Kathleen . . . I told Kathleen about her father.' But I know who killed her."

"Who?"

"Someone Elizabeth hired to assassinate her. Anna sold the information of your whereabouts. That's the only possibility, the only motive for her murder. My wife wanted to prevent anyone else from finding you . . . and protecting you.

"Kathleen, Josie was my only link to you. She loved you as though you were her own child. She protected you and tried to prevent any hurt from coming to you. You must understand that and not condemn her for keeping my secret."

The still silence of the room was almost tangible. I nodded finally, remembering Miss Montgomery's eyes the last time I had seen her. Fear—fear for me—and I had run from her, hated her.

"There is something else you must understand," he said. "To everyone else Elizabeth seemed perfectly sane . . . normal, even charming. Only at times did she lapse into madness and again become obsessed with finding some trace of you. I couldn't commit her. And I couldn't leave her for fear she would find some way to you. I hoped that I could find some way to have her institutionalized. God forgive me, I even wished she would die. Again and again, I wished for that," he said, his voice a reflection of his torment.

"And there was David . . . my son. I couldn't do anything that would reflect on his life, place him under the shadow of his mother's madness. He was innocent of everything that happened. He still knows nothing of his mother's madness.

"Kathleen, David is an arrogant young man at times, as he was with you that day before Riverview. But he is a fine young man also—he has been a loving son."

My father's hand shook as he released mine. "It was all my fault. Everything." He went on with a blunt, self-torturing admission. "When I saw Brianna, I should have left her alone . . . left her to find a young man who could marry her, offer her everything she deserved. But I didn't. I was selfish. I loved her. I wanted her.

"If I had remained faithful to my marriage vows—to Elizabeth—she might never have gone mad and committed the horror she did . . .

"And Brianna . . . my God, Brianna would still be . . ." He stopped abruptly, unable to trust his voice. "Brianna . . ." he spoke the name with tenderness, the name coming so softly from his lips that he seemed to be calling her back to him across the years and asking for her forgiveness. A forgiveness I knew she had long since given from the cries of her soul's love. His eyes filled with tears and my throat constricted as I shared the pain and loneliness of his existence as well as the memories of my own. He faced me, seeing someone else, a woman long dead but still infinitely loved.

"Father . . ." I murmured, and his thoughts focused again.

"Elizabeth is dead now. An attack of apoplexy. She told me she had found you and that this time you'd die and end the curse on her once and for all. A few days later, an Allen Jackson contacted Josephine, asking her questions about a Kathleen O'Reilly. Through him I was able to find you and learn of your marriage to Clinton Matthews. Clinton and I have been in contact since that time. He told me of your longing and your bitterness. I knew I had to see you and explain. I couldn't just remain out of your life anymore."

"Tell me about my mother. Please. I want to know what she was like . . . how you met her . . . Please."

My father's face lit up. "There is no one I would rather talk about more. It's been so many years since

I even dared mention her name aloud . . . though I thought about her . . . dreamed of her all these years." He looked younger, the lines loosening in his face as he remembered his young love.

"She was about seventeen when I first saw her. She was singing in a little theater, an Irish ballad. It was a tragic song, and she sang with such feeling I couldn't get her out of my mind."

"She was an actress according to the file."

"Yes . . . but her talent was singing. There was something almost indescribable about her voice . . . an empathy with the people about whom she sang. Most actresses were fighting to get to the top, any way they could. They were usually hard and experienced with life by her age. Well acquainted with the easier ways of getting parts in plays. Your mother was never a successful actress. She wasn't like the others. I don't think she even liked being on the stage, except when she sang."

"How old were you?"

"I was twenty-six . . . celebratnig my birthday with some friends. They wanted to go to the theater and see women. That was their idea of showing me a good time. I was quiet, a little cynical already. I had been married to Elizabeth for three years. She was a beauty in her own way, high-strung and vital. She was also ambitious and calculating. My father had insisted on the match, and I was too vacillating to refuse. I didn't love her, but agreed to the marriage to merge the Hale and Benson shipping lines.

"But when I saw Brianna O'Reilly . . . I forgot everything. I was young, in love, and selfish. I wanted her no matter what the cost to her. The miracle was that she loved me."

My father sat silent for a long time, his face relaxed and reminiscent. The gray hair seemed only an attractive part of his masculinity. His eyes were soft and dreamy and he smiled fleetingly.

"I returned to that theater night after night. Just to sit there and watch her. Finally I sent a note backstage saying how much I wanted to meet her." He smiled again. "She was dressed in a white dress, a red silk rose sewn on the skirt. And her eyes were so dark and blue. She looked young and defenseless. I wanted to make her life easier, to care for her, make her happy. I wanted her to let me buy her a little house and give her expensive gifts, but she said that would make her nothing more than a mistress. She wanted to give her love to me freely. She had no family left and the only person she knew from Ireland was Josephine Montgomery. Her brother had been killed soon after he paid her passage to America. She had no one but me and Josie . . . and then she had you. She was so happy . . . when you were born. I was with her. I was afraid she would die giving you life . . . and then I held you. You were just a little bundle of white.

"We only had a year . . . one short year," he said sadly. "I've never been so loved . . . or loved so again." His face became agonized. "And then she was dead."

"Father . . ." I remembered my dream and had to ask the question. It was neither malice nor shallow curiosity—I had to know. "How was my mother murdered?" My voice was hushed with dread.

"Elizabeth stabbed her . . . in the back . . . over and over." His voice seemed to tear from his throat and then die in anguish. I slid down to my knees before him.

"Oh, my God . . . I saw it all in my dream . . . I saw . . ."

He reached down and pulled me against him, all his pent-up agony coming forth in a shuddering sob. And in the minutes that followed, it was I who comforted and reassured him with my love.

XXII

Time melted away during the hours I shared with my father. The childhood insecurities and rejection seemed from another lifetime. I had a father who loved me, who had always loved me.

Now, finally, I could look back on my childhood with different feelings. I no longer held the bitterness and loneliness that had filled me during those days after Anna's discovery. I had all that I could ever want, a man I loved beyond anything in the world, his baby snuggled deep and safe within me, soon to be welcomed into our world, and my father—a father I had longed for.

The night after my father's confession to me, I wrote a long letter to Miss M. begging her forgiveness for my misunderstanding and cruelty to her. Realizing now that her love had always been genuine, I knew the torment through which I must have put her after my disappearance. Now I could accept her love without suspicion, without fear of falseness or loss.

During the hours my father and I shared walking

in the garden, sitting in the study, riding with the children, we seldom talked of my childhood. My real happiness had started at Las Posas with Clinton and the children, and it was of them that I spoke.

And my father listened.

When I pressed him to tell me of himself, he said little of his life after my mother's death. Once he compared himself with "Prometheus on the rock" and I never again asked him uncomfortable questions.

He spoke often of my mother, and I never tired of hearing the love that lifted his voice during these moments.

While Clinton sometimes joined us on an afternoon ride, my half-brother never did.

David Benson remained reclusive. My father apologized for his behavior, attributing it to shyness and perhaps even a mild jealousy of me.

Not insensitive, I realized that it was a shock for him to find he had a half-sister. And even worse for him, he would realize now that my father had loved my mother above all else in the world—even David's mother, Elizabeth.

When David and I did converse at all it was with shared reluctance.

David was ever polite and pleasant, but never personal, never wanting to delve beyond the border of simple friendliness.

Priscilla and Steven did not offer their usual friendliness to my half-brother. They stayed away from him, and watched him with a curious mixture of emotions when his company was beyond avoidance. At the dinner table, they darted uneasy glances in his direction, glances that he met with a casual smile.

I asked them one day why they evaded him.

"I don't know," Priscilla said, distressed. "There's something strange about him . . . he's polite and nice . . . but I don't like him."

336

"I'll ride with him if you really want me to, Aunt Kathleen," Steven offered generously. I did not press the suggestion.

The longer my father and half-brother remained at Las Posas, the stranger became the aloofness of David Hale Benson. He began riding out alone, not returning to the ranch house until late in the afternoon. He became more silent and pensive when with others. Sometimes he didn't even appear to hear when questions were addressed directly to him.

My father became concerned and annoyed by the apparent rudeness of his heir. But he hesitated to approach him because I asked him not to do so. David needed time. He had just learned something which I had learned some time previously. He needed time and unconditional love from his father. And he needed acceptance and friendship from me, still a stranger to him though we shared our blood.

Then David's behavior began to change suddenly.

One evening, later than usual, he came in from riding by himself. His usually quiet manner was replaced by a sparkling enthusiasm to join in our conversation. He smiled often and with sincere pleasure.

"I'd like to apologize for my self-ostracism," he said quite unexpectedly, "but I've had a lot to adjust to with what's been happening over the last few months." He looked directly at me as he spoke. "I am sorry, Kathleen, if I have made you at all uncomfortable with my behavior." Then he lifted his freshly filled wineglass. "I'd like to propose a toast . . . to the discovery of my sister." He drank the wine in a dramatic flourish, setting the glass down and smiling at me.

"And to my son . . . and heir," my father added as he drank his wine. Clinton hesitated, and then followed suit. He watched David with a studied eye and then smiled at me.

337

The next morning David joined us for breakfast. He appeared to have lost all his taciturnity.

"Why don't we go riding together this morning, Kathleen?" he suggested. Clinton tensed, looking across the expanse of the dining-room table at me, trying to convey some silent message. I knew he did not trust David. But David was my half-brother and I wanted to overcome the barrier that our mothers had unknowingly constructed between us.

"I'd like that very much, David," I answered brightly, pleased that he was giving me an opportunity to be alone with him. We would have time to talk, to reach an understanding of one another. Perhaps, in time, we could even share the affection a brother and sister should have.

I smiled down the table at my husband, hoping he would understand. He met my glance, with a lassitude uncharacteristic of him.

David and I rode several miles from the ranch house, few words passing between us. Those that did reach utterance, were common, unimportant observations about the weather and countryside. My half-brother's previous reserve was again taking control of his personality. The farther we rode from the ranch house, the more tangible and embarrassing became the silence.

Every now and then David would look back over his shoulder as though he felt we were being followed. Then he spurred his mount on faster toward the hills.

"Is anything wrong, David?" I asked, urging my mare to keep up with David's spirited mount. I had to call out the question, for he did not seem to hear and he was moving out in front of me as though to hasten his arrival at a destination.

"No, nothing," he answered curtly and his eyes caught mine for an instant. A chill went down my spine as it had when he had touched me the morning of his arrival at Las Posas. Had I been sensible, I would have turned and ridden back to the ranch house and safety as fast as my mare could take me. But I did not.

I did not want to trust my intuition. I did not want to offend or hurt him, especially since he had made the effort to reach out to me.

Soon after I called out to him, he reined in his horse and waited for me. He smiled almost pleasantly as I came up next to him.

"Let's talk," he said simply. We had ridden five hard miles from the ranch house, and I stared at him half in anger, half in frustration. The area through which we were now riding was rocky and dangerous. And now, when our attention should be on our riding, he wanted to talk.

"Why don't we ride over . . ." I started to suggest, riding to a nearby meadow, but he cut off my suggestion with a question so abrupt and loaded that for a moment I was speechless.

"What has my father told you about my mother?" David asked again, something in his manner and voice making me shudder. What had the children said about him? He was strange. Polite and nice, but there was some undercurrent of unexplainable menace which eluded you when you faced him, yet permeated your imagination.

"Not very much," I answered. It was the truth, but not all of it. I flushed and he smiled unpleasantly.

"Well, then, I'd like to tell you about Mama," he replied. He urged his mount on at a slow, cautious pace and I followed. "I know my father has told you he never loved my mother . . . but that is not the truth. He always treated her with kindness."

"David, must we—"

"Oh, don't let this embarrass you, Kathleen. It had nothing to do with you after all," he said, turning his horse toward a clump of sycamore trees. I followed, though premonition told me not to do so.

"She used to talk to me about her marriage to my father. He was kind . . . in some ways. But he never gave her anything of himself. I never saw him touch her. I hardly know my father myself," he said with a shrug that conveyed his lack of concern in that matter.

"I'm sorry, David."

"Sorry?" he laughed, looking at me incredulously. "What a kind thing to say," he commented sarcastically. He reined in his mount as we reached the trees, boulders scattered around as though tossed by an angry giant eons before. "This is far enough," he said flatly, swinging down from his horse.

"Far enough?" I repeated, feeling uneasy.

"We're by ourselves. No one to interfere while . . . we talk. Come on," he said with sudden impatience, "get down!" He turned a strangely radiant smile on me almost instantly after his demand. Then he reached up and took me by the waist, lifting me easily from the saddle and setting me down in front of him. Something jumped inside me and scurried in panic through my veins. His eyes were sparkling in a way that did not match his friendly smile.

Though we were two years apart in age, he seemed much older. He was much taller than I, and his shoulders were massive under his rich shirt. His hands felt like steel bands on my waist.

He took my hand, leading me toward the center of the copse. And as we walked I watched his face from the corner of my eye, wondering why I was suddenly so terrified of him.

Why had I ridden so far with him?

"Father loves you, Kathleen," he commented drily, sitting down on the grass near a small cluster of boulders jutting sharply from the ground. He leaned back studying my face above him and plucked a piece of wild wheat. He broke the stem in several places while he continued to stare with that fixed smile on his face. My throat dried.

"David, why did you suddenly want me to ride with you?" I managed to ask.

"Because I found Ted Berns finally."

"Ted Berns?"

"Uh huh . . . He won't spoil things now."

"Spoil things?"

"He can't . . . he's dead."

"I think we should ride back to the ranch house," I said casually, wanting to laugh suddenly. What madness was this? What madness had brought me here with him in the first place? I fought to control the hysteria that threatened me.

'No, not yet." He reached up and clasped my hand tightly in his before I could step away. "Sit down, dear little sister." I strained to break the lock on my hand. "Sit down!" He yanked hard and I was jerked to the ground. "I haven't finished, yet, dear, sweet little sister."

He sighed with heavy drama, leaning back again while still holding my hand in an unrelinquishing grasp. "You look very much like Brianna O'Reilly, you know."

"You don't know anything about—" I remembered my father assuring me that David knew nothing of my mother other than the fact that my mother had been a loved mistress. David knew nothing of the horrid end which had befallen my parent by Elizabeth's hand. David knew nothing of Brianna . . . nothing of the threatened divorce of his mother . . . not even her name which was never spoken in the mansion by the river.

"Oh, I know all about Brianna," David said, smiling. "My mother told me all about her. She talked of little else when we were alone. She talked of the woman who destroyed her marriage, her happiness, her very life. I grew up with Brianna O'Reilly, sitting like a vulture on my mother's dying shoulder . . . waiting for her last breath of air." His face twisted in a half-grin, his eyes glinting.

"I'm sorry . . ." I murmured, imagining the bitter hatred that his mother must have felt toward mine. I could see David sitting by his mother, longing for her affection and hearing her talk of her unhappiness and hate, weaning him on bile.

"You're sorry," he laughed.

"David, I want to go home."

He sneered, mocking my voice in a high-pitched version of his own. "I want to go home . . . I want to go home."

"You know only part of the story."

"Shut up! Shut up!" His hand slammed across my mouth so fast and hard I did not have time to dodge away. His fingers dug cruelly into my cheeks, making a steel clamp over my jaw. "She was nothing but a cheap little theater tramp, you know," he said, his voice calm and casual. His eyes were burning into mine. I tried desperately to pull his fingers from my face, but he pressed even harder with my efforts, smiling diabolically at the pain and panic he saw.

"She got what she deserved," he whispered, smiling still. He looked like an angry beast, teeth bared in a grin of vicious delight at the cruelty it was about to inflict on its unwary victim. "Brianna's child," he breathed. I squirmed frantically, remembering my dream.

"It was so easy," he went on casually. "So very easy. My mother told me all about it . . . a hundred times at least. She waited outside the theater . . . and when Brianna came out she asked to talk with her.

It was all over in a few minutes . . . and no one ever knew it was Mother that killed her."

Cold sweat beaded on my forehead.

"I knew who you were that day at Riverview. My mother had a picture of Brianna O'Reilly from the theater advertisement. She kept it hidden from my father. She showed it to me many times. You look just like her," he observed.

"My mother was so happy when I told her I knew where you were. Your friend, Anna Bowen, said she'd tell for a thousand dollars. She told me but she didn't get her thousand dollars," he announced with a laugh. "My mother and I planned how we would kill you. It was her idea to hire someone to do the job, but I knew whoever it was would mess it up," he growled with disgust. "Hired help isn't very satisfactory nowadays. They just want their money and don't want to perform to standards." He went on as though he were discussing an everyday businessman's complaint. "Well, I could hardly leave the man to roam around after threatening to tell people who hired him to kill you. Three times that damned fool botched it! God, what a stupid bastard!" His face clouded. "He used up all our time. If you'd died sooner, my mother would have been happy again . . . Brianna would have been gone finally and my father would have come back to her." His voice became childlike and whining.

With a terrified effort, I broke one hand loose and raked my nails down his face. He cried out, grabbing at me as I scrambled away from him running for my mount. David overtook me easily, winding his hand in my hair and yanking me back. I screamed and kicked, my hands flailing at him. His hands grasped my shoulders and he started to shake me violently, jerking my body about like a rag doll.

"Since I was five, I've waited for this, you bitch!"

he yelled in my face, sheer hate ringing in his tone. I fought frantically to break his hold on me. Kicking, screaming, hitting, pulling. His fingers just dug into my arm harder. He dragged me away from the nervous horses, my heels digging into the rocky soil as I yanked and tugged frenziedly against him. He jerked me again.

"I'd like to talk with you, Brianna," he said in a falsetto voice. I shuddered, looking into his mad face. I stopped struggling, just looking at him, frozen into immobility like a rabbit before a snake. His grip loosened slightly. "Come over here, Brianna, what I have to say will only take a minute." Even in my panic I knew that he was addressing not me, but my mother—and that in his madness he was re-enacting a scene out of his own vindictively murderous mother's life.

As soon as his fingers slackened their grasp, I whipped myself away, spinning to run. I screamed as I darted away. He caught the collar of my jacket. His hand doubled into a rock-hard fist and he hit me across the jaw. I could taste the blood in my mouth as yellow and black spots danced before my eyes.

Fighting to remain conscious, I continued to fight and started to scream again. Before the sound could issue from my lips, his iron fingers closed on my throat.

My ears rang with the blood pressure building in my brain. He pressed down slowly, his face contorted with insane pleasure above me.

Slowly, like a drying collar of leather, his fingers tightened, choking the life from me.

A loud crack rang in the air as I clawed at his hands, fighting for air. His face showed surprise and then flooded with fury.

"No!!!" he screamed. "No! . . . I . . . am . . . going . . . to . . . kill . . . her! . . . Once . . . and . . . for . . .

all . . . damn you," he screamed. The words strained through his gritted teeth.

Through the buzzing in my ears I heard another sharp report. Then another. David jerked up, his fingers slackening only fractionally, his face twisting with rage. Blood spattered my blouse and he squeezed down on my neck again.

A numbness floated over me, consciousness a retreating fog. My head felt blood-heavy. David lurched forward at the distant sound of a fourth report, his hands still grasping me, his weight crushing me against the rocky soil.

XXIII

When I opened my eyes, I was not sure where I was. I could hear voices, low and indistinct, in the dim light surrounding me. My body ached, and I could still feel the horror of David's fingers around my throat. Then I remembered the grotesque contortion of his face as he pitched forward onto me, his blood spattering across my face and chest.

I opened my mouth to scream and no sound issued from my lips. My throat seemed to tighten even more, almost cutting off my shallow breath. I wondered if I were dead and this was Hell. Pain blurred my vision. Fear made me cold and immobile.

Clinton's face appeared above mine, his eyes dark with concern. He brushed a stray lock of hair from my forehead.

"Don't try to speak, darling," he said, his fingers still tracing my face tenderly. I heard another voice behind him and my eyes widened with fear as I thought perhaps my brother was not dead but there in the darkness waiting for another opportunity to kill me. My father leaned over Clinton and looked down at me. His face was haggard. It did not seem possible that he could have aged so much during a few short hours. I wanted so much to tell him I would be all right now, that I was sorry about David, but I could not speak through the pain in my throat.

"You'll be fine in a few days," Clinton reassured me as he caught the hand I reached toward him. "Try to relax completely. Mabel is making some broth for you to drink. That will soothe your throat." He leaned down and kissed me gently. When he would have left, I clutched at his hand.

"I'll only be gone for a short time. The sheriff is here now to ask some questions. Then I'll be right back with you. Your father is right here and he'll stay with you, Kathleen." He leaned down and spoke in a whisper only I could hear. "You're safe now, darling. There is no one to harm you. David is dead."

While I felt reassured by Clinton's words, I felt a deep sadness surge through me. It hurt dreadfully to know that my own half-brother had hated me so much he wanted me dead. I had wanted a family, and was now the cause of destroying one.

Still I would not let go of Clinton. There was something I had to know. He saw the plea and leaned forward again.

"The baby . . ." I managed. Clinton smiled and kissed me.

"Our baby is fine. He has a fine, warm nest that he won't give up so easily."

I sighed, relaxing back into the pillows. I heard Clinton leave the room and felt my father's hand press mine. I smiled, too exhausted to open my eyes again. My father was here with me. He did not hate me for being the cause of his son's death.

I must have slept, for when I opened my eyes again my father was gone. The room was lighter, dawn approaching. Clinton was asleep in a chair he had pulled up next to the bed. His hand rested near mine.

As I carefully slipped my hand into his, he opened his eyes and leaned forward. His expression relaxed as he met my smile.

"Why didn't you come to bed?" My voice was barely a whisper but the pain in my throat had diminished.

"I didn't want to awaken you." He kissed me, his fingers winding in my hair and pulling almost painfully. "I thought I'd lost you!" he said huskily. "If I could, I'd keep you tied to me every second so I could be sure nothing would ever happen to you."

"You said I was safe," I reminded him.

"Safe from intentional harm. But you'll probably find other ways to frighten the wits out of me!"

"You sound as though you believe I brought everything on myself," I said, tracing the line of his jaw with my finger.

"No, love," he stroked my hair. "It all began before you were even born. Your father has explained."

The mention of my father reminded me that I was the cause of his loss. My face clouded. "How is he, Clinton?"

"He's in a state of shock, of course. But he's surprisingly calm under the circumstances. He loved David, and he never suspected the insanity he had inherited from Elizabeth Benson. He blames himself for not seeing what was driving his son. He blames himself for what almost happened to you."

"You knew it was David, didn't you?"

"No, not really. There was just something about him that made me uneasy."

"He made the children uneasy too," I remembered.

"Children can be very perceptive," Clinton agreed. "We should listen to their instincts more often."

"I wanted David to like me."

"I know, darling," Clinton said quietly.

I leaned back into the pillows, looking at Clinton. The last few days had taken a toll on him. There were lines about his eyes and mouth that showed the apprehension he had harbored. And I had been the cause.

"I'm sorry," I smiled apologetically. "You've worried about me so much."

"I love you," he said simply.

"And I love you."

We looked at each other for a long time, content with the quiet and the closeness.

"What made you follow David and me?"

"I found Ted Berns," Clinton answered, his eyes skipping away from mine for the first time.

"And he told you about David?"

"In a way."

"What way?"

"I found him in the ravine just a mile beyond the springs."

I stared at my husband, not sure I understood his implication. After hesitating, Clinton continued, and his meaning was horrifyingly clear this time.

"His neck was broken."

"It couldn't have been a fall from his horse?"

Clinton shook his head, his face controlled. "He was too good a rider for that kind of accident. And there were other things, Kathleen. Things only a madman would do to his victim." He rubbed his hand across his face as though trying to push away the image still engraved on his mind. "Everything seemed to fit then. David's long rides as though he were looking for something or someone. Then his jubilation when he returned yesterday, and his sudden turnabout when he wanted you to ride with him. All I could think of when I found Ted Berns was that you were alone with that madman and he might do the same things to you. I cursed myself a thousand times for being so blind. And then I thanked God when I found you were still alive."

"He thought I was my mother, Brianna," I told Clinton. "He kept calling me Kathleen . . . using a strange, high-pitched voice." I shuddered at the memory.

"Elizabeth Benson must have weaned her son on hate and malice. Even in the grave that woman had the power to destroy."

"She thought that if my mother and I were both dead, my father woud turn to her . . . would love her."

"From what he has told me, he never loved her. Their marriage was one of those arrangements between two powerful, wealthy families."

I turned my face and looked out the window to the garden beyond. "It's strange, Clinton. But I pity her. Maybe if she had been allowed to marry someone who really loved her . . ."

"You're more forgiving than I am then. She murdered your mother in cold blood and then drove her own son insane with her obsessive hatred of you. She made her husband miserable almost every minute of his life." He shook his head. "I doubt if she was capable of love, Kathleen. Possession would have been closer to what she wanted."

"What will Father do now, Clinton? I can't imagine him returning to that cold estate I saw. There's nothing there but grief."

Clinton's face colored slightly and he smiled almost sheepishly. "He has spoken of buying land here in California. I suggested he make an offer for the James ranch. Monte has accepted."

"So Cybil will be going away," I sighed with relief.

"And Michael."

"You never had anything to worry about where Michael was concerned," I assured him with a smile.

"Nevertheless, I'll feel much better when he's out of the valley," he commented.

"How did Cybil take the news?"

Clinton grinned. "What could she say? I imagine she did her screaming until her father promised her a tour of Europe and a nice home on the East Coast. That brightened her outlook considerably. I would make a bet that she will be married to some aging millionaire by the end of next year."

"I hope so . . . and I hope he's not too old," I muttered. Clinton laughed.

"What is Father going to do about his business back East?"

"He's transferring much of it to San Francisco. He believes that San Francisco will be one of the greatest seaports in the world. He already has a hundred ideas of how he is going to set up an import-export business."

"Then he won't be living at the James ranch," I said with regret.

"He will be there a good part of the time. He made it very clear that he wants to be close to his daughter and grandchild."

My eyes and throat burned with tears as I smiled at Clinton. He leaned down and kissed me.

"Clinton? If our baby is a girl . . . may we call her Brianna?"

He smoothed the tears from my cheek with his thumb. "If our first child is a boy . . . you'll just have to wait for your Brianna," he smiled.

I laughed. "And how many children do you want, Mr. Matthews?"

He raised his brows and grinned. "Enough to fill

our home from basement to rafters with resounding laughter," he answered.

And with that glimpse into our future, I felt all the old shadows fade away.